The Better Angels

Bette Bono

The Better Angels

Copyright © 2019 by Bette Bono

ISBN: 9781733444859

Library of Congress Control Number: 2019953701

Cover Design by All Things that Matter Press

Cover photo by Douglas Biklen

Published in 2019 by All Things that Matter Press

To Jessie and Andrew because we always share stories.
And to Alex, my remarkable companion,
who encouraged me to write this one.

Prologue ~ New York City, April 1882

The sound of his wife's scream, rising above the howling wind, tore into Gabe's heart. Desperate, he peered out the bedroom window into the dark yard. *Where was the midwife? Why hadn't she come?* He had sent the stable boy to fetch her over an hour ago when the pains started. Lula was too old for a baby, especially a first baby. She needed help.

The moonlight, flickering as clouds scudded across the sky, added a silver outline to the barn and glinted off the glass panes of the small greenhouse. He had finished building it just that morning. It was his gift to her, a place to grow her flowers. She had planted wildflowers around the house, here and there, little patches of columbine and milkweed and bee balm. He had helped her with the lilac bushes that shaded the side yard.

But he had seen the way she talked about the gorgeous blooms in tall vases adorning every room in the East Side mansion where she had worked for so many years. Roses, carnations, and peonies, *blossoms as big as melons*, she had said, and they had laughed at the frivolity and joy, the sheer opulence displayed in growing such splendid and luxurious plants.

When she had told him there would be a baby—something neither had imagined possible—he had planned for the tiny greenhouse. He crafted it using photographic plates taken from Mathew Brady's studio. Why keep the glass squares stored in a chest? What value did they have now? The war was long over. The battle that had torn two fingers from his hand lay twenty years in the past. Mr. Brady himself was gone from the city, his gallery closed.

Most of the plates were portraits: uniformed boys with unlined faces, boys who had given that *last full measure of devotion*. Their leaders were there, too, caught in the minutes of stillness required to hold and record them in the camera's wondrous eye. He had hesitated with a few of the portraits. Was this the son of a family bereft? The beloved of a wife or sweetheart? But the knowledge that the sun's rays would erase the images forever didn't deter him. People wanted to forget, and surely it was not unkind to let the faces become one with the light.

Lula cried out again, and he turned to her. Her face was convulsed in agony, her dark hair drenched with sweat. What could he do? A man with only one good hand? He took a last, despairing glance out the window. Clouds flew across the sky, and the etched images on the greenhouse glowed in the night. The ghostly eyes of the soldiers stared into his own. No one was coming.

Chapter 1 ~ Junket

Alzheimer's offered a rational explanation for the strangeness that began that summer. Time travel didn't. It wasn't real, and Aggie May had spent most of her sixty-plus years dealing with what was real.

Aggie was newly retired after decades spent working in a dilapidated high school tucked into a part of Connecticut characterized by double-digit unemployment and a Rust Belt landscape of shuttered factories. She had never looked far beyond her own gritty school in her own small town. Surely, teaching science to kids was its own reward. Especially when many of those kids made it to class without the benefit of clean clothes or breakfast. Granted, helping a teenager build a simple robot or use a prism to create a rainbow was pretty basic science and hardly a remedy for all of life's ills. Still, she had been trained in science and trusted science, trusted its ability to explain and inspire.

Aggie hadn't wanted to retire. She was childless, a widow. There were no grandchildren to tend. She didn't have a bucket list and had no interest in compiling one. But things changed at the teacher's union spring meeting. The union president, wearing a rumpled suit and an unaccustomed look of defeat, had spelled out the bad news to the restless faculty members crowded into the cafeteria. Negotiations on a new contract had not gone well, and state arbitrators had rubber-stamped the Potatuck School Board's austerity plan scheduled to take effect in the fall.

Running a hand through his thinning hair, he bluntly explained how a slew of new contract provisions would eliminate most of the longevity benefits senior teachers counted on to help in retirement. The board didn't see any point in rewarding a veteran's years of experience when an enthusiastic twenty-two-year-old could be hired for half the price.

"So, it's pretty much bad news coming outa' arbitration, ladies and gents," he concluded. "The town cried bankruptcy and retrenchment, and the panel handed 'em a big box of tissues to dry their eyes and mop us up. Bottom line: If you're anywhere close to retiring, file for your pension while the current contract is still in force. If you don't, it's going to cost you."

It had been a troubling message, and Aggie prayed he was wrong. But that night, sitting at her kitchen table, she ran the numbers herself and reached the same bleak conclusion. She submitted her "intent to retire" notice the following day, shocked at how quickly and completely her world had been upended. She loved her boisterous and unruly students. Even Conor Pulaski, who had distinguished himself by ejecting a fully loaded, three-drawer, metal file cabinet from the principal's second story window in a fairly effective protest of the largely negative material contained in his permanent record. Then there was Jacki Swenson, who had plagiarized an entire essay on climate change due to the mistaken belief that a teacher as old as Ms. May would never successfully navigate her way to the relatively obscure online source of the elegantly worded article she had submitted under her own name.

"I've been teaching longer than you've been living," Aggie had informed the girl calmly. "Don't try that trick again."

Jacki pretended confusion about the red *NC* penciled on her paper. "And this is supposed to mean …?"

"*No Credit*, bird-brain," Conor called out, having eavesdropped on the whole exchange. "Also *Not Cool*. Miz M ain't stupid, yo."

Aggie's last weeks at school had passed in a blur. She took down posters from her bulletin board, handed back student portfolios, and attended one final graduation ceremony in the gym. The seniors had been beautiful: the girls in pastel dresses and the boys self-conscious but proud in their blazers and ties. With *Pomp and Circumstance* playing over the tinny sound system, the ROTC cadets marched in with the flag, the students received their diplomas, and then it was over.

A few weeks later, Aggie stood at her kitchen window on a blistering mid-summer day sipping iced tea and gazing out at her garden. She felt uneasy. Now what? Something didn't feel right. She was not "Miz M" anymore, not a teacher, not employed. Not anything, really. Outside, a robin hopped about near one of the tomato plants. A fat bumblebee disappeared into a pink gladiolus.

Aggie finished her tea and set the glass on the counter. It was time to accept her new reality. She had come to terms with loss before: her husband's premature death, the fact that there had been no children. Most people liked retirement. She could garden, volunteer, visit her siblings. All good. And yet, *something didn't feel right.*

***

As the summer progressed, some odd incidents stoked her concern. Preparing for her weekly grocery run, Aggie sat at the kitchen table to write out a list. The window was open, and from somewhere outside the sound of a radio came to life. Irma Thomas was finishing up "Time is On My Side," and there was a seamless transition to the Drifters crooning "This Magic Moment." Nice oldies, she thought, and waited for the next song, but there was a commercial break, and the words of a jingle floated in. A jingle about Junket rennet custard.

Junket. She hadn't thought about Junket in years. She remembered her mother making Junket, pouring the custard pudding into pink melamine cups and placing them in the refrigerator to set. Her little brother Roscoe loved having Junket for dessert. It was strange the company would reuse that old commercial with its decades-old tune.

Aggie glanced back down at her list, but an odd flash of double vision blurred the words. It was like peering through a View-Master and discovering the cardboard reel was bent and stuck between two pictures. She had owned a View-Master in her childhood and remembered those out-of-kilter images: the Statue of Liberty listing to one side, Mount Rushmore with a few extra shadowy faces superimposed on the originals.

Aggie pulled off her glasses and rubbed her eyes. The radio had been snapped off. The odd feeling was gone.

In the store, she pushed her cart along, checking off items as she found them. In the aisle featuring baking ingredients and mixes, she paused. Did they even make Junket anymore? Apparently they did because there it was: small boxes available in raspberry or vanilla. Feeling silly, she tossed the vanilla in her cart.

At home that night, she had a simple dinner of chicken and salad. She had made the Junket that afternoon. The four dessert dishes sitting demurely on the top shelf of the refrigerator confronted her as she stored the leftover chicken. Too bad there weren't four people to serve, or three, or even two. Is this what retirement was about? Vanilla Junket for dessert, four nights in a row. Why had she bought it anyway? Why was that old jingle on the radio? She shut the refrigerator door a tad forcefully.

That evening, Aggie sat through a nature documentary before heading up the narrow wooden staircase to bed. She lived in an old carriage house that she and her late husband, Jacob, had converted to a home. The bottom floor had a small kitchen and a sitting room with a fireplace. The second floor contained two bedrooms with slanting ceilings separated by a tiny bathroom.

The carriage house was the last remnant of a long-gone Victorian estate constructed in the post-Civil War years by the owner of a corset factory. Once there had been a grand house with a porte-cochère and a conservatory overlooking rose gardens. But when the factory shut down in the twenties, and the last family member died, the house had fallen into disrepair.

In the 1970s a developer bulldozed the main house, most of the outbuildings, and the rose gardens, in order to put up rather blocky condominiums. The carriage house had only been spared due to its proximity to a marshy area that the new Potatuck Conservation Commission had designated as wetland. Informed that if he razed the carriage house, nothing could be constructed in its place, the developer had cut his losses by offering it for sale "as is."

Aggie and Jacob—newly married and full of dreams—had bought it the first day it was listed, undeterred by stalls on the first floor and the smell of hay in the air. They performed much of the renovation work themselves, laughing at their setbacks: an overturned can of paint, a ceiling fan that crashed to the floor the first time they turned it on. Happy hours were spent planning where to place the table and bookshelves, the loveseat and rocker—maybe, at some point, a crib. It was all so long ago. They had been so young. There was nothing to hold them back and nothing to worry about. Certainly not the dry cough that sometimes caused Jacob to pause and catch his breath.

With memories drifting like motes of dust, Aggie washed her face and examined her reflection in the mirror. Unremarkable. She looked like a thousand other women her age. Her hair retained its natural red-orange color, but there were silvery strands mixed in. Her round face was made rounder by rather old-fashioned wire-rimmed glasses.

She turned sideways and considered her profile. Ten pounds overweight she concluded, then immediately recanted. Who was she kidding? Twenty pounds overweight, at least. You can't fudge your data. Facts were facts. She moved her face closer to the mirror and studied her brown eyes. If something was amiss in there, could she discern it? She might have a few wrinkles, a few gray hairs, but her mind felt sharp. Surely, of the many problems in the world, Junket was not one to stay awake over any longer, at least not on that particular evening.

***

Aggie had almost forgotten about Junket, the old jingle, and that odd double vision by the time she set out to run errands later that week. A prescription was waiting at the pharmacy, and she had assembled a load of clothes—all too tight—to drop in a donation bin. She might pop into AAA, too. Her sister, Minnie, was coming in from California for a visit, and they had planned day trips into New York City for shopping and sightseeing. A tourist guide would be handy.

As Aggie drove by the striped awning of the Busy Bookworm Bookshop, she considered stopping to browse. They had a good local section. Maybe she could pick up a tourist guide there. Then she remembered. The Busy Bookworm had closed twenty-five years ago. The striped awning was long gone. The space had been converted into a video rental place, then morphed into a dog grooming salon. It was a Dollar Store now. She shook her head. *Don't daydream while you drive.* That's how seniors lose their licenses. At the pharmacy, she collected her prescription, along with aspirin and a plastic jar of Tums. She felt queasy and hoped she wasn't coming down with something.

In the following days, Aggie made an effort to stay busy and focus on her sister's visit. She restocked the refrigerator—thank goodness the Junket was gone by now—made up the bed in the spare bedroom and set out jars filled with flowers from the garden. She verified Minnie's flight information and wrote it on the wall calendar in the kitchen. She dusted everything and took a lint roller to her cat Hubble's favorite chair.

The evening before her sister's arrival, Aggie drove to the Mobil station to fill up her old Honda. She was picking up Minnie at JFK and wanted to set out with a full tank. As she stood at the pump, she spied a man entering the phone booth that stood on the far side of the station, just below the red Pegasus sign mounted high on the wall. The man fed coins into the slot, dialed, and held the phone to his ear, shutting the door of the booth for privacy.

At that moment, the handle of the gas pump clicked, signaling a full tank. She hooked the nozzle back on the pump, wincing as she checked the total. Pulling out of the station, Aggie felt a twinge of nausea. Gas fumes, she thought. She had always been sensitive to gas fumes. But the part of her brain that was still, even in retirement, devoted to science, set off a buzz, as if a game show contestant had produced the wrong answer. It was a breezy evening, not too hot. On a night like this, fumes were not a problem.

Wait. What the heck?

She knew then, and a chill ran down her spine. At the next corner she stopped at the light. There was right turn on red, and a right turn would take her home. But with heart pounding, she sat at the deserted intersection, not moving. Carefully, as if it didn't matter, she put on her left blinker. When the light changed, she turned left and drove around the block. This time, she pulled into a parking space next to the gas station restroom. She turned off the engine and lowered the window.

The insistent, repetitive buzz of cicadas filled the air. She was parked directly under the flying red horse, right where the phone booth used to be. *Used to be.* It was gone. It had been gone for years. But the scary part was, she was sure she had seen it, just a moment ago. Sitting in the darkness, Aggie gripped the wheel so tightly her knuckles turned white. With the tiny light over the restroom door flickering in the night, she tried repeating a reassuring mantra: Your memory is playing tricks on you. This happens to everyone, doesn't it?

She didn't have an answer, and maybe didn't want one. Didn't want to contemplate the possibility that she had encountered a problem far bigger than Junket. Didn't want to confront the fact that it didn't happen to everyone. It only happened to people who were, as her mother used to say, losing their marbles.

Chapter 2 ~ Super Constellation

In the morning, things seemed better, as they always did when the sapphire morning glories opened outside her window. On her way to pick up Minnie, Aggie was gratified to see that the only thing standing beside the Mobil station was a sandwich-board sign promoting the sale of lottery tickets and beer. Driving through town, she felt no confused uncertainty about the array of shops on Main Street.

Her sunny mood dimmed when she arrived at JFK only to have her cell phone announce that Minnie's flight had been delayed by well over an hour. Circling back to the short-term lot, she parked and resigned herself to a wait.

The sidewalks outside the terminal and the lanes of traffic beyond were jammed. Cars, taxis, courtesy vans, and shuttles zoomed up to the curb, disgorging travelers with varying amounts, sizes, and shapes of luggage. To the sound of honking horns and roaring jets, car doors and trunks popped open or slammed shut, people hugged in greeting or farewell, backpacks were hefted, and suitcases rolled away.

After negotiating the crosswalk, Aggie stepped onto the sidewalk next to an elderly woman with a fire-engine red walker who was peering out at the whizzing traffic as if searching for someone or waiting for a ride. Suddenly, a taxi swerved to the curb directly in front of them. The back door was flung open and a man jumped out, a carry-on bag in one hand and a briefcase in the other. Instinctively, Aggie put her hand on the elderly lady's arm to steady her as the late traveler slammed the cab's door shut with his foot and offered a hasty, "Sorry," to the women as he dodged around them and bolted inside.

Aggie felt a second of disorientation, then the thunderous roar of a plane struck her, and she was enveloped in sound. It was not the scream of a jet. It was a low-pitched, buzzing growl like you heard from planes in old movies. She looked up. Directly above her a giant metal bird was rising into the sky, its propellers whirring in liquid silver circles. It was a vision from another era. She couldn't recall the last time she had seen a vintage propeller plane take off, and she watched in wonder.

"Now that's something you don't see every day. It's pretty, isn't it?" The elderly lady had also lifted her face to the sky.

"It's magical," Aggie replied. "It looks like a DC-6 maybe?"

"No, it's a Super Constellation. Like President Eisenhower's Air Force One. Look at the tail. My brother had the model airplane kit, and I remember that tail."

Aggie squinted against the light, watching the plane climb with ponderous grace until it disappeared in the clouds. "I think you're right. I remember those models, too. Only it wasn't my brother who had them. It was my sister. She wanted to be a pilot. Or an astronaut. Not an easy goal for a little girl back then. But she grew up to be an engineer, so she came pretty close. Actually, I'm here to pick her up. She's coming out from California for a visit."

Aggie realized she still had a steadying hand on the woman's arm. She also realized, with a huge sense of relief, that she wasn't hallucinating. Someone else had seen the plane, too. She released her companion and smiled. The woman with the walker was older than Aggie, in her seventies, at least, with an oval face, perceptive green eyes, and wavy, shoulder-length white hair. With her pearl earrings and lace blouse, she seemed delicate, almost fragile. But she gripped the handlebars of the walker with assurance.

"I'm just back from California," the woman said. "I was visiting my little brother." She laughed. "It's odd to call a seventy-year-old my 'little brother,' but old habits die hard. We keep the airlines rich flying back and forth between LAX and Idlewild. Are you a New Yorker?"

"No, a Nutmegger. I'm from Connecticut. Potatuck."

"I live in Connecticut, too. Up near Ledyard."

The steady stream of traffic and travelers continued to flow past them as they talked. Aggie didn't like leaving the woman alone in the midst of such a crowd. "Is someone picking you up? Or do you need a hand getting somewhere?"

"No, no, I'm fine," the woman said. "My place in Connecticut is an assisted living community. They're sending one of their shuttles to get me."

"Well, that's convenient. Do they let you go off whenever you want?" She stopped, embarrassed.

The white-haired lady laughed. "They do. I know assisted living sounds *institutional,* but in our community the residents stay in charge, and—oh, here they are now."

A gleaming white minibus pulled up to the curb in front of them. Stylized birds and flowers were painted on the side along with the words *"Remarkable Enterprises"* done up in an art nouveau script. With a whooshing sound, a wide door opened, and a wheel-chair platform descended to the sidewalk. The driver, a young man with farm-boy freckles and straw-yellow hair pulled into a ponytail, waved to the white-haired lady.

"Hey, Lily, welcome home! How was your trip?"

"Thank you, Wells. The trip was lovely. Hold on a minute, I'll be right with you." She turned to Aggie and held out her hand to shake goodbye in an old-fashioned sort of way. "I'm Lillian James. It was nice chatting with you."

"Aggie May. It was nice chatting with you as well, and welcome home."

"Thank you," the woman said, then maneuvered the walker onto the lift. As the platform ascended, Aggie could hear the young man's eager questions.

"How was *Hollywood*, Lily? Did you see any stars? How was your brother? How was your *flight?*"

Aggie smiled. Nice kid, she thought, and headed into the terminal.

***

Minnie gave a whoop when she saw Aggie and folded her in a hug. "I'm so glad to see you," she exclaimed, then released her somewhat abruptly as a giant blue suitcase cruised by on the luggage carousel. "That's mine," she said as she grabbed the handle and wrestled it from the conveyor belt. "You'd think they'd design these things better," she said with a disparaging gesture at the machinery. "They're too slow, and it's too difficult for short people and seniors to get their bags."

"Why didn't you just bring a carry-on?" Aggie asked bluntly.

"Just because I'm short, doesn't mean I have to carry a small bag," Minnie huffed.

"Well maybe your team at Hytech can do a redesign."

"I'll suggest it at the next management meeting," Minnie said, then burst out laughing and hugged Aggie again. "I'm so happy I'm here."

Minnie stood just over five feet tall, but she had a real presence. Fluffy auburn curls surrounded her face like a halo, and her wide eyes and high cheekbones added to her angelic look. In her youth, Minnie's appearance had worked against her, but she had bucked the well-meaning suggestions of the high school career counselor — *You'd make a wonderful receptionist, dear, or a stewardess if you're looking for adventure* — and enrolled in a Big Ten computer engineering program.

"It's hard to be taken seriously," Minnie had confided to Aggie at the time. "The professors assume I've walked into the wrong class. Or they think I'm only there to find a husband. You know, earn my M-R-S. When they realize I'm there to learn programming, they look at me like I'm a *freak*. Like a two-headed calf."

"I've always thought you *did* look a little like a two-headed calf," Aggie had said, as if giving the matter serious consideration. Minnie stuck out her tongue and persisted in her dream, graduating with honors and landing a position at a leading engineering and aerospace company. She had risen quickly through the ranks. She had also, as it turned out, earned her M-R-S, but not by pairing up with a crew-cut colleague. She had met her husband, Joe, at his auto body shop, and their first date involved a hands-on effort to complete a rather tricky bit of work on a 1968 Mustang.

On the way back to Connecticut, Aggie told Minnie about the woman with the walker and the ascent of the Super Constellation.

"Oh, I wish I had seen that. That plane's a beauty."

"Do you remember the airplane models you used to build?"

"Not just planes. Cars. Ships. I hung that Revell 'Moon Ship' model by fish line over my bed. God, I was such a nerd."

"You're still a nerd, sweetie."

"I know," she sighed. "But what do all those Facebook posts say? *Follow your dreams! Reach for the stars!*"

"Facebook wasn't invented when we were kids."

"Well, maybe I was inspired by Hallmark, then. But enough about that. I want to hear about you."

For the remainder of the trip, Minnie plied Aggie with questions and coaxed her into reciting the whole story of the union contract and the factors that had forced her to retire. It had been good to talk about it, but it also confirmed Aggie's suspicion that sisterly concern had motivated Minnie's visit as much as a desire for sightseeing in New York.

Back at the carriage house, the sisters dragged the suitcase up the narrow stairs where Minnie hoisted it onto the bed in the small guest room and commenced unpacking. Aggie looked at her fondly. "You don't need to worry about me."

"Of course I need to worry about you. What happened sucks."

"I'm going to be all right."

"Of course you're going to be all right. You're a *rock*. I know that. But you didn't want to retire. And you don't exactly have hobbies, except for gardening, which is only a summer thing, and you're—"

"Alone," Aggie said. That was the heart of the matter, after all.

Minnie studied her. "I just thought you might need cheering up. And don't give me that big sister look. I'm not here solely on your account. I really did need a break. Work's been *crazy*. The next release of our control product is coming up, and Hytech wanted to beef up the algorithm group, so I've been on five a.m. phone conferences with India for days. And the boys have been driving me crazy, too. Having three teenagers, at my age, is a teensy bit fatiguing."

"That's what you get for not paying attention to your biological clock until you were past forty."

"That's what I get for going to one of those fertility clinics and ending up with triplets. I was so naïve about being a working mother. A working *older* mother. Well, I love them to pieces, but when Joe said he would pack them in the camper and take them to Monterey for the car show, I knew it was my chance for a break."

"Taking a break in Potatuck is not exactly the same as, uh, the Hamptons. We don't have a spa here. We have a Walmart, of course. And there are rumors we might get a Chipotle."

"Believe me, a spa is the last thing I need. I just need some good old-fashioned East Coast sights, and people, and conversation, and *food*. Like a New York City bagel. What passes for a bagel in California is just *sad*. Whenever I make the mistake of ordering one, I'm never sure whether I should actually eat it or just pitch the poor gluten-free thing and put it out of its misery." She paused in her unpacking. "You don't mind that we're spending most of the time in the city, do you? I'm not knocking Potatuck, spa or no spa. I love Potatuck. It's your home, and it's got character, and charm, and—"

"An abandoned brickworks."

"Well, that's kind of historically picturesque, isn't it?"

"I'm sure the First Selectman will be thrilled with your endorsement," Aggie said dryly.

"And Potatuck's close to Metro North, so it's easy to commute to New York."

"Yes, there's that. A major selling point for Potatuck has always been that it's easy to leave and go somewhere else more interesting."

"Remember that George M. Cohan song?" Minnie spread her arms like a vaudeville soloist, cleared her throat, and began singing "Only Forty-Five Minutes from Broadway."

"Cohan was writing about New Rochelle, not Potatuck," Aggie observed.

Minnie paid her no attention and continued the song. Aggie watched with amusement as the number went on. At the conclusion, her sister gave a twirl and landed flat on her back next to the suitcase on the bed.

"Okay, I believe you."

"About what?"

"You did need time away."

Minnie grinned, sat up, and resumed unpacking. "Ah, here it is." She pulled a printout from the suitcase and handed it to Aggie. "I did a schedule for us on Excel."

Aggie scanned the spreadsheet which listed the sights they had talked about visiting, with columns set up for locations, entry fees, hours of operation, and whether a senior discount was available. "My sister the engineer is back," she murmured. "I wonder what happened to the Ziegfeld girl."

"I have no idea what you're talking about," Minnie said with dignity. "Now pay attention. We'll want a full day at the Metropolitan Museum of Art. Less time for Tiffany's and Teddy Roosevelt's house. We'll see Grand Central every day when we go in, of course, but we'll need a few hours for the self-guided tour. I scheduled that for the afternoon I leave, so we can eat supper at the Oyster Bar before my shuttle back to the airport."

"Minnie? What's *Comic Convocation*? You penciled that in for tomorrow morning at the Javits Center."

Minnie wrinkled her nose and looked guilty. "That's a stop I have to make for the boys. It won't take long, I promise. It's a comic book festival. They have booths and vendors and exhibits, I guess. The boys want me to pick up some early editions of," she referred to another list, "Superman, Batman, and Aquaman. They gave me the numbers. Do you mind? When the boys found out I'd be in New York at the same time as this, um, convocation, they begged me to shop for them."

"By 'the boys' I assume you mean your sons, who can be forgiven, and your husband, who ought to have outgrown this stuff."

"Exactly."

"Do we have to dress up or something?"

"God, no. Who would we dress up as anyway? Really old Wonder Woman and really old Batgirl? Nope, we'll just pick up the comics then do something more age and gender appropriate. Like lunch and Tiffany's."

"Sounds like a plan."

Minnie set the empty suitcase on the floor then pulled out her phone and started typing.

"Say 'hi' from me."

"I'm not texting the boys. I did that when I landed. I was just checking," Minnie paused then typed a bit more, "about that plane you saw. I wonder if it was here for an airshow. Hmm ...."

Suddenly Aggie's heart was thudding uncomfortably. "What?"

"There are only two Super Constellations still flying. One is in Australia, so you must have seen the other one. But I don't see anything about an airshow. Are you sure it was a Super Constellation?" Her thumbs moved quickly as she started a new search.

Aggie got up, went into the bathroom, and splashed cold water on her face. She recalled the old woman's words: *Look at the tail.* Aggie had looked at the tail. She knew what she had seen.

"Hey Ags," Minnie called, "maybe it was just a commuter plane."

Aggie looked into the mirror. "Maybe," she said. She picked up a brush and ran it through her hair. Wasn't there more gray than there used to be? And lines around her eyes and along her collarbone. "Maybe," she repeated in a whisper.

Chapter 3 ~ Comic Convocation

Aggie awoke early. Troubling thoughts had followed her to bed, but they dissolved in the light, and by the time she had made tea and fed Hubble, she was able to enjoy a feeling of happy anticipation. *Anticipation*. Something she hadn't experienced all summer. It was good to look forward to a few days of companionship. Good to look ahead to a day of adventure—even if the adventure involved nothing more intrepid than a ride into New York, a bit of sightseeing, and a nice lunch.

After breakfast the sisters made the short drive to the Metro North station and boarded a mid-morning, off-peak train. Minnie turned her attention to the window where the shoreline was rolling by and sighed happily. "New York City is always magical. Kind of like Sodom and Gomorrah meets the Land of Oz."

"Speaking of the Land of Oz, you know Roscoe's started rehearsals for *Wicked*?"

"I know! Our darling baby brother is over the moon," Minnie laughed. "Or over the rainbow, I guess. He's thrilled a man 'his age' got a part. Plus, he gets to sing and wear a costume."

"Two of his favorite things."

"We have to get to Chicago when the show opens. Seriously. I'm springing for front row seats."

She chattered on, and Aggie foresaw another Excel spreadsheet taking shape in her sister's mind. Finally, Minnie broke off. "Look. We're almost there."

The familiar splendid skyline of Manhattan glittered against the glass of the window, and they watched in silence until the light disappeared abruptly as the train entered the underground tunnel leading to Grand Central. There was always something a little mysterious about the minutes of darkness preceding arrival at the terminal. At intervals, dim lights appeared, illuminating strange set pieces, each visible for only a few seconds: a ladder leading to the tracks, a pile of bricks in a corner, a single abandoned boot. Then a final stretch of blackness before the yellow glow signaling their arrival.

Outside the station they caught a taxi and asked to be taken to the Javits Center. The driver grinned, swooped gracefully into a break in the traffic, and zipped off. On the way across town he provided helpful advice evidently having ferried others to the same location all morning.

"That long line that snakes around the corner is *Will Call*." He glanced into the back seat. "But since you ladies have your badges, you can go right in through the Crystal Palace." Aggie handed over the fare and added a nice tip. The driver grinned again. "Have fun in Area 51."

"That's the plan," she replied.

The Javits Center was a sight to behold. Masses of people—many wearing costumes—gathered in the huge outdoor plaza where inflatable cartoon characters towered thirty feet in the air and the buzz of thousands of excited voices competed with the honking of traffic and amplified pop music. Aggie and Minnie joined the crowd streaming toward the entrance. Once inside the building they joined a security line. When they reached the guard checking bags, he took one look at them and waved them through.

"Age profiling?" Aggie asked.

Minnie scanned the crowd. "Age and gender."

"There are plenty of women here."

"There are plenty of *younger* women, hardly any older women. Although, I do see quite a few older guys."

"Judging by your own family, guys don't always age out of this phase."

As they entered the cavernous exhibition hall, Aggie gasped in amazement. Scores of booths had been arranged into an entire city of narrow lanes like a mammoth medieval bazaar. Throngs of people meandered along the pathways, pausing before display cases and crowding around tables piled with merchandise. Vendors hawking t-shirts, video games, toys, collectibles, posters, and comic books waved people forward. At one booth, a young man peddling hats held a mirror up for a teen who had placed a warrior's helmet on her head. At another, tote bags emblazoned with glittery unicorns were handed to passersby. Huge banners fluttering overhead advertised shows about zombies and dragons.

"Oh. My. God," Minnie exclaimed, covering her ears to block the din.

A young woman clad in fishnet stockings and a skimpy satin costume sauntered forward and pulled two campaign-style buttons featuring female cartoon characters from a wicker basket she carried over her arm. "Girl power," she declared, offering them to the sisters before wandering off again.

"I guess I'm Wonder Woman after all," Aggie said examining her button.

"Here, switch with me. I got Poison Ivy, but you're the redhead with a kickass garden."

Aggie traded with Minnie then studied the image on the button. "I'm not exactly sure how *girl power* is advanced by a bustier and thong."

"Well, feminism is a *process*. One step at a time."

"True. But I couldn't take one step if I had to wear those stilettos. But what the hell," she grinned, pinning the button on. "When in Rome ...."

Minnie had pulled out her shopping list and opened a map of the exhibition hall she had grabbed at the entrance on their way in. "Comic books and graphic novels are in the next aisle. Shall we head over?"

Aggie hesitated. Booths displaying illustrations of science fiction and fantasy scenes had caught her attention. Several artists were seated behind tables, or at easels, some autographing copies of their work, others sketching portraits of costumed convention-goers. "I think I'll hang out here and watch the artists."

"Okay," Minnie said, "I'll be right back." List in hand, she set off and was swallowed by the crowd.

Aggie drifted along the aisle and stopped at a booth where four young people seated behind easels were drawing caricatures. A giant banner on the wall behind them featured an illustration of gleeful artists waving from the back of a cartoon-like van careening madly along a comic book street. The words "Van-Go Designs" and prices for black-and-white and color portraits were lettered on its side.

Aggie paused near one of the easels. The artist seated there sported a full, 1970s-era Afro and was in the process of putting the finishing touches on a portrait of a young man dressed in a Robin Hood-style shirt. The Robin Hood was an angular teenager with rather prominent ears and the beginnings of a black beard shadowing his jaw. A scattering of shallow pits across his cheeks gave evidence of an adolescent battle with acne.

Young as he was, the artist had wounds of his own. A scar on his cheek, light against his dark skin, showed the crosshatching of stitch marks. The scar was old, and Aggie wondered what childhood mishap had created it. She hoped it was something like a skateboard accident, not an abusive adult.

She stepped to the side to get a better view of the portrait, and, seeing it full on, caught her breath. In the sketch, the gawky, young fan in the homemade costume *was* Robin Hood—a real Robin Hood with acne scars and a scruffy beard—a gallant, reckless young man perfectly capable of robbing the rich to give to the poor. The artist hadn't made him handsome or square-jawed. Hadn't bulked him up. He had done something infinitely more magical. He had found the spirit in the teen that perfectly mirrored the legendary character.

The artist's hands moved across the paper adding the final shades of color. Solemnly, he held the portrait up to the fan for inspection. Aggie moved a step closer.

"Dude, it's awesome," the teen exclaimed, straightening his shoulders, as if taking on the mantle of Sherwood Forest.

16

The artist's eyes rose to look at the teen, and a brief smile lit his face. Two of the teen's friends pulled Robin Hood to his feet and patted him on the back, sensing something about the moment, sensing he ought to be congratulated. The teen paid for the drawing, then the friends threw their arms across each other's shoulders and walked off into the crowd, a band of Merry Men. The artist watched them leave, and another quick smile flashed across his face. Oddly, Aggie felt her eyes sting, and she wondered what it was about the scene that had affected her so much.

As she watched, a young woman in a Princess Leia costume took the chair vacated by the teenaged Robin Hood. The artist turned his attention to this new customer, clipping another sheet of paper to his easel and arranging his pencils. He studied his subject for a minute then his hands moved to the paper, and a new sketch began.

"He's good, isn't he?" A man in a *Van-Go Designs* t-shirt stood at her shoulder. He carried a cardboard tray holding four cups of coffee. "Did you want a portrait, ma'am?"

"Oh, no thank you. I was just admiring his work."

The man slid one of the coffees out of the tray and placed it carefully on the table next to the artist. "Tyrece is a real magician and already getting a following. Some of the New York magazines have picked up his work," he said proudly, "although certain celebrities aren't always happy with how they end up." He tilted his head toward the back of the booth where samples from the artists were displayed.

Aggie studied Tyrece's work. A conservative TV host had been transformed into a fussy toddler. A well-known executive was Cruella de Vil. In a stunning rendition of the Charlottesville mob, every face was recognizable. Politicians and pundits held Tiki torches, Confederate flags, and Nazi banners.

"Hey, big sis, I found *everything* on the list." Minnie was suddenly at her side. "Good prices, too. Plus, I got to eavesdrop on a fascinating dispute between a couple of honeymooners about whether they should spend three hundred dollars on what one of them called 'those fucking idiotic bobble-heads.' Are you ready to leave? I mean, we could walk around a little if you want."

"No, let's go. Wait a sec, though." Aggie picked up a postcard from a stack sitting on the table near the young artist. The Van-Go logo was in the corner, but most of the card was devoted to an ink sketch in which the artist had drawn himself as Leonardo da Vinci's *Vitruvian Man*. "Tyrece Vinci," she read aloud.

The artist let his eyes flick in Aggie's direction. He examined her face quickly, as if sizing her up for a portrait. His brow furrowed, and, for a fraction of a second, he looked troubled, as if he detected something in her that was disquieting.

"Look again." Aggie was surprised and embarrassed by her whispered words. *Look again*. The words she used to encourage a student struggling with an experiment.

It was over in a flash. The artist's eyes scanned her face once more, and the look of concern faded. He seemed a little perplexed, as if he had seen something unexpected, but then showed that brief, stunning smile and turned back to his easel.

Aggie opened her handbag and tucked the postcard inside. She saw that Minnie was paging through one of the comic books she had just purchased.

"Learning anything useful?"

"Yes," Minnie declared. "Here's the basic idea: Sometimes it's no fun being a superhero. On the other hand, sometimes it's freaking awesome."

"Words to live by, I suppose."

"I think it's time to head to Tiffany's. Did you know Tiffany's made swords and surgical instruments for the Union Army during the Civil War?"

"No, but I did know you always recite odd facts about every place we visit."

Minnie beamed. "Of course. Now let's go look at pretty things made from silver and gold. Then I need pastrami."

Chapter 4 ~ Grand Central

They devoted their second day in New York to the Metropolitan Museum of Art. Here, Aggie took charge. "We're going to look at statues and paintings, not armor or mummies."

"My taste in art is not totally shaped by the boys," Minnie said, looking offended.

"You could have fooled me. Especially after yesterday. And we don't need to look at jewelry today because we're done with that, too."

"Yes, well, okay." Minnie fingered a new silver pendant—three intertwined hearts that she assured Aggie represented the boys—purchased the previous day at Tiffany's flagship store on 5th Avenue. Aggie hadn't seen much she could afford, but it didn't matter. What was the point in purchasing an expensive new bauble at her stage in life? Also, after the explosion of noise and color at the Javits Center, the hushed aisles of Tiffany's had seemed curiously pallid.

They started in the enormous sunlit pavilion of the Museum's American Wing. While Minnie snapped pictures of a bronze of Diana, Aggie wandered away among the light beams that angled down from above. She was drawn to a huge circular limestone pulpit, its sides carved with angels, all of whom seemed rather industrious as they went about the work of swinging censers, strewing flowers, and playing musical instruments.

"It's from All Angels Church. By Viennese sculptor Karl Bitter," Minnie said, appearing at her side. "I just googled it. All Angels was founded in 1846, but this pulpit is more recent. The first church was just a wood structure in Seneca Village, which was—"

"A nineteenth-century interracial community. One of our history teachers wanted to take the students to the site, but there was no money for buses. It was the first place in New York City African Americans owned property. But it was demolished when they created Central Park."

"That was in 1857," Minnie said, consulting her phone again. "So, the church moved to another building, and this pulpit was done in 1896."

Aggie studied the pulpit. "I like this. The angels look busy, like they have jobs to do."

"Are we drawing an analogy to our current situation?"

"I've been busy all summer," Aggie shot back defensively. "Gardening takes time. And housework. I have plenty to do," she stopped, then added reluctantly, "until September when I'll have nothing to do."

"Well, maybe you can find work," Minnie eyed the pulpit, "spreading incense or something. Come on, let's go see Madame X."

"You saw Madame X the last time you were here."

"I know, but I love Madame X."

Aggie led the way to a quiet gallery where Minnie made a beeline for the famous John Singer Sargent painting of a young socialite in a black gown. The portrait had scandalized the Paris Salon in 1884 because Sargent had painted one of the gown's straps sliding off the model's shoulder. Shocked criticism of the "sexually suggestive" pose had forced Sargent to repaint the strap, placing it back in its proper position.

"He should have left the strap down," Minnie declared. "Sometimes you have to break the rules."

"Sometimes you break the rules and get clobbered."

"Sometimes you follow the rules and get clobbered. Isn't that kind of what happened to you?" She consulted her phone. "Wikipedia says Sargent 'wearied' of portraiture in his later years, so he 'forsook' portraits for landscapes and architectural subjects."

"Pretty highfalutin language for Wikipedia."

Minnie laughed. "Apparently Sargent hated having to chat up his high-society clients during sittings."

Unbidden, Aggie's thoughts flashed back to the Javits Center. Robin Hood sitting for Tyrece Vinci. Such a different kind of portrait, created by a different kind of artist, in a different light-filled gallery.

***

The last day of Minnie's visit dawned bright and sunny. The sisters arrived early at Teddy Roosevelt's birthplace home on 20th Street and joined a tour, learning the house had been recreated to look as it had at the end of the Civil War. The Park Service guide shepherded them from room to room then directed them to the small adjacent museum. Strolling past the exhibits, they paused before a photograph showing New York's funeral procession for Abraham Lincoln winding past the Union Square mansion owned by Teddy Roosevelt's grandfather. By looking closely, two small boys could be seen peering at the solemn parade from an upper-floor window: Teddy Roosevelt and his younger brother, Elliott.

"The original was a stereogram," Aggie said. "You put them in a stereoscope, and they look three-dimensional. Like a View-Master."

Minnie peered at the card by the photo. "'Photographer unknown.'"

"Well, whoever it was, he didn't know what he had, did he?"

"What do you mean?"

"He didn't know *all* he had. It was Lincoln's funeral procession, but he also captured seven-year-old Teddy Roosevelt, a future president.

And Elliott, the father of Eleanor Roosevelt. The photographer knew the funeral was important, but Teddy was just an anonymous little boy looking out a window. Then time passes. He's elected president. And one day someone looks at this picture again and sees something more." Aggie examined the picture again. "You know, all those other anonymous people were part of history, too, even if they never became famous. There must have been Civil War veterans in the crowd. And maybe people who would, I don't know, see *wonders*." She noted the expression on her sister's face. "I'm rambling?"

"Undeniably. Let's check out the gift shop."

It was still beautiful—sunny and clear—as they walked back to Grand Central. Their plan was to tour the station and grab an early supper at the Oyster Bar before Minnie's shuttle to the airport. They stopped on 42nd Street to admire the enormous sculptures crowning the roof.

"The statues are Mercury, Hercules, and *me, Minerva!*" Minnie informed her.

"You hate your given name."

"I'm not alone. When was the last time you introduced yourself as Agatha? Anyway, I like *this* Minerva."

Once inside, they surveyed the massive empty space of Vanderbilt Hall. "This used to be the original waiting room," Aggie said, "but the chandeliers and those wood benches in the corner are all that's left of the original fixtures."

"Too bad it's empty now."

"It's used for a holiday market in the winter. And it can be rented out."

"Look," Minnie said pointing to a poster mounted in a brass frame. "There's going to be an art show here."

Aggie read the gilt letters on the notice:

Coming in September
In cooperation with the Metropolitan Museum of Art
Portraiture in New York:
From John Singer Sargent to Cartoon Caricatures

"Gosh. We just saw both of those things," Minnie said. "How very trendy of us. I think I read something about Sargent that relates to the station." She tapped on her phone. "Ah, here it is. He set up an art school here in the twenties. There was painting, sculpture, murals, and costume design. It closed in 1944. Norman Rockwell attended, and Willem de Kooning, and Bob Kane!"

"Who's Bob Kane?"

"*Who's Bob Kane?* Didn't you learn anything at the Javits Center? He's one of the creators of Batman."

"Oh, *that* Bob Kane."

Minnie laughed. "You're hopeless. Come on, let's explore."

In a moment, they were standing in the massive cathedral-like main concourse, gazing up at the curved, teal-green ceiling decorated with the constellations of Orion, Taurus, and Gemini. Minnie snapped a few pictures with her phone then opened an article and read from the screen. "This says the ceiling has complicated astronomical inaccuracies. Some of the constellations are internally reversed and out of position or something."

Aggie looked up. "That's right. Funny I never noticed. I always looked at it as, you know, art. Not astronomy." She had been rotating slowly to get a panoramic view but felt lightheaded. "I'm getting dizzy," she said, rubbing the back of her neck. "I think my brain's getting internally reversed and out of position."

"Keep your head down a minute and stand over there so I can get a picture."

Dutifully, Aggie posed in front of the circular information booth crowned by the brilliant, four-sided, brass clock, each opalescent face pointing in a different direction.

"Let's go look at the whispering gallery," Minnie said. "You're the expert on that one."

"Yes, I am," Aggie said, pulling her sister toward the wide marble ramp leading to the lower level. "It's right in front of the Oyster Bar."

That last school year, Aggie had brought her class to the whispering gallery after pleading for permission from Potatuck's stodgy school board which didn't hold with spending money on field trips. It had taken a phone call to Minnie and the promise of a small grant from Hytech's Science for Schools program to sway the board members, who grudgingly okayed the trip since it wasn't going to cost anything.

She had prepared the class by setting up experiments to investigate the way sound waves could cling to a wall and follow the curve of an arch. Once in the city, the students had spent nearly an hour in the whispering gallery, awed by Grand Central and by the fact that they had been granted this unexpected furlough.

Conor Pulaski and a few of his fellows had relished every moment, dawdling in the gallery's broad passageway, gawking at the commuters, and peering through the glass panes in the doors of the Oyster Bar. Periodically, they'd saunter to a corner of the vaulted space to whisper obviously off-color messages to clusters of female classmates gathered in the opposite corner. The girls would shriek in pretend outrage, then hang on each other laughing raucously.

As Aggie led Minnie down the wide ramp, she expected to find the usual crowd of sightseers and summer camp children in matching t-shirts, but the corridor was unexpectedly open with only a few stray commuters and tourists standing about. Minnie paused to admire the four graceful arches framing each side of the intersection and the tan, rectangular ceramic tiles that covered the domed ceiling.

Two giggling teenage girls stood in opposite corners of the square gallery, facing the wall as if they were toddlers on a time out. "See how you do it?" Aggie drew Minnie's attention to the girls. "You face the corner diagonally across from your partner and whisper. The other person hears you, no matter how quietly you speak, and no matter how many other people are in the room. Want to try?"

"Let's do it." Minnie gave her a thumbs up and headed across the gallery.

Aggie waited until the teenage girl finished then took her place and faced the corner. A brass rail provided a handhold, and she curled her fingers around it. Then, without warning, she was hit by another wave of dizziness. It was bad, and she felt a sudden terrifying confusion.

"Is this where you whisper?" The speaker was a young woman wearing a smart brown suit with a longish skirt, a jacket with padded shoulders, and a hat ornamented with a veil of white netting. She had wavy, honey-colored hair falling to her shoulders and a twinkle in her big brown eyes. *Veronica Lake*, Aggie thought. She looks like Veronica Lake from those old movies.

Suddenly a whispered male voice emerged from the corner. "Hey babe, are you going to say something extra sweet to me now that we're married? You've been Mrs. Jackson for a whole twenty-four hours, so I think you should know—"

The blonde shot Aggie a conspiratorial look and leaned toward the corner to whisper. "Careful, honey, I'm standing here with another lady who can hear every word you say."

Aggie managed a wobbly smile. "Congratulations!"

"Thank you. I think I'm going to like being a married woman."

Afterward, Aggie couldn't be sure why she chose to turn around just then. Maybe to catch a glimpse of the blonde's new husband? Check on Minnie? Whatever the impetus, she turned, then blinked, stunned by what lay before her, and what didn't.

The whispering gallery was gone. No, not gone—transformed. The nearly empty space she had entered a moment ago was jammed now with people moving in all directions. They had appeared out of nowhere, out of nothing, all at once. Why hadn't she heard their voices and footsteps, seen them clutching briefcases and shaking umbrellas. *Umbrellas?* When had it started to rain?

Her eyes widened as she registered details. There were men wearing baggy suits and fedoras. Women in knee-length dresses and high-heeled shoes. She had an unexpected impulse to laugh as a formidable-looking matron bustled by pushing a massive baby carriage that looked as durable as a Conestoga wagon. And there were *soldiers*. Soldiers wearing uniforms of khaki, brown, gray, dress blue. World War II uniforms.

It was 1942. The knowledge landed with a thump, as if a heavy object had been dropped at her feet. She wasn't sure how she knew, but she knew.

"There he is." The Veronica Lake look-alike pointed to the far side of the room where a dark-haired man in a navy ensign's uniform was waving at them.

A man with a dripping umbrella walked by and gave it a shake, throwing droplets of rainwater on the women.

"Hey, watch it, buddy," the blonde said, inspecting the sleeve of her jacket. She smoothed her skirt then checked her stockings. With a snort, she pointed to her calf where the seam had twisted into a zigzag line. Reaching down, she tugged it straight then glanced back at Aggie, her brow wrinkled in concern. "Are you okay, honey? You look a little pale."

"My sister went to the other corner. I think I lost her in the crowd," Aggie said unsteadily.

"You can't see a thing in this crush," the blonde said and turned back to the wall. "Johnny, this lady is waiting to whisper to her sister. We better let someone else have a turn."

"Okay, babe. And we've got a train to catch. I don't have much leave, so we can't waste time."

"Time for what, Johnny?" the blonde teased.

"Time for the most important person in the world," he whispered back.

The blonde blushed but hesitated, shooting a worried look at Aggie.

"Go," Aggie urged. "I'm fine." The woman gave her a quick smile and set off into the crowd. Aggie watched her disappear then turned again to the corner. She gripped the handrail. *What if she couldn't get back?* "Minnie?"

Immediately, the sounds around her faded. She was falling, untethered, like plummeting down on the Parachute Jump at Coney Island.

"Aggie? *Hello?* Testing, one, two three, four." It was Minnie.

"I can hear you," Aggie whispered. She pressed her forehead against the cool marble of the wall.

"You're coming in loud and clear."

Aggie drew a shaky breath. "How can a whisper be loud and clear?"

"You know what I mean. I'll come over and meet you, okay? Over and out."

Aggie straightened and turned around. The gallery—like she knew it would be, *must* be—was empty again. Or very nearly empty. A small band of tourists was listening to a guide, but Veronica Lake, her ensign, all the others were gone.

Minnie arrived grinning. "That was awesome."

"Awesome," Aggie echoed. Her sister had pulled out her phone and was taking pictures. It was obvious that, for Minnie, nothing out of the ordinary had occurred.

Aggie walked to the center of the domed space and rotated 360 degrees, then went to the doors of the Oyster Bar to peer in the tinted windows. A few customers were seated at the counter, but none were soldiers, none wore fedoras.

"Are you hungry yet?" Minnie appeared at her elbow. "I've got a while before the airport shuttle, but I wouldn't mind eating early and getting off my feet. How about we split some Oysters Rockefeller and fried calamari?"

"Okay. Um, did you notice …?" Aggie stopped midsentence. How could she put into words what had just happened? She didn't know what had just happened.

"Oh look," Minnie said. "Something spilled on your blouse."

Aggie looked down at her silk top and saw a spray of dots where the raindrops shaken from the man's umbrella had landed. "It's just water," she said mechanically.

"Here," Minnie said, pulling a tissue from her handbag, "blot it."

Aggie dabbed at her blouse, but the water had already dried, so she stuffed the tissue in her pocket. "Let's go in," she said. "I need to sit down."

Chapter 5 ~ Welcome Wagon

A week later, sitting in her doctor's office, Aggie hoped—feared—an answer was at hand. She had called her doctor immediately after seeing Minnie off on the shuttle. After listening to her carefully rehearsed concern about "memory issues," Dr. Sterling had arranged for her to be examined, screened, and scanned. Now was the moment of truth.

"You can cut to the chase," Aggie said. "I need to know what I'm dealing with."

Dr. Sterling glanced at her over the top of his glasses, then looked at his laptop. She tried to read his expression. Was that a scowl? Was he trying to find the words to tell her she was crazy as a loon? Finally, he met her eyes. "You're fine, Aggie. Everything is completely normal except—"

"Except?"

"Vitamin B levels are low. That can affect memory. I want you to pick up some Super B Complex, and we'll do another blood test in eight weeks."

Aggie shook her head in disbelief. "What about getting confused at Grand Central? What about," she almost choked on the word, *"Alzheimer's?"*

Dr. Sterling folded his hands on his desk. "Aggie, when you were young, did you ever daydream? Adults daydream, too. So do seniors. Thoreau would daydream sitting in a sunny doorway. Einstein would daydream listening to music."

"How many great minds daydreamed in big city transportation terminals?" she asked with a sniff of frustration.

"Maybe you're an original. You're certainly not suffering from anything as tragically unoriginal as Alzheimer's. I'm giving you a clean bill of mental health."

"Why do I feel like this is an exit interview?"

"Because it is. Go home. Read a book. Work in your garden. Sit in a sunny doorway and listen to music. You're *fine.*"

And that was that. But it wasn't, of course. For a day or two, Aggie attempted to embrace the diagnosis of daydreaming with a Vitamin B shortage. She dutifully tried reading, gardening, music, and sunny doorways. It didn't work. She couldn't forget Grand Central.

Sitting at her kitchen table, she considered other options. Opening her laptop, she did a quick check of her email and learned her sister was fine, her brother was fine, her nephews were fine, *everyone was fine.* After a moment of thought, Aggie pulled out her wallet and extracted her red-

and-white AARP card embossed with the words "Real Possibilities." She entered the web address listed on the card, and the cheerful home page appeared along with a dizzying array of choices. This was more like it. There were tabs for work, retirement, money, driver safety, and— *Bingo!*— brain health.

She located a search box, and, after some reflection, entered the words "imagining history." A new page appeared—it looked like one of those pop-up ads—featuring magazine-quality seniors waving from cruise ship balconies and curled up on rugs in front of fireplaces sipping champagne. A line of text in art nouveau lettering caught her eye: *Remarkable Enterprises—Have you ever imagined traveling through the most fascinating events in history?*

She clicked on the link, but, after a minute or more in which the little circle icon did nothing but circle, an error message appeared. Lost in the woods and down a rabbit hole, she thought, blowing a wisp of hair out of her eyes. She hit the X at the corner of the screen and shut down the computer.

***

One of the younger teachers at Potatuck High had once made known—with a gentle smile aimed at the older faculty members—that stress and anxiety could be reduced if one was "mindful." It was, perhaps, a sign of Aggie's determination to get on with things that she made a dogged effort to follow this advice. In the next few days, she mindfully weeded around her tomato plants and dead-headed the red petunias that spilled out of a clay pot that stood outside her door. She mindfully sent Minnie photos of their New York City excursions, with copies to Roscoe. The approach worked less well when it came to housework, however, where it was a bit more difficult to remain "present" and "aware of her incoming thoughts and feelings" as she folded laundry and mopped the floor. So, when the doorbell rang just as she finished scouring the sink, it was a welcome interruption.

The man on the doorstep was tall, over six feet. He was a senior, like herself, but handsome, nonetheless. He reminded her of Harrison Ford. He had that same general look, that same kind of smile. An Indiana Jones smile. He appeared a bit more professorial than swashbuckling, but still, charming. The man wore a linen sports jacket and held a straw hat somewhat awkwardly in his hands.

"Ms. May?"

"Yes. May I help you?"

"I'm here from the AARP. The tristate regional office."

She narrowed her eyes. "You're not collecting money, are you? Because I just renewed my membership. For three years. They sent me one of those little red travel bags because I renewed for three years."

"Oh, no. It's nothing like that. I'm just following up on your online profile. It's a kind of Welcome Wagon thing for members who might be interested in some of our more active educational programs."

Aggie looked at him blankly. *Welcome Wagon?* "Are you selling something?"

The man looked abashed. "No, Ms. May. Not at all. I'm just here to find out if you'd like to attend some seminars on a variety of very informative topics."

"What kind of topics?" Aggie asked suspiciously. "I don't need a forum on the long-term advantages of a reverse mortgage."

"There aren't any long-term advantages of a reverse mortgage," he replied promptly. "They provide income in the short run but deplete it over time. But this is not about anything like that. It's just a series of lectures on history. The program is called Remarkable Travelers."

An image of stylized birds and flowers materialized in Aggie's brain. She considered the man in front of her. Oh, what the hell, she thought. "Would you like to come in?"

The man flashed a grin and suddenly looked very much like Indiana Jones. Stepping through the door, he held out his hand. "Ms. May, my name is Abraham Irving. I'm very pleased to meet you."

They sat in the kitchen. Abraham had accepted iced tea, and Aggie had found and opened a tin of shortbread. For the first time in a long time she was aware that her home was a bit shabby. A hole in the tablecloth had been darned. The blue and white kitchen curtains were faded. A rinsed-out jam jar served as a vase for a bunch of daisies. Everything was neat, and, after her recent efforts at the sink, scrubbed, but kind of old.

"Nice place," Abraham said, as if reading her thoughts and seeking to reassure her. "Nice view. Very impressive plantings along the driveway."

"I put the gardens in when my husband and I first moved in."

"Not everyone mixes vegetables and flowers."

"Are you interested in gardening? My husband wasn't. The good part of that was I had a free hand to do what I wanted."

"I love gardening," Abraham responded easily. "Not that I have much scope for it. I'm in a fairly small place right now. There's just a little patio in the back."

"You must do container gardening then."

"Oh, I have a few things. Some flowers," he said vaguely. "Would you mind giving me a tour? I thought I saw heirloom tomatoes out there?"

"You did. I was growing heirloom tomatoes before they became a *thing*." Smiling, she got to her feet. "I'll show you if you're really interested."

"Believe me," he responded, picking up his straw hat, "I'm interested."

They went out the kitchen door and walked back toward the street. Aggie regarded her handiwork with satisfaction. Both sides of the long brick driveway were crowded with a myriad of flowers, vegetables, and herbs. There were ten-foot-tall sunflowers and tiny radishes. Geraniums shared beds with cabbages and beets.

"It's all companion-planted," Aggie began, "which is why the sunflowers are there. They help the corn, along with the clover and pigweed. The corn works with the pumpkins. The nasturtiums and marigolds help the cucumbers, and that combination repels raccoons."

"Pigweed?"

"That stuff." She pointed to a tall plant with dark green leaves. "It's edible. My heirlooms are over here. These tall ones. They're all indeterminates, but I expect you know that. I have family heirlooms and a few mystery heirlooms, but no commercial heirlooms."

She glanced over her shoulder and saw Abraham studying her with a funny expression on his face. He had put his hat back on, so she couldn't see his eyes, but she had the strangest feeling he was making a judgment about something.

"I get a little carried away when it comes to plants," she said apologetically. "When I was teaching, I started an organic garden at my school. Nothing like a pile of compost filled with worms to capture the attention of your average teen. I hope they keep it up next year." It hurt to acknowledge such a simple thing was no longer within her control.

"Tell me more," Abraham said. "I'm *enchanted*. Show me one of those tomatoes?"

Aggie surveyed the staked plants then gently pulled a fat striped tomato from its stalk. "This is a family heirloom. The patterns are as individual as fingerprints."

She held the tomato out to Abraham and their fingers met. In the next instant, it was the Parachute Jump all over again. Only this time, there was no dizziness, not even when her vision blurred for a brief second. When it cleared, she was still there and so was Abraham. But everything else had changed.

The street was now paved in brick like the driveway. A small, horse-drawn wagon rolled by, its wheels clacking over the bumpy surface. Letters painted on the side of the wagon spelled out the words *Burton's Dairy – Milk, Cream, Butter, Cheese*. Aggie noticed a coolness on her skin and looked up. She was standing in the shade of an elm tree, its branches rising fifty feet overhead. A nicker from the direction of the house made her look back. The building was still there, but it was back to being a true carriage house. The wide barn doors stood open. A horse, poking its head over the front of a stall, waggled its neck.

She was conscious of the fact that Abraham was holding her hand, tomato and all. She saw him scan their surroundings with interest, and an appreciative grin lit up his face. He glanced her way, his look quizzical, asking her a question.

Without quite knowing why, Aggie grinned back. *Yes. I see it. It's real.*

"Look at the tomato," he said. Glancing down, she felt them parachute out together. Her garden returned. Her house was back to normal. She heard a car pass on the street.

She let go of the tomato, leaving it in Abraham's hand. "Welcome Wagon?" It was a challenge.

He met her eyes and nodded. "Ms. May, may I trouble you for another glass of tea? I would like to talk to you a little more about the AARP and those classes. If you don't mind."

"Not in the *least*," she replied wryly. "I'd be *enchanted.*"

Chapter 6 ~ The Other AARP

They sat again at the kitchen table. Aggie had refilled their glasses from the pitcher she kept in the refrigerator. Abraham stirred in a spoonful of sugar. He had brought the striped tomato inside and set it on the table next to the sugar bowl.

"Ms. May—"

"I have two questions first," Aggie interrupted.

"That's to be expected."

"You don't know a damn thing about gardening, do you?"

"Not a thing."

"And you're not really from the AARP."

"Well, not from *that* AARP."

"What do you mean 'not *that* AARP'?"

"Our group—we *are* all seniors—our acronym is the same. But it's a slightly different organization. A different AARP."

"What does AARP stand for in *your* organization?" For the first time that morning he looked embarrassed. "'Fess up," she demanded.

"The American Association of Remarkable Persons."

"You're kidding."

"It seemed like a good idea at the time," he said apologetically.

Aggie stared at the man across the table from her. Picking up the tomato, she rotated it in her hand until she had seen all its sides. "Mr. Irving," she said at last, "let's put our cards on the table. I don't really know you, so it doesn't matter if I make a fool of myself. The seniors you represent, these 'remarkable persons,' you're—"

He interrupted her. "What happened out in the garden just now, I suspect it's happened to you before. And you should know it's happened to other people, too."

She digested that. "Tell me what you saw," Aggie commanded. "Tell me *specifically*."

"Your house was a stable. Your garden was gone. There was a milkman's wagon in the street. We were standing under a tree."

"An elm tree." Aggie had taught her students about Dutch elm disease. It had arrived on the continent in the 1930s, eventually killing nearly 80 million trees. There were no elm trees left in her town. Not now anyway.

Aggie thought about his description. She had seen those same things. Those things and more. Things he wouldn't have known about if it was all some sort of trick. She had smelled the roses from the long-gone Victorian estate. And spied the horseshoe. There was no way to explain away the horseshoe. She had seen it nailed under the eaves of the carriage house roof, barely visible. That's where it had been when they first bought the house. Jacob had taken it down when they painted the exterior. And nailed it back. But not under the eaves. He had positioned it right over the kitchen door, where it still hung, pointed ends up for luck. Luck that hadn't materialized, as it turned out.

Abraham was fiddling with his teaspoon. "Some people, a very few people, as they *age* ...," he shot her a look as if worried she might take exception to the word, "as they age, they develop the ability to move into the past."

"I take it you're not talking about reflecting back on a lifetime of happy memories," she said dryly.

"No, I'm not talking about that."

"You're talking about time travel." There, she had said it out loud.

Abraham picked up the tomato and turned it in his hands as Aggie had done. "We don't call it that. We just say we're travelers." He put the tomato back down and looked her straight in the eye. "So, cards on the table, I'm here because it came to our attention that you might be one of us. And we wanted to see if you were interested in cultivating your gift."

"Wait a minute. *It came to your attention?* How *exactly* did it come to your attention? I haven't told *anyone* about what's been happening. Only my doctor. Sort of. And he said I was *fine*. You haven't been poking into my medical records, have you?"

"No. Nothing like that," he responded quickly. "That wouldn't be ethical."

"So?"

"We place ads. We put things online. And we track inquiries, hits, on a few sites popular with seniors. We look for particular keywords, and that gives us a starting place for finding people beginning to experience the kind of thing you obviously have been experiencing." He gave a wry smile. "I'm afraid I'm not explaining this as clearly as usual."

"*As usual*. Then you've done this before?"

Suddenly he was serious. "Dozens of times. Scores of times."

"You found me after I clicked on that brain health link? How is that possible?"

"Hackers."

"I thought hackers were young," Aggie said a bit caustically.

"Hackers who get caught are young. They're always in a hurry, so they make mistakes. But in your case, we had a bit of a fortuitous occurrence. Another contact."

It took Aggie a minute to recall the name. "Lillian James."

He nodded. "She's one of the directors of our group."

"So, at JFK, when I saw the old plane, the Super Constellation—"

"Was that what it was? Yes, you saw it. You just didn't see it *in the present*. Was the plane the reason you did a web search? Lillian told me the trip you shared was just a flash, over in a few seconds. The kind of thing that could easily be explained away."

"Is that what some people do? Explain it away?"

"All the time."

"To answer your question, no. That's not why I did a web search."

"There have been other things then? Things that were not so easy to explain away? That actually helps. It makes time travel easier to accept. Although sometimes it makes it easier to believe you're nuts. Can you tell me where it happened?"

"Grand Central Station."

Abraham looked delighted. "Bravo! A New York landmark. Time period?"

"World War II. There were soldiers in uniforms from that era."

"If you do decide to join us for a few classes, I hope you'll share what you observed."

Aggie put her elbows on the table and folded her hands together. "In that case I think you ought to tell me about those classes."

"We meet quarterly, up near Ledyard. The fall session starts right after Labor Day and runs for a month. There's an AARP campus there. *Our* AARP. We have senior housing and a community center. Our neighbors in New London County believe we're just one more rural retirement village. And we are, in a way. As for the classes, new recruits get basic training so they can control their time travel. For veteran travelers, there are fieldwork opportunities."

Every school year, day one, Aggie began her classes with a lecture. Lectures weren't in vogue anymore, but she had always felt the need to make sure her students understood certain principles right off the bat. And so, the lecture. *Science doesn't start with an experiment. It doesn't start with a hypothesis. It starts with a question, a central question.*

Sitting at her kitchen table—in the face of one of the more extraordinary and unexpected experiences of her life—she pondered. What was her question? The central question. If one put aside the fantastical and surreal, what was left?

"I need to know," she began finally, "what the training is for. If you are training seniors for time travel, the question becomes *why*? What is your mission?"

Abraham smiled ruefully. "Teachers always get right to the point. They're often the best recruits, but they make you answer a million questions."

"Well, now that we've established that the dog didn't eat your homework, tell me what your AARP is trying to accomplish."

He was silent for a long moment, his eyes moving toward the window, then back to Aggie. "We're observers of history. We endeavor to document parts of the past that have been lost or are unknown. We're thirty years into the computer age, yet parts of history are still forgotten, or misremembered, or misreported, or turned into some sick conspiracy theory. The moon landing was a hoax. The Holocaust never happened. Sometimes young people assume that everything can be found by googling. That it's *all there*. And if you can't find it online, or what you find isn't accurate, it's almost as if it never happened at all."

"And the training?"

"Basic training is about control. If you can control where you go, then sometimes you will be in the right place, at the right time, to learn what history books missed and the internet never learned."

Aggie leaned forward. "What about the butterfly effect? Changing history? Because I don't—"

"Now that's something that's both simpler and more complicated than you might suppose. What I can say, as a preliminary matter, is that history can't be changed by our travelers. It's not something we can do, and we're not about that." Abraham leaned forward mirroring her position. "But we can observe. We can be eyes and ears. We can find ways to document people and events, even when memories—people's memories and institutional memories—fade."

Aggie couldn't put a name to what she was feeling. But it was strangely familiar. It was like the first time she had examined a slide under a microscope or gazed at the sky through a telescope. It was the feeling of adventure one got when peering into a new world.

Abraham had fallen silent now and appeared completely at ease, waiting patiently for her to think it through and come to a decision. *I must be out of my mind*. But Dr. Sterling had already put the kibosh on that eminently sensible theory. What should she conclude if a reasonable explanation didn't hold water, while one that was totally crazy was at least serviceable?

Maybe, for the first time in her life, go with crazy.

"What do people tell their family and friends? You can't just announce you're leaving for a month to learn how to time travel."

"Most of our folks say they're attending residential adult learning classes. Some say they're going on a senior bus trip or a retreat. We also find the more you talk about going on a seniors-only excursion, the more lots of people tune you out. *More is less*."

"No one listens to old people?"

"That's not what I meant," he said reproachfully. "And we actually do have a bus up to our campus. We pick up new recruits, and some of our veterans ride along because we pair everyone up with a mentor. Kind of a Big Brother-Big Sister thing."

"But doesn't anybody ask questions? I mean, here's a bus full of seniors going to—where did you say the campus is?"

Abraham grinned. "Up near *Ledyard*." He waited for her to put it together.

"You don't mean—"

"No one thinks it's strange to see seniors on their way to the casino."

"Do you get a rewards card to use at the slots?"

"Ms. May," Abraham said in a dignified manner, "we don't actually meet at the casino. That's just a cover story. Our campus is *near* Mashantucket Pequot land, but that's about the extent of the contact." He cleared his throat before continuing. "I should also tell you that there's no cost. Remarkable Enterprises is a foundation. We have donors, an endowment …." He waved his hand in a vague manner, dismissing the subject as unimportant.

Aggie stood, brought the now empty glasses to the drainboard, then reached up and took the wall calendar down off its hook. It had pretty garden photos on the pages. July's picture was a close-up of heirloom tomatoes arranged in a basket. She flipped to September, which featured brilliant blue bachelor's buttons, and picked up a pencil.

"Okay, Mr. Irving. Tell me the date. And where to catch the bus."

"You'll join us for the fall session?"

"I'm going to think about it. I assume you don't need an answer today."

"No. That's not necessary. I can leave you my card."

"Am I going to continue seeing things?"

Abraham rose to his feet and picked up his hat. He nodded. "Once you are open to the idea, it tends to keep happening."

"And if I decide all of this is just …." Aggie wasn't sure how to complete this thought.

Abraham looked serious again. "Some people, if they really want to suppress it, they make it stop. They make it go away." He studied her. "I hope you won't do that."

"The date," she directed.

"After Labor Day. We begin right after Labor Day."

Aggie circled the date on the calendar.

Back in January, when things were so different, she had filled in all the important dates for the year—her siblings' birthdays, Spring Break, June Graduation. The Tuesday after Labor Day already carried her penciled notation marking it the "first day of school." She didn't erase the words but added a coda under one of the blue flowers: *Catch the bus.*

From somewhere a stray fact drifted into her consciousness. In Victorian times, bachelor's buttons were thought to represent anticipation.

Chapter 7 ~ The Notebook

In the blink of an eye, it was August. Aggie tended the garden, completed household chores, and had an occasional lunch with friends. But resting in the back of her mind was the penciled notation on her calendar: *Catch the bus.*

Another reminder greeted her every day in the kitchen: Abraham's card clipped on her refrigerator, right next to a photo of her nephews at Dodger Stadium. He had handed her the card before leaving, seeming, at that moment, a little less like Indiana Jones and a little more like Elwood P. Dowd. She didn't believe in six-foot-tall white rabbits but realized she had somehow subscribed to something even more unlikely: *Remarkable Persons, the other AARP.*

She also realized that the anxiety and fear that had plagued her since Grand Central—since Junket, really—had receded. Her reward was a series of incidents that both surprised and beguiled her.

One occurred on a walk to the mailbox on the corner. Aggie had just deposited cards to her siblings when she heard the distinctive rattle of roller skates on pavement. She looked up to see a child of about eight zigzagging toward her with the characteristic swaying motion of the confident skater. The child had braids and wore a thin cotton dress with a narrow sash. One knee sported a red Band-Aid sprinkled with white stars. A piece of cotton string holding a skate key hung around the girl's neck and swung from side to side as she sped along.

Of course, Aggie thought. The skates are attached to her Buster Browns with metal clamps. You need a key to adjust the clamps. The girl approached, glanced up with a grin, and swerved around Aggie. At the end of the next block, she glided around the corner and disappeared.

Only then did Aggie think to look around. She found herself in a Polaroid snapshot from her childhood. Trees were dressed in their autumn reds and yellows. A woody station wagon drove by, and a man standing near the curb tended a pile of burning leaves raked into the gutter. As the scent of smoke reached her, she sneezed and closed her eyes. When she opened them, it was gone—the station wagon, the man with the rake, the pile of burning leaves—all of it.

Aggie was charmed, but disappointed to have returned so quickly Back at home she rummaged about in a drawer and, among the clutter, found a practically new spiral notebook and a ballpoint pen emblazoned with the Hytech logo. Opening to a blank page, she jotted the date in the upper right-hand corner and began to write.

1. *Junket jingle on the radio*
2. *Busy Bookworm Bookstore*
3. *Gas station phone booth*
4. *Super Constellation*
5. *Grand Central Terminal*
6. *Welcome Wagon trip with Mr. Irving*
7. *Roller skate girl*

She reviewed her list. Each item would need a fuller description. What had she observed? What was the time period? She started to write. An hour later, she poured herself a glass of lemonade and opened a can of cat food for Hubble who had come into the kitchen to investigate. She closed the notebook but left it on the table. Something told her there'd be more to come.

Her hunch was confirmed on her weekly visit to the Potatuck Public Library, a small Classical Revival structure built in 1908 with the help of a $20,000 grant from Andrew Carnegie. The library sat on one side of the rectangular village green which featured a rather weather-beaten Civil War monument whose anonymous soldier stood in a patch of flowers badly in need of water.

"Good morning, Aggie," the librarian greeted her cheerfully. "That mystery you wanted came back in yesterday."

"Thanks, Phyllis. I'll just take a quick look to see what else I can find." Aggie made her way to one of the narrow aisles at the back of the building and checked the shelf of new releases. Selecting a book, she glanced inside at the summary. Three sentences in, she knew it was a romance and slapped it closed. It wasn't that she never read romance novels, but too many seemed to feature clueless heroines who did reckless things and had to be rescued.

She shelved the book and scanned the other titles, but in that instant something happened. There was something odd about the books now. It was like that game in the Sunday comics: *What's wrong with this picture?* Then it came to her. Not a single book had a large colorful title on its spine. Not one exhibited a glossy plastic cover.

Someone else had joined her in the aisle, and Aggie peeked at the newcomer. It was a woman in an ankle-length skirt, a long-sleeved blouse, a hat, and high-button shoes. As Aggie watched, the woman turned away, moving toward the alcove where the card catalogue used to be. The distinctive scraping sound of a wood drawer being pulled from a cabinet informed her that the card catalogue was back, and the woman was leafing through the cards. Such a simple task. A task no one did anymore. Libraries everywhere, even in Potatuck, had online catalogs.

Aggie shifted her weight, the floor creaked, and she was back. The spines of the books glimmered again with a plastic shine. Returning to the front desk, she picked up the mystery and walked out into the sunshine.

At home, she opened the spiral notebook and added a neat number eight to her list. Eight sights? Visions? She wasn't sure what to call these events, but finally settled on the word "trips." She glanced at the wall calendar—the picture for August was sunflowers—noted the date and started writing.

***

Aggie's next contact with Remarkable Enterprises arrived in her mailbox in the form of a bulky, ivory-colored envelope embossed with the now-familiar stylized flowers. When she opened it, she discovered the bulkiness had been caused by a silver lanyard with a plastic card clipped to the end. The card—looking suspiciously like a casino rewards card—was imprinted with her name, the picture of a silver bird wearing a flowered hat, and the words "Ledyard Lucky Lady." There was also a letter:

Dear Ms. May,

We look forward to seeing you in September for our Remarkable Traveler classes. Our bus will pick you up at the South Norwalk train station at 10:15 a.m. Please plan for a four-week stay. In addition to clothing, toiletry articles, and your medications, you may wish to consider packing the following:

1. *Your cell phone, computer, and any other electronic device you know how to use. Wi-Fi is available throughout the campus.*
2. *Paper, envelopes, pens, and pencils, if you continue to appreciate this classic form of self-expression and communication. We have stamps at the front desk.*
3. *Several free reading books. We have a small lending library but offer no guarantee that your favorite authors are represented. The New York Times is delivered daily to all residents.*

Important Reminders:
- *If you play a musical instrument, please advise our staff, so you can be housed in an end unit or one of our cottages.*
- *If you are planning to bring your dog or cat, you may be assigned to one of our "pet-friendly" floors.*
- *Attention golfers: Bring your clubs! There are several public courses nearby.*

If you have any questions, we can be reached by phone or email. If you have determined that you will be unable to attend, please contact us.

Aggie raised her eyebrows. Not exactly reassuring. Nonetheless, she dropped the lanyard and card in a kitchen drawer and clipped the letter to the refrigerator next to Abraham's card. Her eyes scanned the last line: *If you have determined that you will be unable to attend ….* Funny. Through some peculiar alchemy, she had determined just the opposite.

In late August she called her friend Sally, one of the English teachers at Potatuck High, and invited her over for the day. Sally was twenty years her junior but shared her love of gardening. Together they began harvesting the produce from Aggie's garden: preparing pesto and tomato sauce, blanching beans for freezing, drying herbs, and making refrigerator pickles with the last of the cucumbers.

"So, tell me about this trip you're going on," Sally said, wiping her hands on her apron. "It doesn't really *sound* like you."

"What kind of trip sounds like me?"

"Well, don't you usually go sightseeing with your sister?"

That, indeed, was what she usually did. It was how she had spent most of her vacation time in the more than two decades since Jacob's death. It was time for a little misdirection.

Aggie remembered Abraham's advice. *More is less.* "Well, my sister's been really busy at work, so I thought I'd try something new. And since I'm retired, I'll be free in September. This program is held at a retirement community up near the casino. It's like a senior retreat, and there's lectures and social events in the evening. They have a bus pick you up. It's all retirees."

"Sort of like those free college classes for seniors? Sounds nice."

Aggie shot a furtive glance at Sally. Her friend was using cotton twine to bundle stems of oregano. At best, she was listening with half an ear.

Sally frowned as she looked out the kitchen window. "Gee, Aggie, what's going to happen to all this stuff? The herbs and jars will keep, but there's still a million tomatoes out there."

"I haven't figured that out yet. My across-the-street neighbor said she'd look after things, but she has a new set of twins. The best solution would be a house-sitter."

"Aggie!" Sally looked up from the oregano, a huge smile lighting her face. "Oh, I am so brilliant. I have the answer. Eva's got another student teacher this fall. Darling girl. Keen to change the world."

"That was us not too long ago."

"I know, I know. But listen, she's from Wallingford, and she'll have an awful commute, and she asked if I knew anyone who had a room to rent or needed *housesitting.*"

"She's with Eva? So, freshman biology, right? She should be able to handle the garden. Do you think she'd take care of Hubble, too?"

"I bet she'll jump at the chance. I'll call her *now*." Sally dropped the oregano and began fishing through her handbag for her phone.

In less than ten minutes, it was arranged. With her usual efficiency, Sally made the proposal, outlined the details, handed the phone to Aggie to close the deal, then took it back to jot down names, numbers, emails, and dates.

"Problem solved," Sally announced with satisfaction dropping her phone back in her bag. "She is *thrilled*. And she *adores* cats. Isn't that just the luckiest thing?"

"She hasn't met Hubble. I love my cat but have no illusions about his character. He's not entirely happy about being rescued from a feral existence, but he sticks around for the food."

"He won't be a problem, will he?"

"No. He'll love living with a student teacher who gets up at the crack of dawn. Hubble hates waiting for breakfast."

***

As Aggie prepared for bed on Labor Day, she wondered if she had forgotten anything. Though her clothes were packed, her suitcase still lay open on the bed. She had tucked in the spiral notebook after adding a few more sentences about the events of the previous week. On Friday she had glimpsed early twentieth-century townsfolk gathered on the green for the unveiling of the statue of the Civil War soldier. On Saturday she had noted something odd about the flag outside the post office. Later she realized there were only 48 stars.

Scanning the room, Aggie's eyes fell on a framed photograph of Jacob. He was standing in front of the Bethesda Fountain Angel in Central Park, his arms spread like wings. Roscoe had taken the snapshot after encouraging his normally serious brother-in-law to adopt the pose. It wasn't the best picture of her husband, but it was her favorite. His wild black hair and reluctant grin somehow captured who he was, who he had been.

"What do you think?" Aggie said, looking into his eyes. "Time to call the men in the white coats and turn myself in?"

So many of their conversations had begun this way. She'd pose questions in a storm of enthusiasm, or outrage, or delight, or curiosity— ah, how young she had been. Jacob would think things through. Then they'd talk. For minutes, or hours, or days. As long as it took.

Aggie picked up the photo and sat on the bed. "Should I go through with this? Be sensible or throw caution to the wind?" Since Jacob's death, she had spent years being sensible. But now things were different.

"I don't know why I'm asking," Aggie said at last. "For better or worse, I've decided."

She looked at her husband's handsome face. The smoke from his cigarette curled lazily toward the sky. "Those things will kill you one day," she said with a catch in her voice. "Stupid habit for a smart person."

He said nothing, of course. The time for talk, that beautiful time, was gone forever. Gently, she placed the picture in her suitcase, folding a cardigan around it to protect the glass.

Surprisingly, she slept well that night. As she awakened the next morning, she realized the air had become crisp. Lacy veins of yellow and orange adorned the leaves. It was September.

Chapter 8 ~ On the Bus

Aggie looked around nervously. She was standing at the curb in front of the ground transportation area of the train station. A northbound train on its way to New Haven had just disgorged its passengers. A much larger group of travelers on the far platform waited for the train to New York City.

She couldn't help wondering if anyone else was here to board the Remarkable Enterprises bus. Clearly not the three giggling twenty-somethings snapping selfies. Not the half-dozen people carried off by a city bus. Perhaps the elderly woman clutching a Macy's shopping bag? But, no, she entered a taxi and was whisked away.

That left two men with suitcases standing nearby. One had wispy white hair and resembled Albert Einstein. The other was a tall African American man who wore gray slacks and a maroon cardigan sweater with a little polo player embroidered on the front. In addition to his suitcase, he had a large zippered golf club travel bag.

Aggie studied the men discreetly, then realized they were eyeing her in the same surreptitious manner. *Time to fish or cut bait.* She opened her handbag, retrieved the Lucky Lady ID card, and looped the cord around her neck. The white-haired man gave her a tentative smile. The effect on the taller man was more pronounced. He grinned, unzipped a pocket on his suitcase, and extracted his own lanyard. His ID card bore the words "Lucky Ducky" and the image of a mallard duck improbably clothed in a vest and top hat.

"Kind of embarrassing, isn't it?" he commented with a rueful grin. "But I guess it fits the cover story." He squinted at her ID. "Agatha? I'm Benjamin Hale. From Danbury."

"Aggie May," she replied. "Pleased to meet you." She turned to the other man who had yet to speak. "Are you waiting for the Remarkable bus?"

The white-haired man gave them a slight bow. "Ms. May, I'm delighted to make your acquaintance. Mr. Hale, a pleasure. I'm Edgar Jaworski. My daughter thinks I'm crazy."

Aggie wasn't exactly sure how to respond. "Um, did you explain you were going on a senior retreat? I mean, she doesn't know about—"

"Oh, goodness no. I *would* be crazy if I told her I was starting to move through time. No, I told her I was going on a senior excursion, just like that helpful Mr. Irving suggested. Then I made a mistake and said there might be a side trip to the casino, and she got it into her head I was about to fall into the hands of card sharks. I can't really blame her. I've never gambled a day in my life. An irrational thing to do, really, when you think about it. Just look at the odds."

"Unlike time travel," Benjamin said, his eyes crinkling in amusement.

"Point taken," Edgar responded. "Actually, Mary's concern—Mary's my daughter—was very sweet. I just had to work around it a bit. I'm not used to dissembling, though. I live with Mary, and she takes good care of me. I'm quite fortunate having a caregiver who actually cares. Did you see that article in the *Times* about robot caregivers for the elderly? *Dreadful.*"

A honk from an approaching coach bus made them look up. Aggie exchanged nervous glances with the men as the bus turned into the circular drive and pulled to the curb. Wide doors opened, and a young woman with short-cropped, black hair stepped out. She held an acrylic clipboard and wore a scoop-neck t-shirt with the words "Lucky Lady" outlined in rhinestones.

"Ms. May? Mr. Hale? Mr. Jaworski? I am Mirlande Allaine." The woman spoke with a lovely Haitian accent. As each of them nodded, she made check marks on the clipboard then surveyed their luggage. "Just one set of clubs? Any other bags? Walkers?" They shook their heads, and she smiled. "Easy as pie then. Wells," she called to the driver, "three suitcases, one golf bag."

"Okay, Mirlande. I'll load 'em up." The driver bounded from his seat and jumped to the ground. It was the freckled young man with the blonde ponytail that Aggie had seen at JFK. He grinned at them then stowed their luggage in the storage compartment on the side of the bus.

Mirlande stepped back onto the bus and beckoned to Aggie and the two men. "Our first Connecticut recruits are here," she announced to those inside, and clapping and a few cheers could be heard. Aggie took a deep breath and mounted the steps.

Seats upholstered in navy blue and silver furnished the spotless interior. There were about thirty people on board. Apart from Wells and Mirlande, no one was young. Aggie pegged most of the passengers as sixty-somethings, but a few were much older. One plump little lady with permed blue-white hair and a pink-flowered cane looked about eighty.

"Listen everyone," Mirlande said. "This is Ms. Agatha May, Mr. Benjamin Hale, and Mr. Edgar Jaworski. Now bear with me. I need to give my welcome speech. You've heard it before, but they haven't, so please hush." She gave a spectacular smile and began. "Welcome aboard. We are so excited you will be joining us for the fall session at Remarkable Enterprises. The trip to our Ledyard campus takes about ninety minutes. We will make one additional stop to pick up our last recruits in New Haven. Now, to answer a few of your questions, we have brought along some of our old hands—"

"Look out folks, she's using the *O word!*" a smiling, brown-haired woman called out.

Mirlande pointed her pencil at the woman. "Julie, no catcalls, please. We have brought along a few of our *veterans,* and each of you will be paired with a Big Brother, or Big Sister, to act as a mentor for you on the trip, but more importantly, during your stay in Ledyard. We know you have questions. All of our mentors have been through basic training, so they are well suited to help you through the next days and weeks." Mirlande consulted her list. "Ms. May, you'll be with Julie, and good luck trying to get a word in edgewise."

The brown-haired woman who had interrupted Mirlande waved and Aggie headed down the aisle. When she reached the seat, Julie surprised her by pulling her into a hug. Benjamin was paired with a strong-looking older man with a crew cut sitting near the front. They shook hands, and the man gave Benjamin a friendly slap on the shoulder. Edgar's mentor turned out to be the plump lady with the flowered cane, who Mirlande introduced as Viola.

With everyone seated, Mirlande turned to the young driver who had settled back behind the wheel. "Ready, Wells?"

"I'm always ready," he replied shooting her a slightly suggestive look.

"Focus," Mirlande scolded. "Very close is not home yet."

"Yes, ma'am," he said with a grin. Putting the bus in gear, he drove out to the street.

Aggie gave her mentor a tentative smile. Julie looked to be in her mid-fifties, with a plain face, hazel eyes, and glasses. Her clothes and shoes looked expensive, but not particularly fashionable. Her mother would have called them "good quality" and "sensible."

"I'm Julie Wright. Should I call you Agatha? I can't believe I'm a *mentor.* Abe said I was ready, though, and thought you and I would hit it off, that you were *special* and would have a lot of questions. I thought for sure he would pair you up with one of the science or engineering guys, but he said teachers need to deal with people who can *communicate* and, well, when was the last time you read anything written by an engineer and had any *clue* what it meant?"

"Call me Aggie. My mother was the only one who called me Agatha and then only when I was in hot water. Were you a teacher, too?"

"Nope. Lawyer. Same kind of thing really," Julie responded with a grin. "You spend your time explaining complicated matters in a simple way to people who are absolutely convinced they know more than you do. I guess we senior citizens have to learn that particular survival skill as well."

"Mr. Irving arranged the mentor pairings?"

"Along with Lillian and Maurice."

"Lillian James?"

"Yes. Abe told me you ran into her at the airport, and that got them interested in finding you. Abe, Lillian, and Maurice are the directors and do most of the recruiting. Then they compare notes and assign veterans to be mentors. Now our mentor training said to 'let the recruit lead the conversation because each person will have his or her own concerns and questions.' So, what can I tell you about the Remarkables? That's what we call ourselves. Do you have any concerns and questions we should begin with?"

"Have you been doing this long?"

"Two years. I was recruited by Lillian. First time I did time travel, I thought I'd had a stroke."

"I thought it was Alzheimer's."

"Most of us have similar reactions." Julie nodded knowingly. "I was sure something was *wrong* with me. There I was, walking along the boardwalk in Atlantic City, and I stopped to look down at a tourist map. When I looked back up, there I was. Late thirties, maybe early forties."

"How did you *know*? After you ruled out a stroke, how did you know?"

"Well, my doctor said I was—"

"*Fine*," Aggie said.

"Exactly. Fine. But the experience wouldn't go away, and I kept trying to make sense of it. I woke up at night thinking about it."

"What convinced you?"

"The evidence. Details I never would have come up with on my own if I was just imagining it. I saw a group of women on the beach wearing old-fashioned swimsuits and bathing caps. Remember bathing caps? Women don't wear them anymore."

"For me, it was a woman straightening the seam of her stocking."

"Yes, that would do it," Julie said. "And there was something else. I saw things that *I know I didn't know*. I saw the names of shops, and I looked them up later and found them. I didn't know anything about restaurants or vendors along the Boardwalk. It was my first visit *ever* to Atlantic City. It wasn't a memory. I was seeing it for the first time. And I was seeing it accurately."

Aggie thought about this. Outside the bus window, the Port Jefferson Ferry was chugging sedately out of Bridgeport Harbor on its way across the Sound to Long Island. "Could it have been from a book you read a long time ago? Or a picture you had seen?"

"No," Julie shook her head emphatically, "I *know* I didn't know. If I had read about it before, I would have remembered. But I'm getting off track. We're supposed to be talking about basic training. That's what you'll do first. Fieldwork and acting come later."

"Acting?"

"Well, it's not really *acting*. It's more like practicing time-period-appropriate behavior. You know, so you don't speak or behave in a way that's unsuitable for the time period and draw attention to yourself. That can get you evicted back to the present." Julie shot an anxious look at Aggie. "I'm not being clear, am I?"

"You're doing fine," Aggie said reassuringly. "But let's take a step back. Tell me about the place we're going, the campus."

Julie grinned. "Oh, you'll like it. Wells says it's a cross between an Embassy Suites and senior housing, and he's kind of right. But it's really nice. The directors and some of the veterans live there year-round, but new recruits, and those of us who only come in for the quarterly sessions, we're given apartments. All accessible, of course. For meals, you can prepare something in your apartment, but most people eat together in the Lodge which is a giant clubhouse kind of building. It has a dining hall, meeting rooms, and the library and gym."

"There's a gym?"

"Yes, there's exercise equipment, but it's also used for focus class and acting."

"Yoga class?"

"No, *focus class*. It's part of basic training, the way the process begins. It's rather like yoga, now that you mention it. Or meditation. To travel, you focus on an object and kind of tune out the rest of the world. Then you think about your destination and let go. Focusing helps you limit input to your brain. What were you looking at when you traveled with Abe?"

"A striped heirloom tomato. He said he was interested, so I passed it to him, and he kept hold of my hand. The next thing I knew it was about 1905. I figured out afterward he didn't know a thing about tomatoes, or gardening for that matter."

"Well, he usually doesn't know what the potential Remarkable is interested in and what object might be used for focusing. Abe's one of the best. Exceptional, in fact. He can focus on just about anything, but someone who's starting out needs a little help. He pretends to be interested in something the prospect is interested in and waits to see what happens."

A short, grandmotherly-looking passenger across the aisle had clearly been eavesdropping. "Yes, that's what I imagined must be going on," she said. "After all, you don't find a lot of older gentlemen who want to talk about embroidery."

Julie started to giggle. "I would *love* to have seen that interview. We kid him a lot, you know. We call him 'Honest Abe,' a bit sarcastically, because he's anything but. Wait till you talk to Sal. Salvatore. He's the guy with the crew cut sitting up there with Benjamin. He's a five-year veteran. Owns his own masonry business in Waterbury. Abe went out to recruit him and couldn't get Sal to focus on *anything*. He finally spun some tale about how Sal had won a contest and was entitled to new vinyl siding. They went outside to talk about matching gutters and bang. They were off to the Roaring Twenties."

"Do the recruiters always get it right?" Aggie thought back to her Welcome Wagon visit, Abraham studying her in the garden, making a judgment.

"Not always. Sometimes they get false hits. You know, people might do an internet search using key words from the algorithm, and get picked up as potentials, but they're just not travelers. Ask Abe to tell you about the guy in Jersey with the stamp collection. Sometimes Abe just wings it, but he prepped for that visit, and was there for like three hours looking through scrapbooks and discussing 'accountancy marks' and 'cylinder flaws.' It turned out the man had no ability at all. It just wasn't happening."

Julie drew a breath and went on. "That two-person travel thing, where he goes with you into the past—we call it *companion travel*—it's rare. Very, very rare. Most of the time, when you travel, you go alone."

Aggie raised her eyebrows. "Explain that."

"It's like the past only makes room for one traveler at a time. But Abe, Maurice, and Lillian can go with another person, at least for a few minutes. They're the only ones on the East Coast who can do it. It makes them wonderful recruiters."

Aggie glanced out the window. They passed the giant IKEA that faced the coastline, then the Knights of Columbus building. A new question occurred to her.

"Do the recruiters ever encounter someone who doesn't want to pursue it? Someone with ability, but no interest?"

"It happens. Usually for understandable reasons like family or health. Sometimes one spouse has the skill, but the other doesn't, and it becomes way too complicated. Some people are afraid. Some can't believe the evidence. Some just don't care to pursue it. I mean, some seniors are content spending time with the grandchildren or going on a cruise."

Aggie understood. She knew her own unhappiness—her outrage and despair upon being forced from her job—was not a feeling universally shared.

"And even when people join the Remarkables, it's accepted that no one can train or do fieldwork 24/7. It's too intense. We have clubs and social activities, so people can relax. There are musicians, golfers, aerobics. A couple of the guys play poker. Some folks actually do go to the casino." She reached across the aisle and tapped the arm of the grandmotherly woman. "There's a needlework group, too. And those ladies really do know something about embroidery. They'll be thrilled to have a new member."

The bus had turned onto the exit ramp heading into New Haven. "How many are we picking up here, Wells?" Julie called to the front of the bus.

"Just two, Jules. Maurice recruited them. We're getting them at Yale, by Dwight Hall."

The bus rolled into town, passed a Starbucks, then turned under a stone archway ornamented with a giant clock and sculpted angels.

"Dwight Hall was designed by Henry Austin and built in the 1840s. It used to be the library," Julie said. "It became Dwight Hall—the old YMCA—in 1930. Old buildings can help you travel, you know. They have *auras*. You'll hear about that. Say a house was built in 1925. You can travel back to that time, and the house is still there, and it's less jarring than having everything around you disappear and get replaced by a completely different structure."

"What if you miscalculate?" Aggie asked curiously. "Say the building has been renovated, and you materialize inside a brick wall or something?"

Julie laughed. "Boy, that would be distressing, wouldn't it? Very Edgar Allan Poe. But no worries on that account. If there's no room for you in the past, or there's any kind of danger, you won't be able to time travel. You'll stand there focusing, but you won't budge. Like, you can't take an elevator to the top of the Empire State Building and then go back pre-1930. There's no safe space for you. At least not at that time, at that height. And once you do get to the past, you're still protected. First hint of trouble and you get evicted back to the present, no harm done."

The bus had pulled up next to a Gothic Revival building on the edge of the Old Campus. An elderly couple stood at the curb, her arm looped through his. Wells opened the door, and Mirlande stood up, clipboard in hand. "New Haven recruits are here," she called. Aggie clapped along with the others.

In a few minutes, the couple, looking slightly shell-shocked, had boarded the bus. "Ladies and gentlemen," Mirlande announced, "let me introduce Flora and Fred Hopewell. Take note. They're not Mr. and Mrs. They're *twins*."

"Gosh," Julie whispered. "They have the same eyes and nose. And the same terrified expression, poor dears."

"Does that happen often? Siblings?" Aggie could not picture her organized sister roaming through time although free-spirited Roscoe would probably see it as an adventure: a new part in a new play.

"Siblings are not unknown, but they don't usually develop the ability simultaneously. I *have* heard of it happening with identical twins. But it's cool Maurice found fraternal twins."

While Julie had been talking, Mirlande had finished her welcome speech and assigned mentors to Flora and Fred. Wells settled into the driver's seat again. "Next stop, the Lodge," he called and set the bus in motion.

Chapter 9 ~ The Lodge

In less than an hour, the bus pulled off the highway and began winding along two-lane country roads. They passed a few farms and a vineyard before turning into a wide driveway flanked by stone columns. A carved wooden sign stood to the side. Its gilt letters read "The Lodge – A Remarkable Enterprises Senior Living Community."

"This land was a family farm until not too long ago," Julie said. "Then a real estate outfit bought it and put up some condos and a community center, but the crash in '08 killed that project. Then they thought it might work for corporate retreats, but the market was shaky, and the area is rural, so that deal fell through, too. Abe bought the whole place for a song."

The bus entered a circular driveway and slowed to a stop under a portico. Aggie got to her feet, shouldered her handbag, and took a deep breath.

"You'll be *fine*," Julie assured her, and Aggie laughed. She thought Dr. Sterling might be rather disconcerted if he knew she was out in the middle of nowhere having signed up for time travel lessons with a group of "remarkable persons."

Mirlande was already out of the bus, clipboard in hand. "Come along, don't be shy," she called. "Your luggage will be brought to your apartment. There's a buffet waiting inside, so head on in. The teachers and residents are excited to meet you."

Aggie stepped off the bus and examined her surroundings. The building before her displayed an odd mixture of elements, as if the architect had been unsure whether to design an English manor house or an L.L. Bean ski resort. The gabled roof rose above tall multi-paned windows, and neat flowerbeds filled with purple and maroon chrysanthemums flanked the wide double doors. To the right of the entrance was a brass plate engraved with the words "The Lodge."

Beyond the main building, three long residential structures, connected by covered walkways, formed a "U" around a green featuring a wooden gazebo. A path leading away from the green wound past a rather picturesque-looking barn and ended at a cluster of cottages that sat at the foot of a hill.

Julie noticed Aggie studying the barn. "The developers weren't sure whether to tear down the old barn or leave it up as a 'landscape element.' They went bankrupt before they made up their minds. Abe left it up. He's crazy for that barn. He says it was the deciding factor in his decision to purchase. We use it for basic training."

"The barn?"

"Sure. Like you might have a practice session where you try traveling back to the early twentieth century to make observations about raising chickens or milking cows. You know, before it was all mechanized." Julie started giggling. "Last year one of the rookies was practicing and saw a couple of early-century teens going at it like rabbits in the hayloft. Well naturally, after that, everyone had a go, but no one got back to that exact moment, so all they had were a lot of boring observations about old-time farm implements."

"Did you try it yourself?" Aggie laughed.

"Of course. No luck though. Come on, let's go in."

Aggie let Julie steer her through the front door. The room they entered was large and open, with a high ceiling supported by dark wooden beams. Sofas and armchairs faced an enormous fieldstone fireplace. A long, polished counter, such as might appear at a posh hotel, stood to the side. Wells was already in position behind the counter, overseeing the distribution of white paper badges with the traditional *"Hello. My name is ____"* lettering. A trio of white-haired ladies stood nearby, handing out dark blue gift bags stuffed with silver tissue paper.

"Take a goody bag, dearie," one of the women said, handing Aggie a small paper tote. There's orientation material in there and some nice little products."

Across the room a wide arch led to a spacious dining room, where a long table laden with sandwiches, salads, and fruit awaited them. An easel near the entrance displayed a poster with the Remarkable Enterprises flowered logo and the words "Welcome Tri-State Trainees!"

Mirlande reappeared, having disposed of the luggage. "Ladies and gentlemen, you can head right into the dining room. If you want to freshen up first, the ladies' and gents' rooms are down the hall."

Aggie excused herself and headed to the ladies' room. Inside she noted that all of the stalls were wheelchair accessible. Heavy paper guest towels and china dishes holding pastel soaps sat next to each basin. She washed her hands and took a moment to study her reflection. Who was the woman looking back? Not the same woman, anxious and adrift, who had stared from the mirror as the summer began. But not the confident teacher, either. She was somewhere in the middle: cautious, curious, ready to see this experiment unfold. She pulled a comb from her handbag and ran it through her hair.

As she headed for the door, she saw a small bulletin board with a pretty wicker frame mounted on the wall. A notice printed on pink paper caught her attention, and she stopped to read.

Question of the Day:
Which sales pitches are the most annoying?

Four choices were offered, and a pencil was secured to the board with a piece of pink cord so people could vote. Aggie contemplated the options:

1. *Claims that a product contains an "anti-aging" formula.*
2. *Reprimands about "style mistakes that age you."*
3. *Promises to "repair" your lines for "younger-looking skin!"*
4. *Advice to put on "shapewear" because no one wants to see you sag.*

There were check marks next to each choice, although the first two were the biggest vote-getters. Picking up the pencil, Aggie put a mark on the third line. She had never liked the word "repair" when it came to face cream. It sounded as if those with lined skin needed an Angie's List handyman to set things right. Pushing through the door, she met Benjamin coming out of the men's room. He was chuckling and shaking his head.

"I'd compare votes," he said, catching sight of Aggie, "but I'm sure you had a different list."

In the dining room, dozens of people clustered in small groups, moved along the buffet line, and gathered at long "family-style" tables covered in crisp white linen. Everyone seemed to be talking at once.

Aggie selected a roasted vegetable sandwich and a glass of iced tea then headed across the room toward Julie who was waving her over.

"Here's my Little Sister," Julie cried. "Have a seat and meet some folks. This fine-looking gentleman is Sal. He was on the bus with us. And this is Bernice." She pointed to a short, gray-haired woman whose placid expression reminded Aggie of Vivian Vance from *I Love Lucy*. "She completed basic training last winter."

Aggie nodded to each in turn. Across the room, she noticed two young men wearing dark blue, double-breasted chef's coats peeking out from a door she assumed led to the kitchen. They were joined by a much older African American man with a white beard who scanned the room with a critical eye, then pointed to a nearly empty platter of fruit. One of the young men scurried out and removed the platter, while the other disappeared back into the kitchen, emerging a moment later holding a bowl piled with berries and garnished with sprigs of mint. He held it up to the older man for inspection, and, after receiving an approving pat on the shoulder, delivered it to the buffet table.

Aggie took a bite of her sandwich. It was delicious. For a few minutes she concentrated on the food, before the clinking of a spoon on a goblet brought conversation to a halt. Abraham stood at a table near the big front window. He looked just as he had last summer, Aggie thought, although his linen jacket had been replaced by a corduroy one, very much in professorial mode. He smiled broadly as he raised both hands in greeting.

"Ladies and gentlemen," he began, "old friends and new, we are thrilled to welcome you to the fall quarter of Remarkable Enterprises. To our new recruits, we hope your mentors have filled you in a bit, although, judging by past experience, I'm sure you still have many, *many* questions." Here he glanced over to where Julie and Aggie sat together. "Once you've all had a chance to finish up and get a piece of Maurice's fine chocolate cake, we'll reconvene next door and have a little chat about what exactly we do here."

Aggie and Julie brought coffee into the room with the fireplace where they found seats in comfy armchairs near the front. In a few minutes every chair, loveseat, and sofa was filled. A few of those gathered sat in wheelchairs or on the flip-down seats of their walkers. Most in attendance were gray haired and neatly dressed. They were the kind of people you saw at senior centers, Aggie thought, or in the audience at a C-SPAN Book TV broadcast.

Two women lounging in a doorway stood out, however. One was tall, with a beautiful figure, and long hair as black as a raven's wing. She wore an emerald green, scoop-neck top and form-fitting black pants. Next to her stood an equally striking blonde with a very fashionable blunt cut and rather a lot of jewelry. The blonde had one hand on her hip, displaying manicured nails painted with rose-pink polish. Aggie stole a quick look at her own fingernails which were clean but clipped short and unpolished. She rarely bothered to get her nails done, what with handling chemicals at school and digging about in her garden at home. Nonetheless, looking at the blonde, she wondered if perhaps it might have been worth it to invest fifteen dollars at Glamor Gloss back in Potatuck.

Abraham had positioned himself behind a podium placed in front of the fireplace and rested his coffee cup on the mantelpiece behind him. Next to him, seated on her fire-engine red walker, was Lillian, the elderly woman from the airport. The third person joining them was the man with the white beard who had been directing the young chefs in the dining room.

The room grew quiet, and Abraham grinned at the assemblage. "For those of you who have not met me, my name is Abraham Irving. The lovely lady next to me is Lillian James, and this gentleman is Maurice

Kingston. You did, of course, meet one us during your Welcome Wagon visit, and, in quite a coincidence, one of our newcomers, Ms. Agatha May from Connecticut, met both Lillian and myself. Wave your hand, please, Ms. May, so folks will know who you are."

Self-consciously, Aggie raised her hand then quickly put it down again.

Abraham grinned at her before resuming his talk. "What we want to do now is go over a few basics for our newcomers and explain what will take place in the next four weeks."

"Abe?" It was Wells calling from the back of the room. "Are you sure you don't want to use the screen and projector? It will only take a minute."

"Thank you, Wells, but *no.*" Turning back to the gathering, Abraham explained. "Wells very kindly put together a PowerPoint presentation for orientation, but I pointed out that we seniors are perfectly capable of listening attentively to a live speaker, and—" He stopped abruptly. "Vi," he said to the woman with the blue-white permed hair, "wake up Frank."

Viola turned to look at an armchair behind her, near the wall, where an athletic-looking older man with a buzz cut was seated. He wore a baseball jersey and had his arms folded across his stomach and his feet stretched out in front of him. A Yankees cap on his head had been pulled down to cover his eyes. A gentle snore rose from below the cap.

Picking up her flowered cane, Viola gave a resounding thwack to the side of the chair. The man jerked and sat up abruptly, pushing his baseball cap back on his head. "Morning, sunshine," Viola said cheerfully.

"I wasn't sleeping," Frank protested. "Jeez, Vi, you don't have to wallop my chair every time I rest my eyes."

"As I was saying," Abraham continued smoothly, "I know this audience will listen attentively to what we are going to go over this afternoon. As you know, we are here because we have discovered in ourselves the ability to travel in time. In his later years, Einstein concluded that the past and present exist simultaneously, and our experiences seem to provide evidence that Einstein was right. Although we use the term 'time travel' because it is simple and convenient, what is happening in fact is a far more complicated process—a process that is not completely understood even by those of us who are veterans. What we do know is that the brains of some people, as they get older, develop the ability to perceive the *simultaneousness* of time. Once that happens, it becomes possible to move between those simultaneous worlds."

Deftly, Abraham retrieved his coffee cup and took a swallow. "Your mentors have undoubtedly explained that what we hope to accomplish in basic training is some degree of control over those movements. Generally, the new time traveler begins by getting quick glimpses of different time periods based on stray thoughts, or personal interests, or random memories, or perhaps the effect of *auras* that seem to collect in certain locations."

"You're getting a little mystical there, Abe," Wells called from behind the desk.

"*Thank you*, Wells," Abraham said. "I'm sure I don't know how I would ever explain this without your *invaluable* input." He finished his coffee and placed the empty cup back on the mantel. "Some may quibble with the concept of auras, but we shouldn't get bogged down by terminology. We have anecdotal evidence suggesting that there may be a locational element involved in some of our journeys. And a few of our statistical folks have worked up a geographic analysis and found a definite correlation between certain historic sites and successful time travel experiences. For example, we can cite many cases associated with the Empire State Building and the Brooklyn Bridge. The D.C. chapter points to the Capitol Dome and the Lincoln Memorial. Philadelphia, Boston, Chicago, Los Angeles—they all report clusters of cases tied to historic structures. Here in the Tri-State Chapter we know the Big Apple seems to turbo-charge the time travel process, and we've gotten a steady stream of recruits from the city. But I'm digressing." He made an apologetic gesture toward the other directors. "Perhaps it's time for Lillian and Maurice to give you a run down on basic training."

"Yes, I think so," Lillian agreed, rising to her feet and smiling at the gathered seniors. "As Abraham explained, and as your mentors have no doubt discussed with you, we hope to help you learn control over your time travel. As a preliminary matter, let me say that henceforth I will endeavor to speak of what we do here as 'travel' rather than *time* travel. I encourage you to do the same. It is a helpful habit that allows us to talk about what we do without raising concern should we chatter on a bit thoughtlessly when we return home or are out in public. Those of you who recall World War II—and I know there are some here who do—remember the posters that said, 'Loose Lips Sink Ships.' We are not at war, but we do find that discretion helps us avoid unwanted attention."

A murmur of whispered comments traveled across the room. Lillian waited patiently until it was quiet again. "Maurice will be working with our new recruits this session. He will review a few basic training principles with you now, and then your mentors will escort you to your apartments. Tonight, we'll get together in small groups after supper to socialize a bit and share our experiences before classes begin tomorrow."

The man with the white beard stepped to the podium next. He rolled forward onto the balls of his feet and back again, before an engaging grin spread across his round face. Aggie's brow wrinkled. The man looked familiar, but she couldn't place him.

Julie noted her expression and leaned over to whisper. "Do you have his book?"

"His book?"

"*Kingston's Kitchen.* It's a collection of his best recipes."

"He's *that* Maurice Kingston? The celebrity chef?"

Julie giggled. "Yes, but don't call him that. He says the word 'chef' is inherently dignified, but the word 'celebrity' is not."

"Good afternoon, everyone." Maurice's deep voice extended to every corner of the room. "Welcome. We are happy you're here and look forward to getting to know you better. Now, for most of our recruits, control over your travel can be achieved, but it takes practice. Youngsters enter elementary school and learn their ABCs. Here we are no longer youngsters, but we are, nonetheless, learners. Our goal at Remarkable Enterprises is to learn the *Three Ds* that allow us to regulate our travel: Destination, Distance, and Duration."

"I should've gone over this with you," Julie whispered, "but Maurice will explain it better."

"Your mentor will have told you that travel begins by focusing on an appropriate object," Maurice continued. "The first time I traveled I was contemplating a rather nice microplane zester. But be that as it may, once you're on your way, the three Ds put you in the driver's seat. Proficiency in *Destination* allows you to arrive at the exact point in history you wish to visit. With *Distance* you can move from your arrival point and step out into the past. *Duration* permits you to extend your visit beyond the few short minutes generally accorded the novice traveler. And that about covers it. I'll be working with our rookies this fall, and I want you to rest assured that all of us on campus are here to support you."

Applause broke out. Maurice acknowledged it with a wave, then stepped to the side as Lillian moved to the podium again. "Thank you, Maurice. Naturally, we're hopeful that once you have learned control, you'll wish to join us in fieldwork to support our central mission which is to observe and report on parts of history that have been lost through the passage of time."

Lillian stopped, and her eyes swept the room. Nearly everyone was attentive, although the raven-haired woman in the doorway was whispering something to her blonde companion, who giggled in response.

"We want you to know, however," Lillian continued in a more serious tone, "based on quite a few years' experience, what we are not hopeful about, and what you should not be hopeful about either." At these words, the room grew still. "You must not be hopeful about changing the past. The past cannot be changed. You cannot alter the great sweep of history. You cannot prevent a war, or a disaster, or even a single death. Any interactions you have with others in the past are, at best, tenuous and ephemeral. That is why our missions are limited to observation and documentation.

"You should also not expect to spend time on personal time travel. *It is not possible to see yourself in the past.* You cannot take a nostalgic trip back to a childhood birthday party or your high school prom. We are not sure why this is so, but to borrow Abraham's rather awkward word, it probably has something to do with the *simultaneousness* of our travel. You cannot look through a telescope and be a star in the sky at the same time."

"Nice metaphor," Abraham commented.

"Thank you," Lillian replied gravely. "What we would like you to concentrate on in the next few weeks, is what you *can* do. As Maurice said, we are here to support you." There was another round of applause which Lillian acknowledged with a nod. "Now, Wells and Mirlande have a few announcements then your mentors will show you to your apartments."

Wells had come forward from his spot behind the reception desk. Mirlande stood next to him, her hands folded in front of her and a tranquil expression on her face.

"Okay, folks," he said, rubbing the palms of his hands together. "First, Maurice says there's lots more cake, so help yourself to seconds. Then when you're ready, your mentors will take you to your apartments and go over your class schedule. If you need anything at any time, just pick up the phone and dial the operator. I'm the operator—"

"That's the truth," Mirlande said softly.

Wells shot her a wounded look and continued. "That is, I'm the operator along with a really good service we've brought on board, so don't hesitate to call."

Mirlande addressed them next. "You should also use the phone if you need any kind of medical assistance. Some of you have already made arrangements for reminders about your medications or help in the shower, but if you would like to be added to our list, just speak to me. So, mentors, whenever you're ready."

"Let's go, Aggie," Julie said. "Time to check out your new digs."

Chapter 10 ~ The Apartment

Julie led Aggie down a wide hallway and out a side door. They emerged on one of the covered walkways that linked the three apartment buildings adjacent to the Lodge.

"We're in this first building," Julie said. She hit a button positioned on an ornamental post, and the door to the lobby opened automatically. "The construction crew Abe brought in thought they were modifying the apartments for assisted living, which they were, of course. Just assisted living of a slightly different kind."

The rustic décor of the building's lobby echoed that of the Lodge. A sitting area held sofas upholstered in fabric patterned with leaves and flowers. The flat weave carpet appeared wheelchair friendly. An oak handrail was mounted on the wall along the hallway.

"You're right down here." Julie led her to a doorway a short distance down the hall. "Unit 103. You were going to be on the second floor, but after your Welcome Wagon visit, Abe insisted you be on the first floor so you could have a yard and patio, not just a balcony."

Aggie opened the door to the apartment and the Embassy Suites image faded. The living room contained a sofa, armchair, flat screen TV, and coffee table. At the end of the room, a kitchen area was set off by a marble-topped counter. A wooden table sat in front of a picture window covered by lace curtains that filtered the late afternoon sunlight. A wide sliding glass door led to a patio.

Aggie crossed the room, slid the door open, and stepped outside. The patio was set in a small yard enclosed by a stone wall. It featured a wooden bench, a large pot of white chrysanthemums, another of blue-purple asters, and smaller containers with herbs. A gate in the wall opened to a sloping lawn. The barn and cottages were visible in the distance.

Julie spoke from behind her. "Abe thought you'd like having a bit of a garden, but he can't tell a dandelion from a daylily, so he asked the Garden Club for help. Marla and Ted put their heads together and potted up a few things."

"It's beautiful," Aggie said, taking it all in. She felt an unexpected wave of emotion. Someone—Abraham—had given thought to what she might like.

"Come and look at the rest of the place," Julie called.

The sunny bedroom had a dresser, nightstand, reading lamp, and rocker. The queen-sized bed was covered in a gorgeous crazy quilt fashioned from flowered fabrics.

"Needlework Club," Julie said gesturing toward the bed. "We seem to get a lot of quilters. A few years back they told the directors the apartments needed to be homier, so everyone gets a quilt. They talk to whatever director did the recruiting then pick something out." Julie giggled. "One of the ladies told me Abe's input on your quilt was 'give her one with lots of flowers.' Check out the bathroom."

Aggie peeked through the door. There was a walk-in—or roll-in—shower and two sinks, one at wheelchair height. A deep tub had a little door in the side for easy access, a built-in seat, and whirlpool jets. Aggie had seen tubs like this advertised in the weekly magazine that came with the Sunday newspaper. But this one was sleeker. And a little out of place. Like a Ferrari in a handicapped parking space.

"Um … wow, I guess," Aggie said.

"Wells had so much fun with these," Julie laughed. "He thought those senior walk-in tubs were cool, but he wanted to fiddle around with the concept. He said they shouldn't look institutional, so he talked to some of his geeky friends from M.I.T., and they played around with the engineering and design."

"M.I.T? Wells looks like he's seventeen."

"He's nineteen. He graduated from M.I.T. last year."

Aggie looked at her in disbelief.

"Smart kid, that Wells," Julie said, then started giggling. "He had one of these installed in his own apartment. He said there was no reason to wait till he was a senior to enjoy the perks of old age. Then one weekend when Mirlande was away he had one installed in her place. It's *pink*. She pretended to be annoyed, but I caught her coming back from the mall with matching towels."

"Is he sweet on her?"

"Totally smitten. She thinks he's too young and treats him like a bothersome puppy."

Aggie snapped off the bathroom light. "The course of young love …."

"Let's look at your schedule," Julie said. "And check out your goody bag."

They found the schedule—printed on lilac-colored paper—clipped on the refrigerator then sat at the wooden table in front of the window. Julie dumped out the contents of the goody bag which included lip balm, an energy bar, a travel-sized bottle of sunblock, a keychain with the Lucky Lady logo, a postcard-sized map of the campus, and a CD in a plastic case. Julie inspected the CD. "*Tunes for Travelers*," she read. "Oh God, Wells has gotten clever again. We may as well put it on while we check your schedule."

Julie popped the disk into a CD player on the counter and hit play. Pete Seeger's voice wafted into the room, singing the opening lines of "Turn! Turn! Turn!"

Returning to the table, Julie picked up the lilac-colored sheet and ran her finger down the page. "Okay, Abe has us all down for Show and Tell tonight. It's listed as the *New Student Reception,* but don't be fooled. It's more like Show and Tell. We break into small groups with vets and rookies in each group. Rookies take turns talking about their first serious time travel experience. You know, the one that convinced you."

Pete Seeger finished, and Cyndi Lauper's "Time after Time" came on.

"After tonight you have the normal classes," Julie continued. "There's Focus and Control in the morning and a history elective in the afternoon. Let's see. They're offering electives on Prohibition, the Great Depression, and the home front in World War II. Good choices." She passed the lilac sheet to Aggie. "Evenings are usually free, and clubs, sports, and off-campus trips are listed on the back."

"Will you be in some of the same classes?"

"No. Veterans do fieldwork. Some do projects on their own, but most fieldwork is with a group. I'm with a Civil War photography group that Lillian's leading. I'm not sure what the exact mission is yet. We'll find that out tomorrow."

"You said most travelers go back alone. So how does a group work together?"

Julie propped her chin on her hand and considered. "It's all about coordination. Let's say you want to study the construction of the Empire State Building. You have just over a year to work with—from March 1930 to April 1931. You could have people go to different months then compile their observations and get an overview. A lot of travelers can be out there at once because they're all at different points in time.

"If the event occurs in a short time period—like the Wall Street crash in 1929—it's a little trickier. You have to take turns. So, you send the first traveler out. Say she arrives at 9 a.m. on Black Tuesday and is able to stay until 9:30. She comes back and reports to the next person in line. That person goes back to 9:30, stays until 10, and so on. Of course, some can stay for longer periods, some shorter. But it's all about working in shifts.

"Sometimes you use both methods. Like last year we did fieldwork on the intake process at Ellis Island. We could all go out at once because we all went to different years then compared notes. But," Julie hesitated and shot a look at Aggie, "some of us found out that Sal's grandma arrived on a particular day in 1921 when his father was just a baby. His dad was killed in the Korean War when Sal was young, and they didn't have it easy after that. His mom went to work, and his grandma helped raise him. A couple of us thought he might like to see the day she arrived."

Aggie studied her. "A couple of you ...."

Julie paused for a good long minute. Tony Bennett was crooning "Just in Time." Aggie waited.

"You heard Lillian," Julie said at last. "She has strict notions about personal travel—travel that doesn't advance the mission."

"You did it anyway."

Julie looked uncomfortable. "We did. Look, you can't tell anyone. I don't like being less than totally honest, but it didn't feel like an inappropriate thing to do. It wasn't easy. We knew the day, and the name of the ship they came in on, and we had a picture of his grandma, but that's a big building, and it took *forever* to find her, what with the crowds and the lines and people getting pulled into rooms for physical exams. We worked in shifts, and everyone that went back had to record their time and the part of the building they were in." She colored slightly. "It was also complicated because there are differences in skill levels, even among veterans. Some have trouble with the first D, *destination*. You know, getting to the day and time you're aiming at. Some can get there but can't stay very long. That's a *duration* problem. Some arrive and try to take a few steps then get dropped right back to the here and now."

"A *distance* problem."

"Yes."

"Does practice help?"

"Sometimes yes, sometimes no."

Aggie looked at Julie's flushed cheeks. "Isn't it true that some travelers are better observers than others? Aren't the observations themselves the important thing—no matter how good or bad you are at the Three Ds? I mean maybe you're great at getting there, and staying there, and walking around. But if you're not perceptive, or you misinterpret what you see, that's just as big a problem."

"Yes," Julie agreed. "Sometimes that's the biggest issue. Abe tells me—tells all of us—that the most talented travelers are those with good observation skills."

"Did you find Sal's grandma?"

Julie's face lit up. "Yes. It was amazing. We saw her holding the baby, Sal's father, and we told Sal the time and the right window to go to. He saw them reach the front of the line and saw the guy behind the desk check their names on the ship's manifest. The clerk couldn't understand their accents very well, but he was incredibly patient and kind. Sal's a traditional kind of guy, but he had tears in his eyes when he came back."

"And the larger mission. Was that successful as well?"

"Definitely. There's so much you can learn by *being there*, seeing an event as it's happening. And with traveling, you see it, and hear it, and smell it."

"What did you do with the information? How do you pass it on? I take it you can't just swipe a couple of interesting artifacts or whip out your cell phone and take a photo."

"No. Nothing like that is possible. You'll figure that out when you start training. You can't use modern technology. And nothing can be carried out. Nothing at all. Not a single object. That's a hard reality at the beginning. You find out you have this incredible power. Then you learn the limits. But for Ellis Island, it was pretty straightforward. We weren't looking for lost treasure. Just lost information. After each visit, we recorded our observations. Next we assembled everything and drew conclusions. Then Sal composed letters to the Ellis Island Foundation and a few historians who had studied immigration. Oral history is given a lot of respect, especially at a place like Ellis Island. Sal said he had oral history from family stories that he wanted to share, and he composed a narrative of what we had all seen, making it sound like something his grandma told him."

"But that wasn't so."

"I know. But the information was truthful, even if we lied about how we obtained it."

Aggie was troubled. In science you had to follow the rules. Procedure was the foundation: control of variables, careful observations, multiple trials, honest reporting of results.

Julie studied her face. "I know. It's not perfect."

"It's not even close to perfect."

"But—"

"Julie, there are no 'buts.' You experiment objectively, or you don't. You report accurately, or you don't."

"Aggie, what alternatives do we have? We don't know what happens when we travel. We don't know why it only affects certain seniors or what scientific processes are at work. It's only been a decade or so since travelers figured out there were others out there like them. Before that it was an isolated experience. People thought they were the only ones who could do it. Or, they thought they were crazy. If we were honest about how we acquired our information, other people would think we were crazy, too. Right now, lying is our only option."

Aggie leaned back in her chair and crossed her arms. "I don't like it."

Julie ran a hand through her hair in frustration. "Sometimes there's no other choice. If the mission locates an artifact, something tangible, then we can return to the present and send an archaeologist off to find what we know is there. But even that requires subterfuge, doesn't it?

We've got to invent a cover story that explains how we know where to look."

Aggie studied her mentor. "What happened?" she said at last. "With Sal's letter, I mean."

Julie smiled. "He got a tremendous response. One professor even came out for an interview. Sal felt," Julie paused to search for words, "that he had given a voice to his grandma. Explaining things she never had an opportunity to explain herself."

The sound of voices came from the hallway. They had left the door ajar upon entering the apartment. *"Hello?"* Abraham appeared in the doorway, Wells by his side. "Ms. May, how delightful to see you again. How are things here? Everything shipshape?"

Aggie smiled. "Everything is perfect, thank you. Wells, I understand you did the engineering on the tub. It's quite impressive."

The young man broke into a smile. "See, Abe. I told you they'd be popular."

"Especially when they're *pretty in pink*," Julie said sotto voce.

Wells blushed, but Abraham didn't appear to notice.

"And thank you for the plants," Aggie added, gesturing toward the patio. "They're so lovely. That was very thoughtful."

Abraham glanced outside, then met her eyes and grinned. "Container gardening, right? Isn't that what you called it?"

Aggie laughed. "Yes, that's what it's called. I'm impressed you remember the term."

"I remember everything you told me, Ms. May. I was particularly enchanted to learn about pigweed. But actually, I stopped by to find out if Julie explained about our little reception tonight. I was hoping you would do us the honor of leading off."

Aggie hesitated. "How about I go second?"

Abraham pulled himself up to his full six-foot-whatever height. "Ms. May, you're a *teacher*. You're *used to this*. Most of our recruits have no experience with public speaking."

"Teaching high school isn't the same as public speaking."

"You're right. This will be easier. And this will be fun."

As if echoing the sentiment, the CD player started pumping out the big number from Dirty Dancing, and Bill Medley's baritone started in on "The Time of My Life."

Julie started giggling, and a reluctant smile appeared on Aggie's face. "All right, Mr. Irving, I'll go first."

"Splendid! Now, if you'll excuse us, we need to check on the Hopewells."

Abraham and Wells marched off down the hall, heads together, both speaking a mile a minute. As they waited by the elevator, Abraham looked back, and Aggie saw him studying her with a speculative look in his eyes.

"Mutt and Jeff," Julie remarked. "I'm going to head off, too. If you need me, my place is on the third floor, 309. I'll come by and pick you up for dinner, okay? At seven or so?"

"Seven is perfect. I can unpack and watch the news."

"You're sure you're okay? If you want company—"

"I'll be fine," Aggie assured her, "I've been on my own for years. I think I can make it through the next few hours."

Julie grinned then impulsively threw her arms around Aggie. "Oh, I could just kiss Abe for pairing us up. When he said you were special, I was sure he would give you a more experienced mentor."

Aggie drew back, puzzled. "What did he mean by that? Why am I *special*? Isn't everyone here because they can travel?"

Julie shrugged. "One thing I've learned is that no one really knows what Abe means. But no one has better instincts about travelers. If Abe says you're special, then you're special. I don't know what he saw when he recruited you, but I'm not betting against him." Julie paused a moment before continuing. "Some people get fooled by Abe. He comes across as gregarious and transparent, but he holds his cards close. I trust him, though. Most of the time, anyway."

It wasn't a bad working hypothesis, Aggie thought. Trust him. At least for now.

Chapter 11 ~ Show and Tell

With Julie gone, Aggie inspected her apartment more carefully. In the kitchen cabinets she found china plates, bowls, teacups, and saucers featuring a pattern of delicate blue flowers. The refrigerator held butter, half-n-half, orange juice, several cans of Ensure—all chocolate, no vanilla—and a bottle of chardonnay. How did they know her wine preference? A package of English muffins and a box of teabags sat on the counter. The tea was the same brand she used at home. There was also a tin of shortbread like the kind she had served to Abraham.

She rolled her suitcase into the bedroom and started unpacking. She stored her sweaters in the dresser and hung her tops, slacks, and coat in the closet. She put Jacob's picture on the nightstand then sat on the edge of the bed, bouncing tentatively to test the mattress. It was comfortable. It might be a good idea to close her eyes and clear her head, she thought. She wouldn't nap. She never napped. But she set the alarm on her cell phone, just in case.

When the alarm rang, it startled Aggie out of a deep sleep. Getting up quickly, she washed her face and assessed her outfit. It was past the point of no return. She considered her options. What was appropriate for a time travelers' meet and greet? Settling on navy blue pants and a white, square-necked top, she pulled them on and added plain gold earrings. Everything matched and was comfortable, but the mirror told her she more closely resembled a Carnival Cruise passenger than a fledgling remarkable person.

As she brushed her hair, she was glad she had splurged the previous week on a visit to the salon. All the May children reflected their parents' Irish heritage in their hair. Aggie had always considered it a bit unfair that her siblings had an attractive auburn color while she ended up with a shade that, in childhood, had earned her the nickname "carrot-top." She had never dyed her hair, and hadn't on this last visit, but at least her red-orange waves were neatly trimmed.

Julie knocked on her door promptly at seven, and they walked to the Lodge together through the mild autumn evening. The women entered the dining room to be met with the cheerful clatter of cutlery and buzz of conversation. The tables had been rearranged and covered with cranberry cloths. Dozens of diners were already seated. A petite young woman with chestnut hair pulled into a ballerina bun was delivering plates to the tables.

"The staff members," Aggie whispered to Julie as they sat down, "are they from town, or do they live here?"

"Well, some come in part-time, but tonight it's just Maurice's kids."

"His employees?"

"No, his kids. Adopted, fostered …. I'm not sure of the legal status of all of them, but Maurice just seems to collect kids. Especially throwaway kids. God, I hate that term, but maybe it conveys something about what they've experienced. Some are older and out on their own, but the four youngest are still here. Carlos and Angel are training with him to become chefs. Erin helps out, too. She's the young woman bringing out the food. She's not aiming for culinary school, but she likes to boss her brothers around. And then there's Wells, of course."

"Wells, too?"

"Wells has been with Maurice since he was about twelve."

"Do they all know?"

"They know all right. Maurice put his foot down about that right from the beginning. He insisted his children deserved total honesty. 'You have to show you trust them and are trustworthy yourself.' You're lucky to have Maurice for basic training. Wait till you hear some of his stories. He did an Upton Sinclair kind of trip a while back—I wasn't doing fieldwork then, but he told us about it—and let's just say *The Jungle* was a pretty accurate version of that reality. The folks on that mission kind of went off their feed for a while, but seeing as how we're about to eat, I'll spare you the details."

The young woman with chestnut hair appeared before them, balancing plates on a tray. "Evening, Jules. Glad you're back. Is this your mentee? I heard Abe made you a Big Sister."

Julie made the introductions as Erin set plates before them.

"Nice to meet you, Ms. May. Now ladies, we have a beautiful pan-seared salmon for you. Carlos is in charge in the kitchen tonight, so if it's good, tell him. And I know it's good—no one is better at seafood than he is. Angel and I are trying to build up his confidence. A kid with that much talent doesn't need to be shy. He should be a little more like Wells. And Wells should be …." She laughed. "Wells should be a little less like Wells. And oh, Jules," she leaned in and lowered her voice, "Serena's on a tear, complaining to Abe because she isn't chairing a group tonight, seeing as how she has a *gift*. Looks like she's already in full-diva mode." She grinned and gestured to the food. "Enjoy your meals, ladies."

Aggie picked up her fork and started in on the salmon. How pleasant, she thought, and how unusual, to enjoy two meals in a row she hadn't prepared herself and didn't eat alone. "Who's Serena?" she asked.

"Did you notice the tall woman leaning in the doorway this afternoon? You probably did because Serena always makes sure she's positioned right where the spotlight falls."

"Black hair? Green top?"

"That's our Serena."

"Does she have a gift?"

Julie allowed an expression of distaste to show on her face. "She's got good control," she stated colorlessly. "She learned how to focus in about a minute and a half. The three Ds are a snap for her. She's only about fifty—and she won't even admit to that—and her skill level is already high. And …." Julie stopped, closed her mouth, and looked around the room.

"And?" Aggie prompted.

Julie scanned the room again then lowered her voice. "Serena claims she'll eventually be able to *intervene*."

"Intervene?"

"Among Remarkables, *to intervene* is a technical term. A term of art. It carries a special meaning for travelers. But we shouldn't be talking about this. Not here anyway. Lillian just gave her little lecture. She regards the whole idea as futile and dangerous, and thinks it sets people up for crazy experiments that waste time and drive them nuts. She gets seriously displeased when anyone even jokes about it."

"But what is it? You need to explain."

Julie surveyed the dining room again, assessing whether anyone was within earshot. Many of the tables were full, but, judging by the noise level, people were engaged in their own conversations. No one was paying them any mind.

"So, here's the deal." Julie leaned toward her and spoke in a near whisper. "We're all here because we can travel. But we're not all equally adept. We can't all get exactly where we want to go. We can't all move around much once we get there or stay very long without getting dropped back to the present. Still, all travelers pretty much play by the same set of rules."

"Pretty much?"

"Well, you know about the directors. The three of them are companion travelers. Ninety-nine percent of Remarkables go back alone because the past typically makes room for only one person at a time at any particular destination. But Abe, Lillian, and Maurice can all travel *with* another person, if they start out holding hands or touching them in some way. And they can stay in the past with that other person, at least for a few minutes. So, they can *break* the rule about traveling alone."

"If they can break it, maybe it's not a rule at all. Maybe it's just something that's hard to learn how to do."

"That's possible, but they all maintain they didn't practice or train in any way. It was just a trait they always had," she cast an eye at Aggie, "like being born with red hair. Now, when Serena boasts she's going to *intervene*, that's a different way to break the rules. A different skill. A different rule that's getting broken."

Aggie narrowed her eyes. "What's the rule?"

"The biggest rule of all. The rule that says *you can't change the past*. To intervene means to change the past."

"Lillian said the past can't be changed."

"And she's right. There aren't any documented cases where it's happened. And Lillian feels—a lot of travelers feel—it's a *ruinous* obsession."

"But, wait a minute." Aggie was confused. "I intervened at Grand Central, at least in a minor way. I talked to a young woman. I spoke to her husband. Wasn't that a change to the course of history?"

Julie picked up her coffee, sipped, and put it back on the saucer with a decided clink. "No. Let me see if I can explain. When we travel back in time, we can see and be seen. We can hear and be heard. We can even smell the roses or the coffee or whatever is there. But when you try to be more than a passive observer, or have more than the most superficial of conversations, you get pushed right out of the past, and you're back in the present. *And nothing has changed.*"

Aggie put down her fork, folded her hands together on the table, and studied her mentor. "So, Serena has tried to intervene. Do other people try?"

"Of course they do. Even with Lillian's warning and knowing it won't work. Even with strict admonitions to color inside the lines. We might look like a bunch of old folks ready for Bingo, but most travelers are adventurers. If we're ready for anything, we're ready to break the rules, or at least give it a shot. And once you learn control, it's natural to try. But you can see Lillian's point. We all wish we could change something. We want to pull a child out of the street when we know he will be hit or raise an alarm in advance of a fire. But when you try and fail, and try again and fail again, that's a dark road to travel."

"You've tried?"

Julie fiddled with her coffee cup a minute. "At Ellis Island. I saw this man. He was carrying a beat-up old valise. And at one point the handle just broke off, and the valise hit the floor and popped open, and all his worldly belongings—and they were pretty pathetic belongings—were strewn across the floor. It was not a tragedy or anything, but he looked so tired and confused and embarrassed. That's what got to me. This poor man's embarrassment. So, I tried to warn him the next time I went back. I thought the very *insignificance* of the moment might mean I could intervene in some way. Change this tiny, little bit of history. So, I knew the handle was going to break, and I went back to just before it happened, but I simply couldn't make a difference. I tried talking to him.

69

I tried gesturing at his suitcase. Nothing worked. I was just one part of a faceless crowd in a chaotic—and to him, incomprehensible—situation."

Aggie eyed her mentor shrewdly. "How many times did you try?"

"Twelve times. I tried twelve different approaches. No luck." She met Aggie's eyes. "I hate failure. Even over something small. But that's what trying to intervene gets you."

Aggie turned the information over in her mind. "Are there other ways to intervene? Apart from trying to warn someone? Like moving something—"

Julie finished her thought. "Yes, moving something from the past to the present, or vice versa, would change the past. It can't be done." A wry smile settled on her face. "It sure would make fieldwork easier, though. Go back in time, pick up an artifact, carry it home, and give it to a museum. Or leave something in the past you know would be of help. But look, here's what happens." She picked up her teaspoon from the table and held it in front of her. "This is a valuable artifact," she intoned. "You found it in 1950, or 1920, or 1895. It's a priceless silver teaspoon, or a diary, or a letter, or a rare coin, or a piece of jewelry. You pick it up, if you can. Some people get evicted for just trying. But say you're able to pick it up. You know there's a historian who would love to see it. It's important. It belongs in a library, or a museum, or an art gallery. You slip it in your pocket." Julie placed the spoon in the pocket of her blazer. "Nothing could be easier. You return to the present and reach in your pocket, and—" she paused dramatically, "it's not there. Not anymore."

Julie took a sip of water and screwed up her face in concentration. "Nothing gets carried. *Nothing comes out of the past.* Not even accidentally. You could be standing in a mud puddle in the past, but when you return, your shoes are clean. Not a speck of mud comes back with you."

"And I take it you can't leave anything behind?"

"Nothing at all," Julie repeated solemnly. She pulled the spoon out of her pocket and regarded it thoughtfully. "Abe tells a story about a traveler who went back to the Depression. He talked to a man in a breadline. A man with nothing. A man who was desperate. On impulse the traveler pulled off his own wedding ring, thinking he could leave it behind. It was gold. The man could sell it. He reached out to slip it into the man's pocket, and the ring dropped to the ground. And the traveler was evicted."

"What happened then?"

"Nothing. The ring was on the ground. The traveler picked it up and put it back on his hand and learned he couldn't be a Good Samaritan."

"I asked about the butterfly effect during my Welcome Wagon visit," Aggie said.

"Abe usually says something equivocal about it. There's so much going on during a recruitment visit that people don't focus on intervention. Between you and me, I think Abe doesn't want to give up on the idea. He's been traveling so long, and he's seen things he wishes he could change. But in the end, he's on the same page as Lillian. What's the use of talking about something no one can do? No one's ever heard of a traveler with the power to rearrange furniture in the past. And maybe it's for the best. If Remarkables could change the past, who'd set priorities? Or limits?"

"It's interesting, though." A flurry of hypotheses swirled through Aggie's brain.

Julie nodded and made circling motions with her spoon as if turning the crank on a machine. "I know. If you *could* intervene, and if you were in the right place at the right time …."

A tall young man holding a pot of coffee was at Julie's elbow, regarding her curiously. "Refill, Julie?" he asked. "Um, something wrong with your spoon?"

Julie broke out of her reverie and realized she was still twirling the silver utensil like a magic wand. Sheepishly, she put it back on the table.

"No thank you, Carlos."

He turned to Aggie. "Would you like coffee, ma'am?"

"No thank you," she said, holding her palms out to indicate she was finished. "But please give my compliments to the chef for that wonderful meal."

The young man blushed furiously, his brown cheeks turning to mahogany. "Uh, yeah, cool. I mean, I will," he said and escaped back to the kitchen.

Julie smiled. "Maurice encourages him to interact with people and not just hide in the kitchen." Rising to her feet she gestured to Aggie. "I think it's time for Show and Tell, and you're up first."

Aggie grimaced.

"Abe made me go first, too," Julie said sympathetically. "He fed me this line about how I was a *lawyer*, and lawyers have to speak in front of judges and juries, so he was sure I wouldn't mind starting off."

It occurred to Aggie that Mr. Abraham Irving had developed effective people manipulation skills in addition to his time travel skills.

"Our group is in the library," Julie said. She led the way down a wide hall to a pleasant room lined with bookshelves. Cozy armchairs had been arranged in a circle, and a table along the wall held computers and a small yellow cone displaying a warning: *Caution! Seniors Online!* The only person online, however, was Wells, who was typing away at lightning speed.

He looked up as they entered. "Hey, Jules, Ms. May."

They took chairs in the circle. Aggie recognized a few of the others in the room including Benjamin, Edgar, the Hopewell twins, and Jane, the lady who liked embroidery. Their mentors were present as well, and others she assumed were veterans. "Why don't the veterans speak first?" she asked Julie. "That way we could learn a bit before presenting ourselves."

"Interference." The answer had come from Frank, the man caught sleeping earlier. He had shed the baseball cap and jersey and was nattily attired in a blue sports coat and a tie emblazoned with the Yankees logo.

"What does that mean?"

"Well, think about it. A rookie hears a vet describe a trip—what they saw and what it was like—and the next thing you know the rookie's saying the same thing. They get it in their heads that that's the way it's supposed to be, and it interferes with their own memory." Frank had brought a Corona into the library and paused to take a drink. "It's much better to let the rookies tell it fresh."

He had a point. She had addressed observer bias with her students. *Don't go in with rigid preconceptions. If you expect to see a particular phenomenon, you'll see it, or think you see it.*

"All set in here? Shall we get started?" Abraham had entered the room. He took a seat in the circle and smiled at the group. "Ms. May has kindly volunteered to start us off tonight. So, Ms. May." He gestured in her direction.

Aggie was ready. From her handbag she extracted the notebook she had kept on her kitchen table, the one in which she had recorded the details of her trips. "Please call me Aggie," she said to the group, "and just so we're clear, I was asked to speak first, and I agreed, but that's not the same as volunteering, is it?"

"She's got you on that one, Abe," Frank said.

Abraham grinned in much the manner of a student caught throwing an eraser cap. Aggie opened the notebook to the page headed "Grand Central" and took a few seconds to review what she had written about that singular experience.

"It was a sunny day," she began. "My sister was in town on a visit, and we were exploring Grand Central Terminal."

"Grand Central," a wiry, gray-haired man piped up. "Talk about *auras*. That place should be in the *Guinness Book of World Records* for sending more people back in time than any other structure on the East Coast."

"Hush, Ted," Viola said sternly, thumping her cane for emphasis. "You're interrupting the flow of events. Go on, Aggie. You were exploring Grand Central."

Aggie resumed the tale, describing how she and Minnie had examined Vanderbilt Hall and the main concourse before going to the whispering gallery. "I was standing in the corner, and I had this funny feeling in my stomach, like I was on the Parachute Jump at Coney Island."

"Yeah, that can happen when you're a rookie," Frank interjected. "Sal threw up in his hydrangeas after his first trip."

"Hush!" Viola chided. "Let her finish."

"Then a young woman spoke to me. I noticed she was dressed differently, but I didn't set much store by it. It was New York. People dress differently. But something made me turn around, and everything that was there before had been replaced."

Several other seniors nodded their heads. Aggie proceeded to recount what she had witnessed: the soldiers, the unmistakable 1940's clothing, even the formidable matron with the baby carriage. She repeated her conversation with the blonde and her new husband.

"That's pretty cool, having a conversation on one of your first trips," Wells commented from his seat by the computer. He had swiveled around to face the group. "Did you take any steps away from the corner? How long do you think you were gone?"

"I didn't take any steps," Aggie said. "All I did was pivot. And I don't think I was gone for more than a minute. Two at the most. Otherwise, my sister would have noticed."

Abraham spoke for the first time since introducing her. "Why were you so sure you had gone into the past? There are always crowds in Grand Central. And those—what do you call them—flash mobs? Maybe you just saw a few people dressed unusually and jumped to the wrong conclusion."

"People don't do flash mobs anymore," Wells noted.

"I'll take your word for it," Abraham said dryly.

"It wasn't just the clothing," Aggie said. "When my sister and I walked down the ramp, the whispering gallery was almost empty. Then, out of nowhere, there was a crowd. And the weather was different."

"You were inside," someone commented.

"Yes, but we had arrived not ten minutes earlier, and there wasn't a cloud in the sky. The people I saw in the whispering gallery had wet hats and coats. One man shook his umbrella and threw water droplets on us."

"What was the exact date you were at the terminal?" Wells asked. Aggie told him, and he tapped briskly away at his computer. "No rain at all in New York City on that date, Abe," Wells reported.

Aggie nodded. "That's pretty much it. I knew something had happened, and I knew it wasn't normal. I resolved to see my doctor, but I didn't say anything to my sister because I didn't want her to worry."

"That's what most of us do," Frank said. "We see a doctor, then go online, then get a Welcome Wagon visit."

Viola leaned toward Aggie. "Do you have any regrets?"

It seemed an odd question, but she gave it her consideration. Perhaps if she had been happy in retirement, she would feel, if not regret, then ambivalence. But that wasn't her story.

"No regrets," she said. "Well, one tiny regret," she laughed. "I was wearing my favorite silk blouse when that man shook his umbrella. I never got the water spots out."

Viola's reaction to this comment caught Aggie by surprise. Leaning forward again, she gave Aggie a searching look, then lifted her eyes to glance at Abraham who had an arrested expression on his face. The two of them seemed to be sharing a message only they could hear. No one else reacted.

"Let's give Ms. May—Aggie—a hand," Abe said abruptly. Everyone joined in then he raised his hands for silence. "Now, who would like to go next?"

Benjamin, the tall man Aggie had met at the train station volunteered, and, after a brief introduction, launched into his tale. "It all began at the Westchester Country Club. I had chipped up onto the green on the ninth hole and had a good chance for a birdie."

Aggie settled back to listen.

Chapter 12 ~ Intervention

Despite the lateness of the hour, the fullness of the day, and the astonishing events that had brought her to the Lodge, it took Aggie a long time to fall asleep. She had crawled under the flowered quilt at midnight, far later than her usual bedtime, only to toss and turn as she replayed the events of the evening. Finally, she sat up, turned on the light, and retrieved her notebook.

Turning to a blank page, she wrote the date and began recording her impressions from the Show and Tell session. Benjamin had indeed made a birdie by sinking a ten-foot putt. What greeted him on the next tee was a well-to-do foursome dressed in plus fours.

"They all had caddies," he said, "and for a moment I assumed they were some New York City bigwigs dressed like Payne Stewart. But then the first guy goes up to the tee, and the caddie hands him a driver and it's *wood*. A Bobby Jones-era hickory shaft beauty. A longnose if I'm not mistaken, and I don't think I am. So, I take a real good look and see they're all wearing *spikes* which most courses don't even allow anymore. You could've knocked me over with a feather. I figured I'd had one too many blue raspberry Gatorades, if you know what I mean." Everyone had joined in his good-natured laughter.

Edgar told of setting off on his usual morning walk and stumbling on an apple orchard. "It was splendid. Just like it was when I was a boy. But I knew at once something wasn't right. That orchard was cut down when the shopping center was built in 1965."

Jane's trip had started in a New York City Burger King. "I have to confess I like fast food French fries," she said apologetically. "Well, imagine my surprise when it wasn't a Burger King at all. It was a Horn and Hardart automat. All the food sat behind little glass windows: pies, cakes, sandwiches. I don't know why, but I accepted it. My brain just went right to the question of whether I should get macaroni and cheese or creamed spinach, and I wondered if I had enough nickels. You need nickels to put in the coin slots. I was checking my handbag when I came back to the present. I must say I was quite disappointed."

The Hopewells presented next. Flora went first, explaining she had been reading on the back porch when she looked up to see her mother hanging laundry on a clothesline. "Fred and I still live in the same house we grew up in, and somehow it seemed natural to see Mother, even though she's been gone many years now," Flora said softly. "She was using wooden clothespins, the old kind. Mother did laundry for Yale students back then. It was a good way to make ends meet."

Flora had watched for long moments, reluctant to look away. "I was afraid she'd fade like a mirage, but I had to tell Fred." She had run to the front room to find her brother. "I told him what I had seen, and he believed me. We've spent most of our lives together. He's a bachelor, and I'm a spinster, and we know each other well. He just got up from his recliner and went out to see for himself. Then I heard him laughing."

"I didn't see Mother," Fred explained, "but as I looked out the screen door, I saw our dog, Jo-Jo. The dog we had when we were children. He followed me home one day, and I convinced Mother and Pa to let us keep him. There he was in the yard, still just a pup, and barking like crazy at a squirrel he had chased up the oak tree."

Abraham posed the same question to Fred that he had to Aggie. "Why were you sure? Couldn't it have been some other dog? A dog that reminded you of the one you had as a boy?"

"I couldn't mistake Jo-Jo for any other dog. Any boy that's had a dog, grown up with a dog, knows that." Several others murmured in agreement, and Fred continued. "I called to him, and he came right up to the porch steps with his tail wagging. *He knew me*. I went outside, and the screen door slapped shut behind me. I could tell it was our old wood screen door, the one we had before we put the new aluminum one on. The sound broke the spell because the next thing I knew, Jo-Jo was gone."

There were tears on Fred's cheeks. Without a trace of embarrassment, he pulled a large handkerchief from his pocket, removed his glasses, and mopped his face.

Fred and Flora had been the only ones to hesitate when Viola asked about regret. The siblings exchanged a look, then Flora spoke. "Not precisely regret," she said evenly, "but sadness. I wanted to help Mother hang out the laundry. I wanted to tell her Pa would get a job, times would get easier." She glanced fondly at her brother. "And when Fred told me he had seen Jo-Jo—those two were inseparable. I wish they'd had time to play."

Aggie thought a moment then started to write: *Lillian says you can't go back in time and see yourself. Flora's experience shows you can go back and see loved ones.* Recalling Julie's narrative about Ellis Island, she added *Sal saw his grandmother and father.* Mentally she reviewed her own trips to the past. She hadn't known the people she had seen. Not the blonde in Grand Central, the little girl on roller skates, the lady in the library. It was impossible to be dispassionate about any time travel experience, but how much more affecting would it be if you had a connection to the people you saw?"

Feeling restless, Aggie got up, pulled on her robe, and walked into the kitchen. The moonlight was strong through the lace curtains, and she didn't need to turn on the light. She procured the chardonnay from the refrigerator, found an opener, and poured herself a glass. Returning to the bedroom, she sat in the rocking chair next to the bed and sipped the wine.

I wanted to tell her that Pa would get a job. In her mind, Aggie saw the pain in Flora's eyes. Maybe Lillian was right to discourage personal time travel. How do you walk through that kind of emotional minefield?

Placing her glass on the nightstand, Aggie picked up her notebook again and turned to a new page. *What is the role of love? What are its implications?* Aggie wrote the questions then stared at the words dissatisfied. These were not things that easily lent themselves to scientific inquiry. She spent a few moments rocking gently back and forth, considering the questions. Finally, she put down her pencil and closed the notebook. It was almost one in the morning. She had confronted a fair amount of astounding information in the past few weeks but did not yet feel prepared to explore the idea that membership in this "other AARP" involved traversing some rather complicated emotional terrain. Her eyes fell on the framed photo of Jacob in front of the angel in Central Park. After she got into bed and turned out the light, it occurred to her that she knew exactly when that picture had been taken.

***

Surprisingly, she didn't feel tired in the morning. She jumped out of bed as soon as the alarm buzzed. In the bathroom, she eyed the tub designed by M.I.T. but opted for a shower instead. After dressing, she pulled aside the lace curtains in the living room and fixed herself an English muffin and tea. On a hunch, she opened the door to her apartment and was pleased to see the *New York Times* lying on the mat. There was also an envelope with her name on it.

Inside was a lilac sheet of paper, another copy of her schedule. This one, however, bore a handwritten note at the top: "Dear Ms. May: After consultation with Mr. Irving, I would be pleased to have you join my fieldwork seminar. We believe this class will be a good match for your skills and abilities. I have taken the liberty of modifying your schedule to accommodate this change." The note was signed "Lillian." Aggie scanned the sheet. Her Focus and Control class and the elective block had been replaced by the words *Fieldwork: Civil War Photographic Portraits.* Now what was this about? Julie had said fieldwork was reserved for veterans.

She pondered the problem while finishing her tea. Why would this advanced group be a good match for her skills and abilities? As a science teacher, she understood the rudimentary principles of photography but had never explored it in depth. And she was certainly no expert on the Civil War. Did Lillian think she had taught history?

Skills and abilities. Familiar words. When she first began teaching, quarterly report cards were done by hand. Teachers assigned letter grades and then composed short narratives assessing students' *skills and abilities* and their *areas in need of work*. It had been time consuming but a good way to reflect on each individual.

Suddenly, Aggie began to laugh. Thinking about her students had brought Conor Pulaski to mind. She had learned quite a bit about his skills and abilities the day he orchestrated that metal file cabinet's plunge to earth from a second-floor window at Potatuck High. The cabinet had landed at just the right angle to throw the metal drawers along their slides and free an explosion of accumulated papers that launched into the sky like a flock of white pigeons. It had helped that there had been fifty-mile-per-hour winds, the early warning of a nor'easter which arrived later that week and closed the school for two days. The cloud of fluttering pages overhead had completely halted the afternoon football scrimmage, as players and coaches alike stared in wonder as random gusts produced miniature tornados of paper that formed and reformed across the field.

Aggie hadn't joined the frantic guidance counselors sent on the ultimately doomed effort to recapture the precious confidential records. Rather, she pulled out her cell phone and snapped a series of pictures documenting the chaos.

Later, when asked to testify at Conor's expulsion hearing, she had angered and dismayed the principal — who had hoped to finally rid the building of what he termed "a criminal element" — by describing the teen as a "really good kid with admirable scientific curiosity and an interesting approach to the scientific method." She had emphasized his desire to tackle even the most challenging material. "He's endlessly curious," she said earnestly, adding a sunny and innocent-looking smile.

When asked whether he ever exhibited disruptive classroom behavior, she had feigned consternation and reported that his behavior was just fine. She had kept her hands in her lap during the hearing, so no one could see she had crossed her fingers in a nod to the childhood practice intended to excuse a bald-faced lie.

The committee members, "faced with contradictory evidence," had concluded the hearing with a determination that Conor's offense did not rise to the level needed for expulsion, and the furious and disappointed principal had to settle for handing out a two-week, out-of-school suspension. Aggie knew the only thing the principal was endlessly curious about was why any teacher would go to bat for "a kid like that."

Upon Conor's return to class, Aggie had delivered a rather good lesson on the Beaufort Scale and the awesome power of gale force winds. Her slide show with scenes of hurricanes and windstorms included one of the more impressive images she had taken of the paper storm on the football field. Conor, slouching sullenly in the back of the room, had leaned forward in his chair as exclamations of glee erupted from his classmates.

He had eyed Aggie as if trying to determine whether she was making fun of him, but she had carried on with her commentary on what could be learned from the photo. After class, Conor waited till the others left before rising from his seat. She preempted him.

"Conor, may I have a word?"

His expression was carefully neutral.

"It would be quite an accomplishment to *engineer* something like that," she said casually, almost as if discussing a proposed science fair project. "There are a lot of variables to take into account, like the height of the drop and the weight and construction of the cabinet. Then there are unpredictable things like the angle when it hits. And getting the drawers to open and eject the contents would necessitate some advance preparation, maybe the use of levers or springs. It's quite a complex problem."

He looked at her stonily for a moment, then walked out of the room, but not before she saw the tiniest smile flit across his features. "And ya gotta listen to the weather report," he mumbled, almost as if he was talking to himself.

***

A tapping on the patio door interrupted her thoughts. Looking up, she saw Abraham. He was wearing a baseball cap, sweatpants, a Yale t-shirt, and sneakers. She unlatched the door and slid it open. He had apparently come from the direction of the barn and the cottages down the hill.

He saw her inquiring look. "I was just finishing my walk and heading back to my cottage, but I saw your curtains were pulled and thought you might be up."

Aggie nodded. "Most teachers, even retired ones, rise early."

"I usually get out early, too. I try to walk three miles every day, rain or shine. Wells suggested wearing a pedometer, but I told him the accumulation of data, while often admirable, was not necessary in every instance." He fell silent, but his eyes took in the table littered with the breakfast things and the lilac sheet of paper. "I wondered if you had any questions about your new schedule."

She regarded him appraisingly. "Maybe it's time for another cup of tea, Mr. Irving."

"Please call me Abe."

"Abe, then. Come in. Have a seat."

Abe removed his baseball cap and settled at the table while Aggie cleared her plate, put the kettle on to boil, and took another cup and saucer from the cabinet. She collected the half-n-half from the fridge and brought the sugar bowl to the table. Abe was silent, his eyes scanning the room. At one point, he picked up the lilac sheet, read the note at the top, then placed it back on the table.

When the kettle whistled, Aggie poured and brought the two steaming cups to the table. Setting one in front of Abe, she took a seat across from him. He busied himself dunking the teabag up and down and doctoring the cup with sugar and half-n-half. He seemed to be avoiding her gaze.

"Mr. Irving—Abe—I take it you are here to enlighten me with respect to the change in my schedule. Julie explained the normal regimen. Basic training first, then fieldwork. Now Lillian writes," she gestured toward the lilac sheet, "that after consultation with you, she believes her fieldwork class on Civil War photographic portraits would be a good match for me. How can I do fieldwork when I don't know the first thing about getting to a specific time and place? All the time travel experiences I've had so far have been random. I see World War II soldiers or a girl with a skate key or a woman wearing high-button shoes."

He didn't answer directly. "Ms. May, would you let me take a look at that notebook you had with you last night? Am I right in thinking you've been recording details from your journeys?"

"If I am going to call you Abe, you should call me Aggie. And yes, I'll get the notebook." She went into the bedroom and returned with the spiral notebook. She handed it to him, then picked up her blue-flowered teacup and took a sip. Abe placed the notebook in front of him and regarded it pensively. Then he turned to the first page and began to read.

Aggie had expected him to skim the pages, but she was wrong. He appeared to tune out everything around him giving his complete attention to the text. At certain points he turned the notebook at an angle to better read the stray comments she had added in the margins. At times he turned back a few pages and reread some of the narrative. On one occasion a smile flitted across his features, and he lifted his eyes to her face before letting them drop back to the page. He didn't rush, and his tea grew cold. After what Aggie estimated to be about twenty minutes, he reached the last page, which he read twice before closing the notebook and setting it aside.

"*The role of love*," Abe said. "Yes, there definitely are implications."

Aggie felt a flush on her cheeks but regarded him steadily.

"How long have you been with us?" Abe continued. "Twenty-four hours? A little less? It strikes me as interesting that you're moving rather quickly toward some of the more complicated issues inherent in what we do here."

Aggie studied his face. The mantle of easy-going charm he normally wore was gone. The man before her looked serious, troubled.

"All of us struggle with the kinds of questions you are asking," Abe said, "but I want you to put that aside for the time being. I wish us to discuss a different matter."

She didn't reply but nodded, signaling him to go on.

"Remarkable Enterprises exists to preserve history. Maybe it's just bits of history, tiny details. But who's to say tiny details are unimportant? Sometimes it's the smallest things that make the biggest difference. Captain Smith ignores an iceberg warning and the *Titanic* sinks. A New Yorker gets stuck in traffic and doesn't make it to the World Trade Center on 9/11. And within our small group, within the hearts and minds of our people, details matter as well. Those who join us bring with them a diversity of backgrounds and life experiences, a diversity of skills and abilities. And so, when time travel becomes available, it manifests itself differently in different people. As a teacher you must be familiar with this sort of thing. Some kids will take to your class like fish to water. Some need coaxing and support. And every now and then you stumble across someone who is brilliant, unique."

"*Each one* is unique," Aggie countered.

Abe nodded. "Yes, each one is unique. Sometimes we forget that. We oversimplify time travel, try to make it more understandable, I suppose: focus and control, the three Ds. But in reality, time travel is slightly different for everyone. Yes, there are general rules that apply to all, but there is also a complexity we ignore at our peril. The details of the traveler will invariably mix with the details of the moment in time he or she explores." He drained the last of his tea, not seeming to mind it was cold. "Details matter."

"You don't need to convince me on that score," Aggie said. "But what's the detail that made you change my schedule and assign me to fieldwork?"

"What I told Lillian was that I had a hunch about you. That you'd be a fast learner and wouldn't need to spend the whole session on the basics. Lillian agreed. That meeting you had at the airport convinced her."

"You moved me on a hunch?"

"No. But that's what I told Lillian."

"Then we're back to the original question: the detail—the real reason—you changed my schedule."

He looked her straight in the eye. "Did Julie talk to you about intervention?"

"I thought that was something that was off the table," Aggie responded evasively. It sounded lame, even to her own ears.

"You needn't worry Julie will get in trouble for telling tales out of school. Dostoevsky said if you try not to think of a polar bear, the cursed thing will come to mind every minute. Intervention is the elephant in the room, or the polar bear if you will."

"That's quite a menagerie."

"Look, we know mentors and rookies talk about intervening and changing the past. It's to be expected. Everybody has read enough science fiction to know about the butterfly effect. It's usually the first thing people ask about. They want to know if they can go back and undo a mistake. Or they're terrified they'll change history in some horrible way. But since experience has taught us it's not going to happen, or not going to happen in the way it happens in a fantasy story, we don't want folks to get sidetracked or obsessed."

Abe glanced out the window, and Aggie followed his gaze. A flock of starlings had descended on a maple tree, their dark, iridescent bodies giving the illusion of animation to the branches. Raucous whistles and trills filled the air with sound, as if the birds were engaged in a wild conversation. In a moment, they lifted off in one dark cloud and soared away.

Abe turned back to Aggie. "Tell me what Julie said about intervention."

"She said interventions cannot succeed because of the rules of time travel. You can't change death. You can't give a warning. You can't move objects back and forth between time periods. If you stand in a mud puddle in the past, when you return your shoes are clean. You're unchanged, and the past is unchanged."

"That's all true, with very few exceptions."

"Julie said, and Lillian certainly implied, that there are no exceptions."

"They're probably right. They're almost certainly right." Abruptly, Abe got to his feet and began to pace back and forth in the small dining area. He seemed engaged in an internal struggle, trying to sort out what he wanted to say. She watched him without speaking. After a moment, he stopped pacing, returned to the table, and sat down.

"But think for a minute," he said, as if there had been no interruption, "what's the journey from myth to reality? From Icarus to the Wright Brothers? For Leonardo da Vinci, flying wasn't a myth, it was an engineering problem. In 1865, Jules Verne wrote about a moon shot. Until NASA, it was just fiction, just a story. Then Neil Armstrong took that one giant step." Abe gestured expansively. "I don't think we've even begun to understand all the different kinds of remarkable abilities that can be exhibited by remarkable people. And that means we must pay attention to every single detail."

"Then what is the detail—the detail about me—that explains this," Aggie pointed to the lilac sheet, "and explains why you were less than forthcoming with Lillian, and explains why you are sitting here now?"

Abe ran a hand through his hair. "I need to tell you a story," he said. "But I also need and hope that you, like me, will be less than forthcoming. With Lillian. With Julie. With everyone." He stopped talking and scanned her face.

To Aggie's eyes, he looked extraordinarily uncomfortable. She chose her words carefully. "I can't make any promises. Not until I know more."

Outside the window, the starlings had returned to the tree. They rustled uneasily for a few moments then rose into the air again. Aggie spoke without thinking. "It's called a murmuration, when the starlings do that."

Abe watched the swirling cloud of birds move off over the barn and toward the woods beyond. "Why do they do it?"

"A few reasons. Safety in numbers. When they roost together at night it's warmer. They exchange a lot of information."

Abe examined her face a moment and nodded. She wasn't sure if he was acknowledging her facts about starlings or agreeing to her terms. At last he spoke.

"My father was a tailor. The whole family was in the clothing business. Tailors, seamstresses, retail. One of my uncles had a men's clothing shop in Vienna before the war. It's gone now, of course. They're all gone now. On Kristallnacht ...." He stopped. "Some made it out, but most didn't. My father got away. My grandparents could see what was coming, and they had a little money. More important, they had a little luck. A lot of luck, if truth be told. They couldn't save themselves, but they saved their son. What parents wouldn't believe themselves fortunate to have accomplished that?"

He paused, but Aggie said nothing. Where was this going?

"I didn't follow in my father's footsteps, but I learned from him. I can use a sewing machine. I can measure a man for a suit. I know something about fabric. My father made the most beautiful shirts and suits. Made-to-measure and bespoke suits. And men's silk ties. Most tailors, even the best ones, don't bother with the ties. They offer a selection to their customers, certainly, but don't construct the ties themselves. No need to, really. But my father had a real eye. He knew what color and pattern would work. He knew which tie would fit the shirt, and fit the suit, and fit the man. His customers always came back. They were loyal. And sometimes they would bring in a favorite tie, one he had made, and they had spilled wine on it or been caught in the rain, and they would ask if there was anything he could do to restore that tie. A man can get attached to a favorite tie. But it's almost impossible to clean a silk tie. He'd usually end up making them a new one if he still had the same fabric."

Abe's eyes met hers. "Do you know why it was so hard to clean those ties? Why he had to make new ones? Silk is hard to clean because liquid causes the fibers to expand. Even a single drop of water can cause this to occur. And once you've made that change happen, it's nearly impossible to undo." He stopped and looked at her, his expression unreadable.

"Aggie, your blouse got ruined at Grand Central, got ruined by drops of rain that fell before you were born. It shouldn't have happened. Julie was correct. 'You stand in a mud puddle in the past, and when you come back, your shoes are clean.' Raindrops fall in the past, and when you come back, your clothes are dry. But yours weren't. And now I have to figure out what it means."

Abe stopped speaking. He spread the fingers of both hands on the surface of the kitchen table as if to indicate he had nothing more to say. After a beat, he pushed himself to his feet, picked up his cap, and headed out the patio door. Aggie watched as he strode down the hill and out of sight.

Chapter 13 ~ Fieldwork

The room designated for Lillian's fieldwork group was situated in the back of the Lodge and resembled the kind of elegant but generic space usually found in an upscale hotel. The walls were sage green, and the tall windows showed pretty views of the barn and cottages. A mahogany credenza near the door held a massive coffee machine flanked by a row of mugs and a basket filled with a variety of coffee pods. The chairs had been arranged in a circle, as they might be for an AA meeting. Maybe they would introduce themselves in the same way: *I'm Aggie, and I'm a time traveler.*

Lillian was already in the room. She wore a dramatic and, to Aggie's eye, expensive, black maxi-dress, accented with a red beaded necklace and matching earrings. Sal, the man who had seen his grandmother at Ellis Island, stood chatting with Frank, the Yankees fan. Raven-haired Serena and her blonde friend were checking their phones. The *I Love Lucy* woman—Bernice—hovered by the door.

"Get coffee if you want it, friends," Lillian called out. "We'll wait a few minutes for stragglers, but we'll be getting started soon."

"I'm not a straggler," a quavering voice announced from the doorway. "Blame Wells. He drives like an old lady." It was Viola. She was seated in a sleek, blue, aluminum wheelchair, although she had her pink-flowered cane with her as well. A pink shawl draped around her shoulders set off her blue-white hair.

"Complaints, complaints, Granny," Wells grumbled as he maneuvered her toward the circle of chairs. He leaned over and kissed her soundly on the cheek, making a loud smacking noise.

"Silly boy," Viola scolded.

Bernice, looking a little anxious, scurried forward. She peered into the older woman's face and adjusted the pink shawl.

"Now, now, Bernie. No need to fuss," Viola said.

"Painting the town red last night?"

"Nonsense. It was just me and the kitty. We had a glass of wine and watched Rachel Maddow."

"Fibber," Bernice countered.

"My former student should accord me more respect."

"My former mentor should stop gallivanting about at all hours and act her age."

Aggie smiled at the exchange. She had been lingering near the credenza, studying a poster which presented step-by-step instructions for the coffee maker. Selecting a pod of dark roast, she snapped it in the machine, and pressed the start button. Behind her, she heard a whoop and felt herself hugged. It was Julie.

"Aggie! Abe just pulled me aside and said you were joining our group. He was infuriatingly stingy with the particulars, as usual. Typical Abe. What happened? Tell me everything. Wait, let me guess. He didn't give you any details, and you're just supposed to go with the flow. He does this now and then when he gets it in his head that someone's a fast learner. God, I need some coffee." Julie turned to study the basket of pods so missed the color that rose in Aggie's cheeks.

"I'll get us some chairs," Aggie said and made her escape. Abe had left that morning without reiterating his request that she be "less than forthcoming." Nonetheless, she didn't feel prepared to discuss what he had shared.

By the time Julie joined her, Aggie was more composed. "You're right about Abe. I got a note from Lillian and a new schedule with my morning paper. Then he dropped by and said he had a hunch fieldwork might suit me. I hope I won't be a drag on the group. I haven't learned anything yet. I'm no expert on photography, or the Civil War, for that matter. I'm not sure what he was thinking."

"Believe me, no one knows what he's thinking half the time. Don't worry about focus and control right now. Abe said he would clue in a few people, and we can meet at my place this afternoon to tutor you in the basics. Like I said, Abe has good instincts. If he believes you're ready for fieldwork, he won't let you waste time in a beginner's class." Julie's eyes narrowed. "Still, I'd love to know what factors he considered."

To Aggie's relief, Lillian interrupted the conversation. "Find chairs please, ladies and gentlemen." There was a bustle of activity as people selected seats while Lillian scanned the gathering and consulted a list. "Welcome everyone. I see most of the veterans from the Ellis Island group have elected to sign on to this project. We also have a new traveler with us," she indicated Aggie with a wave of her hand, "so let's begin with introductions."

"We're working with a rookie?" Serena let her eyes travel from Aggie's wavy red-orange hair to her rather unfashionable shoes. "Where is she from? New York?"

"Connecticut," Aggie said.

"Fairfield County?"

"Potatuck."

Serena sniffed. "And your expertise is …?"

"I'm a high school science teacher. Retired."

Serena leaned toward her blonde friend whispering audibly. "A schoolteacher from Palookaville? Bet she had an interesting change of life."

Now what was this about?

Viola intervened. "She doesn't mean *that* change of life, dear," she explained to Aggie in a reassuring tone. "She's talking about your first big excursion to the past. What you were sharing with us last night. Which was very interesting by the way," she said in louder voice, directing the comment toward Serena. She turned back to Aggie. "We used to call those first travel experiences our *change of life*, as a little joke, because finding out you're a traveler can change your life. But some of our gentlemen members pointed out the term was a bit *sexist* and they felt *excluded*, so we try not to refer to it that way anymore."

A few side conversations started up until Lillian called for order. "Ladies and gentlemen," she said with a touch of asperity, "we were introducing ourselves."

Viola nodded and started off. "Now you all know me," she said brightly. "I'm Viola, from Old Lyme. I'm a grandmother and great-grandmother. And Sadie just sent me pictures of the new baby!" She pulled a cell phone out of a cleverly crocheted bag fastened to the arm of her wheelchair, but catching the expression on Lillian's face, immediately dropped it back in. "I'll show you later when we take a break," she said then pointed to Serena with her cane. "Now introduce yourself properly," she commanded.

Serena sighed and glanced at her own cell phone before speaking. "I'm Serena Staunton. I work in fashion media. This is my fourth mission."

The introductions proceeded around the circle. Serena's blonde sidekick announced she was "Kat Padgett, originally from Bel Air." She regarded Aggie in an appraising manner. "I run a morning aerobics class in the gym. It's an advanced class, though …."

Frank announced he was a retired high school coach. "Football, baseball, girls' softball, a couple of years of lacrosse. Did some track and field."

Sal, "short for Salvatore," was more voluble. "I try to make it here for the fall and winter sessions. My business slows down then, and my boys can handle things without me. Plus, it makes for a nice change." He pulled his wallet from a back pocket, reached in, and extracted a card which he handed to Aggie. *Tosi & Sons: Concrete and Masonry.* "What we do here is a little far afield from my line of work. But I must say it's been quite an interesting coupl'a years. Course my buddies at the Chamber rib me about neglecting my bowling team to spend time with a bunch of eggheads, but that's okay. They don't know what's really going on, and I gotta say, there's more important things than sticking one more trophy up on a shelf."

When it was Julie's turn, she rattled off her resume points in a surprisingly efficient manner: Yale Law, partnership at a large firm in Hartford, service on a number of local boards and commissions, semi-retirement. "I'm still 'of counsel,' but since I started with the AARP, I've been trying to cut back."

The *I Love Lucy* woman who had fussed over Viola was next. "I'm Bernice," she said flatly and stopped. After a moment she noticed the group expected her to continue. "I worked at Yankee Metal." She stopped again, and another thirty seconds passed. "Before it shut down," she added. There was a pause while everyone waited to see if Bernice had more to contribute. She didn't.

They had come full circle. "Thank you, all," Lillian said. "As you know, our job today is to discuss our mission and, if we can, begin to develop a strategy and timetable." She turned to Aggie. "I'm sure Julie will have explained that travelers are unable to transport artifacts from the past to the present, and, much as we might wish to, cannot deposit explanatory material in the past to provide guidance in subsequent years—"

"Like the Western Union guys from *Back to the Future*," Wells called from the back of the room.

"Thank you, Wells," Lillian said repressively. "We all have favorite time travel movies and books, but it's important for Aggie to know we operate here within the realm of reality."

"I wish we could go back and save JFK like that guy tried to do in Stephen King's book," Kat interjected suddenly. "He's my favorite."

"Stephen King or JFK?" Sal asked.

"Stephen King, of course," Kat stated. "I bet he's a traveler himself. He's just the type."

Aggie's curiosity was piqued. "Is there a type? Perhaps this is something you all know," she said apologetically, "but I'm interested. Do you have statistics on this sort of thing?"

"We have yet to identify any characteristic which is a reliable marker of traveling ability," Lillian said. "Last year we analyzed data from Remarkable Enterprises' first decade and were unable to correlate *anything* with *anything*—not education, not income, not race or ethnicity, not health, not lifestyle choices."

"Well, there *is* the age thing," Sal said, "and the gender thing."

"Gender may not be relevant," Julie noted. "The differential in life expectancy means there are more women travelers because women, on average, live longer."

"Age is the one factor we know about," Lillian agreed, "and the one factor that is, therefore, germane. All our research, our whole recruitment system, our organization's name, *everything*, is based on that one fact. To our knowledge, the rare gift of travel is conferred only upon seniors. The youngest recorded age for a traveler is 46, but most of us are well beyond that milepost."

At the mention of 'the youngest recorded age,' Serena sat up and tossed her hair back.

"But we need to get back to work," Lillian stated firmly. Turning her walker, she again directed her comments to Aggie. "Fieldwork begins when we see an opportunity to add to our knowledge of a particular historical event, figure, or artifact. Sometimes this happens as the result of questions raised by historians. But often our starting point is information from a *source*. A source may be one of our fellow Remarkables, or a family member, or friend. With that in mind, let's talk about this mission. Where we are going and what we are trying to find."

"It's a treasure hunt, isn't it?" Sal asked. "I know you don't hold with that terminology, but it is what it is. If it is."

Aggie gazed back and forth between Sal and Lillian. The contrast could not have been greater: Lillian was elegant and beautiful, her shoulder-length hair as white as snow. Even the lines in her face were beautiful, like the striations in old porcelain. Sal was solid as a brick and nearly as weather-beaten. Lillian's green eyes met Sal's gray ones, and a smile played on her face. "It's a treasure hunt," she conceded.

A buzz traveled through the room. Julie shot an excited look at Aggie. Frank sat up and grinned. Viola patted Bernice's arm. Even Serena lost her air of calculated disinterest.

"What are we looking for?" Kat asked.

"What's the name of this group, Kat?" Julie prompted in a patronizing tone of voice.

"We're looking for a picture," Lillian interposed smoothly. "A photographic portrait that dates back to the Civil War."

"A picture? How is a picture valuable?" the blonde asked. "Is it somebody important?"

"Yes, Kitty Kat, it's undoubtedly somebody important." This time it was Viola who answered. "But we're going to be patient and let Lillian tell us in her own way, aren't we?"

"Want me to start the show, Lillian?" Wells called.

"Wells and I put together a slide show to provide an overview of the era we will be working within," Lillian explained. She nodded to Wells, and he pressed a button mounted on the wall. With a soft whirring sound, drapes closed over the windows, overhead lights dimmed, and a screen descended from the ceiling. Some of the seniors adjusted their chairs for a better view. Sal reached into his pocket for a pair of glasses.

An image of the nighttime Los Angeles skyline appeared on the screen, complete with roving Hollywood spotlights. To the sound of trumpets, the familiar movie logo materialized, but it had been altered to read '19th Century Fox.' A few giggled in appreciation, but Julie wrinkled her brow. "Nineteenth century, Lillian?"

"Those are the 1800s," Kat said smugly.

"I know that," Julie snapped, "but most of us have never gone that far back."

Aggie was confused. "But this mission is about Civil War photography. Doesn't that require travel to the 1860s?"

"Well, it doesn't have to," Frank began. He waved to Wells. "Pause it a sec," he said. Obligingly, Wells clicked a remote and froze the image on the screen. Frank turned to Aggie. "On treasure hunts we go to the last known location, but that's not always when the object was created."

"I need an example," Aggie said.

Frank scratched his head then raised a finger to indicate he had an answer. "Okay, listen. My brother had a baseball signed by Jackie Robinson. He got it in 1952, when he was a kid. That baseball was stolen during a break-in at his house in 1995. Now if I wanted to find that ball, I wouldn't go to 1952, would I? I'd plant myself outside my brother's place on the night of the robbery and try to follow the thief. See what I mean? Last known location."

"That's helpful," Aggie admitted. "But are you telling me no one has traveled to the nineteenth century?"

"We'll get to that," Lillian said, "but there's a lot of ground we need to cover first before we hear from our source."

"We're talking directly to the source?" Viola asked eagerly.

"Yes." Lillian checked her watch. "He'll be here later this morning."

"Then let's get this show on the road," Viola ordered.

Kat leaned over to whisper to Serena. "Who's the important person in the picture? Did they say?"

Serena smoothed the sleeve of her blouse. "I think we're about to find out."

Chapter 14 ~ A Time of Wonder

Wells clicked the remote, and a handsome young man appeared on the screen. He had dark curly hair, a broad brow, and thin metal-framed spectacles. Aggie knew that face. It was Mathew Brady, the Civil War photographer. Seeing it like this, the only bright image in the darkened room, brought home its striking similarity to another face. The face in the framed photograph that was sitting on the nightstand in her room. Jacob's face. Aggie twisted her wedding ring around her finger. There had been a day—years and years ago now—when the history teacher at her school had remarked on her husband's resemblance to the famous photographer. He had shown her Brady's picture in a textbook, and they had laughed because Jacob did, indeed, have *that look.*

Pain shot through her, the kind of pain that had been part of her life ever since her husband's death, especially in those early years. It came at moments when she knew she needed to talk to him and knew he was gone forever. *I'm dealing with a lot right now, Jacob. A new place, new people, new information. And this crazy new ability ....*

"Our mission is tied to the life and work of this man." Lillian's voice brought Aggie back. "Mathew Brady's photography studios in New York City and Washington, D.C. created and displayed portraits of the great figures of the age: writers and inventors, politicians and generals. Brady also sent teams of photographers to the battlefields of the Civil War, then shocked the world by exhibiting the first-ever images showing the true devastation of that war. The middle of the nineteenth century is a time of tragedy," Lillian continued. "The moral plague of slavery tears the country apart and triggers America's deadliest conflict. The Civil War will last four years and cost over 620,000 lives. But it was a time of wonder, as well.

"Walt Whitman publishes *Leaves of Grass,* and Darwin writes *The Origin of Species.* Forty thousand people meet the opera singer Jenny Lind at the dock in New York City as she arrives for her American tour. Faraday experiments with electricity, and Marie Curie begins research on radioactivity. Pasteur develops the first vaccines. Thomas Edison invents the light bulb, and Alexander Graham Bell earns a patent for the telephone." As Lillian spoke, the screen showed a collage of images illustrating her points. "The world's first transcontinental railroad is under construction," she continued, "and, before the century is over, Henry Ford will be building automobiles."

"And go on to become one of America's leading anti-Semites," Viola called out in a tremulous voice. "A lot of people don't know that."

"Yes," Lillian replied gently, "a lot of people don't know that. But before struggling with the great evil of the twentieth century, America will have to confront the great evil of the nineteenth." Viola nodded, and Bernice reached over and patted her arm.

"The work of Mathew Brady must be understood from the perspective of his times," Lillian went on. "In the early 1800s the photograph *did not exist.* This is hard for us to imagine. Today, everyone photographs everything, the monumental and the mundane. But think — really think — about the fact that prior to 1839, no one had ever seen a photograph of anything. Not the Colosseum, or the Pyramids, or the Great Wall of China. There are no photographs of famous persons or singular events. All the images in books and periodicals, on posters and signs, in museums and galleries, all are the work of artists and illustrators. On a personal level, no one has a photo of a loved one. The wealthy commission oil portraits of their family members, but for most people, it is only memory that preserves the image of a loved one who has traveled far from home or passed away."

"Until Niépce and Daguerre." Aggie spoke aloud, surprising herself. What she had told Julie was true. She was no expert in photography. But she had helped more than one student construct a pinpoint camera or a primitive stereoscope for the science fair. She understood the basic principles and knew the story behind the development of the technology.

Lillian signaled to Wells, and two faces materialized on the screen. "Yes, as Aggie says, two Frenchmen will introduce photography to the world: Nicéphore Niépce and Louis-Jacques-Mandé Daguerre."

"Now those are a couple of complicated monikers," Frank commented.

"Daguerre," Lillian went on, "is remarkably generous with his invention. In 1839 he publishes a pamphlet outlining the process. In short order he receives a visit from Samuel Morse, still in Paris after demonstrating his own invention, the telegraph, at the Paris Observatory. By the time Morse returns to New York, where he holds a professorship in painting and sculpture at NYU, he's prepared to lecture on the process and pass on what he has learned. One of those to whom the knowledge is passed is Mathew Brady. Brady is fascinated by the new miracle and recognizes its implications immediately. For a small charge, almost everyone can possess the portrait of a loved one, can see the face of the president or Queen Victoria, can view an image from halfway around the world.

"Brady moves quickly, establishing a studio in New York City at 205 Broadway, a few steps from St. Paul's chapel. The chapel is still there. It was used as a place of refuge—"

"On 9/11," Julie said.

Lillian regarded her with a curiously compassionate look. "Yes. That is so. Brady's studio is also near the Astor Hotel, which is an ideal spot to rub elbows with the wealthy and important clients he will convince to come and sit for him. He is across the street from Barnum's American Museum, the most popular tourist attraction in the country. Brady commissions a large sign to draw those tourists into his studio.

"But Brady is more than a clever promoter. He has a vision. He talks with Walt Whitman about how photography is *history*, how sketch artists and illustrators create subjective images, but photographers produce objective truth. Now, of course, we regard this idea as naïve."

"It was pre-Photoshop, Lillian," Wells noted.

"Yes, and perhaps their naïveté is understandable. They stand in awe at the dawn of a new age. Brady felt it. He became intent on photographing the important people of his time as a way to chronicle history. Of course, it will soon be evident that even the 'objective truth' of a photograph can be manipulated. In the studio, the lighting, the pose, the clothing and objects included in the frame—all are carefully chosen to give a certain impression. A case in point is Brady's first photograph of Abraham Lincoln, taken right before the Cooper Union speech. Brady places Lincoln's hand on a book to make him appear wise and pulls up his shirt collar to hide his long neck."

A shaft of light from the back of the room cut across the screen, then quickly disappeared. Someone had opened the door and entered the room. Aggie glanced back, but it was too dark to make out who had arrived.

"So," Lillian continued, "with an eye on history, and dreams of glory, Brady photographs Andrew Jackson, John Quincy Adams, Daniel Webster, and Henry Clay. He does portraits of Nathaniel Hawthorne, Washington Irving, and Edgar Allan Poe. Here's the portrait he did of Jenny Lind in 1852."

"The dress is good, for that era." The comment came from Serena. "Overly embellished but an interesting silhouette." Her voice, so sharp earlier, now had a pleasant but business-like tone.

"By the time of the Civil War, Brady had become famous," Lillian said. "He's called 'Brady of Broadway,' and has relocated to a more fashionable area of the city. He has also opened a studio in Washington, D.C. His first portrait of Lincoln will be followed by others."

A series of Lincoln photographs appeared on the screen. As each image was replaced by the next, the hopeful man in the prime of his life became the ancient figure carrying the weight of the world on his shoulders. Aggie studied the familiar, fascinating features.

"Remarkable clarity on those pictures, Wells," Lillian commented quietly.

"Thanks, Lillian. It was an honor to work on them," he replied.

Lillian turned from the screen and resumed her narration. "Seven states secede from the union before Lincoln is inaugurated. His inaugural address contains a plea that the union be saved by 'the better angels of our nature.' But, a month later, shots are fired at Fort Sumter. Brady feels called to chronicle this momentous history. Two innovations affect this task. First, one-of-a-kind daguerreotypes are replaced by photographs that utilize glass plate negatives. This allows the images to be easily reproduced. A young man leaving for war can give a picture of himself to his family or sweetheart and can carry their pictures as he faces battle.

"The second innovation is a change in behavior. Photographers venture out of the studio to document events where they happen. Brady's first move in this direction, however, is a failure. In 1861, he brings a wagon of photographic equipment to the first Battle of Bull Run but loses it all when the Union forces are routed and forced to retreat. Brady realizes he is not well-suited—physically or mentally—for work in the field. His solution is to hire others to go to the front lines to take the pictures that will give the country a window into the war."

"*A window into the war*," Frank repeated. "It must'a been like when they started showing Vietnam on TV."

Lillian nodded. "In the fall of 1862, Brady exhibits a series of stereoscopic pictures taken at the Battle of Antietam. Antietam was the bloodiest single day in that bloodiest of wars. The *New York Times* review of the exhibit said it was as if Brady had laid dead bodies along the streets." There was silence as photographs from Antietam emerged before them.

"What Brady did was unprecedented," Lillian said emphatically. "Historians regard the Antietam exhibit as the beginning of photojournalism. But as the war drags on, the bloodshed takes its toll. More soldiers are needed, and Lincoln initiates conscription. You can buy an exemption for $300. But $300 is far beyond what most laborers see in a year. The result is a draft riot in Manhattan. For four days a mob of mostly Irish immigrants, who are at the bottom of the economic ladder, target African Americans, who also reside on the bottom rung and become scapegoats. Over a hundred people die. Most of them black. Some by lynching. The homes of African Americans and abolitionists are ransacked, interracial couples are attacked, and two churches are destroyed. One of the ugliest incidents is the torching of the Colored Orphan Asylum at 44th Street and Fifth Avenue. That's two blocks from where Grand Central Terminal is now, two blocks from where the New York Public Library will be constructed.

"The war takes a toll on Brady as well. He's in financial trouble having invested over $100,000 to send photographers to sites around the country. Brady had bet the government would purchase his collection, but at the war's end, the country is determined to look away. Ten years after the war, James Garfield tells Congress that Brady's collection of Civil War photographs is worth $150,000. What Congress offers is $25,000. And by this time, some of the collection, including some of the most valuable images, have been scattered."

"I think I see where this is going," Sal said glancing around at the others.

Lillian nodded. "As Brady ages the debts mount. His priceless compilation of portraits, prints, and glass plate negatives, slips from his control. Creditors take possession of some of the most valuable portraits. Vendors take glass plates in lieu of payment. In 1896, Brady dies alone and nearly penniless. While many of his images survive — thousands are in the National Archives and others make it into the hands of collectors — many are scattered, misplaced, or lost." Lillian looked around the room at the gathered seniors. "Our mission is to locate one of these lost images. That is the treasure we are seeking."

The screen went blank, then slowly rose into the ceiling. The lights in the room came up. Lillian smiled. "Let's take a break. Get coffee, stretch your legs, and be back in fifteen minutes."

"But whose picture are we looking for?" Kat asked.

"Our guest is going to go over that," Lillian said. "He'll pick up the story from here."

Aggie stretched and looked over at Julie. Her talkative and exuberant mentor had remained quiet and nearly motionless throughout the presentation. As some of the seniors got to their feet, Julie blinked and shook her head, as if coming out of a trance. "Wow, a treasure hunt. This is going to be good. I have to use the facilities. Need to go?"

Aggie nodded. "Lead the way."

As they walked toward the door, Aggie saw Abe and another man sitting off to the side in an alcove. They must have been the ones who entered during Lillian's presentation. Abe's companion was a powerfully built, older man, with straight gray hair clipped short, a broad square forehead, and small pale blue eyes set in a face that looked as if it had been carved from stone. The man's eyes followed her with a glance imbued with both intelligence and calculation. When he noted that she returned his gaze, his eyelids lowered, hooding his eyes in a manner reminiscent of some prehistoric reptile sunning itself on a rock. Aggie's eyes moved to Abe. He was watching her as well. He gave her a half smile then turned to speak to his companion. Julie was already out the door, and Aggie hurried to catch up.

In the bathroom, several of the women were examining a new survey posted on the bulletin board. Aggie studied the options.

Question of the Day:
Which situation do you find most annoying?

1. *Being addressed as "Honey" or "Sweetie" by a total stranger. (I know the person is probably just being nice, but it gets a little patronizing, right?)*
2. *Dining with friends and having the waitperson assume it's your birthday because why else would a senior be at a fancy restaurant with a large group of people.*
3. *Having someone raise his/her voice and speak to you ... very ... slowly.*
4. *Hearing people behind you in line sniff impatiently because you (very sensibly) carry coins and like to pay (in cash) the precise amount charged rather than just swiping a card or using your phone.*

"Three used to happen to me even before I got old," Bernice stated flatly. "Foreman used to bug the hell out of me doing that."

"Sign me up for number four," Viola said. "That's the one that happens to me the most."

"I'm with you on using coins," Aggie agreed.

"Put me down for the first one," Julie said. "One of my first times in court, the judge called me 'Missy.' There weren't that many women litigators back then, but *really*. It's not exactly the same thing, but close enough."

Bernice dutifully marked their votes on the sheet then pushed Viola's wheelchair out into the hall.

"Feeling poorly today, Vi?" Julie asked solicitously.

"My arthritis is acting up. I need to do better with those exercises Mirlande taught me."

"Does Mirlande work with Kat on her aerobics class?" Aggie asked.

Viola giggled. "No, Mirlande is a doctor. The only thing she does with Kat is try to steer her away from high kicks and head stands."

Aggie shook her head. "A doctor. My goodness. I try not to make snap judgments. I should have—"

"Don't beat yourself up, dear," Viola laughed. "Most of us made that same mistake. I think it's that 'Lucky Lady' rhinestone t-shirt she wears on the bus."

"Who is the man who came in with Abe?" Aggie asked. "Is he joining the group?"

None of the women said anything for a moment, then Viola spoke. "Hold up a minute, Bernie." Bernice stopped the wheelchair and turned it so Viola could face Aggie. "Now that is an interesting little conundrum. The gentleman's name is Axel Bajek. He's a year-round resident and has pretty much been here since the Remarkable campus was established. The odd thing is no one knows very much about him. He doesn't usually come to the Lodge for meals. Sometimes he drops by a fieldwork group, but he never joins in. He seems to prefer running his own operations, but no one knows what those operations are. The only one he really talks to much is Abe. And Abe is closemouthed about him."

"What's his background?" Aggie asked.

"It's a mystery," Viola answered. "Some of us had a little guessing game about him, but," she hesitated and looked troubled, "all of the guesses involved crimes or things that were unsavory. So, guessing wasn't much fun anymore, and we didn't want to slander the man."

"He's Polish," Bernice offered unexpectedly. "You'll hear the accent if you talk to him. Not that he talks much. Lots of folks in my local were Polish. Big Polish community in the Valley. I don't think he's from Connecticut, though. I once heard Abe say something to him about his family in the city."

"He scares me," Julie said bluntly. "I don't know why. I just never see him smile."

Lillian poked her head into the hallway. "Ladies, we're about to get started."

When they entered the meeting room, Aggie glanced at the alcove. It was empty. Axel and Abe were gone.

Chapter 15 ~ Panes of Glass

A newcomer had joined the group. Seated next to Lillian was a man as old and crooked as a wind-blasted tree. He was nearly bald, although he had tufts of gray hair along his collar and around his ears. He was dressed in a dark suit, a white button-down shirt, and a narrow tie. He held an old, leather-bound book in his lap.

Lillian smiled encouragement at the man then addressed the group. "I want to introduce Mr. Daniel Buckley, our source for this mission. Mr. Buckley has a story to share with us. And a request. Please give him your attention."

All eyes turned to the ancient man. His eyes moved from face to face around the room before turning to Lillian. "You're right," he said. "They look like everyone else, even with their … special powers."

He gave the group members an apologetic grin. "I've known Lily here a long time. We were neighbors, and she was good friends with my Sylvie. The gals did everything together, and she was strong for us when the polio came through and hit our oldest girl." Daniel stopped and cleared his throat, staring wordlessly at the assembled seniors to see if they understood.

Heads nodded. They all remembered the time before the vaccine—the time when every parent was afraid.

"Sylvie figured out what was going on with Lily and this traveling business," Daniel continued. "She tried to explain it to me, but I didn't pay it much mind. Sylvie was always a mite fanciful. She'd weave stories for our kids filled with elves and fairies and leprechauns, and half-believe them herself. Now, with Sylvie gone, maybe I'm a mite fanciful myself. And I started to think on the old days, the long-ago days, and wondered if it might be possible to find out more about my family and some of the things my grandpa told me. I knew *I* couldn't do it, couldn't go back and see it myself. But maybe someone else could. So I called up Lily, and here I am."

He glanced over at Lillian who nodded in a reassuring way. "You told me that when a man gets older …" she prompted.

"Yes. When a man gets older, he starts to think about what he can leave behind. I'm not talking about money, though, if you can make things easier for the kids and grandkids, that's a fine thing. My granddaughter is a *doctor*," he said proudly. "Graduated top of her class. Sylvie and I paid her tuition."

For a moment he sat taller in his chair. Then his brow creased in confusion, and he looked to Lillian again. "What do I tell them now?"

"Tell them your story. And how you need help."

Daniel straightened again. "When a man gets older, he thinks about what he has to leave behind," he repeated. "I figured what I had to leave was a story, and maybe something more. It was a story my grandpa told me when I was a boy. I don't know the whole story, and what I know, I don't have any proof for. That's why I'm here. I got as far as I could on my own, but now I need help from folks who can search where I can't go."

Daniel looked down at the book cradled in his lap, running his hand across its cover. "Grandpa owned this book. It's a family Bible. It was the only thing of his they gave me when I left the orphanage. Likely it was the only thing he owned. It's helped me remember my last days with him and some of what he was trying to tell me. So, about a year ago, I started putting the pieces of the puzzle together, and I got pretty far. But then there were questions I couldn't answer and things I suspected but had no way to find out. *And time is running out.*"

The old man rocked back and forth in his chair, his eyes still resting on the Bible. Aggie regarded his distress with compassion.

"Now tell about your grandpa," Lillian prodded gently. "Would you like your notes?" She picked up a slim packet of stapled pages. Aggie saw the text was printed in a large-sized font, making it easier to read. Daniel placed the Bible on a side table and reached for the packet. His anxiety eased as he scanned the first sheet. "Daniel did some research," Lillian explained, "with the help of his daughter and granddaughter."

Daniel looked out at the assembled seniors and began. "Gabriel Aaron Buckley, my grandpa Gabe, was an important man in my life. He raised me, you might say, even though I was only with him till I was nine. See, I was born in New York City in the twenties. The 'Roaring Twenties' they called it." He shrugged. "Maybe the twenties did roar, but I was just a child, so what did I know?

"I don't remember my momma and daddy. Grandpa Gabe told me they died together of the influenza. Not in the worst years, when thousands died. In the years after, when it was supposed to be over, but it came back and took more. Grandpa said life can be like that. You think 'the fearful trip' is done—that's what he called hard times—but death and grief can lie in wait.

"And he was right about that. When the Depression came, he tried to hold on for me. But he was terrible old by then. There wasn't much food, and what there was he gave to me. I was nine when he died. Did I tell you that?" He looked around uncertainly.

"You're doing fine," Lillian assured him. "Explain what happened when he died."

"It was 1932 when he died," Daniel said. "I was sent out of the city to the orphanage. They gave me education and meals and a family of sorts. I survived, and when I left at eighteen, they gave me that book there, Grandpa's Bible.

"But before the orphanage, all my early years were with him. And Grandpa was a good parent. He took me fishing and helped me with my lessons. We went to the museums and Central Park. He took me to Yankee Stadium in the Bronx. And a jazz club in Harlem. Me, just a boy, but he got me in to hear the music. Oh, he was an educated man. Not from college, but he had seen a lot. At night, we sat at the kitchen table, and he read to me—*Dr. Dolittle* and the *Hardy Boys*, those were my favorites—and told me stories. Stories about being a teamster, and watching the Brooklyn Bridge go up, and the Statue of Liberty. And sometimes, when he judged I was able to listen carefully enough, he told me about joinin' the Union cause and meeting Mr. Brady. Just before he died, that's all he would talk about. He repeated the same stories, over and over, like he knew he was going to go and wanted to pass on something to me that he wasn't sure I was ready to understand."

Kat shifted in her chair, and Sal adjusted his glasses. The slight movements distracted Daniel. He stopped speaking and again looked about as if confused about where he was. Quietly, Lillian leaned over, scanned the notes in Daniel's hand, and pointed to a section.

He gave her a grateful look and went on. "Grandpa was a young man when the Civil War began, and young still, at least in years, when the war was over. But the war changed him. Grandpa was at Antietam. September 17, 1862. The most lethal single day in America's history. Twelve thousand casualties on the Union side. That many or more on the Reb side. Antietam ended Lee's first invasion of the North and gave President Lincoln the victory he needed to issue the Emancipation Proclamation."

Daniel raised his eyes and spoke directly to the group. "When the war started, people thought it would be over in three months. And some thought it was about preservin' the Union and nothing else." He snorted. "Grandpa was smarter than that. He knew what all that dying was about. 'You can't be preservin' the Union with four million souls enslaved.' That's what he'd say to me. He knew about slavery from growing up in Seneca Village."

"He grew up with Indians?" Kat asked.

"No, dear," Viola said patiently. "He's talking about the little town that was on land taken for Central Park. And I'm not sure you should refer to native people as Indians."

Aggie sat forward. *Seneca Village.* She recalled the history teacher's futile effort to organize a field trip there and the carved angels on the pulpit in the Metropolitan Museum of Art.

"The lady's right," Daniel said, nodding toward Viola. "Seneca Village was smack dab in the middle of land that got made into Central Park. Before the City Fathers decided to make a park, it was just acres of rocky, swampy land. But it wasn't all empty land. A section of it was *owned* by free black people. Think of that! Those folks built homes and a school. Three churches, too. Maybe they were able to do it because the land was so far from the center of the city back then. People thought of it as out in the countryside."

"All Angels was there," Aggie offered. The name had come to her.

"Yep, that's right. The church and school were integrated. This is before the Civil War, mind. When other folks came to settle—other outcasts, you might say—the black folks that started Seneca Village had nice comfortable relations with the newcomers. The Germans came. After the potato famine, the Irish came. That's how my grandpa got there.

"And that's how he understood about the Civil War. Like I said, Grandpa was Irish, but most of his neighbors were black. Some had been born in New York. It was a free state after 1827. But some had escaped from states that held people in chains. Course, when construction started on the park right before the Civil War, they were all kicked out, and Seneca Village was destroyed."

Daniel stopped. Again, Lillian drew his attention to the right paragraph. "So, Grandpa was at Antietam," Daniel read. "Antietam was where he left his childhood. He also left his best friend and two fingers off his left hand."

Sal flinched and looked down at his own giant hands resting on the arms of his chair. Bernice surreptitiously spread the fingers of her left hand, then folded down two fingers and studied the effect.

"It happened when Grandpa carried his friend Billy out of the cornfield and over to where the nurses were. The bullets were flying everywhere. The nurses were that close to the action. He laid his friend down right next to the Lady, Clara Barton herself. Billy had been hit in the shoulder, so the Lady and Grandpa started with the buttons on his shirt. The bullets flew, their hands worked, and then the next bullet came. That bullet tore through her sleeve, and through Grandpa's hand, and through Billy's heart."

Daniel sighed heavily. "The Lady looked at Billy and looked at Grandpa's hand and kept working. She never looked at the bullet hole in her own sleeve. Her hands moved from Billy's buttons to Grandpa's hand. And she was so calm that Grandpa stopped being afraid. She had a *bandage.* Grandpa told me what a miracle that was. The nurses had brought supplies to the battlefield. Before they arrived, the wounds were dressed with corn husks.

"It was because of his hand that Grandpa met the photographers sent out by Mr. Mathew Brady. Grandpa didn't go near the place they called the field hospital. Hah! It was a couple of filthy blankets held up with sticks. He just walked a ways off and sat hisself under a tree and waited to see if he'd live or the infection would come and take his life."

Daniel's eyes lifted, his gaze suddenly hawk-like as it swept the group. "McClellan *dithered* after that first day. He had fresh troops arriving but didn't use them. Lee retreated across the Potomac. Left the Rebel dead for the Union boys to bury. Two days after the battle, the dead still weren't all buried. But Grandpa said except for the smell and the flies it was almost peaceful. At least there was no shooting and no one screaming anymore.

"And his whole self was focused on his hand. His good hand cradled the one that was shot apart and bandaged up. He didn't belong with the living, and he didn't belong with the dead. He was superstitious about the bandage put on by Clara Barton. He figured it would work, or it wouldn't, but he didn't want anyone else to touch it. Sitting under a tree in that quiet, he heard the horse and wagon come along the road. It was Mr. Gardner and Mr. Gibson."

"Brady didn't go to the battlefield himself, right?" Sal asked.

"Mr. Mathew Brady was what you might call an 'offsite manager,'" Daniel said dryly. "He was an entrepreneur. He put up the money, paid for the equipment, and sold the pictures, of course. He photographed the important people that came to his studio, but he hired others to get the job done in the field. Grandpa never said anything against the man. Brady had the idea after all. But the only battle he went to hisself was the first big one, First Bull Run. Manassas is what the Rebs called it. He said *a spirit in my feet said Go and I went*. Well, he went all right, but you know what happened, don't you?"

"I explained it was a rout," Lillian said, "and Brady realized he wasn't suited for work outside the studio."

Unexpectedly, Frank spoke up. "It was a rout, all right. Stonewall Jackson held his ground, and the Confederate forces chased McDowell through the woods and back to D.C."

Daniel bobbed his head in agreement. "I don't fault Brady for staying away from the front lines after that, even though he wanted to be part of history."

"He wanted the euphoria of advancing his art in service to the country and making it a truthful medium of history," Julie said quietly, then reddened as all eyes turned in her direction. "I read that in one of the books Lillian recommended," she explained. "That line stayed with me. It's kind of like why we're travelers."

"That's the right word," Daniel agreed. "*Euphoria.* That's the feeling, at least at the start."

Frank grunted. "Funny how *euphoria* evaporates when the shooting starts."

Daniel pointed in Frank's direction. "Yep. Grandpa had no euphoria after Antietam. But sitting under that tree, he made a resolution. He told me about it before he died, repeated the words so I wouldn't forget: 'I wasn't going to be useless.' That's what he kept saying. There he was, a kid, his hand shot apart, and he determines not to give up on livin' a *useful* life. The way he told it, the minute his mind went in that direction, he heard the wagon coming along. Mathew Brady's wagon with Mr. Gardner and Mr. Gibson inside.

"The photographers stop right near Grandpa's tree. They come out with their camera mounted on a tripod and work fast, as a team, almost not talking. Gibson prepares a plate at the wagon then gives it over to Gardner. The exposure would take ten or fifteen seconds, then the plate goes back to the wagon. That wagon smelled of ether and collodion. Attracted flies, too. Grandpa thought it fitting the wagon had the same death smell as the fields and ditches."

Daniel sat forward. "This is where Grandpa's story comes together with the story of those pictures. Each time, while Mr. Gibson was preparing the plate, Mr. Gardner was movin' the camera, getting ready for the next shot. Well, it comes to a point when Gardner hesitates. Remember, the dead were everywhere, still lying unburied. It was almost as if he wasn't sure he should be doin' what he was doin'. But he knew he *had* to."

"He knew that camera was the eye of history." It was Julie again.

Daniel nodded. "Gardner and Gibson were the first to make photographs on a battlefield right after the battle ended. It's not like now with everything *instant*. Not even like World War II with those G.I.s in *Life* magazine, or Vietnam with those boys on the nightly news."

At the mention of Vietnam, Frank rubbed his hand along his shoulder as if trying to ease an old pain.

"So Mr. Gardner hesitates and stares across the land. And Grandpa gets up from where he's been sittin' and walks up to him and says, 'Come with me.' Mr. Gardner looks at Grandpa, and looks at Grandpa's hand, and nods his head. Then Grandpa goes over to the camera and indicates to Mr. Gardner to take one side, and together they get it and the tripod."

"Musta' hurt like a sonovabitch," Sal commented sympathetically.

Daniel considered this. "The way Grandpa told it, the moment he picked up that camera, the pain in his hand stopped botherin' him. It wasn't gone. It just stopped botherin' him. He'd made up his mind. He wasn't goin' to be useless."

Lillian put her hand on Daniel's arm. "A lot of us here have made that same resolution."

Daniel patted her hand. "That's right, Lily. Grandpa knew he had to get up and use what was left of his hand. So, he showed Mr. Gardner and Mr. Gibson places to take their pictures, helped with the camera, and drove the wagon. The photographers telegraphed for more glass plates. When Brady's teamster showed up, Grandpa unloaded the supplies, loaded what was ready to go, then hopped up in the wagon and headed out. The fighting was over for him, and he left it all behind.

"That's when his relationship with Mr. Brady began. He arrived at the gallery on Broadway like he had a right to be there. When he met Mr. Brady, he pulled off his hat and reached out to shake his hand. Mr. Brady does like Gardner. He squints down at Grandpa's other hand then looks at Grandpa's face, and they shake. And that was that. In the days that followed, he let Grandpa work in the studio, set up the stereo viewers, make deliveries with the wagon. Grandpa is there when the exhibit opens." Daniel leaned back in his chair and closed his eyes.

"Do you need a break?" Lillian asked softly.

"No, I want to finish it. Maybe I could have a cup of tea?"

"I'll have some brought in," Wells said. "How do you like it?"

"With a little lemon if you have it," Daniel answered. "Now let me get to the point. I seem to take longer and longer to get to the point these days."

He referred again to the notes, and this time found the place without Lillian's assistance. "For a while, Grandpa was content working for Mr. Brady. But he didn't stay. A year after the Antietam exhibit, the draft riots came. The rioters were mostly Irish, the victims mostly black. They even went after children. Maybe because he grew up in Seneca Village and was repelled by a mob burning an orphanage, he felt he needed to get away.

"Grandpa went north, to the West Side, right near Harlem. Back then it was just a few buildings and homesteads and some open space. He found a little place and set up a livery stable. He also got hisself a wife. Lula was her name. When Grandpa asked her to marry him, he was sure she would turn him down because of his hand. He even said as much when he proposed." A delighted look came over Daniel's face. "Lula's answer was to slap him so hard he nearly fell to the floor. Then she says, 'I don't care about your hand, fool. I care about your *heart*. If that's what you're offering, I'm of a mind to accept.' Oh, they were happy. I could tell by the way Grandpa talked about her.

"He was up near the north city limits most of the time. But he came south if business brought him. Or history. Grandpa was there when sixteen gray horses pulled the hearse with Lincoln's body through the streets. And he did jobs for Mr. Brady if there was occasion, though mostly he got hired by farmers and shopkeepers. He said he liked working with horses more than people. The horses didn't care about his hand."

Erin had entered the room carrying a steaming cup of tea. She handed it to Daniel who smiled at her gratefully.

"The last job Grandpa works for Mr. Brady, it's a different time. Lily said she was going to tell you about Brady's money troubles. Grandpa said Brady was always orderin' things he couldn't pay for. Ignoring his bills. Falling behind on paying his employees. By 1872 he owes everybody and his brother. So, he starts to use his pictures as currency. He can do that with the important ones, the portraits of presidents and generals. He signs some over to pay for supplies. He gives others to creditors. A bankruptcy lawyer gets hold of some and passes them out to his friends." Daniel put his teacup down and referred to his notes. "Listen to this," he said, pointing to the page with a shaking finger. "Some of his plates are taken by one of his photographers, and they get passed to the photographer's wife, then get passed to her executrix, then get passed to the executrix's son, who stores the plates in a barn, and they don't get found until 1948."

"I read that some plates were sold for the glass alone," Julie said. "Did your grandpa say that happened?"

"It happened. Portraits of anonymous soldiers were sold to anonymous dirt farmers scratching out a living. The glass was used for cold frames or greenhouses. Course, used that way, the images fade because the sun bleaches the glass."

Daniel had reached the last page of his notes. Fatigue caused his head to drop. Gently, Lillian took the notes and picked up the Bible from the side table. Opening the front cover, she placed it in his hands. He looked at her, confused.

"Read it," Lillian said.

Daniel cleared his throat. *"Lincoln buried at home. Brady's soldiers to stand guard. With the angels as our witnesses, April 1882.* That's what it says here, right by the list of all the marriages and births and deaths. I'll pass it around so you can see." Daniel handed the open book to Viola, who was seated next to him.

"Now tell us what you think," Lillian directed. She handed him the packet again, still turned to the last page. Read from where you wrote about what you suspect."

Daniel studied the page, his lips moving silently as if rehearsing the words of a script. But when he began reading aloud, his voice grew stronger. "I believe Grandpa took some of Mr. Brady's glass plates. Grandpa was an honest man, and he respected Mr. Brady, but I imagine Mr. Brady owed him, like he owed everyone. I believe it happened in 1872, when the bankruptcy was going on, and the assets—the equipment and pictures—had to be taken to a warehouse for storage. Grandpa knew some of those pictures were valuable, and creditors were lining up. I believe Mr. Brady asked Grandpa to use his wagon and move load after load. But I believe there might've been a last load, a smaller load. A load that made it into the wagon but never made it to the warehouse. I would like to believe Mr. Brady nodded to Grandpa, and Grandpa nodded back before slapping the reins and heading north."

"But if he got the plates in 1872, why is he burying them a decade later?" asked Sal, holding the open Bible and studying the inscription. "If it was to keep them safe, why wait?"

"And if he had a portrait of Lincoln, why didn't he just sell it when he needed money?" Serena asked.

"We don't know the answers yet," Lillian explained. "The upper West Side was changing in those years. For a time, 110th Street was a rough area known for its saloons and brothels. Homesteads were being replaced by apartment houses. The fields where cows grazed would become Morningside Park. We don't know what challenges Gabe was facing in that period."

"If you have valuable glass plates, it's not something you take down to the bank to deposit," Frank offered. "Especially if you didn't exactly get them in a totally legit sort of way."

The Bible had been moving from person to person around the circle. When it was Aggie's turn, she admired the beautiful handwriting and the carefully placed names and dates.

"Grandpa was a brave man," Daniel said. "He had seen war and riots. Seen people killed and done some killing hisself. But maybe, as he got older, he learned to be afraid. Afraid to lose his home again like what happened when he was a child. Afraid to move the plates. Afraid they would be broken or stolen."

Aggie handed the Bible back to Daniel, and he nodded his thanks.

"Grandpa once told me, 'Your fears are like ghosts.' The ghost that's chasing me now is age. The doctor says I don't have long. And I've known that for a while. There are things I can't remember. Things that are confusing." He looked around at them, helpless and pleading, but determined at the same time. "I'm here to ask you folks to find those panes of glass. Lincoln and his soldiers. I'm asking you to find the end of the story. I need to know before I enter the time when I can't know, and the place where I will never know again."

Chapter 16 ~ Study Group

"What does everybody think?" Julie asked.

The group members were gathered around a table in the dining room. Lunch was buffet-style again, and they had already helped themselves to sandwiches. Serena was absent, having begged off with a breezy reference to a session with her trainer. Daniel had politely refused an invitation to join them as well. He left arm in arm with Lillian, announcing they were going to find a diner and talk about the old days.

"Isn't that what we were just doing?" Kat asked.

"Not *those* old days," Viola explained, "*their* old days. When they were young."

"So, what does everybody think?" Julie pressed. "I think we'll have to do a stakeout, like we did for Sal at Ellis Island. It's odd the inscription lists just the month and year. That narrows it, but it's not ideal."

"We've got a bigger problem, don't we?" Frank said. "You're suggesting a stakeout. Well, a stakeout *where*? We need to know exactly where they were living and whether there's a big old fat building sitting there now. That's going to take some research. And another thing—and this is a big thing—we don't know what Daniel's grandpa looked like. Wells says he hasn't found a single picture of the man. With Sal's grandma we had a couple photos."

"We know he had a messed-up hand," Kat said.

Julie lifted her eyes to the heavens, but before she could respond, Viola intervened. "Yes, kitten, but it's not always easy to be close enough to see a person's hand."

"We've maybe got another thing to figure out," Sal said slowly. "We're going on conjecture here. I mean, what do we really have? Maybe Mr. Buckley is remembering what he was told, but maybe he's filling in the blanks with what he wishes was the case. Finding a portrait of Lincoln, especially a rare one, would be a big deal. And the reference to soldiers, look at who Lincoln's soldiers were: Grant, Sherman, Meade, McClellan. Finding pictures of any one of them would make headlines. But face it. We're kind of relying on a man whose memory is faded."

"Do you think he's demented?" Kat asked.

This time even Viola looked exasperated. "The term is *dementia,* and even if he has it, which we don't know, that doesn't mean his story is worthless. It just means we have to work harder to pull things together."

"Last known location," Aggie said suddenly. She turned to Frank. "For Gabe, his last known location is the Antietam exhibit. We know when it opened and where it was located. We could … attend. Verify that he worked for Mathew Brady. See what he looked like."

"Now that's a darn good idea," Frank said. "It would be a start."

"Julie," Aggie had remembered something from earlier that morning, "you questioned Lillian about traveling to the nineteenth century. What's the issue there? Are there limits on how far back you can go?"

"There's always some kind of limits," Sal replied a little ponderously. "Limits on the three Ds, limits on who's going to get traveling ability in the first place. We don't even know all the limits out there. But what Julie said is true. No one in our group has gone back that far—"

"Except the directors," Frank said.

"Yes," Sal agreed. "But the rest of us …." He shrugged. "It took a lot of practice to get our whole group to Ellis Island. But Lillian must think we can handle the job, or she wouldn't have organized this mission."

Aggie began to feel uneasy. A lump was forming in her stomach that had nothing to do with the food on her plate. "Julie, you said Abe arranged for some folks to tutor me?"

"Yes. You guys are going to help out, right?" Julie asked. "I thought we could meet at my place after lunch and give Aggie some pointers on focus and the three Ds. Time travel 101 stuff."

"Count me in," Frank said.

"I'll be there," Sal added.

"Bernice and I are coming, too," Viola said. "It works out well because acting won't begin until tomorrow."

"Tell me about acting," Aggie interposed. "Does fieldwork require you to learn lines or something?"

"No, it's more about blending in," Julie explained. "If you don't act appropriately for the time period, you draw attention to yourself and are prone to eviction. Elizabeth—she's the acting teacher—helps you fit in. Little things, like the way you sit, walk, or gesture. We practice conversation skills, too, but there's no memorizing."

A dreamy expression spread across Viola's face. "In the past, you're background, unimportant. Others don't pay you much mind because the time they're in is so much more vivid. You're not someone anyone will remember. Your clothes don't matter much, or your hair. If you can act in a way that fits the time, you can increase your duration and soak it all in."

"Is that why my Grand Central trip happened even with my modern clothes?" Aggie asked.

"Yep," Bernice answered promptly. "That blonde gal you talked to in 1942 wasn't looking at your clothes or your hair."

"Except at some point, once you travel back eighty or ninety years, people *do* start to notice if your clothes are wrong, or your hair, or you use an expression that hasn't come into usage," Julie added. "Elizabeth helps with costumes for when you go back far enough to need them. We all wore period clothing at Ellis Island."

"It's funny," Viola said. "An actress works to be the one no one can take their eyes off. A traveler must be the one no one notices. It's hard for some to get used to."

"I *know*," Kat exclaimed. "Serena was evicted a bunch of times because she's gorgeous and people look at her."

Julie started giggling and choked on her iced tea.

Kat looked offended. "It wasn't her fault. And won't Aggie have trouble, too? She was a teacher. They always want you to look at them and pay attention."

"Had trouble in school?" Bernice suggested. "Me, too. Got caught smoking in the bathroom."

Julie was overcome with laughter. Mystified, Frank and Sal looked at each other and shrugged.

Wells appeared at their table munching on an apple and holding a spiral-bound book. "Jules, you're going to prep Ms. May, right?" he asked.

"Yes, we're going to grab some cookies from the kitchen and head to my place."

Wells glanced around the dining room before turning to Aggie and holding out the book. "I put this together last year," he said. "Lillian doesn't like it being written down, but I think it's useful. Just, you know, don't circulate it or anything."

Aggie took the volume and looked at the cover. *Remarkable Travel for Dummies*. "Ah. Thank you, Wells," she said. "I'm sure this will help."

He beamed and turned to Julie. "Did you say there's cookies?"

***

Aggie found Abe leaning against the wall in the hallway outside her apartment. Without saying anything, she unlocked the door and entered. He followed her in and shut the door. She dropped her sweater on a chair, then pulled her notebook from her handbag.

"I'd offer you some tea, but Julie's convened a study group at her place. I'm heading up there in a few minutes. Are you joining us?"

"No, but you'll be in good hands with Julie, Viola, and the others. I have a sense you'll pick things up quickly. You pay attention." He tilted his head toward the notebook.

"Maybe it's one of my 'skills and abilities,'" she said with a smile. "I didn't take many notes this morning, though, so there's not much new here. Just questions on time travel basics."

"I'm sure the study group will cover everything. Actually, I didn't come to read your notes. I just dropped by to make sure everything went all right this morning. And I wanted to hear your opinion of Daniel."

"Everything went well. No one asked any uncomfortable questions. As for Daniel," Aggie paused as she mentally reviewed the old man's story, "I believe him. We'll have to see what the facts show as we start our research. But right now, I think there's something there."

Abe nodded. "That's what I felt when I first met him."

Aggie studied Abe. He was dressed in blue jeans and a denim shirt. He looked more at ease than he had that morning. "You left this morning before securing my agreement to be 'less than forthcoming' about what we talked about."

He shrugged. "I couldn't make the deal, so I just bet on your discretion."

She nodded, considered him a moment, then held out her hand. "I can make that deal now. As long as you keep me posted on your thinking."

"Thank you," he said with a grin. Reaching out, he shook, but then kept hold of her hand. His eyes dropped to look at their joined hands, and his brow furrowed as if he were considering a complicated problem. Then the moment was over. He dropped her hand and smiled. "Good luck with the study group," he said, then went out the door and was gone.

Arriving at Julie's apartment a few minutes later, Aggie saw that the layout was similar to her own but with modern furnishings and decor. Most of the fieldwork group members were already there, and the cookies Julie had secured were artfully arranged on a platter that sat on a glass-topped coffee table. Frank and Sal were on the leather sofa happily munching away. Aggie eyed a macaron, but resolutely seated herself a safe distance from temptation and turned to a fresh page in her notebook.

"Who wants coffee?" Julie called from behind the kitchen counter.

Bernice raised her hand.

"Got any beer?" Frank asked.

"It's too early for that, and you know it," Julie scolded.

"Okay, Mom," Frank said grudgingly. "Coffee's fine."

"Too much caffeine is bad for you," Kat said in a preachy sort of voice. "And I don't think those cookies are gluten-free."

"God, what a shame," Frank responded as he stuffed a gingersnap in his mouth.

The door to the apartment stood ajar, and Serena appeared in the hallway. She was wearing a smart-looking workout outfit and was focused on her cell phone.

"Coffee, Serena?" Julie called out a trifle impatiently. "You want to come in? We're going to start."

Serena entered and selected a chair opposite Aggie. "No coffee, thanks," she said, then returned to a study of her phone.

Aggie regarded the woman. Kat was right. She was very pretty, indeed. It was hard to believe she qualified as a "senior citizen." Her skin was smooth, and Aggie wondered if she used one of those lotions that "repaired" wrinkles. Her long hair shone glossy and full without a single silver strand in evidence.

Julie emerged from the kitchen balancing a tray with coffee cups, a sugar bowl, and a pot of cream. She slid the tray onto the coffee table and took a seat. "Okay, let's get going."

"Tell us what you've already told Aggie," Viola suggested. "We might be able to save some time. Do that lawyer thing. You know, *sum up*."

Julie sat up straighter in her chair, folded her hands in her lap, and smiled at Viola. Then the smile was gone, and she began speaking, ticking off points in a precise, methodical manner.

"Okay. Aggie knows that only a very few seniors become travelers. You go back in time by focusing on an object, like you're meditating. Generally, only one person at a time can go to a particular destination in the past. The exceptions in our chapter are Maurice, Abe, and Lillian who can *companion travel*, which allows them to accompany another traveler that they are touching and stay with that person for a few minutes. Some places—old buildings, historic sites—have *auras* that facilitate travel. You have protection in the past. You won't materialize inside a wall, or in a fire, or in the middle of a battlefield. If danger develops during a trip to the past, you'll immediately be dropped back to the present. We call that getting *evicted*. So, for example, if a bullet flies in your direction in the past, you'll get evicted. You can also get evicted for random mistakes such as trying to use something modern or drawing too much attention to yourself."

Julie paused and drew a breath. Viola had pulled some fuzzy yarn out of a little cloth bag and was serenely crocheting what looked like a baby bonnet.

"Travel requires skills in three areas," Julie continued. "We call them *the three Ds*: destination, distance, duration."

"Some people find that part challenging," Serena murmured.

Julie turned slightly pink but continued her recitation. "*Destination* is the ability to get where you want to go, the exact date and time. *Distance* is the ability to move around in the past, to go from place to place. *Duration* is the ability to stay in the past for a period of time without getting evicted."

Julie stopped and looked at Aggie, assessing her comprehension. Aggie looked up from her notes and nodded.

"Now, here are things we haven't discussed at all," Julie continued, "or not discussed in depth. When you begin your journey, if someone is looking directly at you, you can't travel. Another person's concentrated attention holds you in the present. But if you're alone, you can travel. If you're unnoticed, you can travel. If you're just a face in a crowd, you can travel. Finally," Julie looked sideways for a moment, as if retrieving information from storage, then returned her gaze to the room, "you can't change the past."

Aggie's mind flew to her early morning conversation with Abe. *What's the journey from myth to reality? From Icarus to the Wright Brothers?*

"You can't prevent a death," Julie elaborated, "or give a warning, or move things around, or bring objects forward, or leave things behind." She paused, spread her fingers wide, then refolded her hands in her lap. "Okay, that's it."

"I love it when she does that," Frank said admiringly.

"Very nice," Viola agreed. She turned to Aggie. "Is that about where you were?"

Aggie had been scribbling notes as Julie talked. "Tell me more about not being able to begin a trip to the past if someone is looking at you."

"Ah," Viola responded. "Isn't that a funny thing? But I suppose it serves a purpose. It certainly would be disconcerting to be talking to Great Aunt Matilda or old Cousin Fred and have them disappear on you with a little *pop*. Lucky for us people don't tend to look too closely at seniors."

Sal cleared his throat. "If you do happen to be the kind of lady that attracts attention … I mean if you catch the eye of a gentleman … uh …." He stopped in apparent confusion and waved a hand helplessly in Serena's direction, then looked back at Aggie. "Not that I think you'll have that kind of trouble," he said, then, realizing the implication, blushed furiously. "I mean … it's not that … no offense meant."

Aggie took pity on him. "None taken. But what do you do if you *are* being observed, and you want to travel?"

"You gotta wait till you're alone," Sal replied.

"Yeah, or you excuse yourself and go to the john or step into a closet," Frank added.

"What happens if you're being photographed? Or filmed?" Aggie probed.

There was an awkward silence, then Julie spoke. "If you're being filmed by a *live* cameraman, or you're on a security camera and the feed is being viewed, obviously someone is looking at you, and you can't travel. You're stuck in the present. But ...." She hesitated, and Aggie jumped in.

"What about a security camera that no one is looking at right then? You know, it's not being monitored?"

"You can travel, but the film will show you disappearing," Sal said bluntly.

Julie nodded in confirmation.

Abruptly, Bernice spoke up. "Wells tested it without telling anyone. Lillian was *royally pissed.*"

"I think you mean properly incensed, dear," Viola suggested calmly, not bothering to look up from her crocheting.

"It happened a long time ago. Wells used hidden cameras," Julie explained unhappily. "He set them up in secret at the barn where we practice. He didn't live monitor them but reviewed the film later."

"*Poof,*" Frank said, raising his hands in an expansive gesture. "It was *now you see him, now you don't.* Pretty mind-blowing." He saw the disapproving looks aimed in his direction and turned his palms out in surrender. "But wrong, you know. Definitely wrong."

"Lillian felt—strongly felt—that an experiment like that undermines *trust,*" Viola said with some heat. "And she's right. It would have been different if there was *consent.* You have to go about things in the proper way."

Bernice gave a sarcastic little snort.

Viola ignored her and continued. "Not that I'm unmindful of the fact that he discovered this teensy little problem. We can't have video recordings of old people popping in and out of view all the time without raising suspicions. And if you're not aware of a security camera, that's exactly what will happen. Think about places that are monitored all the time. There are bank cameras, traffic cams, even police cars with dashboard videos."

"So how do you address the problem?" Aggie asked. "What if you don't know whether a particular location has a hidden security camera?"

"Or drones," Bernice said. "Wells is worried about drones."

"Wells is worried about a lot of things that will probably never happen," Viola scoffed. "It's far more likely a Remarkable will get caught disappearing off a nanny-cam."

"So how do you manage," Aggie insisted, "if a camera, or drone, or whatever, records a traveler leaving on a trip?"

"Well, it was rather a tempest in a teapot when it came down to it," Viola said tranquilly, "apart from Wells treating people like guinea pigs. You see, when we found out we dematerialize if we're caught on film, we chatted a bit and decided we would try to be careful."

"*You try to be careful?*" Aggie said. "Isn't that awfully loosey-goosey?"

114

Viola nodded. "But it works fine in practice. We try to avoid places that are likely to be monitored, but if we're caught unawares," she paused for a moment to attend to a particularly complicated maneuver with the crochet hook that produced a lacy flower on the baby bonnet, "well, it's a curious thing. People have such faith in technology, especially young people. But at the same time, they don't trust what it's telling them. Or showing them in this case. Tell me, what would you think if you watched a video showing an old lady disappear into thin air?"

Aggie tried to address the question seriously. After a moment, she enumerated possibilities. "I'd think it was a trick. Or a prank. Faulty equipment. Doctored tape. Special effects. Something for Facebook or YouTube. Film erased by mistake. Rosemary Woods and the eighteen-and-a-half-minute gap."

"You see?" Viola said. "No one would ever give credence to the evidence on the tape. No one would ever believe what was really going on."

"Who's Rosemary Woods?" Kat asked.

"I'll explain it to you later, dear," Viola said.

"All right," Aggie continued, "what you say makes sense, sort of. Now tell me about returning from the past. I assume you don't appear without warning right in front of someone? What if you need to come back to the present, and the place you're going to return to is occupied?"

"Now that's a cool thing," Frank said enthusiastically. "You *never* come back in a suspicious way. Even if you appear in a room full of folks, no one is ever looking in your direction, or they blink, or their attention is drawn to something outside the window, or *they feel the need to go get a beer*," he said with a meaningful look at Julie, "and walk right out of the room, so they don't see the Remarkable appear."

"The present always makes room for you," Sal agreed. "Coming home is never a problem. No one ever suspects a thing."

"You just tap your heels together and say, 'There's no place like home,'" Viola sighed.

"Yes," Julie said, "returning is easy, and you don't need ruby slippers. You simply form the intent to return, and you're back. Don't worry," she added, seeing Aggie's dubious look. "No one has trouble with that part."

"So, are you taking her out to practice?" Sal asked.

"Yes, we'll go out to the barn when we're done here," Julie said. "Any advice on focusing and the three Ds?" Almost resentfully, she turned to Serena.

"Well, I'm not sure what to advise," the pretty woman drawled turning to Aggie. "I just seemed to be a *natural*. Went right into fieldwork."

"That's what Aggie's doing, too," Julie said tightly.

"Well," Serena sniffed, "I'm sure she'll be fine then. Stranger things have happened."

"Look," Frank said, "maybe I can help. See, first you focus on something. Some of the gals think it's like meditating, but all you really gotta do is look at something without really looking at it, you know? Like, when I was a rookie I was practicing in New York, and I started focusing on the box scores in the paper and thinking about where I wanted to go. That's the first D, *destination*. I say to myself, Wouldn't it be something if I slid a few decades back … to 1956, say … October 8th, say."

Aggie was confused. "Uh, you mean …?"

"Game five of the World Series!" Frank exclaimed. "*The perfect game.* Yankees versus Dodgers at Yankee Stadium. Yogi Berra leaping into Don Larsen's arms. What could beat that? I let my eyes slide along the box scores and thought about the date and felt myself moving back. Easy, right? This was early into traveling for me, and I was still getting that upset stomach business. But I had some Tums with me, so I chewed on a coupla' those, and everything was hunky-dory until I forgot to keep my mind in the right place. With destination, you have to keep your mind in the right place."

Bernice started to giggle.

"What happened?" Aggie asked.

"Well, I thought I was okay. I imagined getting to the old stadium, *The House that Ruth Built*. But that's where I got off track. Took my eye off the ball and started thinking about Ruth—the Babe—and his career. Then I thought about what it would be like to see one of *his* games, and the next thing I know, I've overshot my destination, and it's about 1915, and all these lady suffragettes are marching down the street with signs demanding the right to vote. I'm standing in their path like an idiot, chewing on my Tums. I guess they thought I was trying to block the march or was against the cause or something because before you know it, wham! They're whacking me with their placards."

Bernice and Viola were convulsed, and even Julie was grinning.

Frank pulled out a handkerchief and wiped his brow. "Those females were terrifying. Awesome, of course, but terrifying. Naturally, I got evicted. Considered giving it another go, but I was a touch unnerved, so I went home, put my feet up, and watched the game on TV. The one in the present, that is."

Sal was shaking his head. "You can't let stray thoughts distract you when you're working on destination. That's the point of a focus object."

"What about the other Ds?" Aggie prodded.

"Distance is about confidence," Frank continued. "Say I'm in the past, and I want to find out if there's beer in the fridge. Well, I've gotta cover the distance between where I'm at and where I want to be. I have to kinda' mosey across the room into the kitchen. That's distance. Want me to demonstrate?"

Julie held up her hands in surrender. "Help yourself, Coach. I guess it's not too early."

"And I'm *retired*," he said, vaulting to his feet and taking exaggerated tip-toe-like steps toward the kitchen. Halfway there he glanced back at Aggie. "See? Distance is like walking a tightrope." He held his arms out to the sides as if for balance. When he reached the refrigerator, he faced the group and executed a brief bow before opening the door and peering inside.

"And duration?" Aggie asked.

"Well, duration is a combination of skill and luck," Sal said, thoughtfully. "Like Julie said, if danger appears, you'll get dropped back to the present faster than you can say Jack Robinson. That's just bad luck, like Frank getting into a melee with those suffragettes."

"But if you're not in danger?" Aggie pressed.

"Well, some can stay for an hour or so," Serena said unexpectedly, "and some get evicted after a couple of minutes. It's like the other skills. Some have a gift, and some don't."

Julie frowned but stayed silent.

"Um, does that cover it?" Sal asked.

"Did you tell her about intervention?" Kat asked. "Serena's tried a few times." When no one responded, a stubborn look appeared on her face. "Oh, come on, guys. Lillian is too strict. We aren't even supposed to *talk* about it?"

"You can't change things," Frank said dismissively. "Intervention ain't real and ain't happening."

"Well, when Serena was in California last year, she went to the sixties and almost did it."

"She tried to get a *tattoo*, Kat," Julie snapped. "And nothing happened."

Serena's eyes flashed. "Nothing happened? My lower back was *extremely sensitive* all week."

"Jeez, how come you're always going to the sixties?" Frank asked.

Serena tossed her hair. "A lot was going on culturally in the sixties."

"Yeah," Frank said acidly, taking a pull on his beer. "A lot was going on. I was in 'Nam watching my buddies get blown to bits and wondering when my number would come up."

Serena looked annoyed. "I don't want to start anything," she said rising to her feet and picking up her bag. "I'm just saying, maybe it's easier to learn interesting things when you're in an interesting time period."

"Maybe the sixties are squishier than other decades," Kat said. "Like, more open."

"Must be all the LSD," Bernice commented from her seat in the corner. "Summer of '68, I was stoned out of my mind."

This astonishing pronouncement was met with stunned silence. Sal was shaking his head, and Frank's jaw had dropped open. "Can't judge a book by its cover," Bernice remarked blandly.

"Well," Viola managed to say with cheerful determination, "we're not going to spend time on this. Everyone tries to intervene at the beginning, and everyone fails." She stopped crocheting, pulled a length of yarn through the last stitch so it wouldn't unravel, then stowed the yarn and bonnet in her needlework bag. "But now we need to adjourn, so Aggie can practice."

Before Viola had finished speaking, Serena was on her way out the door. Kat bolted to her feet and hurried to catch up. "Thanks, Julie," she called over her shoulder.

"Yeah, thanks, Jules," Frank said, draining the last of his beer and rinsing the bottle at the sink. "Catch you later." He ruffled Julie's hair on the way out, in much the way an older brother might take leave from a kid sister.

Viola was the last to go. "Good luck, dear," she said to Aggie. "I'm sure you'll do fine. And if you ever want to talk, my apartment is right down the hall from you. My door's always open."

Chapter 17 ~ The Barn

Aggie helped tidy up after the others had left. While Julie rinsed the coffee cups, Aggie plumped the throw pillows and polished the glass surface of the coffee table. "Your place is very stylish," she remarked as Julie emerged from the kitchen. "Did you do the decorating?"

Julie looked around in a satisfied way. "In part. I said I wanted something very modern. No chintz, nothing Early American. This is what they came up with, the furniture at least. After my first session, when I knew I was coming back, I picked out rugs and paintings."

"Did you want it to be more like your home?"

"Actually, I wanted it nothing like my home," Julie responded emphatically. "My home is filled with all the big traditional pieces of furniture my husband and I picked out together. Expensive. Built to last forever. The furniture outlived the marriage, as it turned out."

Aggie looked a question.

"They used to call it a mid-life crisis when a man divorced his first wife and married someone twenty years younger. And they used to call that young thing a 'trophy wife.' Is that still what they say? I just remember the turmoil caused by the whole sordid business and his stupid, self-justifying monologues accusing me of caring more about my career than him and 'limiting his heart's ability to explore.'"

Aggie looked at Julie. Someone who didn't know her, someone who had never talked to her, would probably describe her as plain in every respect: her face, her hair, her figure, her clothing. "Should I say I'm sorry?" Aggie asked carefully.

She was surprised when a grin appeared like a ray of sunshine. "Don't you dare. I definitely got the better deal at the end of the day. I don't mean money. His family was loaded, but so was mine. I just mean I got custody of our daughter, which was all that really mattered to me. He didn't want the house or the furniture, all that big expensive furniture. I didn't, either, except it meant my little girl wouldn't have to deal with a move on top of everything else. She's grown now, of course. She's a lawyer, too. Here's her picture."

Julie picked up a framed photograph from a bookshelf and passed it to Aggie. The photo showed Julie with a tall young woman wearing a graduate's cap and gown. "What's her name?"

"Dorothy. It was my mother's name."

"She's beautiful," Aggie said, handing the photo back.

"Oh, my gosh, look at the time," Julie said. "We should get out to the barn and start you on a practice session. Why don't you pick up a sweater from your apartment, meet me in the lobby, and I'll walk you over. Maurice will have coached the rookies through their first practice sessions already, so it should be free."

"Does it have an aura?"

Julie snickered. "Nothing so exotic. It's rather prosaic, in fact. Still cool though. Perfect for learning 'destination.' You'll see. And amazing that Abe figured it out."

In a few minutes time, they were on their way down a paved walkway that followed the curve of the hill toward the barn. As they got closer, Aggie could see why someone might decide to leave it standing for purely aesthetic reasons. It was a giant structure with a fieldstone foundation and vertical planks painted red. The years and weather had softened the color to a warm rust hue, like the fur of a fox, and there were hints of gray where the paint had worn away completely. Huge double doors opened on the gable end, and a scattering of windows along the side glittered in the afternoon sun. Shading her eyes, Aggie looked up. The roof was crowned with a cupola containing long rectangular panes of glass.

"It's pretty, isn't it?" Julie said. "A cupola actually has a function on a barn. Farmers knew a well-sealed barn in the winter meant they didn't need as much feed for the animals. Better insulation equals lower grain costs."

"Makes sense."

"But tight barns lead to problems. You can't just place a barn over a manure cellar without allowing for proper ventilation. Hence, the cupola. Early designs were just grates, but later they installed windows and screens which enabled an enhanced ability to control temperature, air flow, and humidity. The cupola on this barn coincides with the Queen Anne style, and—" Julie stopped abruptly. "Sorry, I didn't mean to give you a treatise on barn insulation."

Aggie studied her mentor. "That bit about barn architecture sounded memorized."

"From Honeyburt's *Discourse on New England Farm Structures*. It sort of stuck in my mind."

"*It sort of stuck in your mind?* Stuff like that doesn't stick in people's minds. You need to talk to me about how you became the smartest girl in the class."

Julie looked defensive. "No one likes the smartest girl in the class."

Aggie shook her head in frustration. "God, doesn't that drive you crazy? Since when is a man deemed unlikeable because he's smart? In my opinion you can usually rely on the smartest girl in the class. She'll give you the straight scoop. And lots of people do like the smartest girl in the class."

Julie responded with a wan smile. "We can talk about that later. Right now, it's time to practice. Come on. We need to go around the side."

A track covered in woodchips and lined with wildflowers took them around the corner. Clusters of lilac bushes stood along the side of the barn. A low window was visible about halfway down the length of the building. Beyond the bushes a gentle slope led to a brook that wound around piles of rocks and the roots of a willow tree.

"Look in the window," Julie directed.

Aggie walked forward and peered inside. She saw a small room that had been roughly walled off from the main part of the barn.

"What do you see?" Julie had come up behind her.

"An old workshop or tack room maybe?"

"You'll find out when you go back."

"When I go …."

"I told you. You're here to practice. Now, look over by the door. On the right."

Aggie peered in again and examined the rough boards. "I don't see anything."

Julie said nothing, but a glance at her face informed Aggie she needed to look again. Studying the wall, she perceived a series of small holes in the wood. It looked like the bulletin board in her classroom after student papers had been taken down.

"Something was nailed or tacked up there. Over and over again. The holes are clustered together."

Julie smiled in a satisfied way. "Okay. Now listen. Controlling your travel depends on the three Ds. And the first D is?"

"Destination," Aggie replied dutifully. "Getting to the date you want."

"What's the best way to know the date? And don't tell me you check your phone."

Suddenly Aggie understood. "A calendar. You check a calendar. She looked in the window again and studied the nail holes. You don't mean …."

"That's exactly what I mean. I told you, prosaic, but still cool. A garage in Ledyard handed out promotional calendars starting about 1908. And guess where the farmer tacked up his calendar? If you pick a destination any time during the years the farmer had a calendar up, you can look in the window and see if you made it, or overshot, or didn't go far enough. Now, are you ready? I'll go sit on one of the benches behind the Lodge and wait for you. Take your time." Julie laughed. "Well, of course you'll take your *time*. Have you picked your destination?"

"Yes."

"What will you focus on?"

Aggie studied her surroundings. A large boulder rested in the sun at the edge of the brook. "I'm going to focus on that boulder."

Julie considered it. "It's a little far away, but I think it will work. Remember, focus on the object. Keep your destination in the back of your mind. Narrow it down."

"Like adjusting a microscope."

"Yes, imagine you're turning the dial. The decade first. Then the year. Then the month. Then the day." She patted Aggie's arm. "You'll do fine. I'll see you soon."

Aggie put out a hand and held her back. "I don't know why I didn't think to ask this before, but how does time pass when I'm gone? If I'm gone for ten minutes, will you be waiting ten minutes?"

"Yes. You don't come back to the exact time you left. Whatever time you spend in the past, you lose from your life in the present. It sounds a little disturbing to say it that way, but it's just the price you pay."

"I understand," Aggie said. "But what happens if I can't do it?"

Julie shook her head. "Abe wouldn't have moved you to fieldwork if he thought you couldn't do it. Just keep trying. I'll meet you at the benches." With that, she turned and headed back up the path, disappearing around the corner of the barn.

Keep trying. The same message Aggie gave to students frustrated by an experiment. *You can't give up before you begin. You don't know anything until you try. If you try, and still don't know anything, you try again. You persist.*

Resolutely, she leaned back against the planking of the barn and studied the boulder, ignoring everything else in her field of vision. It looked a bit like an enormous frog. She kept her eyes on the frog but tried to look through it, playing with colors and light. Slowly, almost lazily, she turned the dial of an imaginary microscope. *The decade—1950s.* Saddle shoes, Elvis Presley, turquoise cars with big fins. *The year—1952.* The Korean War rages, Elizabeth becomes Queen, Stalin is aging and murderous. *The month—July.* Summer on the farm. *The day—4th of July.* Cities and towns have planned fireworks.

She made one more fractional turn of the dial and stopped. The light on the stone frog seemed brighter. The sun was high in the sky. Aggie noted the sound of insects and birds, other animals, too. A cow, maybe, and chickens. Carefully, slowly, she turned to face the barn. The paint on the planking was no longer soft rust and gray. It was darker, the bold red not newly applied, but not peeling away from the wood. From the front of the barn came the buzz of a tractor.

She surveyed her surroundings. It was hard to tell whether the clusters of lilac bushes were different. Less dense, perhaps. The grass was thicker and taller, and there was an abundance of weeds. Summer weeds.

Not the same weeds that lingered into the fall. Dandelions and clover carpeted the banks of the brook. In September—she had started off in September—these plants had pretty much died away. Here they flowered in full force.

Aggie turned toward the window. She would need to move closer to peek inside. What had Frank said? *Distance is about confidence.* Slowly, she moved her right foot forward, shifted her weight, and moved her left foot forward. One step out on the tightrope. The paint on the barn was still dark red. She had not broken the spell. Again, she moved her foot, shifted her weight, took another step. A film of dust covered the windowpanes. It hadn't been there before. Placing her hands on the sill, she peered through the glass.

A thrill went through her. A calendar was tacked up next to the door. It featured an illustration of a forest scene showing a herd of deer in a clearing surrounded by massive oak trees. A buck with enormous antlers stood as a noble guardian, his head raised toward a distant hill. The legend *Smitty's Automobile Service* was lettered across the top. Underneath, the year and month appeared. It was July. July of 1952. She had made it. She was here.

Moving her face up against the glass, Aggie took a closer look. The days were printed in fat black numerals, and—*no, too good to be true*—tacked next to the calendar was a piece of cotton twine with a pencil tied to the end. The first three days of the month had X's penciled through the boxes. But not today. *Today, Friday, July 4, 1952.*

Aggie closed her eyes and opened them again. It was all still there: the red barn, the dusty window, the calendar and pencil. She felt a surge of confidence. Destination, check. Distance, check. Did two steps count as distance? Turning from the barn, she began moving cautiously down the slope to the creek. She kept her eyes on the boulder and counted her steps: one, two, three, four …. It took fourteen steps to get there, fourteen slow steps.

On an impulse, she turned and sat on the boulder. She felt the warmth of the stone beneath her fingers, a granite souvenir from the great Ice Age retreat of the glaciers across the face of the continent. Reaching down, she picked a long-stemmed dandelion from the grass and sniffed its sweet, distinctive smell. She remembered making dandelion necklaces for Minnie when they were children.

Julie's words from the night before surfaced in her mind. *You put a spoon in your pocket, but when you come back, it's not there.* Aggie contemplated the dandelion for a moment before unbuttoning the top button of her sweater and threading the flower stem through the hole. Closing her eyes, she thought about going home. "I'm leaving now," she said aloud. Surely sending soundwaves into this quiet spot would carry her back to the present.

Even before she opened her eyes, she knew it had worked. The sun was lower in the sky, the autumn air chillier. The sounds of the insects and birds, the animals and tractor, were silenced. It was time to walk back. As she retraced her steps, a cool breeze sprang up. She shivered and looked down at her sweater. The dandelion was gone. She refastened the top button. When she reached the front of the barn, she spied Julie in the distance, sitting on a bench and reading a book.

Aggie started forward but was startled to see a figure emerge from behind the huge barn door. It was Axel. He wore a faded canvas barn coat, heavy leather boots, and an old-fashioned, plaid wool cap. He carried a hunting rifle under his arm.

Aggie stopped and the two of them eyed each other. It came to her that she had rarely seen such an expressionless countenance, a face so impossible to read. His pale blue eyes flicked back along the path leading to the side of the barn. He grunted and walked forward until he was directly before her.

"Good place for beginners. First day I practice here, there's a spider web in the window. I watch for maybe ten minutes that spider. She building the web, one strand, then another, then another." He held up a giant hand and raised his index finger. He touched the finger to his wrist as though pointing at an invisible watch. Then, moving his hand in a short arc, he lightly touched Aggie's wrist in the same place, through her sweater.

"Each thread is like a tether, tying spider to the web, to the day, to the moment. So, I start to make my own web. I build the lines to where I am going." He touched his own wrist again, then moved the finger back to Aggie's sleeve, as if emulating the weaving motion of the spider.

"What happened when you arrived at your destination?" Aggie asked curiously.

Axel shrugged. "Spider gone. Left her back in the present. Time I go to, is winter. No spiders. All dead." His hand moved back to Aggie's sleeve, but this time he folded his fingers around her forearm. "Interesting business this travel. Many possibilities."

Aggie shivered. Axel released her arm. "Maybe you need to dress better for the cold," he offered tonelessly.

Aggie's eyes moved to the rifle. "What are you hunting?" she asked. "Deer?"

"Not today. When I hunt deer, there is a butcher ready, waiting nearby. Meat goes to freezer for Maurice. Is not a hobby and not a sport. Is just the way of nature, killing to eat. Killing just to kill ...." He shrugged again and fell silent.

Axel held the rifle in a completely natural manner. Aggie could tell he was comfortable with it, used to it. She had never owned a gun, and neither had Jacob. Axel turned from her, his eyes roving beyond the fields to a thicket of trees. Clouds had obscured the sun, and the colors of the fall leaves were muted and somber.

"Sometimes, out in country like this," Axel waved toward the trees, "an animal gets sick. Rabid animal? Nothing you can do. Just need to put it down." In an oddly formal gesture, he tipped his cap, turned, and headed out across the field. Aggie watched until he disappeared from view.

***

"Tell me everything again," Julie demanded.

The two women had retreated to Aggie's apartment. The temperature had dropped, and Aggie agreed with Axel's assessment that she was not properly dressed for the outdoors. As she boiled water for tea, Aggie described her experiences at the barn. She didn't mention meeting Axel, somehow feeling a need to file away his comments on spiders and rabid animals.

"Oh, this is fantastic," Julie exclaimed as she listened to Aggie's account. "Abe was right. You're a natural."

Aggie didn't respond as she pulled cups and saucers from the cabinet and unwrapped the teabags. The kettle started to whistle. "I'm starting to think I'll have to reexamine my notions about what I consider natural."

Julie regarded her sympathetically. "Are you tired? When you begin, it can be overwhelming. Viola says she needs to put her feet up after every trip, and she's a longtime veteran."

"Julie," Aggie said suddenly, "am I a *natural* like Serena? And what does it mean if I am?"

"You're not like Serena. Not at all. Don't get me wrong, I'm happy you don't struggle with the basics. But there's more to travel than the three Ds. A lot more. Serena is interested in Serena. If she's part of a mission, it's because she sees some advantage in it. Frankly, I can't imagine why she's part of the Civil War group, although maybe she's attracted to the idea of a treasure hunt and the publicity that would follow a big find. Say we locate a new picture of Lincoln, or Grant, or Sherman. That would be one of the biggest things we've ever done."

Aggie wasn't sure how to ask her next question tactfully. "What's going on between the two of you?"

Julie colored. She took a sip of tea then put down her cup. "I'm inept. No skills at all. Here I am, a two-year veteran, and I still don't have total command of the three Ds. And everyone knows it. Serena's made sure of that."

"What happens?" Aggie asked curiously.

"For starters, it takes me forever to get to the right destination. Multiple tries. Then the other Ds? Distance and duration? Very problematic." Suddenly, Julie's eyes were brimming. "When I was recruited by Lillian and arrived on campus, I was ecstatic. When training started, I expected it to be seamless. But it wasn't. Not then, not now. It's always awkward and embarrassing. I'll be in a rotation on a fieldwork mission and go off from the group for an hour. But I won't have been in the past for an hour. I'll have made four or five unsuccessful tries and wasted a ton of time just getting to the right place. Then the least little thing pushes me back to the present. Say I try to pick up an object or walk across a room. *Whoosh.* I'm back. I try to talk to someone in the past—anything more than a few words—same thing."

Aggie rose from her chair, located a box of tissues on the kitchen counter, and returned to the table. She plunked the box in front of Julie. "What about when you tried to help the man with the broken suitcase at Ellis Island?"

"The planning that took. I can't even tell you." Julie pulled a tissue from the box and blew her nose. "I'm particularly bad with distance, so I had to calculate where that man would be and try to arrive as close to him as possible."

"You made an accommodation. What's the shame in that? Abe must have confidence in you, to make you a mentor. And, if you ask me, Serena's probably just jealous of you."

"There isn't much that Serena could be jealous about when it comes to me," Julie said dejectedly.

Aggie narrowed her eyes. "Does she know you have a photographic memory? Do the directors know?"

Julie removed her glasses and dabbed her eyes. "There's no known scientific basis for the idea that anyone has a photographic memory," she answered carefully.

"There's no known scientific basis for the idea of time travel either," Aggie countered.

Julie put her glasses back on and met Aggie's gaze. "The directors are the only ones who know. Sometimes they call on me for special little projects like reading the text of an old document or lists of names."

"Why do you keep it a secret in the first place?"

"Oh, you know," Julie waved her hand in a dismissive manner. "People tend to treat you like you're a freak, or they want you to perform parlor tricks. Or—and this one really matters—they give too much credence to what you say, or too little. I have a reputation for talking a

126

lot. Well, I do talk a lot. But on some things, I've always tried to keep my business under my hat."

Aggie studied her mentor, then thought about Abe's visits and their "deal." She wondered whether there might not be quite a few people in this "other AARP" keeping quite a few things under their hats.

Chapter 18 ~ In the Garden

To Aggie's surprise, nothing was on the agenda after dinner. "These first coupla' days are intense," Frank explained. "We understand people need a break. Besides, there's a game on tonight."

Aggie dined with several other rookies. The food, as she had come to expect, was excellent, and her table companions were animated as they discussed basic training. Even the Hopewell twins appeared at ease. Flora had lost her shell-shocked appearance, and Fred was happily discussing dogs with Benjamin.

Edgar had experienced a measure of success in his first efforts at the barn. "I know I went back in time—oops, *traveled*—because of the snow. Kind of hard to miss. I think it was a blizzard. The window we were supposed to look through was covered in frost." He chuckled. "Course I didn't need to look at the calendar to verify I had missed my target destination. I was aiming for the year I got married and the exact day: June 15th."

"You missed your destination, but you got distance, man," Benjamin said admiringly.

"I did take several steps away from the window," Edgar said modestly. "I had to, you know. I was standing in snow up to my ... well, let's just say it was rather uncomfortable."

"You did better than me," Jane said. She turned to Aggie to explain. "Our instructor is Maurice. I can't believe we're working with him. I've been using his recipes forever. Well, he said to pretend we were meditating. I should have spoken up and mentioned I've never meditated. That sort of thing was a little after my time. But I didn't, and the result was I spent ten minutes focusing on a twig, and nothing happened."

Flora smiled at Aggie. "We were told you joined a fieldwork group that's working on a Civil War mission. Will you be practicing with them?"

Aggie was caught off guard, "Um—"

Luckily, Fred intervened. "They probably wanted her because she's a retired teacher. Nice to have some expertise right there in the group."

It didn't seem the moment to mention she had taught science, not history. "Yes, I'll have to do extra practice," she said in an off-hand manner, "but my mentor's tutoring me on focus and the three Ds."

She was relieved no one seemed unduly curious about how her fieldwork assignment had come about, and she was able to join in the laughter as Benjamin recounted being evicted when he tried to take a selfie of himself on his first attempt at time travel by the barn.

"I mean, I was like Edgar," he said. "Just not so dramatic, you know? I knew I had traveled somewhere. The trees were different, and those bushes had flowers. I was aiming for 1970, but it could have been anytime. I thought, wow! Time to make myself a souvenir, but as soon as I pulled out my phone, bam! I was back."

"We were told nothing like that would work," Flora admonished gently.

"Well sometimes you have to see for yourself," Benjamin said with a grin. "Isn't that what we're doing here? Isn't that what this Remarkable stuff is about? Seeing for ourselves?"

Edgar raised his glass. "A toast," he said, "*to seeing for ourselves.*"

They all drank and continued chatting. It was hard not to be caught up in the energy and excitement that filled the room. Happy voices and hoots of laughter echoed from every corner. Aggie tried to work out what made the scene both familiar and exceptional. Then it hit her. Here was a room full of seniors, and it might have been the lunchroom at Potatuck High. People leaned forward, telling stories with exuberant gestures, laughing raucously, asking questions, and interrupting each other in their enthusiasm.

"Doesn't look like your typical retirement home, does it? Good thing no undercover agents are snooping around. They'd know right away something was up."

It was Abe. She hadn't heard him arrive. He was standing by her chair surveying the room and smiling in a satisfied way. "How is everyone? You survived Day One I take it?"

Everyone started talking, happily assuring him things were going well.

"Good. Glad to hear it. Carry on. Best thing to do these early days is to share experiences. We learn from each other."

In truth, no prompting was needed. Benjamin scooted his chair closer to Flora's. "Tell me more about your try at the barn," he urged her. "I want to hear everything."

Flora blushed. "It wasn't anything special."

"You're the first one who saw the calendar. You figured it out. Plus, you got to the year you were aiming for." In no time, they were deep in conversation.

Abe crouched down by Aggie's chair and spoke in a quiet voice. "Maurice was wondering if you would pop by the kitchen garden after supper."

"There's a garden?"

"Right through those double doors." He pointed to the far end of the room. "You can't miss it. *Farm to table* and all that."

She lifted an eyebrow. "Learned that expression before you visited me?"

He was unabashed. "Of course. I've been dying to try it out. Just waiting for the right moment."

Aggie folded her napkin and got to her feet. "I'll go see him now."

"Excellent," Abe said. "I'll show you the way."

They headed for the exit and stepped outside onto a wide stone patio bathed in an early evening glow. She spied the garden immediately. It was a large square lot directly behind the kitchen containing neatly mulched rows and surrounded by a tall chicken wire fence.

Abe put his hands in his pockets and stared out across the back fields toward the woods. Aggie stopped next to him. "Nice view from here."

He nodded and looked down at her. "Julie said you managed the three Ds. First time out."

"I did."

He shot her a look. "I knew you would."

"How?"

He didn't answer.

"You have to tell me, you know," Aggie said. "We have a deal. Here are the terms. I'm 'less than forthcoming,' you can read my notes, and you keep me posted on your thinking."

"We shook hands."

"Yes. To seal the deal."

"No. You misunderstand. I knew you would manage the three Ds because of what I felt when we shook hands."

She looked at him. "Explain."

He met her gaze then looked back over the fields. "Sometimes companion travelers can pick up things through touch. We're not mind readers. But sometimes we get … flashes. It's not precise, so we don't talk about it." He looked at her again. "Have I held up my part of the bargain?"

Aggie narrowed her eyes. "What was the 'flash' you got when we shook hands?"

"I knew you could manage the three Ds."

"Is that all you're going to say?"

"For now." He grinned apologetically. "Besides, Maurice is waiting in the garden, and I have to check on the other rookies."

Aggie gave him a look then headed over to the garden.

Through the fence, Aggie spotted Maurice, Erin, and the two young chefs gathered around a gangly tomato plant and conferring in low voices, rather like doctors around the bedside of a sick patient. Erin saw her first and waved. "The gate's around back."

Aggie walked the perimeter until she found the entrance. Erin grinned a welcome, and Maurice extended a hand. "Thank you for coming out, Ms. May."

"Aggie," she said with a smile.

"Aggie then. I'm Maurice Kingston. So pleased to meet you. I see you've met Erin."

"Carlos, too. He prepared a wonderful meal last night."

The taller of the two young men smiled shyly.

"And this little devil is Angel," Erin said, elbowing the other young man in a friendly way.

Angel was short and stocky with brown eyes and an earring. He grinned broadly, and, copying Maurice, held out his hand. "How do you do? Welcome to the Lodge. I *told* you guys Abe would know if there were any good gardeners in the rookie group. You see we were wondering about these tomatoes here—"

Maurice put restraining hands on Angel's shoulders. "Forgive my son, Aggie. He gets carried away."

Aggie laughed. "I do as well when it comes to gardens. I'm not a master gardener, though."

"Any help you can provide would be welcome," Maurice said. "The kids convinced me it would be good to have better access to fresh ingredients. I can't argue with that, but it's—"

"Complicated," Aggie offered. "A garden can get complicated. Especially a fall garden. I'm sure you're wondering what you can still harvest and what you need to put to bed."

"Exactly," Angel said. "So, what I want to know first is—"

"Wait," Maurice interrupted. His hands were still on Angel's shoulders, and he leaned down speaking quietly in the young man's ear. "First you ask if she wants to help and has time."

Angel shot a winning smile in Aggie's direction. "Ms. May, would you mind answering a few questions about the garden? If you have time and want to? The Garden Club here is super, but they're pretty much all flower people, and Abe said you had vegetables and stuff."

She couldn't keep from laughing. "Of course. I'd be delighted."

"Great. Here's the first issue—"

Maurice smiled apologetically. "Before this young man talks your ear off, I'm going to excuse myself. This is really the kids' project. I'll let them fill you in."

"Thanks, Dad," Erin said, giving the older man a hug. To Aggie's surprise, the young men joined in. Aggie was touched by the obvious display of affection.

As Maurice headed off to the kitchen, Erin eyed Aggie shrewdly. "Some people don't get us, but I guess Julie told you about our family."

Unexpectedly, Carlos, who had remained silent to this point, interjected. "Before Maurice, we were lost in the system."

"Or on the streets," Angel added. "Me, Erin, Carlos, Wells, the older ones—Timmy, Hattie, and Nate—Maurice found us. Now we're a family, and we stick together."

"Everybody knows about dysfunctional families," Erin noted, "but functional families, different kinds of functional families, can be misunderstood, too. We're not all like *Ozzie and Harriet* or *Father Knows Best* or something."

"Have you ever seen *Ozzie and Harriet* or *Father Knows Best*?"

"No," Erin admitted with a laugh, "but some of the folks here stream those old shows. I know what they're supposed to represent, anyway."

Aggie studied the young woman. "Yes, I think you probably do. And I know a bit about sticking together, too. I have two younger siblings: a brother and a sister. Our parents died in a car accident when we were pretty young, so we had to stick together. We still stick together."

"Hear that, siblings?" Erin said to her brothers. "Now let's talk about the garden before the sun sets."

Indeed, the sun had lowered on the horizon, and shadows stretched across the lawn. The next half hour was quickly consumed by a spirited debate about which plants needed to be pulled and which could be permitted to stay, as well as the relative merits of green tomato relish versus green tomato pie. By the time they finished, it was almost fully dark.

"Can you come back tomorrow?" Angel asked eagerly. "I mean if you have time and want to?"

"Don't forget, Abe wanted her with the veterans," Erin reminded them. "She'll be getting busy with fieldwork."

"Well, I should be able to check back with you, if not tomorrow, then later this week," Aggie said. "I know gardens produce new problems as soon as you solve the old ones."

"Like the drones," Angel said, then shot a guilty glance at Erin.

"She doesn't need to hear about that," Erin said repressively. Angel and Carlos exchanged nervous glances. Aggie remembered Bernice's reference to drones and raised her eyebrows.

Angel started to say something, but Erin quelled him with a look. After an awkward moment, however, she threw her hands up in surrender. "Oh, all right. But you know we aren't supposed to talk about it. Honestly, you guys have no self-control."

"It wasn't me," Carlos said.

"I know, I know. But let's talk inside. The bugs are eating me alive."

They sat at a gleaming table in the Lodge's spacious kitchen. Maurice was at work making notes on a large paper calendar as they spilled in from the garden.

"We're telling Ms. May about the drones," Angel announced. "The subject just sort of came up," he added hastily.

Maurice shook his head in mild exasperation. "I should know better than to expect discretion from my children. Text Wells," he added. "If you're going to do this, you need him here."

With a few quick taps on her phone, Erin summoned the young man to the kitchen. When Wells arrived, he went up to Maurice and gave him a hug. "Hey Pops, what's up?" he asked.

Maurice waved a hand toward the others seated around the table. "Explain about the drones."

"Abe says we shouldn't get people worried about them."

"Abe worries too much about worriers," Maurice said, "and besides, your brother already let the cat out of the bag."

"Okay," Wells said equably. He pulled up a chair and sat down next to Aggie. "Here's the scoop," he began. "It's probably nothing, and Abe doesn't want to make a big deal about it, but we seem to have drawn the attention of—well, we don't really know *who*—but someone has been sending drones over the Lodge and that kind of creates problems, if you get what I'm saying."

Maurice had resumed work on the schedule, but was apparently listening in. "Find out if she knows about travel and cameras."

"I know you can't travel if a person is looking directly at you," Aggie responded, "or even looking at you through the lens of a camera. If the camera's not monitored in real time you can travel, but the film will show you disappearing."

Wells pointed a finger in her direction, indicating she had answered correctly. "You've got it. Drones are pretty much operated by people who are watching a screen. They see what the drone sees. That creates the first problem. A Remarkable can't travel if a drone operator is watching. Being observed thwarts your ability to go. But there's a second problem. Drone technology is changing fast. Pretty soon even hobbyists with an inexpensive drone from Walmart or Target will be capable of programming it to head out and record stuff on its own. The operator can simply view the video later. That means one of those unmonitored drones won't stop folks from time travel, but later the operator will see a whole bunch of strange footage. You know. Boom! Old lady disappears.

Boom! Old lady comes back." Wells stopped abruptly. "Sorry. I don't think of the people here as just old ladies and old men."

Aggie laughed. "It's fine. Keep going."

Wells gathered himself and continued. "Well, obvi, we can't afford that type of scrutiny."

"Duh," Angel agreed.

"Abe says our best protection is that we seem like a regular old senior community that nobody pays any attention to," Wells said. "We don't want anything changing that."

"When did you start noticing drones?" Aggie asked.

"It's probably a fluke," Erin said, "and not related to what goes on here at all. I think it's probably a couple kids out there who like to get together and fly those stupid things around. The scenery around here is pretty with the woods and hills and stuff."

"They're not stupid," Wells interrupted. "The technology is really cool. Not my area, of course."

Erin opened her eyes in pretend disbelief. "Not your area? Really? Never thought you'd admit that *anything* was not your area."

"Cut to the chase, kids," Maurice commanded.

"Okay," Wells said, "I'll try to make it short. We have some natural protection from the barn because most drone operators keep their distance from buildings. Plus, those lilac bushes hide a lot of stuff. But other parts of the campus, that's a different story. A few of the veterans are a little careless about security. Sorta' pop off into the past without taking a quick look around first."

Aggie was starting to get the picture. "Who was it?"

"Viola," Carlos and Angel answered in unison.

"It wasn't her fault," Angel explained in a rush. "Viola's great. She was in the garden one day last summer, working at the elevated bed. On the way out, she went through the gate and got it in her head to take a little trip. Just for fun, you know. She does that sometimes. So, me and Carlos were still in the garden, and we told her we weren't looking in her direction, so she was free to go. But then we heard it."

"A drone." Wells pulled the elastic band from his hair, swept up some stray blonde strands, and re-secured his ponytail. "Right over where Viola had been standing. My brothers heard the whirring and looked up. Carlos did some quick thinking and aimed the garden hose at it. It was out of range but provided a distraction. The drone musta' detected possible interference or something and zoomed off, but I'm a little worried that the damage was done. Viola was back in a few minutes, but what if the camera caught her disappearing?"

"Ever since there's been more fly-bys than you'd expect," Angel added, "especially since we're supposedly just a retirement village with nobody famous living here—except Maurice."

"I'm not famous," Maurice called from his corner.

"Daddy, you are, too," Angel countered. "Your books are still bestsellers. And all those fancy restaurants you worked for just worship you."

"That was a long time ago," Maurice said dismissively. "Thank goodness my career predated the advent of 'celebrity chefs.' It's easier to maintain privacy if you've never been on television, or—what do you call them, Wells?—*digital platforms?*"

"Something like that," Wells grinned. "Anyway, valiant as he is, we can't rely on Carlos and his garden hose to protect us from airborne snoops."

"Axel wants to shoot them down," Angel said. "I heard him and Abe arguing about it."

"Well that's a dumb idea," Wells said. "Nothing like a pissed off drone operator arriving on the doorstep demanding answers. I kinda' get wanting those things to drop out of the sky, but it would have to look natural, so no one's the wiser."

"Nothing natural about a shotgun," Erin said.

"Totes," Angel agreed.

For a few moments there was silence around the table. Maurice, put his calendar aside and rested his head on his hand, looking pensive.

An idea was forming in Aggie's brain. "Wells, I'm supposed to call my sister tonight."

At first, he misunderstood. "Oh, gosh," he said, springing to his feet. "I'm *so sorry*. We've been taking up all your time, and you've probably got stuff to do. It's a free night. Were you going to play cards?" He looked at her doubtfully. "Mahjong or something? Sometimes there's pinochle, canasta, bridge. Got to be careful there, though. The bridge players are a little high strung."

"Calm down," Aggie said reassuringly. "I'm not trying to run off to a card game."

"There's board games, too," Angel said. "And folks go to Frank's when there's a ball game on."

"No, *no*, listen a minute. My sister Minnie works at Hytech. They do engineering, technology, and aerospace. Minnie doesn't work with drones herself, but I'll bet she knows someone who does."

"Hytech? That's awesome," Wells said excitedly. "It would be great to get a couple ideas on drone interference. I've seen some net capture prototypes, but that's way too noticeable. There's this ray-gun kind of thing that looks cool, too, but it's a little conspicuous."

Aggie could almost see the wheels spinning in his head. "I'm supposed to be at a senior retreat listening to TED talks," she said. "How should I explain why I'm asking about drones?"

"We can come up with something. I know! You can say it's for a *robotics competition*. You could say I'm the team coach from your old school, and—"

"Put a lid on it a minute, Wells," Maurice said, holding up his hands as if halting traffic. "Aggie, would that work with your sister? And do you mind asking her?"

"I don't see any harm in asking. Hytech has a Science for Schools program that funds all kinds of projects. They have scholarships for promising high school students, too, and bring them in for internships. I think casting it as a robotics team issue would work."

"All right then," Maurice said to Wells. "Let's hope we can find a way to keep those mechanical pests out of our airspace."

***

Aggie suggested placing the call from her apartment. Wells accompanied her, and Erin tagged along as well saying she'd love to see the quilt the needlework group had picked out for her. On their way out of the Lodge, they passed groups gathered at tables playing a variety of card and board games. One of the ladies distributing goody bags the previous day was shuffling cards with the skill of a Vegas pro. Two elderly men played chess, watched by several attentive spectators. Lillian was concentrating on Scrabble, but Abe was nowhere to be seen.

Aggie unlocked the door to her apartment, switched on the lights, and gestured for Erin and Wells to enter. Pulling out her cell phone, she dialed her sister's work number. Minnie was still at the office, and though she peppered Aggie with questions about her "classes" and whether the accommodations and food were acceptable, it was obvious she was not attending fully. Aggie launched into the agreed-upon story of her school's robotics coach seeking advice on drones.

"Definitely, we've got a couple guys that do that."

"Can I put you on the phone with him? He's right here, as a matter of fact. He was, um, giving a presentation on technology for seniors, and we got talking. That's how it all came up," Aggie offered lamely.

Minnie didn't notice. "Sure, I'll talk to him. If he fills me in on the issues, I'll know who to hook him up with. Actually, one of our tech groups has been playing around with drones. You know, enhancing functionality for different scenarios. That kid you recommended for a scholarship—Conor? He's been here on his internship, and he's with that unit."

"How's he doing?" Aggie asked with some trepidation.

"Oh, great from what I hear. That group is super creative, though none of them have even the most minimal social skills. They're all brilliant and everything, but not exactly housebroken. But they get along with *each other* swimmingly, and Conor seems to fit right in. They did a little project for SpaceFi earlier in the summer, and the team got Conor one of those shirts that says *Actually, it is rocket science,* and he was tickled pink. Very cute. Anyway, put your friend on. I've got to get to a meeting in a bit, but I have a few minutes. Oh, and I'm glad you got there safe and are having fun."

"Love to Joe and the boys," Aggie said, and handed the phone to Wells. He thanked Minnie profusely for speaking to him, then started asking questions.

Aggie gestured for Erin to follow her into the bedroom, switching on the light by the bedside table. "You wanted to see the quilt?"

"Oh, that's a pretty one," Erin said running her hand across the floral fabric. "I love the crazy quilts because each one is different." She plopped into the rocking chair that stood next to the bed and blew a wisp of chestnut hair out of her eyes.

Aggie perched on the foot of the bed. "It was so nice to meet your dad."

"Maurice is ...." A complicated set of emotions moved across the young woman's face. "Maurice *saved* me. Saved all of us. His wife—she passed away a long time ago—they never had kids of their own, so they adopted kids. His 'first family'—Timmy, Hattie, and Nate—they're all grown and on their own and stuff. When his wife died, Maurice kind of lost heart for a while. But after he met Abe and Lillian and started traveling with the Remarkables, he got 'a new lease on life.' That's what he calls it.

"All of us here—me, Wells, Angel, and Carlos—we're his second family. 'Second family but never second best.' That's what he says. You should see us at Thanksgiving and Christmas. We all get together and cook and eat and laugh." She paused in her rocking and looked at Aggie. "What are your siblings like?"

"Well, you heard about my sister. She and her husband have three sons—triplets. They're fifteen now and are named after astronauts: John, Alan, and Neil. And my younger brother Roscoe lives in Chicago. He's an actor, and he just got a part in *Wicked*."

"Wow, that's pretty cool. Brothers can be a pain, but you end up loving them anyway. I did, at least. Is 'Roscoe' his real name, or like a stage name?"

"His real name: Roscoe Richard May. Our parents overdid it on alliteration when it came to naming us. My full name is Agatha Amelia, and my poor sister ended up with Minerva Maude. She switched to 'Minnie' in about third grade and never went back."

Erin laughed. "You know my name? Erin? It's like the composer who did *Appalachian Spring*. I'm Erin Copland Kingston. Maurice let us choose different names if we wanted. He said we *decide for ourselves who we are*. I didn't want the name I had. My old father ...." She stopped, and a shadow passed across her face. "It was *his* name. I wasn't going to have that reminder. So, I tried out a couple different ones, but none of them fit. I didn't *love* them, you know. But one day, I was at Abe's cottage, and he and some of the other people who play music were listening to a *record* on a *turntable*." She said the words carefully, as if proud she knew the names of these obsolete devices. "And the music was so beautiful, not corny or anything, like some of their stuff. I asked Abe about it, and he said it was by Aaron Copland. I said she must have been a happy person to write something like that. And Abe started laughing. Not in a mean way, just like I had said something clever. I didn't know it was a boy's name. Later I told Maurice I wanted that name, and he helped me make it with a girl's spelling. And that was that."

She rocked back and forth. "Carlos kept his name. He didn't have the same issues as me. We all named Angel together. He was pretty young when he came to us."

"What about Wells?" Aggie asked. "Did he pick his own name?"

"Of course. It's like the author. Funny, everyone just calls him Wells, and they're not sure if it's his first name or his last. He wanted Maurice's last name for official documents and stuff, but he likes to go by Wells to the rest of the world. He said if Prince could do it, and Cher, and Bono, then he could, too. I told him they were *pop stars*, and he wasn't, but he insisted anyway."

From the other room they could hear the phone call winding up.

"So, you'll talk to your guys, and they'll expect my call?" Wells was saying. "Okay. Okay. Thank you *so much*. Okay. I'll tell her. Goodbye."

"Hey, Ms. May, Aggie? Your sister said to call later this week. She is freaking awesome."

"Unquestionably," Aggie replied with a laugh.

Erin propelled herself out of the rocker, and they returned to the living room. "Thank you for showing me the quilt," she said to Aggie, "and for the talk." She threw an arm across Wells's shoulders and steered him toward the door. "Let's go, big brother. Wave goodbye."

"Abe is going to be psyched when he hears about this!"

"That's what I'm afraid of," Erin said.

138

Chapter 19 ~ Acting

The next morning dawned bright and warm, a perfect fall day. Aggie brought tea and the *New York Times* out to her patio. She completed the crossword puzzle in a praiseworthy twelve minutes, then started on the front section.

Looking up, she spied Abe walking up the hill. He wore sweatpants and a t-shirt and was apparently embarking on his 'three miles, rain or shine.' At the crest of the hill, he caught sight of her, veered from the pathway, and approached the patio. Pulling off his baseball cap, he leaned his elbows on the surrounding wall.

"Good morning, Aggie."

"Good morning, Abe." She smiled. Hers was a generation where the use of someone's first name had significance. It meant you were getting to know them. It meant the possibility of friendship. "Would you like some tea?"

"Had coffee at home, thanks." Looking about, he inspected the small space with interest, noting the bench and table, the grassy areas around the patio, and the watering can near an outdoor faucet. His eyes fell on the plants. "Are those flowers okay as, uh, *companions*? Did I use that term correctly, garden-wise?"

She laughed. "You used it correctly. And yes, they're good companions. The message is nice."

"The message?"

She blushed. "Sorry, it's a silly gardener thing. In different cultures, at different times, flowers were symbolic. For the Victorians, every flower carried a message. Of course the Chinese had different meanings, as did the Greeks, the Japanese, and so on. And now people just pick out flowers they like, which is much more sensible. I do that myself. But sometimes I look at a garden and 'read' it as a message. Like reading tea leaves."

"So, what's the message here?"

Aggie pointed to the pots. "Chrysanthemums may mean friendship. White ones signify honesty. Asters represent patience. Purple ones stand for love and wisdom. I would read it as … honest friendship leading, with patience, to love and wisdom. See? Nice message. Thank you again for the patio and plants. It was thoughtful. That's the real message."

"I wanted you to come here and feel it was a little bit like home," he said, looking rather pleased. "I understand from Wells that we owe thanks to *you*. He told me about the consult with your sister. His report was enthusiastically garbled, so I gather it was a productive conversation."

"They seemed like kindred spirits," she agreed.

Abe looked at her speculatively. "What we discussed the other day, and our deal about sharing thoughts …. I know there's more to hash out, but—"

"I can be patient," Aggie said tilting her head toward the purple flowers. "The asters will remind me. Right now, I just want to concentrate on the mission."

"This one means a lot to Lillian."

"After hearing Daniel, it means a lot to me as well. To all of us, I think."

He nodded. After a moment, he put his baseball cap back on, gave her a smile, and strode off. Aggie watched until he rounded the edge of the building and was lost from sight. Yes, she could be patient. Nonetheless, she wondered. What had he felt when they shook hands? What did he believe or suspect or know about the significance of those raindrops at Grand Central and how they related to intervention, that forbidden topic?

Aggie carried her teacup inside and rinsed it at the sink. On an impulse, she picked up a sweater and headed out the door. Her kitchen was stocked with English muffins and cereal, but after spending time with Maurice and his sons, she was sure there would be something more tempting on offer in the dining room. She also recognized in herself an unfamiliar desire for company, something that just a few days ago was simply not on her agenda.

At the Lodge, she found she was right about both the food and the company. Chafing dishes on a buffet table offered eggs and bacon. Platters with biscuits and scones had been set at either end. There was fresh squeezed orange juice and urns for coffee. Quite a few tables were occupied. The Hopewells were sitting with Benjamin and Edgar. Mirlande and Wells were conferring over a stack of papers. A large table in the corner accommodated a lively group. Aggie did not recognize any of them. Perhaps it was another group of veterans working on a mission.

Viola was seated by one of the large windows. She was alone at the table, her empty plate pushed to the side, and a newspaper open before her. Aggie filled a plate and went over to the older woman. "May I join you?"

Viola looked up, smiled, and waved to an empty chair. "Have a seat, dear. I'm just finishing the puzzle. Or trying to."

"There's a tricky bit in that corner," Aggie said, pointing to the offending area. "I had to use my eraser. I see you're working in pen, you brave soul."

Viola laughed. "Maybe 'reckless' is more fitting."

"Thank you for the advice yesterday, about focusing and the three Ds," Aggie said, spreading jam on a scone.

"Happy to do it. How did your practice session go?"

"It went well. I saw the calendar, and it was the right year, month, and day. I confess to being a little shocked. I'm tempted to run out there this morning before class just to make sure it wasn't all my imagination. I want to see if I can make it happen again."

"It will happen again. It's like learning to ride a bike. Once you've had a bit of success, you tend to keep progressing."

They were interrupted when Bernice slid into a chair at the table. She was dressed today in plaid slacks and a brown cardigan sweater.

"Good morning, Bernie," Viola said. "There's bacon today. Don't you want to get a plate?"

"Ate at my apartment," Bernice said. She turned to Aggie. "Still get up at five and fix myself oatmeal, like when I punched a time clock."

"Aggie was just telling me about her practice session," Viola said. "She hit her target, first time out."

Bernice turned her gaze toward Aggie. "Took me a good ten days to get that done. Kept getting to the right month in the wrong year. Or the wrong month in the right year." A speculative look appeared in her eyes. "What did you try to bring back?"

Aggie laughed. "A dandelion. My sister and I used to braid them into necklaces. I undid the top button of my sweater and put one in the buttonhole. Does everyone try something like that?"

"Pretty much," Viola answered. "Flowers are a popular choice among the ladies."

"I had been told it wouldn't work," Aggie said. "But still, it was odd to wear that flower one minute and find it gone the next."

"Never learned how to do those daisy chains myself," Bernice commented. "Never learned to braid, to tell the truth. Was usually off playing stickball with the boys."

"They let you play?" Aggie asked.

A rare grin flashed across Bernice's face. "After I knocked their heads together a time or two."

Just then Erin arrived at their table. "Morning everyone. Thanks for your help yesterday, Aggie. Angel, Carlos, and I are putting together a master plan for the garden. Then could you maybe, like, look it over?"

"Of course."

She turned to Bernice. "Morning Bernie. The usual? Anyone else want a cappuccino?" Aggie and Viola demurred, and Erin scurried off.

"Bernie starts her morning with oatmeal," Viola explained, "but she's grown rather fond of following it with a cappuccino topped with whipped cream." She inked in the final boxes in the crossword, refolded the paper, and stashed it in a tote bag. "Look Bernie," she said, pulling an oversized volume from the bag, "Lillian's brought in pictures for us. This has New York street scenes from the 1800s. I've got some sticky notes, so we can study up on what to look out for." She opened the book and slid it over to her friend.

"Looks like the first thing we gotta look out for is horse manure," Bernice said, her eyes on a photograph of a street jammed with carriages and wagons. She peeled off a sticky note and marked the page, then flipped to the table of contents.

A burst of laughter erupted from the group at the large table in the corner. Viola glanced in their direction. "That's the Mark Twain group," she explained to Aggie. "They started together last summer and are picking up again this fall. A lot of English majors in that group. They get a little giddy at times. All speak the same language. Debate the Oxford comma and adjective order—that kind of thing."

Movement outside the window caused Aggie to peer through the glass. Maurice was guiding a small group of rookies toward the barn, walking backward so he could lead the way and talk to his charges at the same time. The rookies looked like a row of baby ducks following in his wake.

Erin arrived carrying a tray that held the cappuccino. Deftly she placed the cup in front of Bernice. "Enjoy, Bernie."

Bemused and charmed, Aggie looked around her—from the rookies outside, to the boisterous group in the corner, the book of old photographs, and the cappuccino on the table. "What am I doing here? What are we all doing here?"

It was Bernice who responded. "No big mystery for me. This is the only place in my life where I've ever had a 'usual.'"

***

Aggie was surprised upon entering Lillian's class. The casual armchairs had been pushed back against the wall. A long table in the center of the room held laptops and dozens of books on Abraham Lincoln, the Civil War, and Mathew Brady. A white board had been set up, as well as three easels, each holding a large map of New York City. The first map bore the heading 1862, the second 1872, and the third 1882.

When the group had assembled, Lillian addressed them. This morning, she was all business. "Let's get one thing straight at the outset. This mission is a long shot. There's more unknown than known. We've got leads that might allow us to find Gabe, verify his story, and locate his treasure, but I don't want anyone thinking this is a sure thing.

"So, we'll start at the beginning. The first thing we need to know is whether you can adjust to the nineteenth century. We're arranging a practice session in New York to answer that question, but we've got preparatory work to do here first. Given the era we're targeting, acting will be important. At Ellis Island, we were primarily observers. This mission may involve more interaction with people in the past. I've discussed this with Elizabeth, and she has developed exercises to help us do that. We also have period clothing for you today. I know it's early, but the outfits will take getting used to, especially for the ladies."

Sal raised a hand to speak. "Say we can all get back to the 1800s, what then?"

"Then we look at possible entry points in Daniel's story. Can we establish Gabe's association with Brady? Did he take some glass plate negatives? If so, where? Obviously, we need clues to the location of Gabe's homestead or place of business."

Lillian approached the maps gesturing to each in turn. "We are working within a twenty-year span of time. Brady exhibits the Antietam photographs in 1862. In 1872 he goes through bankruptcy proceedings and warehouses many of his possessions. Daniel believes Gabe transports some of the portraits to those warehouses, and, perhaps, takes some himself. This last map shows the city in 1882, the year matching the Bible inscription about the burial of Lincoln and his soldiers. So, ladies and gentlemen, we need to know as much as possible about each of these time periods. I'm pairing you up, and you're all getting assignments. Our work starts now."

The remainder of the morning was spent on research. Julie and Aggie were given the job of collecting information on Brady's Antietam exhibition after sharing with Lillian the idea that the exhibit was Gabe's last known location. Other pairs delved into Brady's finances and dated his portraits of Lincoln.

When it was time to break for lunch, Lillian delivered a second pep talk. "I'm pleased with our progress. But moving forward, I want you to remember something. Even if we don't find what we have characterized as 'the treasure,' we are poised to find out more about Mathew Brady and an important period in the history of New York City. This is as much a treasure as any artifact would be. Please feel free to borrow any of the books you see here. And of course, the library is available for research any time, day or night. I'll see you all tomorrow."

After lunch Aggie considered a trip to the barn for another practice session, but one look out the window dissuaded her. The perfect fall day had disappeared with a gathering of gray clouds and spitting rain.

"It's just as well," Julie stated. "I like to sit somewhere quiet and close my eyes before Elizabeth's class. Like I used to do before going to court. I mean, I don't want you to get nervous or anything. It's just—"

Aggie laughed. "You needn't worry about me. I'm not going to let nerves get to me now. Although I've never acted before. My younger brother, Roscoe, is an actor, but it's foreign territory to me."

It was true. She had never tried out for the high school musicals. Neither had Minnie—*Oh, it might be fun, but I've got Calculus this year.* Aggie understood science's logical rules but couldn't fathom acting. How did that soft-spoken kid become Nathan Detroit? How did the shy girl who never raised her hand in class bring people to their feet by belting out that song from *Annie Get Your Gun*?

Aggie studied her mentor. It was apparent Julie was eager to escape to her apartment. "I think I'll follow your lead. It wouldn't hurt to spend a few minutes relaxing."

***

"If you are asked a 'yes-no' question, always go with *yes. Yes* leads you forward. The scene stops when there isn't a *yes* to keep it going. When *you* ask questions, your goal is to elicit that *yes.* A *no* closes the door."

Aggie sat on a folding chair on the shiny wood floor of the Lodge's gym. She hadn't actually rested in her apartment, choosing instead to page through a book on Antietam. Surely, she was too old for a case of the jitters, she thought.

So much for that line of thinking. She couldn't remember the last time she had felt so self-conscious. Viola had tried, somewhat unsuccessfully, to reassure her as they entered class together. "Now don't get into a bother, dear. These little exercises are useful. And Elizabeth's marvelous. Quite intimidating, but marvelous."

Serena was one of the few who didn't look nervous. She had been unusually animated upon entering the gym and had sauntered over to a rack of Victorian-era dresses that stood in the corner. Removing a few of the frocks from their hangers, she held them against herself, pivoting to study her reflection in the gym's mirrored walls. It was only with the arrival of the instructor that she returned to the group and chose a seat next to Kat.

Elizabeth was a slender woman in her sixties with dark, wavy hair and the fluid grace of someone half her age. Her voice was musical yet commanded attention. "When you are traveling in the past, you must bear in mind that you may not have long to establish contact, to converse, to learn what you need to know. Thus, it is incumbent upon you to make every moment, every second, count. That's why you're here. To rehearse. Conversations with those in the past are a strange hybrid. It's not exactly like a play. A traveler may have a 'script' of sorts, but those in the past do not. It is, perhaps, closer to improvisation. For many, that is trickier. You must be resourceful enough to keep the conversation headed toward your goal and obtain the information you need."

Elizabeth searched the expressions of the gathered seniors then clapped her hands together. "So, let's go, folks. We're going to pair up and spread out. Find space for yourselves, and I will give you your roles."

There was an awkward moment as people glanced around uncertainly. Elizabeth shook a dark curl off her forehead and put her fists on her hips. "Come on, guys. It's nothing we haven't done before. Aggie, you're new, so I want you with Viola. She's had the most experience."

With quick efficiency, Elizabeth helped the others select partners, sending each pair to a different part of the gym. "Okay, here is your task. You and your partner are sitting on a bus. One of you plays the role of a person from the past. The other is a Remarkable. If you are the person from the past, you have worked hard all day and don't want to be distracted by a nattering stranger. You're bone tired and thinking about what to make for supper—even you, Sal, you unrepentant male chauvinist. *Pretend* you have to cook tonight."

Sal smiled sheepishly as the others laughed.

"If you are the Remarkable," Elizabeth went on, "your job is to learn something about the person sitting next to you. You seek that *yes*, the opening that will give you information and insight. Is everyone ready? We'll go about ten minutes, then change partners and reverse roles. Okay, begin."

"You'd better be the person who doesn't want to talk," Viola directed.

"Is it that obvious?" Aggie said wryly.

"Oh, you'll learn fast enough. Abe says you're going to be a *marvelous* Remarkable. I've known the man a long time, and he's a good judge of character."

"I'm not sure it's my character at issue here. It's my skill, or lack of it."

"Well, I believe character always makes a difference, sometimes in the oddest ways. But come now, you're not supposed to talk, remember? You're tired, and I'm a gossipy old lady."

The next ten minutes were fascinating. Aggie began by resolutely ignoring her partner and trying to transform herself into someone tired, hungry, and not interested in talking.

After a moment of silence, she peeked over at Viola who sat motionless in her wheelchair, eyes closed. *Had she fallen asleep?* Then,

Aggie heard quiet words. "It's chilly already. Winter's due early this year."

Aggie tried to stay "in character." Isn't that what they called it? But good manners dictated a response. "Yes, time to get out my wool sweaters."

"I got mine out yesterday. A moth put a hole in my favorite cardigan."

"My mother used moth balls. It was before everyone knew how toxic they were. We had to hang our wool clothes out on the line to get rid of the smell."

And so it began. After her first response, Viola led her, one step at a time, into a full-fledged discussion of *what exactly?* From the weather and mothballs, they proceeded to cleaning and cooking, then recipes and family gatherings. Aggie was surprised at how far they sailed and how cleverly Viola piloted the ship. By the time Elizabeth called for them to switch partners, Aggie knew she had been skillfully maneuvered into producing an appreciable amount of information.

Serena ambled forward. "Elizabeth wants you to work with Frank," she said to Viola.

"Do you need a push?" Aggie asked.

"No, no, I'm fine." Viola waved her off. "Serena, are you with Aggie? She was the tired character last time, so let her be the Remarkable this time. Have fun, ladies," she said, and rolled away toward the far side of the room where Frank was waiting.

Elizabeth was conferring with Sal and Kat but looked up long enough to determine that everyone had found a new partner. "All right folks, ten more minutes. Then we'll come back together and debrief."

Serena seated herself, adjusting the chair so she could survey the room. Inspecting the other woman's modish outfit and accessories, Aggie considered the possibility that Serena might never have actually taken public transportation. She had a different designer bag today, and looked stunning in black leggings, a royal blue tunic, and rather complicated lace-up sandals.

Aggie was suddenly acutely aware that her own slacks had an elastic waistband, and her flowered sweater was anything but trendy. Being stylish had never been important to her. At work she had worn comfortable pants and shirts under a lab coat. In warmer weather—her school lacked air conditioning—she replaced the lab coat with a bib apron like her mother had worn to do housework. In her last months on the job, her principal, still chafing over her refusal to condemn Conor Pulaski at the expulsion hearing, had made several snide comments about her lack of professional apparel, but Aggie found she really didn't care.

Confronted with Serena's casual elegance, however, she felt more than a little frumpy. But surely her appearance wasn't relevant to the task at hand. "So, I'm the Remarkable, and you're the tired commuter. Okay?"

Serena shrugged. "Fine."

Aggie thought back to the way Viola had started the conversation and tried a similar gambit. "Weather's chilly already."

Serena picked up her bag and fished through it, finally producing a lip gloss that she opened and applied.

Aggie tried again. "The leaves are turning, and it's only September."

Serena dropped the lip gloss back in her bag and pulled out her phone.

"Put that phone away, Serena." Elizabeth had come up behind them.

A look of annoyance appeared on Serena's face, but she did as she was told. "I'm the person who doesn't want to talk," she said petulantly. "Taking out your phone is a way to signal you don't want to talk."

"We've had this discussion before, Serena. My class, my rules."

"But—"

"Every exercise I give you has a goal. What I expect is commitment to that goal."

"But—"

Elizabeth crossed her arms and waited in gloriously icy silence. Serena eyed her uneasily and held her peace. Elizabeth waited a beat, then stalked back across the gym.

"I was only trying to make it more *realistic*," Serena huffed.

Aggie suppressed a smile. "I understand. I know I'm playing catch-up here. Maybe I wasn't asking the right questions."

Serena looked mollified. "She's not even a traveler herself. I don't know why the directors have her doing these classes."

"Should we try again?"

Serena was not ready to move on. "Her husband was one of the original Remarkables. She only found out about things because he got a little careless and disappeared in front of their home security camera. He was a fun guy, always laughing. He died two years ago, though, and she's still hanging around."

"Two-minute warning." Elizabeth's call echoed in the room.

"Should we try again?" Aggie repeated.

"I suppose."

This time the exercise went somewhat better. Aggie's tentative comments about the weather elicited a few monosyllabic responses, and a query about cooking drew a full sentence. A compliment on Serena's outfit seemed to go over rather well, but then time was called, and they gathered again in the center of the room.

"Okay, time to talk," Elizabeth said briskly.

Frank started off. "Uh, I was paired with Julie when she was the one asking the questions, you know? And man, can she ask questions. I think we did okay, but Jeez. About five minutes in, I was feeling like a criminal being cross-examined in the witness box. Sorry Jules. Just saying."

Everyone started laughing. Julie seemed more amused than mortified, as she covered her face in mock embarrassment.

"There are times when the adversarial approach is effective," Elizabeth said with a smile, "but in most instances, we don't want to grill the person we're questioning. People are remarkably willing to share information if the situation remains casual and nonthreatening. And those bits of information give us leads. They are breadcrumbs that guide us through the forest."

"Where we meet the wicked witch," Bernice added.

Each member of the class shared an observation or two, and Aggie marveled at the insights they had gained during their relatively short conversations. Elizabeth listened intently and offered her own comments and critiques.

When it was her turn, Aggie complimented Viola, and Elizabeth smiled proudly. "Viola has learned the most important part of this process: A gesture, or an emotion, can't be rushed. It takes the time it takes."

Viola was visibly pleased with the praise. "I just try to empathize."

By the time Elizabeth called for a break, the nervousness Aggie had felt at the outset of class had lessened. People stood and stretched, and conversations sprang up. Viola climbed to her feet with the help of her flowered cane and pointed a finger in Bernice's direction.

"Race you around the gym?"

"Three laps," Bernice challenged.

"Do I get a head start?"

"No way. I fell for that last time."

"You're on."

The two women set off, giggling as they promenaded sedately around the room.

After the break, Elizabeth gathered them in the corner by the clothing rack. "As you know, your apparel does not have to be one hundred percent accurate to the time period. Lillian assures me Remarkables are perceived but not closely regarded. Ladies, you will need a dress, a shawl or cloak, a bonnet, and a reticule—essentially a handbag." She held up a black drawstring bag by way of demonstration. "Gentlemen, you will be fine in long pants and simple shirts. There are also jackets and hats here for you to work with. I want you to pick out a few things and try them on. Get a feel for how the clothing affects, and, for the ladies, constrains, your movements."

While the women inspected the dresses, Elizabeth pulled Frank and Sal over to a pile of men's clothing. Serena's preview of the outfits at the start of class had apparently been put to good use, and she quickly selected two dresses apiece for herself and Kat.

"What do you think?"Julie held a plain, brown dress up against herself.

"It looks fine," Aggie said. She inspected the dresses without enthusiasm. It had been a long time since she had worn a dress.

Julie took over. "Here." She pulled out a dark blue frock with wide sleeves and a simple white collar. "This should work. Come on. There's a locker room through that door where we can try these on."

Ten minutes later the class reconvened in the gym, and Aggie studied her reflection in the mirrored walls. The dress was not as uncomfortable as she had feared. But it was strange to feel yards of fabric sweep around her as she moved. Oddly, she thought of her wedding day. She had worn her mother's bridal gown. Its lace bodice and long satin skirt had made her feel beautiful.

Serena had put on a dark green dress with a beautifully gathered skirt. She had her back to the mirror and was peering over her shoulder to view herself from behind. Kat was in a light blue gown that matched the color of her eyes and set off her blonde hair. When Kat saw Aggie, she eyed her critically. "That dress is awfully plain, but navy blue works with your hair. Your palette is kind of limited with that color hair."

"I've always thought so myself," Aggie said agreeably.

Bernice had helped Viola in the locker room, so they were the last to emerge. Both had chosen plain, dark dresses. Viola's pink-flowered aluminum cane had been replaced with an old-fashioned wooden walking stick.

"Nifty, isn't it?" she said, brandishing the cane and adopting a fierce expression.

"Vi's armed and dangerous," Frank called.

"No more than usual, sonny," she retorted.

The gym's mirrors multiplied their reflections, making it appear as if a larger gathering had assembled. Some of the women began twirling in place and experimenting with various ways to gather up their skirts to move more freely. Frank and Sal, wearing rather imposing black jackets and hats, practiced polite bows and handshakes. Julie linked her arm through Aggie's, and, for a moment, they silently observed the play-acting.

"We always get a little silly on dress-up day," Julie explained. "It releases some of the tension, I guess."

The door to the gym opened, and Abe and Lillian entered, followed by Wells. Lillian had on a pretty muslin dress, and Abe was garbed in a

Victorian-era suit. He strolled over, swept the hat from his head, and bowed gallantly. "At your service, ladies."

"Thank you, kind sir," Julie replied with a laugh.

He turned to Aggie, a quizzical look in his eyes. "How are we feeling this afternoon, ma'am?"

She cast an eye over the room. Wells was inspecting Viola's cane and peppering her with questions. Kat was twisting Serena's long hair into an intricate knot on top of her head. Bernice seemed to be practicing a curtsy in front of the mirror. Aggie looked up into Abe's handsome face and caught him eying the fit of her dress. He gave her an appreciative grin, and she was suddenly glad navy blue looked nice with her hair. "I think we're feeling fine this afternoon," she said. She scanned the room again and nodded. "Just fine."

Chapter 20 ~ Steps

As the days passed, Aggie felt herself slipping into the routines of this "other AARP," this other family. It was not unlike the September of a typical school year as each personality became clear, each person more of an individual.

She followed a schedule again. Mornings were spent with Lillian's fieldwork group. Afternoons were devoted to sessions with Elizabeth who had them practice questioning techniques and how to draw inferences based on body language.

When classes finished, Aggie practiced at the barn. Her ability to use the three Ds had grown, and with it her confidence, although, every now and then she hit a glitch, or was troubled by motion sickness or double vision. She had studied *Remarkable Travel for Dummies* and picked up a few useful hints, although it read rather like a trouble-shooting guide for a malfunctioning computer: *Why you might be choosing the wrong focus object. Five things to try if you can't get distance.*

Aggie was satisfied with her ability to get to the date she was aiming for—enjoying the calendar pictures selected by *Smitty's Automobile Service*—and felt she could achieve distance without significant problems. After working on duration, she was pleased to complete a forty-minute trip that allowed her to venture into the interior of the barn where she encountered two enormous, placid horses and a cluster of kittens learning to move about on wobbly legs.

This is not to say all her trips were successful. The study group session at Julie's apartment had alerted her to the possibility of eviction from the past in the face of danger or some other action that contravened the rules of time travel. The *Dummies* guide had an informative page entitled *The Top 25 Reasons Travelers Get Evicted.*

Nonetheless, it was startling when it happened. The first time she was thrown out occurred on a trip to the 1950s. It was an unsettled, humid afternoon with gusts of wind and a heavy cloud cover. Arriving in the past, Aggie walked away from the barn and climbed a small rise to a towering sycamore where she placed a hand against the distinctive green and tan camouflage-patterned bark. Suddenly, there was an earsplitting crack of sound, and, without warning, she was back in the present, feeling like she had just zoomed down a very fast slide.

She knew immediately what must have happened but felt compelled to check. Focusing on a patch of milkweed, she started another trip, aiming for the following week. She arrived amidst the charred remains of the sycamore. It had been struck by lightning. The trunk had literally exploded, no match for the lightning bolt's billion joules of energy.

She told Julie about it the next morning. Aggie and her mentor had settled into the habit of meeting in the library before Lillian's class.

"You were in danger and got evicted," Julie nodded. "See how that time travel rule works? You were evicted before you were hurt."

Aggie pulled on a lock of her hair, twisting it around her finger as she thought. "I was evicted before I was *killed*. You don't survive a direct strike like that."

"Same thing."

"Not exactly. One rule says you won't get hurt. The other says you can't change the time of death. Two different rules."

"Obviously related."

"But not the same."

"What practical difference does it make?"

"I don't know. Maybe none. But when I wrote about it in my notebook, I attributed causation to the rule about death, not the rule about harm." She shook her head and looked at the clock. "Enough on that. We've got a half hour until fieldwork group. We should get back to work."

"You're right," Julie said with a yawn. "But I need more coffee. Last night I fell asleep with the light on and a book in my lap. That hasn't happened since I was studying for the bar."

Aggie understood. Somehow, Lillian's classes raised as many questions as they answered. Each book or article or picture they examined led to another. Even so, she had a sense the group was moving forward.

This sentiment was reinforced when they entered the conference room one morning to find the table pushed to the side and the chairs placed in a semicircle before the whiteboard. Questions had been written on the board under the heading "Next Steps." Aggie reviewed the list.

(1) *Can we adapt well enough to the nineteenth century to carry out our mission?*
(2) *Can we find Gabe (what does he look like?) and verify his connection to Mathew Brady?*
(3) *Did Gabe gain possession of Brady portraits?*
(4) *Were the portraits buried? Where? Upper West Side? Harlem?*

Lillian came straight to the point. "We've collected and shared a huge amount of information. Our destination — the time and place — have become familiar, at least on paper. Now we need to move forward. Look at the board. If we cannot answer question one in the affirmative, the other questions become moot. That's why I've scheduled a day trip into the city for this Friday. It will be a test run. The results will tell us if we can move on."

No one seemed surprised by Lillian's announcement.

"It's time to see if we can become acclimated," she continued. "Most of you worked on Ellis Island, so you know what I'm talking about. Travel to a distant time can be a shock. Abe, Maurice, and I are the only ones in our tristate AARP family who have spent any appreciable amount of time in the nineteenth century. For each of us there was a learning curve."

Lillian looked down at herself then back at the group. "I use a walker," she said, with a trace of defiance. "They came into use in the 1950s. Traveling farther back than that requires me to use a different assistive device. Making that accommodation was part of my learning curve. Each of you will have unique challenges. Your own learning curve. You may be evicted by sights or sounds or smells that disconcert you: horses, gas lamps, peddlers on the street. You might be baffled by a conversation you cannot follow because of an unfamiliar idiom or colloquialism. You may have read Frederick Douglass's autobiography or *The Red Badge of Courage*, but that doesn't mean you understand the vernacular of Civil War-era New York."

Kat chose that rather inopportune moment to announce she had seen *Gone with the Wind* and just knew Rhett Butler was going to beg forgiveness and "get back together" with Scarlett.

"Margaret Mitchell should beg forgiveness for perpetuating myths about reconstruction and romanticizing plantation culture," Julie snapped.

"Who's Margaret Mitchell? Vivien Leigh played Scarlett," Kat retorted.

Aggie covered her mouth to hide a smile and was relieved Kat didn't notice.

"Now's not the time," Lillian said impatiently. "My point is you may encounter unexpected difficulties resulting in multiple evictions. But there are things in our favor as well. The research you've done and the photographs you've examined will be tremendously helpful. Also, New York City still has many Civil War-era structures. I don't fully subscribe to the concept of auras, but I know being in an older building helps some travelers."

"Works for me," Sal noted.

Lillian nodded. "Finally, the city, unlike many rural locations, has an abundance of recorded history. When you know an event happened at a specific time and place, you can quickly double check how you're doing with the 'first D.' It's almost as good as using the calendar in the barn."

"I watched the ball drop in Times Square in five different years," Frank said. "Great way to check your destination batting average."

Lillian tilted her head toward Viola. "Viola watched the survivors of the *Titanic* disembark from the *Carpathia* at Pier 54. History noted the time and place exactly."

"The crowds help, too," Sal said.

"Yes," Lillian agreed. "It's often easy to arrive unnoticed in a crowd."

"In Times Square I aimed for right when the countdown was starting," Frank said. "Everyone's looking up, waiting for the ball to drop, or looking at their sweetheart, waiting for a New Year's kiss. No one notices you drop in. With Vi, everyone was looking at the survivors. Their eyes were on the ship, not on the people around them."

"It was so cold that night," Viola said with a shiver.

"Didn't Abe get mad at you for being out in that weather?" Frank asked. "You got that bad cold—"

"You don't get sick from cold weather, unless you're talking hypothermia," Aggie said automatically. "You get a cold from a virus. Although extreme cold can be a stressor, and there's the indirect effect of vasoconstriction, but …." She stopped and looked curiously at Viola, who, for once, did not meet her eyes.

In her head, Aggie continued the thought. *But it shouldn't make a difference when you travel. You stand in a mud puddle in the past, and when you return, your shoes are clean. If you stand in the cold and rain, you should return warm and dry.* There was something there. An inconsistency. Something connecting Viola catching cold, the droplets on her blouse, the idea of intervention.

Lillian was speaking again. "Wells will be driving us into the city to get the answer to our first question: Can we adapt to the nineteenth century? I want you and your research partner to take about an hour to select a practice location. Then come back here to consult with me about your choice. Are there any questions?"

There were none.

***

"Pairs work well when you're trying to adapt," Julie explained to Aggie as they sat together in the library. "The first person will make an attempt. If she gets evicted, she can tell her partner what the problem was—whether it's horses, like Lillian said, or unfamiliar language, or something else that wrong-footed her. Then the second person takes a turn. If you acclimate quickly—Serena probably will—you can make a few observations on the destination and compare notes with your partner."

It made sense. Aggie looked at her mentor. Julie had come prepared with a pad of paper and a pencil, ready to jot down ideas. Aggie had her spiral notebook. She scanned her most recent entry which detailed observations made by the barn on a lazy autumn day in 1942. Abruptly, she closed the notebook. An idea was forming in her head. "I have a proposed destination."

"I'm listening."

"I say we go to Mathew Brady's exhibit, the one with the photographs of Antietam. We look for Gabe. It's his last known location, and we've been doing research on it for days."

Julie was shaking her head. "I know we talked about going there—and we should, eventually—but practice sessions are designed to be low-key. They're intended to orient you to the era more than anything. Like Lillian said, we need to find out if we can operate that far back and build up our tolerance for the time period before we start collecting information."

"Hear me out," Aggie said. "Normally you conduct an inquiry—any inquiry—by taking it step by step. You follow a protocol. You test for one variable at a time. You conduct multiple trials, gather evidence, and analyze results. But what if we don't have time for that? Lillian put all the questions on the board except the one nobody wants to talk about. What if we find the answer, but Daniel is past the point of being able to understand it?"

Julie was taken aback. For a moment she examined her pencil as if checking whether the point was sharp and the eraser adequate.

Aggie leaned across the table to press her point. "Maybe it won't work. Maybe it's too ambitious. Maybe I'm too new to know any better. But why not try? If we can't get acclimated, then we can't. But if we can, then we need to move as quickly as possible. And the kind of things Lillian said were problems—odd sounds, strange sights—I don't think they're going to be problems for us. You say you're weak on the three Ds. But no one is better at research than you, and the work you've done has prepared us. We know what to expect."

Julie was silent another moment. Her pencil was reexamined. "The Antietam exhibit was well attended," she said at last. "And Brady's studio was on Broadway. The crowds should help."

"Where on Broadway?"

"He moved his studio four times," Julie responded immediately, "always relocating farther north, following the rest of fashionable New York. The exhibit was at 785 Broadway, Brady's last gallery in New York and his most impressive. It was the top three floors of a four-story building. Photographers back then needed the top floor so they could use skylights to improve illumination in the room where they took pictures. The lower rooms were for exhibitions."

"Is the building still there?"

"No. But it was right across the street from Grace Church, and Grace Church is still there. We could use its aura, cross the street, and go up the stairs."

Aggie studied her mentor's face. "Will the distance be hard for you?"

"It might." Julie confessed. "I've never done stairs. The nice thing about Ellis Island was you could do the stairs in the present and then travel back. But look, what you're suggesting is like saying we can skip a grade in school. You're assuming we can acclimate immediately."

"I'd put serious money on you being able to skip a grade."

Julie nodded. "Let's go see Lillian."

Abe was in the conference room when they arrived. He was perched on a corner of the table, his arms folded across his chest. Aggie had grown used to seeing him in the morning. Sometimes she would spot him heading off for his walk. Sometimes he would lean on her patio wall for a chat. He often asked to read her notes.

Lillian stood before a sheet of easel paper taped to the white board. Pairs of names and destinations were listed on the paper. Apparently, Aggie and Julie were the last to check in. Aggie scanned the sheet. Viola and Bernice had chosen Barnum's American Museum. Sal and Frank were headed to Central Park during the period when it was under construction. The final entry puzzled her: Serena and Kat were going to Macy's.

"That'll be the old Macy's," Julie explained, "before they moved to Herald Square in 1902. See the date? Trust Serena to make it all about shopping." She turned to Lillian. "Aggie and I want to go to Brady's studio—to the exhibit—The Dead of Antietam."

Abe frowned and pressed his lips together.

"Let's sit down a minute," Lillian said. "I think we need to discuss this."

They moved to the conference table. Abe and Lillian sat on one side, Julie and Aggie on the other. The arrangement reminded Aggie of a negotiation, and she wondered what each of them had at stake in the outcome.

"I know it's a little *heavy* for a practice session," Julie began, "but even if we don't make it to the exhibit, it's a great location with lots to see."

Lillian's sharp green eyes moved from Julie to Aggie and back again. "Why don't you tell me why you believe you can shortcut the acclimation process."

Julie opened her mouth to answer, but Aggie intervened. "It was my idea. I know it's not a conventional approach. But you and Daniel both intimated that he is beginning to have difficulty understanding things." She paused to gather her thoughts. For some reason her heart was pounding. There was no good way to say this. "I know fieldwork missions generally follow a certain progression—a timeline. But I think we must factor in *Daniel's* timeline, which is going to be shorter. Sometimes you believe you have all the time in the world. To say things to someone, to tell them all the important stories, ask all the questions and hear the answers. And then you don't."

Aggie was horrified to realize tears had come to her eyes. She blinked them away and fought to steady her voice. "I think we have to take a run at short-cutting the process. Julie can pick up information even if she's only there a few minutes. She's brilliant. She notices everything. And I know I'm new, but I want to try this."

Abe was watching her intently, his eyes moving over her face.

Lillian looked to the window. A gust of wind pulled a handful of leaves from an oak tree. "You're right about Daniel's timeline," she said at last. "He may not have long. Abe convinced me you belonged in a fieldwork group. Julie assures me you're doing well with the three Ds. And sometimes success just boils down to desire."

Aggie leaned forward. "I have the desire. I want to try. That's all any of us can do. Try."

Lillian nodded. Aggie looked to Abe.

He regarded her gravely, but then nodded as well. "You're right. All any of us can do is try."

"It's settled then," Lillian said. "But Abe, I want you to go with them. Aggie, you're talented but still a rookie. Julie, this will be more complicated than anything you've done before. If Abe is with you as a companion traveler, he can be a buffer when it comes to adjusting to the 1800s. I would go with you myself, but I'm assisting Bernice and Viola."

Julie put her hand on Aggie's arm and gave it a squeeze. "We've got a green light."

"Put your destination on the board before you leave," Lillian said.

***

If the morning session with Lillian bolstered Aggie's confidence, the afternoon session with Elizabeth drained it away. They had worked on interpreting facial expressions, and, after a fairly poor performance, Aggie found herself standing in the bathroom late that night, making faces into the mirror, endeavoring to analyze the effect of different emotions on her features.

Outside, she heard a clap of thunder and the pattering sound heralding the onset of rain. Climbing under the flowered quilt, she picked up a volume of nineteenth-century photographs of New York. Flipping through the pages, she stopped at a picture of the Angel of the Waters statue that rose above Bethesda Fountain in Central Park. Dozens of men in bowler hats and women in long dresses were gathered at the scene.

From her nightstand, she picked up the picture of Jacob that Roscoe had taken in front of that same fountain. When Aggie and Jacob first became engaged, Roscoe was still a teenager, experimenting with a stunning array of unconventional hairstyles and clothing.

"He's not judgmental," Roscoe had informed her.

"No, dear boy, not judgmental at all."

"Then I approve. You have my permission to wed the chap."

"Thank you," Aggie remarked solemnly, though her lips quivered. "Would you walk me down the aisle?"

"You mean *give you away*?" Roscoe crowed. "Isn't that a bit patriarchal? You're not even changing your name."

"Well, Minnie's maid of honor, and I want you to be part of the ceremony, too. And you're not really giving me away. You're just … walking with me."

"I could be your flower girl."

"Tempting offer, but think I'll pass."

As brothers-in-law, Jacob and Roscoe made an odd couple. Her husband was serious and reserved, her brother exuberant and outgoing. But they had become fast friends. The photograph at the fountain had been taken during one of Roscoe's visits. Aggie's teaching job had precluded her from spending time with her brother during the day, but Jacob had brought Roscoe into New York and together they explored Broadway, wandered through art galleries, and indulged in pastrami at Carnegie Deli.

Jacob had done a feature article about the renovation of Bethesda Fountain, so he brought Roscoe to Central Park to see the beautiful angel standing above a cascade of sparkling water. Roscoe was captivated. He posed by the fountain, spreading his arms like wings to mirror the statue's pose, then insisted on taking a shot of Jacob in the same position.

"You have to be an angel, too," he cajoled. "You married Aggie, definitely an angel. And Minnie's an angel, too. Kind of a nerdy one. Face it, we're a family of angels."

Jacob had reluctantly played along, so there he was, arms spread wide, a sheepish grin on his face, the spray from the fountain creating a halo of light around him.

Outside, thunder boomed again, and lightning flickered through the panes of glass. On an impulse, Aggie reached for her phone and called Roscoe. He picked up immediately.

"Ags! What's up, sweetie-pie? You woke me from my beauty sleep."

Aggie looked guiltily at the clock. It was well past midnight.

"Oh, Roscoe, I didn't realize—" On the other end of the line she heard the unmistakable sounds of laughter and conversation.

"Got you," Roscoe declared gleefully. "After all these years, I'd think you'd know that actors stay up late to philosophize in Bohemian hangouts."

"Are you at a Bohemian hangout?"

"Golden Nugget. Best we could find at this hour. Hey, it's not late for me, but why are you awake? Are you still at that senior retreat listening to graybeards prose on about political trends of the twentieth century? Did it turn out to be a cult? Do you need a rescue? I've always wanted to rescue a lady in distress. Or a lad, of course."

"Well, it's actually political trends of the mid-nineteenth century, and not a cult, so rescue not needed," Aggie laughed.

"You just wanted to hear my dulcet tones then."

"Absolutely. And while I don't need a rescue, I could use advice. There's this acting club here, and I sort of joined. I'm not very good, so I was wondering if you had any suggestions."

"Ags," Roscoe exclaimed delightedly, "are you involved in *community theater*? That's so unlike you. You used to sit out the ice-breaking activities at teacher meetings."

"It's very unlike me. That's the hitch. It's wonderful here, but everyone is very *sociable*, and they wanted me in this club, so I just agreed. Probably a mistake, don't you think?"

"Well, sister dear, you've come to the right place. And you've actually diagnosed your problem and found your solution. You said, 'It's very unlike me.' Well of course it is. It's not about you. It's never about you. It's about the character. You don't need to feel embarrassed or awkward or self-conscious or, I don't know, inept. You just need to feel whatever emotion the character feels. It's a brain thing. You, of all people, can relate to that. You use your own body and voice, but someone else's words and someone else's brain."

"You make it sound like *Invasion of the Body Snatchers*."

"Well, you don't have to think about my noble profession as an alien conquest. Just think about it as *empathy*. You put yourself in someone else's place, feel what they feel. Do you kind of get the idea?"

"I kind of get the idea. I'll let you go, but tell me first, are rehearsals going well? Are you happy?"

"Deliriously. I'll send an email dishing the details."

"I would love that. Now go get some of that beauty sleep you were talking about."

"Will do. Love you, Ags."

"Love you, too."

Aggie ended the call. She felt better as she crawled under her quilt and switched off the light. The storm continued to rage. Somewhat later, another flash of lightning illuminated her room, but she was sound asleep and didn't hear the thunder that followed in its wake.

Chapter 21 ~ Companion Travel

"It's not easy fitting into a bus seat wearing these clothes," Julie grumbled. "I feel hemmed in by all this material." She half stood, pulled the fabric of the long skirt over to the side, and reseated herself with a flounce.

Aggie agreed. The shuttle bus had more than enough seats for the group but seemed crowded that morning. They were all attired in their period clothing, including Lillian and Abe who had boarded the bus after a brief conference with Mirlande outside the Lodge's front entrance.

"I have your meds, Viola," Lillian called to the older woman. "Is everyone set? Wells will be out in a moment."

As if on cue, the young man dashed out of the Lodge. Coming to a stop in front of Mirlande, he greeted her with a grin and formal little bow. Mirlande laughed. At this sign of encouragement, Wells pointed to his cheek and raised his eyebrows in a question. She rolled her eyes but gave him a quick kiss. Clearly ecstatic, he raised his face to the sky as if thanking the heavens for an unexpected blessing, then climbed up into the bus and slid into the driver's seat with a sigh of happiness.

He was about to close the bus doors when they heard a cry outside. "Wait for me." Maurice, wearing loose pants and a jacket similar to those of Frank and Sal, climbed the steps, waved to the others on the bus, and plopped down in a seat near Abe and Lillian.

"Sorry Pops," Wells said, "I didn't know you were coming."

"I wasn't sure myself," he replied, "but Lillian's been keeping me informed about this project, and I thought I'd join you all for a little firsthand exploration."

Lillian reached across the aisle and squeezed his arm. "I'm so glad you're here. Are you going with one of our groups?"

"I'll start out with Frank and Sal. Then I'm going to scout around on my own."

Lillian eyed him shrewdly. "Central Park, about mid-nineteenth century, I expect. That should do it, right?"

"Do what?" Kat asked. She was sitting directly behind him wearing the pretty blue dress.

Maurice grinned. "Let me explore a little place called Seneca Village."

The drive into the city went smoothly. Maurice, Frank, and Sal were dropped off first. Aggie watched them stride into Central Park. Frank and Sal were aiming for the late 1850s. "There were a lotta' workers there, so we should blend right in," Frank had assured them. "Especially Sal.

Just hope he remembers he's not there to advise Frederick Law Olmsted on stonework."

The other drop-off points were farther south. Serena and Kat were let out at 14th Street just down from Union Square Park. "They're aiming for the 1870s or 80s," Viola said. "Macy's was already a big deal though it wasn't a single large structure. They had storefront space in eleven buildings."

"Viola, Bernice, you're next," Wells called as he eased back into traffic.

"We are so looking forward to seeing Barnum's Museum," Viola said, eyes gleaming with excitement. "As soon as we saw it in one of those books of Lillian's, we knew that would be our practice destination. It opened in 1841 and was the most popular tourist attraction of its time. There were zoo animals and whales and magicians and new inventions. A big theater inside held performances of Bible stories and *Uncle Tom's Cabin*. There were all kinds of silly hoaxes, too, of course, like a 'mermaid skeleton' made from the bones of a monkey and a fish."

"Seemed like the place I should be," Bernice added, somewhat enigmatically.

"Will you be able to travel directly inside, or will you have to pay to get in?" Aggie asked.

"We'll see," Viola said placidly. "The layout is a little complicated. As for paying … admission is twenty-five cents, and we don't have any old money. And even if we did—say we had some antique coins and brought them back with us—as soon as we tried to use them, we'd get—"

"Kicked out on our fannies," Bernice finished for her.

"That's because," Julie lowered her voice and glanced toward the front of the bus where Lillian and Abe had their heads together in conversation, "leaving a coin behind is an *intervention*, like the Remarkable who tried to give away his wedding ring."

"Well, I'm sure you'll see amazing things, even standing outside. Or maybe you ladies could sneak in," Aggie suggested with a laugh.

Viola and Bernice looked at each other and started giggling.

"I wouldn't put it past either one of them," Julie said.

In another few minutes, the bus pulled to the side of the street in front of a small, two-story church surrounded by a wrought iron fence. The roof of the church's classical portico was supported by four tall columns. Trees graced the side yards, their leaves just beginning to show autumn colors.

"This is us," Viola said. "St. Paul's Chapel."

"St. Paul's dates back to the American Revolution," Julie explained to Aggie. "It should have a good strong aura, and it's a great starting point for them. In the 1800s, Barnum's Museum was right across the street. And Brady's first studio and the Astor Hotel were nearby."

Using the antique wooden cane for support, Viola rose to her feet. "The nice thing about using a church is that while one person travels, the other can sit inside. And folks usually leave you alone in a church."

She eyed her cane appraisingly. "This baby should work well for me, but I don't want to overexert myself and have to listen to a lecture from Mirlande. Come on, Bernie, let's go in. You can take the first turn and scout things out. I'll bet you my casino winnings—that's $10.55—that I acclimate faster than you."

"You've got yourself a bet," Bernice agreed promptly.

"I'm getting out here, too, Wells," Lillian reminded him.

The three women departed the bus, and Aggie watched from the window as they headed toward the shade of the portico.

"During 9/11 St. Paul's was a sanctuary," Julie said. She was staring out the window but not at the chapel. Her eyes were fastened on the gleaming spire of the new Freedom Tower rising behind the trees in the churchyard. "So many buildings around here came down with the twin towers. But St. Paul's was spared. Rescue workers used it as a place of rest."

"You were here?"

"A little farther away. I saw the second plane hit." Julie turned from the window and fidgeted with a loose thread on a seam of her dress. "It was …." She stopped, seeming unable to find more to say. Suddenly, her eyes fell on something on the next seat. "Oh, look. Viola forgot her reticule." She held up the drawstring bag. "Hold up, Wells. Viola forgot something. I'll run it in to her."

She rose and hurried forward. Wells opened the bus door and let her out. Abe got up, stretched, and headed back down the aisle to sit across from Aggie. She looked out at the Freedom Tower, and a disturbing thought entered her mind. A traveler could go to that terrible day in 2001 and be a witness to the horror that unfolded.

Abe's eyes followed the direction of her gaze, and he seemed to read her thoughts. "Sometimes a traveler will be drawn to an important event. Sometimes by intention, and sometimes because it's hard to keep your mind from making a connection. So you go there by accident. You stumble upon history at its most merciless. When that happens, some leave immediately—"

"But some don't?"

"Some don't."

Aggie turned from the window and looked into his eyes.

"Some stay," he said reluctantly, "even knowing nothing can be done. Even knowing that watching is almost obscene. And when you return, you remember too much of it. Even years later, too much. Maybe that's what history demands, but it is not an easy thing."

"Did it happen to you?"

Abe looked away. When he turned back to her his expression was shuttered. "It was a long time ago. When I was first learning how to travel. Before there was any kind of organization. I was in Poland. That's where my father thought his parents had been sent."

"I can't imagine—" Aggie stopped. The phrase seemed wholly inadequate.

"No one can imagine." He shook his head. "I should have known better."

Julie had emerged from the chapel and was climbing back on the bus.

"Did you find her?" Aggie asked.

"Yes, she was sitting on a chair at the back. Bernice was already on her first trip. That woman doesn't let grass grow under her feet."

Wells waited till Julie was seated and there was a break in the traffic before pulling away from the curb. "Last stop, Grace Church," he announced.

***

Aggie, Julie, and Abe sat next to each other in a pew near the back. A Bach organ piece filled the church with glorious sound. It was Julie who had discovered Grace Church hosted free organ concerts, along with the opportunity to meditate or pray.

"It will be perfect," she explained. "Enough people so we don't stand out, but no service going on, so we won't disturb anyone by moving around."

Upon entering, Julie had headed to a side aisle, pausing before a tall stone column. Aggie lifted her eyes to the stained-glass windows in the majestic vaulted ceiling. Abe slipped into a pew, sat, and began tapping his hand on his thigh in time with the music. After looking about, Aggie sat down next to him, but Julie remained by the column, resting her forehead on the smooth stone surface. She looked, for all the world, like a parent listening to the breathing of a sleeping child. Aggie looked at Abe questioningly.

"Julie's sensing the aura," he explained in a whisper.

"Um, will it take long?"

"No, she'll join us in a minute."

Indeed, by the time the musical piece ended, Julie had entered the pew and seated herself next to them. "We can use one of the columns to focus, she said, "as long as no one else is in the aisle."

Abe nodded. "Do you want to go first?"

"Yes. You're coming with me, right?"

Abe smiled. "I am completely at your disposal."

Julie turned to Aggie. "It's like I told you. I'm weak on the three Ds, especially distance. And I've never gone so far back. With companion travel, Abe can kind of escort me to my destination and drop me off at the right place."

"You're making me sound like an Uber driver," Abe complained, "though I am, of course, pleased to be of service."

"Let's go then," Julie stated with determination. "There's a good place to focus on the far side of that pillar, a little chink in the stone. Aggie, you'll be all right here?"

"I'll be fine," Aggie assured them. Julie and Abe rose and stepped to the side aisle. The organist began a new piece.

Abe extended his arm for Julie. "Ma'am?"

She took his arm and they strolled together toward the back of the church. Aggie watched them go. Julie's long skirt was still visible as they moved behind one of the columns. Aggie returned her attention to the music. Minutes later, she looked back. Julie and Abe were gone.

Aggie blinked. She knew about companion travel—that's how she had been recruited, after all—but it was still startling. Apart from that Welcome Wagon trip, all her journeys had been solitary. She had become accustomed to the feeling of being a lone adventurer on a solo flight. How had the directors perfected companion travel? She wondered if it was something others could achieve with practice. Julie said no. Companions were just born different, like white tigers, or cats with extra toes. Still, Aggie wondered.

After Lillian had decreed that Abe accompany them, Aggie had discussed the matter with Viola who had invited her over to watch *Dancing with the Stars*. "We have an unofficial fan club," Vi had said. Aggie had been greeted at the door by Bernice dressed in a muumuu printed with palm fronds and rather alarming magenta hibiscus flowers. She held a frosted glass with what looked like a frozen margarita. "It's Latin Night," she announced without preamble. From the kitchen came the whir of a blender. Entering, Aggie found Julie, Flora, and Mirlande nestled on the sofa. Erin sat on the rug with a fat orange tabby cat curled up in her lap.

Viola waved from her post at the blender. "Do you want a virgin margarita or a real one?"

"A real one, but light on the tequila." Aggie laughed, dropped into an armchair, and felt herself relax. The evening had been delightful. She was so used to spending evenings alone, reading a book or watching the news. It was a pleasant change to be part of a talking, gossiping, laughing group—like being back in college.

Viola had the largest flat screen TV Aggie had ever seen outside of Best Buy, and the evening passed in a flash. After the show, the other women left, but Aggie stayed to help rinse the glasses and plates. Viola had served nachos and dips as well as margaritas.

"Lillian wants Abe to go with Julie and me for the practice session," she told Viola as she placed a bowl in the dishwasher. "She thinks we'll need help from a companion traveler."

"And you feel like you've been put in a remedial class?" Viola laughed. "You shouldn't. We all use the directors as companions on tricky missions. Lillian's helping Bernie and me."

"Tell me more about companions."

"I don't know everything. I suspect companions have idiosyncrasies about the way they travel, but the three of them are fairly circumspect about that."

Aggie thought back to her handshake with Abe and what he had said about learning through touch.

"But I can tell you about how they do two-person travel," Viola offered.

"Does the companion stay with his, um, partner for the whole trip?"

"Oh, the companion can't *stay* with the traveler," Viola explained, "unless it's a very short trip, like what happens on a Welcome Wagon visit. Still, it's an extraordinary and very rare ability. This is how it works. The companion traveler and his partner look at the same focus object and they have to have some kind of physical contact to start the trip."

"Physical contact?"

"Yes. Say they're on a recruitment visit. They can shake hands or touch the person's arm in a friendly way. People actually touch each other a fair amount without thinking about it. How did it happen when Abe recruited you?"

"I handed him a tomato, and he reached for it and just kept hold of my hand."

"That would work." Viola nodded wisely.

"Julie said the directors do most of the recruiting because they're the only companion travelers."

"They're the only ones in our group. Yes, it's the easiest way to see if someone is a traveler, but it's also helpful in other situations. I wish I could do it," she said a bit wistfully. "I think it's smart to have Abe with you. He'll get Julie to the right destination, and she can concentrate on acclimating once she's there."

"But he can't stay with her?" Aggie asked again.

"No. Well, he can, but only a few minutes. If the trip is short, they might come back together, but usually Abe will just help his partner arrive, and then after a few minutes he gets evicted. His partner will be able to remain in the past longer."

"What if he wanted to stay in the past with her?"

"What he wants doesn't matter," Viola stated matter-of-factly. "With companion travel, it's always the partner who's the driver, the one in charge. The companion traveler has a more tenuous attachment to the location and gets evicted after a little while even if he wants to stay. It's just not possible for more than one traveler to fit into any past event. Not for any length of time, anyway. The companion traveler also gets evicted if he tries to take charge or interfere. You know, wrestle the steering wheel out of his partner's hands, so he can direct where they go and what they do. The only thing the companion can do is ride shotgun."

Aggie placed the last plate in the dishwasher, added soap powder, and pushed the start button. Untying her apron, she picked up her sweater and prepared to leave. "There are a lot of rules I still need to learn."

"Yes, there are a lot of rules," Viola agreed. "And, even when you think you've learned them, you haven't *really* learned them until you try them out yourself. Like driver's ed." She laughed. "I knew the whole manual, all the traffic signs, and the rules of the road. My first time behind the wheel I ran my Daddy's Pontiac into a ditch."

"Manual or automatic?" Aggie asked with a laugh.

"Manual," Viola answered, "but I can't use that as an excuse. It was just bad driving."

***

The organist had started another piece. Aggie heard footsteps approaching then Abe slid into the pew. He didn't say anything but smiled and gave the thumbs up sign. They sat together listening to the music. It was another twenty minutes before Julie reappeared. She looked breathless but elated.

"Amazing! Just amazing." She looked around guiltily and lowered her voice. "It was perfect for me. Easier than Ellis Island. I didn't get to Brady's studio, but I saw where it was, and there was plenty to see, even without moving very far. The horses and carriages, the way people dressed. The vista was so different. Everything was *shorter*, the buildings I mean, and I got as far as this little shop window, and it was something out of Dickens. After all our talk about the difficulties getting acclimated, I kept expecting to get evicted. But nothing fazed me. I had *studied* this, the building, the street, the period. I knew what was supposed to be there. I felt prepared."

"You don't need to take notes, do you?" Aggie said.

"No," Julie grinned, tapping her forehead. "I'll remember. Now you go, Aggie. The date we chose looked good. The weather is mild. There are a lot of people around, but it's not intimidating. And this church has a strong aura. And Abe's a great companion."

Aggie looked at Abe. He bowed his head in her direction. "Anytime you're ready," he said genially. "I'd be—"

"I know," Aggie interrupted. "You'd be *enchanted.* Come on Mr. Time Travel Uber driver. Let's give it a try."

Abe stood and reached out to help her to her feet. She placed her hand in his, and to her surprise, felt herself blush. Julie glanced from her to Abe, then looked down at her lap, hiding a smile.

Aggie and Abe walked down the aisle hand in hand. "Where did you and Julie leave from?" she asked.

"Over here," he said, and pulled her behind one of the columns at the back of the church. "Look," he said, "do you see that line in the stone? Keep your eyes on it and think about where we're going. A full century back, then another half. The Civil War is going on. Brady has received the glass plates from Antietam and put them on display in his gallery. Right across the street. Right now."

Abe's fingers curled around her hand. She put her other hand against the stone column, feeling its coolness. Once more her stomach felt that flying, falling, parachute feeling, and she knew it had worked. She lifted her eyes from an examination of the column and saw Abe studying her face. He smiled. "We're here. Want to take a look?"

They turned away from the column. The organ music had ceased, of course, and the church was empty except for the two of them. Abe kept hold of her hand and together they walked to the entrance, pushed through the door, and emerged into the midday sun.

Aggie drew in her breath. The first things to hit were sounds. The normal sounds of the twenty-first century were gone. The traffic and planes, the screech of brakes, the honking of horns—all had been replaced. Now there were sounds she had only heard in movies: the roll of wooden wheels, the clop of horses' hooves, the odd clink and rattle of wagons and carriages. The smells hit next. Lillian had mentioned this might be problematic, but Aggie didn't find the odor of the animals offensive. The air seemed different, though. She could smell the water, not so far away. There was smoke in the air, but not exhaust, not the puffs of noxious fumes that, in her own time, floated behind every bus and truck. She wrinkled her nose. She did smell garbage, but that wasn't foreign. Garbage and urine. She was a century and a half in the past, but, in certain respects, a city was a city.

In one part of her mind, she wondered how she would ever manage to record the complexity of the scene—the crowds of people in nineteenth-century garb, the horse-drawn vehicles, the buildings of brick and framed wood. She found her eyes darting from place to place, noting the sheen on the coat of a roan horse, a tall gas streetlamp, a pair of barefoot children in crudely fashioned trousers and shirts racing along the sidewalk.

She looked at Abe. He was grinning at her, watching her reactions. "There are two of us here," she said a little tartly. "We should both be making observations."

"What makes you think I'm not making observations?"

"How long can you stay?" Aggie asked politely. *I'm an idiot,* she thought. *I sound like the hostess at a dinner party.*

"It depends," he said. "Usually five or ten minutes."

"What happens if I let go of your hand?"

"I think my feelings might get hurt."

"Well, let's try a little experiment then," she said dryly, and dropped his hand. He was still there.

"I need physical contact to initiate companion travel," he explained. "Once we arrive, we can move about together or apart, but either way, I get evicted after a few minutes. It's essentially your trip, and I'm hitching a ride. I'll be here for a while, then drop out. But let's get started. There are things to see."

Aggie held back. "What if I take a step and get evicted? What if I can't get acclimated?"

"If you get evicted, we'll turn around and come back."

"That wastes time. How do you guarantee success?"

"You can't guarantee success, so don't overthink it. Unless you're like Julie. Then you should overthink it." Abe reached out and reclaimed her hand. "Just look at yourself," he said with a note of challenge in his voice. "You look *fine* in that dress. You look natural. Look at me. We're here because we belong here. We fit in and have things to see. We're ready."

Aggie looked down at the skirt of her navy blue dress. Did she belong here? Wasn't she just a retired schoolteacher wearing a costume? Then she heard Roscoe's voice. *It's not about you. It's never about you. You get to use someone else's character. Someone else's brain.*

Perhaps she could be someone else—someone brave—for a little while at least. She was going to see the first photographs ever made of the dead upon a field of battle, and maybe meet a man who had fought in that battle. That was her role, her mission.

She was aware that Abe was waiting, just as he had waited for her at the kitchen table on the day they met. She could see the photography studio across the street from where they stood. The elegant establishment had a large sign across the front proclaiming "Brady's Portrait Gallery."

"You're right," she said to Abe. "We're ready. Let's go to work."

Chapter 22 ~ The Dead of Antietam

Aggie bent over the large wooden box and looked through the lenses. It was a stereoscope. The photograph inside appeared in 3-D. Rows of the boxy viewers were set out on long tables for the Antietam exhibition in Brady's gallery.

Only a few months ago, she and Minnie had viewed the stereogram of Lincoln's funeral procession. And here she was, two-and-a-half years before that picture was taken. Abraham Lincoln was alive. He had issued the Emancipation Proclamation and was about to replace George McClellan with Ambrose Burnside as head of the Union Army. Thoreau died earlier in the year. He was only forty-four. Harriet Tubman was forty, Teddy Roosevelt a four-year-old, Edith Wharton a baby.

The picture in the viewer showed a group of dead Confederate artillerymen in front of a church. Aggie had grown up when images of war were ubiquitous. Vietnam was on the news every night. Still, the pictures in the stereoscopes were shocking. The boys were so young, too young to have their eyes emptied of life. It was cruelly appropriate the images could only be seen by leaning over, head down. There was a solemnity to this viewing, like looking into a casket.

The gallery was filled with visitors, but the room was quiet. A few spoke in low voices or exchanged whispered comments, but most moved from picture to picture in silence. Several times Aggie heard a sharply indrawn breath, once, a muffled sob.

Julie had found a *Time* magazine article written on the 150th anniversary of the exhibit's opening. It stated that people arrived at Brady's studio with "unconditioned eyes."

The words had stayed with Aggie. The people around her had lived in a world of hand-drawn images. *Harper's Weekly* had already published eight woodcut engravings based on these same photographs. But by peering into the stereoscopes, visitors confronted what all subsequent generations would confront. A photograph was remorseless. It captured the horror of warfare in a way that could not be ignored or made gentler.

Abe had stayed with Aggie for almost twenty-five minutes. From Grace Church, they had crossed to the Broadway entrance of Brady's studio, where a small placard announced simply "The Dead of Antietam." Mounting the stairs, they emerged into a long, extraordinarily elegant salon. Chandeliers hung from the ceiling and row upon row of beautifully framed portraits covered the walls. The pictures near the ceiling were suspended at an angle facing downward, so visitors standing below could see them.

Aggie had caught her breath before a portrait of President Lincoln. He was seated, solemn, not facing the camera directly, a trace of shadow along the side of his face. She had put her arm through Abe's and drawn him close. They studied the photograph in its gilt frame, then joined the clusters of people gathered around the stereoscopes.

Aggie had leaned forward to peer through the first viewer, then stood aside as Abe took his turn. When he glanced up, their eyes met, but they didn't speak. They continued in this manner until Aggie raised her eyes from a photograph depicting a trail of bodies along a fence and realized Abe was gone.

She had known this would happen, but it was unnerving. Her eyes swept the room to see if he had simply stepped away from her side. But he was definitely gone. She couldn't refrain from scrutinizing the people around her, the women in their long dresses and shawls, the men in their formal jackets. Surely someone would notice or remark on her lack of an escort, but it didn't happen. The visitors continued their perusal of the photographs. Their voices remained hushed and reverent.

Now that she was alone, Aggie took better stock of her surroundings. She missed the comfort of Abe's presence, but realized that without him she was not distracted from the job at hand. Stepping away from the stereoscopes, she returned to an examination of the portraits on the walls. She recognized some of them—Michael Faraday, Henry James, Commodore Perry—all stunning in their immediacy. Nonetheless, she was dismayed to scan others, face after face, with no flicker of recognition. These men—for the portraits were predominantly men— were the draw Brady used to get people into his gallery. It was unsettling to think that these famous people had dissolved into obscurity, known in her own time only to historians.

A man's voice interrupted her thoughts. "Ladies and gentlemen, if you are interested in obtaining a portrait or miniature, you may speak to any one of my assistants—there are several here to serve you. They would be pleased to arrange a sitting or discuss a family portrait."

Aggie turned toward the voice and, with a thrill of recognition, saw Mathew Brady standing at the head of the room. He was tastefully dressed in a crisp white shirt and dark suit. She drew in her breath. The resemblance in face and form to Jacob was even more pronounced in person. Brady's high cheekbones and riot of dark curls mirrored those of her husband.

Brady's announcement had prompted a couple to approach him and begin a quiet conversation. After a moment, he signaled the couple to accompany him, and the three moved toward the rear of the long gallery and out of Aggie's line of vision.

She almost followed, took a step in their direction, then wavered. Was it more important to look for Gabe? Examine the framed photographs? Their mission centered on the 'treasure' of a Lincoln portrait, not really on the photographer who had created that portrait. And yet, couldn't something be learned from Brady, too? Little was known of the photographer's inner life. He had never penned a memoir or written long letters expressing his feelings about the extraordinary things he had seen or the notable people he had met and photographed.

Aggie turned to move in the direction Brady had gone, but a tall, black-haired young man stood before her. He gave a polite bow. "Ma'am? Were you interested in making arrangements for a portrait?"

She started in surprise. She had not expected to be addressed. Travelers were generally less noticeable than others in the past, their presence often unheeded. The only person who had ever spoken to her during a time travel experience had been the young Veronica Lake look-alike in Grand Central Terminal. Conversation with someone in the past was certainly possible—hadn't that been the point of so many exercises in acting class? But, even so, it was disconcerting. Out of a roomful of people, he had approached her.

The young man was awaiting her answer. In her head, Elizabeth's voice rang out: *Always go with yes. 'Yes' leads you forward.* Aggie pulled herself together.

"A portrait? Yes. Although perhaps a little later. I don't need a sitting today, thank you, but I wanted to see the pictures from Antietam." She stopped, unsure how to go on but desperate for the conversation to continue. Then another voice came to her. This time it was Viola. *I just try to empathize.* Aggie waved a hand in the direction of the stereoscopes. "Those pictures are important. People need to know."

Brady's assistant nodded and looked at the gallery visitors leaning over to view the images. An elderly woman was holding a handkerchief to her mouth in obvious distress. A man was shaking his head as if to negate what he had seen. "Mayhap the pictures will not rest easy on those that see them," he said.

"Yes," Aggie conceded, "but people still need to know and understand and remember."

"A reminder is not always welcome."

"You may be right. But even so, better to know than be deliberately ignorant and heedless of the cost."

The young man turned again to those gathered at the stereoscopes. Surreptitiously, Aggie examined his features. They seemed familiar in a way they should not. It was like encountering someone at a large gathering, knowing you had met them before, maybe years before, but finding yourself unable to capture that elusive memory.

A suspicion grew in her mind. She looked at his hands, clasped together behind his back. The right hand nearly covered the left, but she could see the scarring, still fresh. She knew then, quite suddenly, that two of the fingers on that hand were missing. With wonder she looked into the face of Gabriel Buckley.

Before Aggie could speak, a young woman approached them. She was fashionably attired in a dark, full-skirted dress, and she clutched a woolen shawl about her shoulders. Despite her youth, and the elegance of her clothing, she had a haunted expression in her eyes.

"Sir, may I speak to you about arranging a portrait by Mr. Brady?"

Gabe bowed to her politely. "Of course, ma'am. May I show you to the studio?"

"Thank you," she replied. "It is for my betrothed. He is a volunteer."

"Yes, I understand. It will be a comfort to him to have your likeness."

With that, the young man bowed to Aggie and turned to lead the young woman to the studio.

***

Aggie found Abe and Julie still listening to the organ music. After her encounter with Gabe, she had lingered in Brady's studio perhaps ten more minutes. But when neither Gabe nor Brady reemerged from the back room, she descended the stairway, crossed the street, and reentered Grace Church. She stood in the rear vestibule and let her mind return to the present.

Julie grinned, and Abe greeted her with the same thumbs up sign he had used earlier.

"Julie, Abe, go ahead with your second trip," Aggie said quickly pulling her notebook from her reticule. "I have to write everything down."

"Right. Let's go," Julie said rising from the pew. Abe looked at Aggie curiously but followed Julie to the side aisle.

There was so much to tell them, but it must wait. Yesterday they had discussed their desire to maximize their travel time.

"Unless we hit a real snag or need to warn each other about something, let's concentrate on getting in as many trips as possible," Julie had said. "We'll operate like a relay team—as soon as one gets back, the other heads off."

Aggie began her notes with a description of Gabe. Tall. *How tall?* Not heavy, but not slim. *That could apply to anyone.* Dark hair. Wavy but not curly. No glasses. Square jaw. *Was that helpful? It wasn't precise.* Too bad she couldn't have pulled out her cell phone and taken a photo. Too bad she didn't have the gift of that artist at the comic convention. What was his name? Tyrece Vinci. That was it. He could have captured Gabe's likeness with a few strokes of a pencil.

She did the best she could, then attempted a transcript of their conversation. Next, she worked on a description of the gallery, the Antietam exhibition, and the framed portraits. She was still writing ten minutes later when Abe sat down next to her. She ignored him and kept writing. *Record your observations carefully. If you can't record contemporaneously, record as soon as possible.* They didn't speak until she closed her notebook.

"Tell me what happened," he demanded.

"I saw Mathew Brady," she said in a rush. "I saw Gabe. He was working in the studio. I saw his hand. I know it was him."

Abe searched her face. He seemed perplexed, as if he could not quite figure out what he was looking at. "Tell me how it happened. What was Brady like? What did he say? What was Gabe doing there? You said he was working? In what capacity?"

She shook her head impatiently. "I can't go through it all now. We're debriefing tonight, right? The important thing for now is that I'm not sure I can describe Gabe well enough to be helpful. What should I do when I go back?"

At that moment Julie returned, her face glowing. "It was marvelous," she said eagerly. "Abe, good suggestion to stay at street level instead of racking up a dozen evictions trying to get up those stairs. I waited for people to come down and listened to the things they said. Well, some didn't say anything, like they were in shock. But," she looked at her watch, "Aggie, do you want to head off? I can tell you all this later."

"Aggie saw Gabe," Abe said abruptly.

Julie's eyes widened. "Are you sure?"

"Pretty sure. I saw his hand. But I want another look. Listen, I should go by myself, and Abe, you go, too. Go alone, not as my companion. That way you can stay longer. We'll separate our destinations by an hour. If both of us see Gabe we can describe him better."

Julie looked from Aggie to Abe then took charge. "Abe, do what she says. It's a good plan. If she got there once with you, she can get back again by herself. Coordinate so you're there at different times." She looked at her watch again. "Go."

They needed no further urging. Abe left, saying he would find a focus object outside. Aggie went to the side aisle to use the same column as before. After repeating the ties that bound her to the destination, she sensed the parachute feeling signaling her arrival. She left the church, crossed the street, and climbed the stairs to the exhibition.

Twenty minutes later, she felt restless and disappointed. Neither Brady nor Gabe had reappeared. She had aimed for a time just after her previous visit reckoning that Gabe would return to solicit more customers for portraits. But it didn't happen. She saw a different young man escorting an older couple to the back room for a consultation, but no other employees. Giving in to the sense that waiting longer would be futile, she headed to the exit. Perhaps more could be learned by exploring the rear of the building from outside.

Descending the stairs, she stumbled on the bottom step. Her foot reached down to the pavement, but she misjudged the distance—or misjudged the way she could move in the long blue dress—and landed a bit wrong.

There was a twinge in her ankle, and her stomach gave a lurch. With a feeling of frustration, she knew the mishap had resulted in eviction. She didn't even need to look about. She heard car horns in the street and found herself on a crowded sidewalk standing before the picture window of a bank. Customers inside were queued up at the teller's counter. She was in full view, but no one gave her a second glance.

Aggie proceeded down the street until she found a small recess next to a shop with papered-over windows and a "for rent" notice on the door. Determined to resume her trip, she stepped into the alcove and looked about for a focus object. For the first time in her life, she found herself grateful for a bit of litter on the ground. It was the wrapper from a Mary Jane, one of her brother's favorite candies. She studied the trademark picture of the little girl in a full skirt and bonnet, and it brought her back almost immediately. The wrapper seemed to lose definition, and, once again, she heard horses and carriages in the street. Looping the strings of her reticule over her arm, she walked back along Broadway, passed the entrance to Brady's studio, and turned the corner.

She had taken only a few steps before a wagon pulled by two horses emerged from an adjacent alleyway. The driver was Gabe. She recognized his face and the disfigured hand with which he held the reins. Aggie stood stock still and tried to impress on her brain a detailed picture of his face. Almost as if he knew he was being observed, Gabe glanced down from his seat on the wagon. Their eyes met briefly. With an awkward movement, he covered his scarred hand. Then his brows drew together as he noted Aggie was studying his face, not his hand.

Without knowing why, Aggie bobbed her head in greeting. It came to her that he was studying her face as she had studied his. What did he see? Lined skin, red-orange hair streaked with silver, round wire-rimmed glasses. Surely not a threat. In a quick movement, he acknowledged Aggie with a nod of his head, then slapped the reins. The wagon moved into the crowded street. Aggie watched until it disappeared.

On the way back to Grace Church, she joined a group of pedestrians gathered at the corner. Stepping forward, she formed the intent to return, and felt a measure of satisfaction that she left the curb in 1862 and was back in the twenty-first century by the time she finished crossing the street.

***

Wells picked them up promptly. As they headed to St. Paul's, Aggie, Julie, and Abe compared notes. Abe had not seen Gabe at the Antietam exhibition. "He left before you arrived," Aggie explained. She told them about witnessing the young man drive away in the wagon.

"How did you know he'd be in the alley?" Abe asked.

"I didn't know. It was a hunch. No, let me take that back. I don't believe in hunches. I just didn't feel it was productive to stay. Brady had a different assistant working in the gallery, so I presumed Gabe was engaged in other duties. I remembered from our research that there was a kind of alley behind that row of buildings, so I decided to check it out."

When the bus arrived at St. Paul's, Aggie volunteered to go inside to collect the others. She found Viola and Lillian sitting at the back of the Chapel.

"Bernice should be back soon. She went for one last trip," Lillian said. She turned to Viola. "Would you mind if I waited on the bus? I'm a little tired."

It was the first time Aggie had heard Lillian express fatigue, and she wondered if the effort to explore the past without use of her walker had worn her out.

"You go ahead, dear," Viola said immediately. "Aggie can keep me company until Bernice gets back."

Aggie took the chair vacated by Lillian. Viola had what looked like a steno book and was writing notes in careful script. She finished a line, closed the book, and dropped it in her bag.

"There, I like to put down my impressions as soon as possible."

"I do the same," Aggie said, "and I always made sure my students took notes during an experiment. Now, of course, they can dictate into their phones. Were you able to get acclimated?"

"Yes, but it took a while. Bernice didn't care much for the horses. But after the first hour, we were stable. How did your group do?"

Aggie was about to respond when Bernice appeared behind Viola's chair and kissed her on top of her blue-white hair.

"Welcome back, Bernie. The bus is here," Viola said. "Aggie was going to tell me about getting acclimatized."

"It can wait," Aggie said, and they headed outside.

Wells navigated his way through the city's congestion, and in short order all the Remarkables were aboard. Aggie had expected lots of conversation on the way back to Connecticut, but the bus was strangely quiet. She was about to ask Julie about this but noticed her mentor had closed her eyes. Then a quiet snore sounded from the seat in front of them. It was Sal. A different snoring sound came from the front of the bus where Maurice sat with Lillian. Only Serena and Kat were still talking, but even these two seemed drowsy. Looking out the window, Aggie closed her eyes. In her mind, she pulled up an image of Gabe's face. Then Brady's face. Then the face she really longed to see. Jacob's face.

She must have fallen asleep because when she opened her eyes, they were pulling into the Lodge's curved driveway. As they got off the bus, Lillian reminded them of the debrief session. "We'll meet in the library after supper to share what we learned."

Aggie was glad to retreat to her apartment, surprised at how tired she felt. She tossed her notebook on the bed and took off the dress. It was a relief to rid herself of the garment.

She eyed the bed. No, another nap would make her groggy all evening. Instead, she picked up her copy of the *New York Times*. She hadn't had a chance to read it before they left for the city. Entering the bathroom, she examined the walk-in tub. The controls looked simple enough and she liked the wide tray that could hold reading material. When was the last time she had read in the bathtub? She couldn't remember. Churchill had often worked in the bathtub, dictating speeches and memoranda to a patient secretary sitting outside the door. If it was good enough for England's wartime prime minister, she decided, it was good enough for her.

She stepped in, placed a pencil and the arts section of the newspaper on the tray, sat, and turned on the hot water faucet. The water pressure was strong, and the bath filled quickly. Well, in for a penny, in for a pound, she thought, and pressed a button marked 'jets.' Bubbles swirled gently. It was like a hot tub, she decided. Not that she had much experience with hot tubs. Very relaxing. Wells and his fellow MIT designers had done a good job.

She pulled the tray closer and worked the crossword puzzle before perusing the rest of the arts section. A headline caught her eye: *Back to Its Roots: Grand Central Hosts Tribute to Portraiture and the City*. She folded the paper back and began reading:

Grand Central Terminal has always been more than just a train station. Since the official opening of the current building in 1913, Grand Central has housed restaurants and shops, a sports club and tennis court. During World War II the USO had an office in Grand Central, and in the 1950s Edward R. Murrow castigated Senator Joseph McCarthy from CBS's television studio located on the terminal's fifth floor.

What many may not know is that from 1923 to 1958 an art gallery operated on its sixth floor. Founded by Walter Leighton Clark and Edwardian-era portrait artist John Singer Sargent, the Grand Central Art Galleries were intended to showcase the works of American artists. The gallery was patronized by many of New York's elite and featured works by prominent painters and sculptors of the era.

Now the Metropolitan Museum of Art, in collaboration with the terminal's operator, has mounted an homage to New York's singular role in portraiture and its evolution through the decades. The exhibition, presented in the terminal's iconic Vanderbilt Hall, salutes the unique way artists have portrayed and memorialized the city's prominent and anonymous personalities —from life-sized paintings of wealthy captains of industry, to gritty photographs of mobsters, to a collection of modern-day caricatures skewering the celebrities of today's Gotham
....

Aggie finished the article. She remembered seeing the poster advertising this exhibit when she and Minnie explored the station during the summer. Several photographs accompanied the piece. One showed a Sergeant portrait of a society lady. Another featured line drawings of speakeasy jazz musicians. A third captured a panel of political cartoons. One of the sketches reminded her, for the second time that day, of the young artist from the Comic Convocation, Tyrece Vinci.

Aggie decided to clip the article to send to Minnie. She noted the exhibit would run another month. She'd be back home before it closed and could run into the city to see it. And yet, it was strange to contemplate resuming her old life, being away from the other Remarkables, away from Julie and Viola. Away from Abe.

The tub water had cooled. She grabbed a towel. It was time for supper and the debrief session.

Chapter 23 ~ Debrief

Aggie arrived at the library as Frank and Sal were pushing the armchairs into a circle. Wells sat typing at one of the computers. To her surprise, Axel was present as well, sitting at a carrel in the corner. He had a laptop open and was scanning a page of dense print. He didn't look up as the other seniors came in, started chatting, and found seats.

Lillian, Abe, and Maurice arrived together. Lillian looked rested. She had changed into a long-sleeved, kimono-like dress. Her eyes sought out Aggie, gave her an approving nod, then maneuvered her walker to an opening in the circle of chairs. Abe walked over to Axel, leaned in close, and murmured in the other man's ear. Axel didn't respond or look away from the screen, but somehow Aggie knew he was listening.

"Heard you had a rare stroke of luck," Maurice said to Aggie as he settled into an armchair. "This mission may not be such a long shot after all."

"We were lucky," Aggie said. "And Julie did a terrific job preparing us. I think it helped us adapt. How was Seneca Village?"

A faraway look came into his eyes. "It was quite something," he said at last. "I hope I can find the right words to explain it."

"Shall we begin?" Lillian looked about the room. "I want to start by saying we've had a truly lucky and successful day. Even though some of you had a rough time at the outset, you all eventually adapted. Before we discuss next steps, I want to hear from each of you. If you encountered any problems that could affect our mission, be honest and share them."

Frank led off. "No bad problems getting to our destination. Sal and I each had a half dozen evictions, but nothing too serious. Not sure what triggered them. Maybe just knowing there should be a skyline around the park, and never seeing the skyline, even from a rise. Eventually we were okay, though, and took turns making observations. Had time for two nice trips apiece. But, man, it was like we weren't in the city at all. I almost expected Davy Crockett to walk outa' the trees."

"Wrong era," Viola said mildly, her hands moving rhythmically as she crocheted. She had apparently finished the baby bonnet and was working on a matching sweater. "And wrong location. New York City is not Tennessee."

Frank grinned, and Sal picked up the tale. "By the time we got to Bethesda Terrace where the crews were working, we felt right at home. A man working with stone is a man working with stone."

"Was the angel there?" Bernice asked. "I've always liked that statue. She looks real down-to-earth. For an angel."

"Nope. It wasn't in place yet," Sal responded. "But let me tell you what they were doing." What followed was an enthusiastic and lengthy discourse on New Brunswick sandstone and Roman brick. "So that's about it," he concluded a trifle apologetically, after detecting Serena yawning daintily.

Lillian had noted the yawn as well and invited Serena and Kat to go next.

"We had a lovely day at Macy's," Serena began. "After getting acclimated, we took turns going through the shops. They were just beginning to organize actual departments." Serena proceeded with a surprisingly entertaining description of the millinery, notions, furnishings, and jewelry the two women had viewed.

"I saw this *darling* little brooch," Kat sighed. "I wished I could intervene—" She stopped as she noted the disapproval on Lillian's face. "Just so I could bring it back to, you know, study it," she finished hastily.

Viola and Bernice reported next. "Barnum's Museum was so not politically correct," Bernice stated by way of introduction.

"Bernice is right," Viola said. "But what a marvelous mixed bag. The sublime alongside the ridiculous. Accessibility was an issue, of course. I was pretty much limited to the lower floors, but there was plenty to see, even without going upstairs. There were quite a few taxidermy exhibits and a rather impressive mastodon skeleton. It was all a little jumbled. The collection, not the skeleton. Still, it was fascinating to see people view things they had never seen before. The Museum of Natural History didn't exist back then. It wasn't opened until 1869. Barnum's introduced other cultures, new ideas—"

"I saw Fiji war clubs and a hat made by a lunatic at Bellevue," Bernice interjected. "Definitely worth the two bits I paid to get in."

"Whoa Nelly," Frank interrupted. "You *paid* to get in? You didn't just travel back into the building? Where'd you get money for the tickets?"

Bernice gave him a deadpan look and didn't say anything. Aggie remembered the problem with commercial transactions in the past. You could bring back money authentic to the time period but couldn't use it. Leaving money in the past by purchasing something would constitute an attempted intervention. The result would be eviction.

"We had to do a little improvising," Viola said airily. "We considered trying to travel directly into the museum, but there's a clothing store on the site now, and it's got security cameras which made us a little nervous. Also, the building is configured differently, and we didn't want to travel right into the tank holding the orcas or a glass case displaying an Egyptian mummy. Bernice had a nice little solution which made things so much simpler. She worked it out for herself then showed me how to do it."

"Come on, Bernice. Spill the beans," Frank pressed. "We'd all like to have a little spending money in the past. What kind of trick did you have up your sleeve?"

Bernice smoothed the skirt of her housedress before speaking. "At Yankee Metal, the boss used to keep the stockroom keys in his pocket, just to piss us off. Said it was for inventory control, but it was all about power. Small-minded little jerk. Trying to yank us around about access to Coffee-mate and toilet paper. Funny thing, though, he kept misplacing his keyring and finding it in the oddest spots."

"You picked his pocket," Frank said in disbelief. "Don't tell me you picked his pocket."

"I didn't tell you I picked his pocket. I just said he kept misplacing his keys."

"So what poor soul misplaced his wallet in front of Barnum's Museum?" Julie asked. "And how do you not get evicted when you do things like that?"

"Bernice never disrupts the flow of events," Viola explained. "She wouldn't just take someone's wallet. That would be too memorable. But if a fat cat loses a coin or two, that's different, don't you see?"

Finally, it was Julie and Aggie's turn. Julie began by explaining their decision to use Grace Church as a staging area. "It has a phenomenal aura. Abe was our companion and helped us cross Broadway to the studio."

"So nice you had help," Serena remarked.

"I was glad to have help," Aggie said. She glanced at Abe, then looked away, remembering her initial embarrassment and the way he had held her hand. "And the point is we arrived and walked around without any serious glitches. Julie, do you want to describe what you saw along the street?"

"No," Julie said, surprising Aggie. "I can share my observations later. It's more important to fill people in on what you saw at Brady's studio. Who you saw." She turned to the group. "Aggie saw Gabe."

Everyone began talking at once, prompting Lillian to call for order. "Let Aggie and Julie continue," she directed, then smiled. "I told you we've had some luck, but let's hear the full story before we talk."

Nodding assent, Aggie related her encounter with the young man at the Antietam exhibition. "But again, I can't say with a hundred percent certainty that it was Gabe," she concluded. "He didn't offer his name."

"Think about the hand," Julie pressed. "It was just as Daniel described. How likely is it that two men associated with Brady would have the same injury? And you saw him driving a wagon. Gabe was a teamster."

Abe sat forward in his chair. "I agree with Julie. We should proceed on the assumption it was Gabe. Daniel's story aligns with what Aggie saw."

"Can you describe him for us?" Lillian asked. "Beyond his hand? It would be an enormous help if we knew what he looked like."

"I was frustrated by this," Aggie confessed. "I don't have the vocabulary to paint a complete picture. But I took some notes." She found the page in her notebook and read aloud. "Tall. Six feet, estimated. Slender. Lanky. Wavy black hair. Eyes dark brown. Straight eyebrows. Thick lashes. High cheekbones. Squarish jaw. No scars or moles. No beard or mustache." She looked up. "I'm sorry. That's all I have. I know it's inadequate."

"Did he have an Irish accent?" Wells asked. He had turned from his computer to join the discussion.

"Maybe a slight one," Aggie allowed. "I noticed a kind of lilt in his voice, a different cadence. At the time I just put it down to a more old-fashioned form of speaking."

"Tens of thousands of other people in nineteenth-century New York had Irish accents," Serena said dismissively.

"Abe," Wells said, "don't you know a guy? Didn't you contact a police sketch artist for that Remarkable from Rhode Island who was researching crime families in Providence? And he helped do sketches of the hoods the Remarkable saw at some 1950's underworld confab?"

Everyone looked at Abe, some seeming rather startled. "Yes," he acknowledged smoothly, "I do know a guy. He's pretty much retired, but I'm sure he'd be happy to assist us."

"That would be very helpful," Lillian said. "Will you make the arrangements?"

"Of course."

"I have a question," Aggie said. "Why don't we have everyone attend the Antietam exhibit and see the young man themselves? I can give you the date and the approximate time."

"The reception gets fuzzy on repeats," Frank explained. "Like when you're listening to the game in the car, and you get too far down the road, and all you hear is static. You fiddle with the channel and sometimes the play-by-play comes back, but sometimes not."

"You don't have SiriusXM?" Serena smirked.

"Why should I pay for radio that I can get for free?"

"But you just said—"

Frank raised his hands in surrender. "Julie, be a pal and explain what I'm talking about."

Surprisingly, Kat spoke first. "Look," she said to Aggie, "if you try to duplicate the exact same trip, it's fuzzy, like Frank said. It's like a smudged carbon copy. You can read it, but it's never as clear as the original. After high school I worked in the typing pool at Woolworth's Corporate, in the city. They always wanted, like, four carbons of everything. You had to be accurate, or you'd have to white out the mistake on every single sheet and that took, like, forever. The bottom copy was always blurry, and the execs would get all huffy like it was your fault or something.

"It's the same thing if you go to a destination where another traveler's just been. Sometimes you get evicted or can't see stuff very good." She shrugged. "I mean it can be done, but it's not ideal. You usually have to make a couple trips to get everything the first person got or wait a long time till the picture clears. That's why on some missions we have to be careful to limit our time and stuff, so no one has to look at a blurry carbon copy."

"Okay," Aggie said slowly, "the sketch artist seems like the way to go."

The others nodded in agreement. Viola patted Kat's arm. "That was very helpful, dear." Kat flushed and looked pleased.

"Are we done?" Serena pushed back her chair and looked around for her handbag.

"No, we're not done," Lillian replied sternly. "Maurice is going to share as well. He walked through Seneca Village, where Gabe lived as a child. It provides an important context for understanding the man we are seeking. We all operate within a framework created in our youth. Those early experiences are carried with us and linger in our character."

"Hold up a minute, Pops," Wells called out. "Let me text the sibs. They wanted to hear, too." He tapped on his phone, and in a minute, Erin, Carlos, and Angel entered the library, pulled up chairs, and settled in at the edge of the circle.

Maurice began by describing how he had parted ways with Frank and Sal, walking north through the park. Leaving the paved sidewalk, he had settled cross-legged on the ground under the branches of an oak tree. "Naturally the tree I sat beneath at the outset wasn't the tree I ended up under when I arrived. None of the trees that are there now pre-date the park. Thank you, Wells, for that bit of research."

"Glad to help, Pops."

"I arrived in a thunderstorm, so I adjusted my destination a few days and caught a nice warm afternoon. I was worried about attracting too much attention. Strangers stand out in a rural area, and Seneca Village was rural—way more like a country village than a part of the city. I walked along the lanes looking like I had a place to go. I saw a church and houses. Nice houses, not shanties, like they called them when they used eminent domain to take the land. The sketchy map Wells found online doesn't give you any kind of sense that the place was a settlement, but that's what it was. A settlement of free black folks who owned their homes and their land and had churches and a school for the children. There were some white folks there, too. I heard a man speaking German to his son. I saw a couple Irish girls. He tilted his head toward Aggie. Leastways, I assumed they were Irish. Redheads, both of them.

"After walking through the little town, I climbed right up the hill to Summit Rock. That was the highest point in the area back then, and it's the highest point in the park today. Olmsted sculpted a lot of other places when he designed the park, but that rock musta' landed there before the dinosaurs. It wasn't meant to be sculpted. You could see all the way across the Hudson from up there. It's a beautiful spot."

"I know an event planner who suggests Summit Rock for weddings all the time," Kat said. "Though why someone would want to walk up a hill in *heels,* I don't know. Plus, with outdoor weddings you never know about the weather. I mean you're going to put down money for the shoes and the dress and get your hair and makeup done, so why take a chance it's going to rain?"

"Beats me," Bernice shrugged. "We used to rent out our union hall for weddings. All it took was setting up the folding chairs and letting people use the kitchen."

Julie started to giggle. "Did you run into any nineteenth-century event planners, Maurice?"

He grinned. "No such luck. But it did seem like it served for romance even back then. I saw a couple of youngsters heading up the hill laughing and holding hands and making cow eyes at each other. It was after I started down, so they didn't see me."

"You naughty thing," Viola scolded. "You didn't spy on them, did you?"

"Oh, I didn't stay but a moment. But, you see, I saw them through the trees and …."

"What was it, Dad?" Erin asked.

"Well, here's the thing," Maurice said earnestly. "It was years before the Civil War, and the boy was white, and the girl was black. And they had just come up from that village where black families had their own homes and land, along with some white folks. And it was almost like the way things should always be. It was like something that still hasn't happened, even today. Maybe I'm not making myself clear."

"Oh, Maurice," Viola sighed, "you're being perfectly clear."

"Think of what they would have to face," Maurice continued. "In a handful of years their town will be gone, along with their churches and school. The war will begin, and the draft riots after that. There they were, maybe twelve, thirteen years old, and they had no idea about the hard times to come."

"They were making out at twelve?" Sal sounded a trifle shocked.

"I was making out at ten," Bernice said to no one in particular.

Maurice smiled wryly. "Well, I'm not sure this makes much sense, given all that, but what I brought back with me, after I saw those children, was *hope*. Despite what I knew was coming. The hope they had for a normal, happy life."

"History would have something to say about that," Viola said softly.

"Yes," Lillian added, "it always does."

***

It was late when the meeting broke up, but Aggie felt restless. Her earlier fatigue was gone, replaced by a strange kind of nervous energy. She had walked back to the kitchen with Erin, Carlos, and Angel who wanted to show her their master plan for the garden.

"We made a copy for you," Angel explained. "There's a list of what's planted and a sketch, and if you could sort of pencil in notes on the different sections, that would be a big help."

Aggie had taken the stapled sheets and promised to submit comments and suggestions. Afterward, she had not returned to her apartment, choosing instead to retreat to the fieldwork group's conference room where she used the giant coffee machine to make a cup of decaf. Sitting at the long table, she reviewed the garden plan. It didn't take long to write out her recommendations. The task was done by the time she finished her coffee.

She was suddenly aware of the lateness of the hour and the emptiness of the Lodge. It must be near midnight. Oddly, she didn't feel uncomfortable in the cavernous building.

The table still held many of the books Lillian had collected for their use. Aggie pulled a volume of Brady photographs toward her and began to leaf through the pages. She realized she had seen some of the portraits just that day and could use the book to identify them. She had recognized Robert Anderson but not John Adams Dix, George Meade but not Elmer Ellsworth. She felt a profound sadness as she jotted names in her notebook. These men had served and sacrificed, but most of their faces were unknown to her. And there were thousands upon thousands more who had served and sacrificed — soldiers, spouses, parents — without ever being memorialized in a single photograph.

Aggie closed the notebook and rose to her feet. She was still restless, but it was foolish to stay up any longer. She'd be exhausted in the morning. She turned off the conference room lights as she left and shut the door behind her.

Walking down the corridor toward the exit, she was surprised to hear the murmur of voices. A patch of light from the library cut across the shadows in the hall. Perhaps a few of the others had been infected with the same restlessness and stayed behind to talk or do research. She approached the library entrance intending to enter but stopped in the shadows. She had recognized the voices: Abe and Axel. She could see them sitting together engrossed in conversation.

"You see the Lincoln picture?" The question had come from Axel.

"Yes. It was like what we've talked about before. You see Lincoln's portrait. He is alive. Countless men are alive. But you know what's coming."

Axel grunted in response. "Nothing to be done. Lincoln pleads, nobody listen. *We are not enemies, but friends.* Good words, but nobody listen."

"I didn't see Brady or Gabe," Abe went on. "Only Aggie did. But I trust what she told us. She's a good observer, incredibly perceptive."

"How long you stay with her?"

"Twenty-five minutes, maybe more."

"Long time for a companion trip."

"I know. With her it's different … easier."

"You see something special in this one." It was a statement, not a question.

"Yes. I think so." He paused. "She's very strong. Smart."

"Would be good to find out more."

Aggie's cheeks felt warm. It wasn't right to stay hidden in the shadows like this. She moved forward into the light.

Axel saw her first. His face settled into a neutral expression, then he tilted his chin toward her, drawing Abe's attention to her arrival.

"I'm sorry," Aggie said. "I didn't mean to intrude."

"Is not an intrusion," Axel said, "but the time is late now. Too late for talk."

Rising to his feet, he nodded to Aggie, placed his wool cap on his head, and left the room. She watched him walk into the darkness at the end of the hall.

She turned back to see Abe regarding her cautiously.

"*We are not enemies but friends,*" she said. "It's from Lincoln's first inaugural, isn't it?"

"The last paragraph."

"How does it go on?"

She had expected him to look it up on his phone or refer to a book. But he didn't. Keeping his eyes on her face, he began reciting.

"We are not enemies but friends. We must not be enemies. Though passion may have strained, it must not break our bonds of affection. The mystic chords of memory, stretching from every battlefield and patriot grave to every living heart and hearthstone all over this broad land, will yet swell the chorus of the Union, when again touched, as surely they will be, by the better angels of our nature."

An emotion she could not name entered her heart. For the second time in a week tears filled her eyes and spilled over, but this time she didn't bother to blink them away.

"I thought Julie was the only one around here who memorized things," she said.

"Julie doesn't need to memorize, but I'm sure you've figured that out by now. As for me, I went to school in the Dark Ages when we all had to memorize. We were given passages and then had to stand in front of the class and recite. Scared the hell out of me as I recall, but it was good discipline."

She gave a small smile. "Helpful training for all that prepared nonsense you spout at your Welcome Wagon visits?"

"It's a skill that's come in handy," he admitted. He saw she had her notebook. "Did you come to use the library?"

"No. I was working in the conference room. I think I can identify some of the other portraits we saw today. I was on my way out when I saw the light."

He rose to his feet, picked up his denim jacket, and joined her at the door. "I think it's time to call it a night." He switched off the library lights. "Come on, I'll walk you home."

***

Aggie arose at daybreak, showered, and dressed. Despite the late night, she didn't feel exhausted. She felt restored. The emotion and intensity of the previous day, and the restless energy they produced, had receded. Her sleep had been deep and dreamless, and she awoke calm, ready for the next steps in their mission.

She was not surprised to hear tapping on her patio door. It was Abe. He was wearing blue jeans and a flannel shirt with the sleeves rolled up. She slid the door open and stood back to admit him.

"I'm sorry to intrude so early," he apologized, "but I wanted—"

She held up her hand to silence him and pointed to the table where two teacups had been placed, along with spoons, the sugar bowl, and the *New York Times*. The kettle began to whistle, and she went to the kitchen to retrieve it.

"Have a seat, Abe," she called.

"How did you know I was coming?"

"I didn't know you were coming. But after yesterday, I thought it likely." She poured the tea then placed her notebook next to him on the table. "I assume you want to see this. I've written out everything I can remember."

"I just came by to—"

"Did you come for some other reason?" she asked. "Because if you did, tell me now. After I finish my tea and the crossword puzzle, I'm going to the Lodge. Erin informed me that she and her brothers are making a full Irish breakfast in honor of our mission, and I intend to enjoy it."

He had picked up the notebook, but she had caught his attention. "A full Irish breakfast, eh? Good thing I walked an extra mile this morning."

She sat down in the opposite chair, picked up a pencil, and turned to the crossword puzzle. She glanced at the clock and jotted the time in the margin. She always tried to finish the puzzle within twenty minutes, sometimes making the self-imposed deadline, sometimes not.

There was silence for perhaps ten minutes before, wrinkling her brow, she erased an answer after recognizing the clue "Really fresh" probably referred to *rude* not *ripe*.

"Viola's good at crosswords, too."

She glanced up and saw Abe watching her. He had apparently finished reading her most recent entries. "Hush. I'm timing myself. I've only got a few more minutes, and I'm having trouble with this bottom section."

"You're on the clock? Who do you compete with?"

"Myself."

"Tough opponent."

She ignored him, finished filling in the last few boxes, and looked at the clock again. "Eighteen minutes. Should've been faster." She put down her pencil and studied Abe. He did look like Indiana Jones, she thought, but there were differences. His build was lankier, his nose thinner, his hair shorter. She didn't know what color eyes Indiana Jones had. Abe's eyes were brown. At the moment they looked quizzical.

"Are you ever going to level with me?" she asked abruptly. "I mean, what are we doing here?"

He regarded her warily. "I've always leveled with you. Except for that necessary bit of subterfuge about the Welcome Wagon. What we're doing here is attempting to discover answers, historical answers—"

She cut him off. "No. What are *we* doing *here*? You and me. These visits. This notebook. If there is something you want to know about my time travel, or about me, why don't you just ask? Tell me what you're searching for, what you're worried about. Isn't that part of our deal? Keeping me posted on your thoughts?"

He sipped his tea in what she suspected was a delaying tactic then sat back and placed his hand on the cover of her notebook. "About this: When you record things, write them down, you're not you. You're a scientist. A trained observer. Most Remarkables don't document the same way you do. It's like you don't even know everything you're seeing until it's on paper."

"But we all take notes. And notes, even if taken shortly after an experience, are not necessarily accurate. People exaggerate or misremember — well, not Julie, of course, but most people — or their biases creep in. What makes these notes different?"

"I'm not talking about other people, Aggie. I'm talking about you. There's something about the way your brain works. I can see what you see because you're looking at what I need to look at. You're not describing what you feel, but your writing is full of emotion."

Aggie felt slightly breathless. "Why don't you spin out your hypothesis, whatever it is."

He picked up his cup, drank the last of his tea, then contemplated the pattern of blue flowers along the rim. "It's not time yet."

She crossed her arms and regarded him solemnly. He didn't look like he was open to argument. "Then I'll wait until you're ready." She pointed to her notebook. His hand still rested on its cover. "Do you have any questions about what's in there?"

Abe didn't answer immediately. Instead, he rose from his chair, carried the empty teacups into the kitchen and put them in the dishwasher. When he returned, he sat down, placed his hands flat on the table and began. "Tell me about how you stumbled leaving Brady's studio."

Aggie was surprised. She hadn't thought anything about it at the time. She had recorded the incident in her notes but hadn't mentioned it at the debriefing session.

"I don't know how it happened. Maybe it was just the long skirt or not paying attention."

"Are you generally a clumsy person?"

"No. Not so far, anyway."

"Tell me exactly where it happened."

"Just as I was leaving. I stumbled on the stairs and got evicted. I walked down the street, found a new focus object, and went back again."

"Did it happen at the top of the stairs? Halfway down?"

"No, at the bottom. The very last step."

"You're sure?"

She raised an eyebrow.

"Okay," he said. "You're sure. Is it possible that the order was different? Maybe you were evicted first, then stumbled when you were back in the present?"

She considered this. "Yes, it's possible. Look," she placed a tentative hand on his arm. "What is bothering you?"

He covered her hand with his. She felt her heart pounding, and for a moment they sat in silence. Then, with a shake of his head, he let go and rose to his feet. "All in good time. For now, shall we go try that full Irish breakfast?"

Chapter 24 ~ Concrete

Perhaps because they had found Gabe and verified part of Daniel's story, the day seemed to speed by. At breakfast Aggie picked up a heightened sense of excitement from every member of the fieldwork group—excitement that couldn't be attributed solely to the lovely spread of sausages, potatoes, puddings, and homemade bread the young chefs had set out in the Lodge dining hall.

Even Lillian, her hair done up in a bun, had abandoned her normal measured pace. When the group members arrived in the meeting room, they found her standing before the whiteboard—one hand grasping her walker and the other an eraser—studying the four questions they had listed before going to New York. She waited only long enough for everyone to find a seat before beginning.

"Look at our first question." She used the eraser to point. "'Can we adapt?' The answer is yes. We may still experience difficulties, but each trip will be easier. Now look at our second question. 'Can we find Gabe and verify his connection to Mathew Brady?' This, too, has been resolved." With a few decisive strokes, Lillian rubbed out the first two questions.

"Now we get to question three: Did Gabe gain possession of Brady portraits, specifically, a portrait of Abraham Lincoln?" To Aggie's surprise, Lillian erased the third question as well, then faced the group. "I recommend we assume Gabe has at least one Brady portrait—maybe more—and jump directly to question four. It is the ultimate question for this mission: *Where are the portraits buried?*

"There are practical reasons to take this approach. According to Daniel, if his grandfather obtained glass plates from Brady, it was probably in 1872. That was a year of financial turmoil for both the photographer and the country as a whole, and Brady struggled to keep his business afloat. Those of you who researched this period found that for months at a time possession of many of his portraits moved back and forth between Brady, his creditors, bankruptcy lawyers, and teamsters bringing things to and from warehouse storage. Consider the logistics of a stakeout under those circumstances. Surveillance of multiple subjects in multiple locations over a prolonged period of time is simply not feasible."

Using her walker, Lillian moved to the conference table, sat down and leaned forward. "On the other hand, concentrating on the final question, gives us a much narrower focus. 'Where are the portraits buried?' The inscription in Daniel's Bible says, 'Lincoln buried at home,

April 1882.' That means a single month and a single location, assuming we can pinpoint the location. Surveillance is possible within those parameters. Does anyone disagree?"

No one did, although Frank murmured something about "a pretty big assumption."

Lillian picked up on his comment. "Wells and Abe are on their way to the city. They left after breakfast. Clearly, we need a short list of possible locations. The place to do that kind of research is the New York Public Library. Daniel believes his grandfather worked as a teamster and lived on the Upper West Side, near Harlem. That's a starting point. Library staff members have assisted us in the past. Once they develop a list of possible sites, and we know what Gabe looks like, Abe can scout the locations. The sketch artist is arriving this morning to meet with Aggie. As soon as we have a picture, we'll text a copy to Abe so he knows who to look for."

"Such nice people at the library," Viola commented. "They have folks who do nothing but work with maps, and they can pull up ownership documents, census records, business names, lot lines, all good material."

"We'll still need a fair amount of luck," Frank pointed out.

"We will," Lillian conceded. "And we've already had more luck than we had any right to expect."

"Some missions, the luck runs the other way," Frank noted, "but maybe this one is destined to be a winner."

Lillian nodded. "We're going to adjourn early today, but I don't want you taking the day off. I want you to pack your bags. We'll head off as soon as we get a location and stay in the city while conducting our surveillance. You'll need to bring your period clothing, as well as modern dress, and anything else required for a two- or three-day stay. That's it, folks. Go get ready."

***

Aggie met with the police sketch artist—an avuncular man with dark-framed glasses and rather unruly hair—in one of the Lodge's small meeting rooms. He introduced himself as Yanni and shook her hand before setting out his drawing pad and pencils.

"Abe may have told you I'm rather old school," he began. "I don't work with those computer-generated features. I find it takes away from the conversation, and, for me, the conversation is the important thing. The more we talk, the more likely I am to find the picture in your head and get it on paper." Yanni pulled out a chair for her at the table, then sat down next to her. He selected a pencil, then gave her a smile. "Now let's see what we can do."

What followed was a series of gentle questions punctuated by swift moves of his pencil across the paper. Fascinated, Aggie watched the penciled lines begin to recreate the face she remembered from Brady's studio. She was reminded of the caricature artist she had watched and mentioned the encounter to Yanni.

"Ah, yes. Caricature artists are our brothers- and sisters-in-arms. They start with a face and look for a story. An ordinary person becomes a samurai or James Bond or Batgirl."

"The artist I saw turned a teen into Robin Hood," she said. "It was wonderful."

"With us, it's the other way around. We begin with the words of the witness. Only the story. We work backwards to find the face."

After an hour of back-and-forth conversation, Yanni held up his sketch pad, and Aggie looked into the eyes of the young man she had seen in Brady's studio. "That's him," she said.

She caught Yanni studying her own face rather than the sketch. After a moment he nodded, satisfied. "I think we've done well, then. I can tell by your expression. If we've caught the right face, there's a look of recognition in the witness."

He left the sketch with her and once again shook hands. As he donned his overcoat, Aggie gave in to her curiosity. "Have you known Abe a long time?"

"We go back quite a few years," the artist admitted. "If he had a difficult job, he might call me in for a consult. Law enforcement is a bit of an extended family in that way."

"He was a police officer?"

"Not exactly. More of a solo operator brought in for special investigations. Undercover stuff. All rather hush-hush. Never shared a lot of information about his caseload, but invariably came in with good access. Red tape cut in advance, that sort of thing. Always enjoyed working with him, I must say. Always had a story to help me find the face."

***

When Aggie passed the sketch to Lillian, the older woman studied the face intently. "Yes, this will help," she said simply. "And I'll have a copy made for Daniel. He doesn't have a single picture of his grandpa. It's hard when a face you love is only in your memory. And Daniel's memory is failing him. This will be a comfort to him and a joy."

After leaving Lillian, Aggie returned to her apartment. Elizabeth had cancelled her class—something to do with a private student—so the afternoon was free. Still, she adhered to Lillian's admonition to get ready for New York. Pulling her suitcase out from under the bed, she began packing. Fortunately, Elizabeth had provided garment bags for their period clothing, so she didn't have to fold the long blue dress into her luggage.

When she finished, she rolled the suitcase into the living room, then looked about restlessly. She was plagued with the feeling that she should be doing something useful. But all kinds of questions were swirling in her brain. Far too many of them, in her opinion, focused on Mr. Abraham Irving.

Outside her window, she saw another roost of starlings gathering in a maple tree whose leaves displayed bright splashes of red. The birds seemed to vibrate with excitement. "I feel the same way," she said. "Ready to take off."

Aggie grabbed her jacket and headed for the door. One thing she could do was practice by the barn. It was windy outside and a little chilly, but the sun was shining and the sky cloudless and blue. The barn, however, was busy. As she approached, she spotted Maurice conducting a practice session with some of the rookies.

Aggie turned back toward the Lodge and walked to the garden. Entering through the gate, she saw Viola, seated on a bench, chatting with Carlos who was harvesting Brussels sprouts.

"Your dad knows just what to do with these," Viola was saying as Aggie joined them. "I love it when he roasts them with parmesan cheese. I used to hate Brussels sprouts. Probably because my own dear mother overcooked them and stunk up the house."

Carlos laughed, and Aggie joined in. "They have sulfur compounds in their cells," she explained. "The compounds break down when you cook them, and new compounds form. Like hydrogen sulfide. Not a pleasant aroma."

"Dad says they're best after they've been hit with a frost," Carlos said. "He said to leave most of them. I'm just supposed to fill this basket and trim off the stems."

"Listen to me, sweetie," Viola cautioned. "I want you to be careful working with those sharp knives in the kitchen. Your brothers and sister are always chattering, and one little loss of attention means you'll be asking Mirlande to sew you up."

Carlos pulled the gardening gloves from his hands and spread his fingers wide. "Let me see," he said, his brow creased with exaggerated worry. "One, two, three, four .... Um, I seem to have all ten fingers still in place." He grinned.

She pulled off her hat and batted him playfully. "Don't get fresh, young man. Now get these into the kitchen, so they'll be ready for

Maurice." Still grinning, Carlos hoisted the basket, carried it to the kitchen door, and disappeared inside.

"Nice kid," Aggie said when he was gone.

"Very nice," Viola agreed. "Were you looking for me?"

"No, just taking a walk. I was going to practice by the barn, but Maurice is giving lessons. So, I thought I'd come by here and see how things looked. Fall gardens need attention."

For a moment, both women surveyed the fenced-in plot. The sun lit every corner, and the gusty wind caused the leaves to flutter and wave around them.

"Did I see Abe coming out of your apartment this morning?" Viola asked abruptly. The question came out of the blue, and Aggie suddenly found herself embarrassed. It hadn't occurred to her that someone might have seen them emerge together that morning. And it really hadn't occurred to her that someone might speculate about what that meant. She recalled that Viola's apartment was just down the hall from her own. She must have seen them as they left for breakfast.

Aggie stumbled into speech. "Well, yes, but it wasn't … I mean … he came in by way of the patio. Not last night," she hastened to explain. "Early this morning." She felt herself blushing. *People her age weren't supposed to feel this way.* "He just wanted to read my notebook."

Viola laughed. "That question came out a little awkward, didn't it? I wasn't trying to butt into your business. I just noticed and wondered what he was up to. He wanted to see your notes, eh? Silly old fuss budget. Not you, dear, *him.* Why don't you come along to my apartment for a bit? It's getting chilly out here, and I can ask Bernice over to make us a nice cup of hot chocolate."

***

Viola arranged the get-together with a quick call from her cell phone. "Yes, at my place," she directed. "Use your key. Can you get things going? It will take me a few minutes to toddle back to the barracks. And, Bernie, bring marshmallows, but don't let Mirlande see you. She's gotten strict since my last check-up. Oh, and see if you can get Sal to join us. Yes, I think so. Okay. Bye."

Viola looked at Aggie and explained. "The three of us, Sal, Bernie, and me, we've done a lot of fieldwork shifts together, so we've gotten close."

By the time they arrived at Viola's apartment, Bernice had the cocoa ready, and Sal was sitting on the sofa, his hands cupped around a steaming mug. Viola's orange tabby had curled up next to him and was purring contentedly.

"Pumpkin loves Sal," Viola said to Aggie.

"Pumpkin loves everyone," Bernice noted. "Except Serena."

"Well, Pumpkin tried to sit on her lap once, and Serena stood up and dumped her off and got all huffy about cat hair on her outfit," Viola sniffed. "Pumpkin took the high road after that little encounter, but she hasn't forgotten."

Aggie laughed and collected a mug of cocoa before joining Sal on the sofa. Viola's living room was decorated in shades of blue. Family photos sat on shelves, and books were piled on the coffee table. Wood blinds on the windows were slanted open to let in the light. Aggie could see an elevated planter ablaze with orange and yellow marigolds on the patio.

"Must be a cold front coming in," Bernice said. "That's why Vi wanted hot chocolate. Some people have joints that ache when the weather turns. Vi's got a sweet tooth." A sly look appeared on her face. "What do you have a hankering for right now?" she asked the older woman. "Besides the cocoa and marshmallows?"

"Ginger cake," Viola answered promptly. "My mother's recipe."

Triumphantly, Bernice held up a tote bag. "Guess what I made?"

"You didn't!"

"Yes, I did. Who wants a slice?"

In another few minutes, they were happily sipping cocoa and eating cake.

"Let me share a story about this cake," Viola said suddenly. "Sal and Bernie have heard it before, but they won't mind hearing it again. When Henry and I were courting—Henry was my husband—he came over one afternoon just as I was getting ready to bake ginger cake. Henry was delighted because he loved that cake. Plus, my parents were out, so it was just the two of us. He put on a frilly apron, and said he was going to help, and we got to laughing. I had already beaten the eggs. They were sitting ready, room temperature, on the kitchen table. But we buttered up the pan, and measured out the flour and molasses, and poured the batter in, and popped it in the oven. Then we kissed. Our first kiss."

She smiled at the memory. "Then Henry looks into my eyes and says," Viola paused dramatically, "'When do we add the eggs?' I had totally forgotten to put them in the batter. Henry pulled open the oven door, and I grabbed the eggs, and we stirred them in and slammed the door shut."

"Were there scrambled eggs in your cake?" Aggie asked.

"Not a one," Viola said with satisfaction. "You see, we got to the cake *quickly*, and stirred before it had set too long in the oven. It was still batter." She waited a beat. "I learned if you act quickly, you can correct a mistake."

Aggie narrowed her eyes, a faint suspicion rising in her mind.

"Yep," Bernice concurred, "like Viola says, with certain things, it's all about the timing. Like putting fruit cocktail in a Jell-O mold. You don't do it at the start because it'll sink to the bottom. You want it kinda' suspended in the middle. You pour in half the Jell-O and stick it in the fridge for ninety minutes to get it part way set. *Then* you add the fruit and top it off. Now Jell-O's a forgiving product. If you miss the ninety-minute mark, and it's ninety-five minutes, or a hundred minutes, you can still add the fruit. You don't have forever, though, because at some point your Jell-O's going to gel."

Aggie looked around uncertainly. "Are you talking about what I think you're talking about?"

"There's certain things we're not supposed to talk about," Viola answered quickly. "But sometimes it's helpful to sort of speculate. Just in case."

Sal cleared his throat. "It's a little bit of a delicate topic around here. With Lillian especially. I don't know exactly what happened in the start-up years with the Remarkables, but I think some of the early folks started going crazy trying to change the past. Got themselves addicted, in a way. All for nothing. I wouldn't be surprised if Lillian kicked out anyone she suspected of spending too much time experimenting with intervention."

"Abe used to talk about it," Bernice said, "but then he didn't anymore. Not much, anyway. Maybe Lillian found a way to shut him down."

"What about Maurice?" Aggie asked.

"Maurice keeps his thoughts to himself," Viola said.

"What are you trying to tell me?" Aggie demanded. "And why me?"

The other three shared a look, then Sal spoke. "Well, first you should understand that what we say shouldn't leave this room."

Aggie raised one hand, palm up, as if taking an oath.

"Okay," he continued. "And 'why you' is because Viola sort of picked up on a coupla' quirks in the way you travel. Like what you said about the raindrops on your blouse. Now maybe you misremembered that detail, but there's other things. Abe had you skip beginners' classes. And he's like a skittish colt every time he's near you. Every time he looks at you."

"Maybe he just likes her," Bernice suggested.

"Bernie, we are not in seventh grade here," Viola said repressively. "A more important thing is he's reading her notes. He thinks something's up." She addressed Aggie directly. "Lillian might have clamped down on Abe's interest in intervention, but he can't really let go of the idea, either. It came to me that you might have something special going on. Nothing to worry about, but I thought it would be a good idea to have this little chat. Sal can explain it better."

Aggie looked at the square-built, tough-looking man. He was wearing a sweatshirt with a "Tosi & Sons" logo on the front. "I don't exactly have a cooking story to share," he began. "The kitchen's not really my bailiwick. I pretty much leave that up to the Missus."

"You're impossible," Viola said.

"I know," Sal admitted without rancor, "but I think I can help get our point across." He turned to Aggie. "You know I have my own contracting business. Masonry, mostly. We build walls, do fancy brickwork, and concrete. We do a lot of concrete. Concrete is one of your most versatile building materials. It's economical and durable, too. Now when we pour a new sidewalk, or a slab for a patio, say, there'll always be a couple kids who come along with a stick and want to put their initials in that brand new slab. And they can do it, too, at least for a while. But then, you know what happens? The concrete hardens. And pretty soon, you can't put your initials in it anymore. Course, if there *are* initials—if the kids acted quick and carved the slab before it was set—then those initials are staying. They're always going to be there."

Aggie looked at the others with a growing sense of understanding and astonishment.

"You see," Viola began, "a few of us have a theory about intervention. Most Remarkables think the idea of changing the past is a pipe dream. But what if a traveler—an especially talented and unusual traveler who has a couple of *quirks* in her technique—wants to change something minor from *the very recent past?* Something that happened ten minutes ago? An hour ago? Our thinking is that maybe those events are more malleable. Most Remarkables think time travel is about going really far back. Decades or centuries back. That's what fieldwork is about. But what if you go just a little way back? Just long enough to add the eggs or the fruit cocktail. Just long enough to carve your initials. What then? It's something to think about."

Aggie didn't know how to respond, but no one seemed to expect her to. There was a moment of quiet before Viola stretched, used her cane to rise from her chair, and gathered up her mug and plate. "No, no," she waved Bernice back to her seat. "Let me do it. If we're going on a mission, I need to move more. I get stiff sitting too long. I'll just put these things in the dishwasher, and they'll be done in a jiffy."

"Has anyone heard from Abe or Wells?" Sal asked.

"No," Bernice said, "but Wells put me on a group text, so I'll get an alert as soon as he hears."

Aggie's thoughts were still on intervention. "What you're suggesting is a theory—an alternate theory—to what Lillian believes. Is it more than that? Is it something you've done?"

"Nope, not me," Bernice said. "Sal and I tried, but—"

A loud chime sounded from Bernice's tote bag. Jumping up, she pulled out her phone and studied the screen before holding it aloft for all to see. "Bingo," she said triumphantly. "They've got a destination."

"Yessiree Bob," Sal exclaimed. He used the arms of his chair to push himself to his feet.

Viola emerged from the kitchen clapping her hands in delight. She gave Aggie an apologetic look. "I know you have questions, dear, but I think we need to adjourn for now. You've probably packed, but some of us," she gestured in Sal's direction, "haven't. We can always talk about this again later. We just wanted you to know we're here for you."

Aggie returned to her apartment with a slab of ginger cake wrapped in waxed paper and a flurry of questions in her mind. She set the plate on the counter, retrieved her notebook from the bedroom, and sat at the kitchen table pondering how to record what she had learned about the alternate theory of intervention. Stories about ginger cake and Jell-O, concrete sidewalks and kids carving their initials—such things were not easily reduced to a set of orderly observations. She tried her best to summarize her thoughts in a few careful sentences, then set her pencil down. *Is it more than a theory? Is it something you've done?* She hadn't really gotten an answer, at least not from Viola.

Chapter 25 ~ Night Visiting

"We're leaving tomorrow after breakfast," Lillian announced. "Double-check your suitcase, and make sure you have your medications."

"Mirlande makes you triple check," Viola noted. "Plus, she gives a list to our chaperone."

"Should I take offense at being relegated to the role of chaperone?" Abe asked mildly.

"Oh heavens, you're not the chaperone," Viola retorted. "That's Lillian. You need a chaperone."

"Actually, Mirlande will be joining us in the city," Lillian said. "She's driving separately and will meet up with us in the afternoon."

"Mirlande likes to be with the fieldwork groups," Julie explained to Aggie. "She watches out for overexertion and dehydration, and meds, of course."

It was the morning following the text alert from Wells. Group members were gathered in the dining room sipping coffee—except for Bernice, who had her cappuccino—while going over their final preparations.

"We're confident about the destination," Wells said, unfolding an oversized street map of Manhattan and spreading it on the table, "and incredibly lucky."

"What'd I tell you," Frank said. "Lady Luck's with us on this one."

"It's not too far from Columbia University," the young man continued, "and the Cathedral of St. John the Divine, and Morningside Park. Right on the dividing line between Harlem and the Upper West Side." He pointed to the map. "Now check this out. In the 1880s, the university's not there, the cathedral's not there, and the park's not there. What you've got instead is Bloomingdale Lunatic Asylum, Leake & Watts Orphanage, and a huge swath of city-owned land that will eventually become the park. Farmers use that land illegally to graze their cows. So, we've got open space here, then you go south, hit 110th Street, and, boom, you're in the city."

"How did you locate the spot?" Sal asked. "Was there a land deed or something?"

Abe and Wells exchanged a look and smiled. "I just love librarians," Abe said. "You know those illegal cows? Guess who was fined two dollars for using city land for his livestock?"

"Oh my," Viola said sadly. "I'm glad you found it, but just think. Gabe fought in the Civil War, had a whole lifetime of experiences, and the one record we find is the nineteenth-century equivalent of a parking ticket."

"Abe, did you actually see Gabe?" Julie demanded.

Abe nodded. "I was scouting along the road, and he drove out in a wagon. Lillian had sent me Yanni's sketch, and it was a good likeness. He was older by twenty years, but I'm sure it was the same man. The area is odd," he continued, shaking his head. "I walked around a fair bit, and one minute you swear you're in the country, the next, you see rows of shops and saloons."

"Can you get close to the house?" Frank asked.

"I think so," Abe said. "There's bushes all along the sides, like the ones out by the barn."

"Lilacs," Aggie said.

Julie's brow wrinkled, and she held out a hand signaling she had an idea. "Daniel said his grandpa called hard times the *fearful trip*. That's from 'O Captain! My Captain!' It's one of Walt Whitman's poems about the death of Lincoln."

The others were looking at her blankly, but Abe leaned forward and signaled her to continue.

"In the poem, the country is the ship and Lincoln the fallen captain. I don't know why I didn't think of it at the time. Daniel said Gabe attended Lincoln's funeral. So the lilacs," she paused and seemed to calculate something in her head, "they're from the other Whitman poem about Lincoln. *When Lilacs last in the dooryard bloom'd, and the great star early droop'd in the western sky in the night, I mourn'd, and yet shall mourn with ever-returning spring.* It's an elegy."

"You're not going to recite the whole thing, are you?" Frank asked a little fearfully.

"Of course not. It's 206 lines. Free verse. It would take too long. But it's beautiful. Everyone should read it."

"I'll put that right on my 'to do' list," Frank grinned, "but what does it mean? Not the poem, the bushes."

"I think it means Gabe and Lula read Whitman and revered Lincoln," Abe said. "I'm beginning to agree with Frank. Luck may be with us on this mission."

"Are we staying at the Yale Club again?" Kat asked.

Aggie leaned toward Julie to whisper. "We stay at the Yale Club?"

"Abe has some kind of pull with them," Julie whispered back. "He gets VIP treatment there."

"Yes," Lillian said in answer to Kat. "We'll check in, then send teams out in shifts." Quickly, she reviewed the plans. Each group member would be assigned to a team. Wells would shuttle one team at a time to the Upper West Side, and the travelers would take turns conducting surveillance. Then they would return to the Yale Club and pass on what they had learned before a new team set out.

"We'll check each day in April 1882, the month listed in Daniel's Bible. We shouldn't need to stay long on any particular day," Lillian added. "Unfortunately, because of the rural setting, there isn't likely to be the same opportunity for conversation that Aggie had at the Antietam exhibit."

"And if a man's got a valuable Lincoln portrait, that's not something he's likely to confide to a stranger that walks up to his place out of the blue," Sal added.

Lillian nodded. "We'll go at night, survey the yard, and see if there is evidence of digging or disturbance to the ground. Once we pinpoint a day, we'll go hour by hour."

Julie was looking thoughtful. "We still have no idea what the precipitating event was. Why does Gabe bury the portraits after having them for a decade? I can't see the answer. Still, I think we're on the right track."

"Yep, it feels like we're getting close," Frank said with a grin, tapping his fingers on the table as if playing a tune. The others seemed to share his excitement. Viola nodded and Bernice raised her cappuccino in a toast. Even Serena was engaged, her phone nowhere in sight.

A shadow crossed Lillian's face. "I know we're feeling lucky, but remember, we're dealing with uncertainty. Sometimes you hit the jackpot—"

"And sometimes you go bust," Sal finished. "Our kind of travel is always a roll of the dice."

At that Abe leaned forward. "Yes, it's a roll of the dice, but even missions that fail give us *something.* You roll a one instead of a six, but a one isn't *nothing.*"

"That's a double negative," Viola said.

Abe laughed. "Okay, but do you see the point? Sometimes we learn things we didn't set out to learn but learn anyway. Sometimes we miss the main prize but find some other reward."

Aggie glanced at the others. No one seemed particularly interested in discussing the philosophical implications of missing the main prize.

"Um, so does that kind of wrap it up?" Wells asked.

"Yes, I think we're all set," Lillian said. "Abe, do you have anything else?"

"Just one more thing. I'm having a little social gathering at my place tonight. About eight. Kind of a send-off for our group. We'll have music, and a few of the rookies are coming, so it'll be a good chance to mingle. I know some of you retire early before a mission, but if you can make it, that would be great."

"Refreshments?" Frank asked.

"Of course." Abe grinned. "Erin is bringing a cheese tray, and I'm putting a few treats together as well."

"Make those little hot dogs wrapped in dough," Bernice directed. "You know ...."

"Pigs in a blanket," Frank supplied.

"I'll see what I can do."

With that, the meeting broke up. In the Lodge's entrance hall, Aggie paused to pull on a cardigan. The wind had picked up, and gray clouds hurried across the sky.

"Will you come tonight?" Abe was at her elbow. He had donned his denim jacket and held a cap in his hand. "Since I've imposed on you for morning tea on more than one occasion, I hope you'll let me return your hospitality."

"With pigs in a blanket?"

"Precisely."

Aggie was caught off guard by the expression on his face. It was as if her answer really mattered. "I'll try to make it," she said.

***

Back in her apartment, Aggie opened her notebook. She put the date at the top of a new page and began writing:

Abe is right. You always learn something, even if it is not the thing you set out to learn. Rolling a one means you have at least one thing you didn't have before. And sometimes rolling a one is better than rolling a six. It depends on the game you are playing.

She stopped and put down her pencil. I'm getting rather obscure, she thought. But the principle was correct. She had talked to her students about learning from failure, and times when scientists found something while looking for something else. Edison's quote on the subject was probably apocryphal, but she liked it anyway: "I have not failed. I have discovered 10,000 ways to not make a lightbulb."

She usually saved her lesson on science's grand accidental discoveries for after Christmas vacation, when many of the kids, especially those from tough homes, returned to school with a load of disappointment. Resentment, as well, aimed primarily at their better-off fellows who appeared in class wearing new name-brand sneakers or flashing a shiny cell phone. January was also a good time to encourage her students to enter the various robotics contests and science fairs held in the spring.

"I've put a list of competitions in the basket on my desk," she would announce. "Check them out. Some offer cash awards and scholarships."

The lesson then began with a discussion of penicillin. "Imagine finding something that will save millions of lives just because you forgot to put the top back on a petri dish, and mold started growing. For humans, it's the most important mold in the world. But penicillin isn't the only fascinating accident. There are so many others, each with its own story: x-rays, microwave ovens, plastic, super glue, the pacemaker—"

"Viagra," Conor Pulaski called out from his seat in the back of the room. Several of the girls covered their mouths in pretend shock or erupted in giggles.

Aggie didn't miss a beat. "You're right," she countered. "What were the scientists actually looking for?"

"A treatment for angina."

"And what is angina?"

"Constriction of blood vessels to the heart. It causes chest pain."

"And does Viagra work as an effective treatment for angina?"

"Nope."

"What does it mean to say that blood vessels are constricted?"

Conor used his fingers to form a circle, then moved his hands together, making the circle smaller.

"Right again, Mr. Pulaski."

The other students watched the quick back-and-forth with fascinated interest.

Aggie had regarded Conor thoughtfully. He had been relatively quiet in class following the principal's failed effort to expel him after his stunt with the file cabinet. She had received a teary, grateful phone call from Conor's mother, who had moved in and out of Polish in a rather bewildering way, but Conor himself had not said much.

"Okay, Mr. Pulaski," she said at last. "Let's explore this in a little more depth."

The rest of the class had gone quite well, with students working in groups to investigate "successful mistakes." But with the clang of the bell at the end of the period, the bubble broke, conversations sprang up, and kids catapulted from their seats heading toward the door.

"How'd you know that shit?" one of Conor's buddies demanded with a laugh.

"Uncle's got angina," she heard him mumble with a wholly uncharacteristic trace of embarrassment in his voice. "I'll catch up with you," he told his friend, then stopped at her desk. Aggie noted that Conor was not one of the students wearing new sneakers. She also doubted he had a new cell phone.

"I'm not a dummy, you know," he said, almost as if reluctant to say anything at all.

Aggie remained determinedly matter of fact but spoke with careful emphasis. "Believe me, Conor, I know—I absolutely know—you are *not* a dummy."

"Okay then." He picked up one of the science fair lists from the basket, folded it carefully, and put it in his backpack.

"Okay then," she repeated as he walked out the door. It was a good memory. One of Conor's first steps toward that scholarship from Hytech.

Hytech. That brought her back to the present. She needed to call Minnie and Roscoe. She hadn't spoken to either of them in a few days. She got hold of her sister first.

"I am so frazzled," Minnie said breathlessly in answer to Aggie's queries. "I have a presentation tomorrow on our new program, so I have to face a roomful of bigwigs. Plus, it's going to be video conferenced to Canada and India and working through the time zone issues was a nightmare. Oh, and to make it even more fun, I'm bringing a couple of the technical people from the development team, and they always manage to be both barely civilized and completely contemptuous when they have to answer questions from mere mortals."

Aggie laughed. "You'll be brilliant. But I won't keep you. Tell me quickly, though, how are Joe and the boys?"

"Oh, they're fine. Joe bought the kids an old pick-up truck to tinker around with and get up and running. They'll have to get it up and running because *at the moment it doesn't run.* Joe had it towed to the house. The boys are acting like they won the lottery. Oh, by the way, our drone group has been in contact with that robotics coach. Wells? Apparently, it's been one big engineering love fest. Our guys here started playing war games out in the parking lot with spy drones and prototype zappers. But then the party-poopers in HR started losing sleep about a drone falling onto someone's SUV and scratching the paint, so they got moved to the back field. The guys, not the SUVs. Anyway, sorry Ags, I've got to go."

Aggie's conversation with her brother was equally brief. Roscoe talked rapturously about rehearsals then asked her how things were going. "Are you enjoying your senior seminars? Should I plan on attending your big community theater opening night?"

"Definitely not. I told you, it's just a few skits and theater games. Most of our time is spent listening to speakers. And they've been very educational. We even took a field trip into the city to see sites related to the lectures. We're going in again tomorrow."

"*The City,*" Roscoe said reverently. "I love the 'second city' but my first love will always be *The City*. A man retains a soft spot for his first love. Are you going to see a show? One of those bargain matinees for pensioners?"

"Did anyone ever tell you you're an ill-mannered boy?"

"Only my big sisters. Well, give my regards to Broadway."

"I'll remember you to Herald Square."

After that, Roscoe had to finish the song. Aggie listened with a smile until the last note.

***

It was nearly eight, and Aggie had not yet decided whether to go to the party at Abe's. Julie was planning to skip it.

"I love Abe, but it would take a hell of a lot more than mini hot dogs and a cheese plate to make me listen to Serena sing."

"Serena's going to sing?"

"Serena always gets someone to beg her to sing."

"Is she terrible?"

Julie was struggling with her feelings. "No. She's quite good. It's just—"

"Galling?" Aggie suggested.

"That's one way to put it. I'm going to get in my pajamas and reread Whitman's poem about the lilacs."

Aggie laughed. "All 206 lines? Frank looked genuinely alarmed. Do you really need to read it again? Isn't it kind of stuck in your head?"

"Reading is different than remembering or reciting. I like to hold a book and turn the pages. Are you going to Abe's? I got the sense he wanted you there."

"I don't know. I said I'd try to make it, but I'll see how I feel."

"Well, have a good time if you go. I'll see you on the bus in the morning."

Ultimately, the decision to attend the party sprang from Aggie's realization that she was too excited to sleep. She had added a toiletry case and Jacob's picture to her suitcase, but then there was nothing more to do, and she didn't feel like getting into bed.

She pulled on a long-sleeved, ivory top with narrow lace trim at the cuffs and neckline—a gift from Minnie she had always considered too nice to wear to school—and set out into the night. Wind was whipping the trees, and she was grateful for the lights illuminating the pathway that led past the barn and down toward Abe's cottage. When she arrived, she stopped for a moment to study the structure. The walls were stucco, and it had a round-top door, steeply pitched roof, and brick chimney. She could see lights behind the blinds and hear the babble of voices inside.

She stepped forward and knocked. The door was flung open by Serena. The younger woman wore a tight black jumpsuit. Her long hair had been pulled into a simple ponytail, accentuating her high cheekbones. There was a hint of displeasure on her countenance when she saw Aggie, but she moved aside to let her in.

About twenty people were crowded into the cottage's cheery main room which featured a leather sofa and an Oriental carpet. Logs blazed in the fireplace, and wooden folding chairs had been set up to provide extra seating. An upright piano stood against one wall. There were books and papers everywhere—crammed into floor-to-ceiling bookshelves, covering a desk, and stacked on one side of a window seat. At the far end of the room, an arched entry led to the kitchen. Aggie could see Erin, Bernice, and Frank gathered around a table loaded with platters of food and a punch bowl.

"You can put your coat in the bedroom," Serena said, indicating a door off the foyer. Aggie walked into the room and added her coat to the pile laid across the foot of the neatly made bed. She took a minute to study the quilt which was adorned with an array of simple four-pointed stars in a variety of gold and blue fabrics.

"It's called friendship star. At least that's what the needlework group told me." Aggie turned and saw Abe standing in the doorway. He had a grin on his face. "I'm glad you could make it."

"I couldn't sleep. I kept thinking about tomorrow. Going back to the nineteenth century."

"I was the same way on my first mission, at least I think I was. It's been a while."

Aggie felt somewhat awkward and couldn't think of anything else to say. Abe seemed a little awkward himself. "Um, I just came to get the violin." He walked to a tall armoire, opened its doors, and removed a slightly battered leather case.

"Abe, you're wanted in the kitchen." Serena had appeared in the doorway, her arms folded across her chest.

"Yes, of course," he replied. He turned and followed Serena out of the room.

Aggie checked her reflection in a mirror hanging over the dresser, then joined the others. She recognized most of the people there and was pleased to see some of the rookies, including Benjamin, the Hopewell twins, and Edgar Jaworski, who was seated on the sofa holding a small plate of miniature hot dogs. Spotting Aggie, he waved her over, patting the seat next to him.

"Ms. May, how nice to see you. Do sit down. Or perhaps you might want to grab some refreshments?"

Aggie laughed and joined him on the sofa. "I definitely don't need refreshments. They look good, though."

Edgar smiled back. "They are good, although I really ought to know better than to indulge. How nice, though, to attend a social function and not just sit home in front of the TV. Flora and Erin are going to provide a little music, and I promised I would come hear them. Flora and her brother are such wonderful people. We're in the same introductory group, you see, and spend a lot of time together. We've even started discussing what sorts of projects we might put together once we're a little more skilled with the three Ds. How are you getting on in your fieldwork group?"

"They've been welcoming, wonderful," Aggie assured him and outlined the investigation they had been pursuing.

"Fascinating," Edgar exclaimed. "That's just the sort of thing I hope to do eventually. Need more practice, though. I aim for Tuesday at noon and end up on Thursday at three."

"You're doing just fine," a voice said. It was Maurice. He had come up behind the sofa and placed his hands on Edgar's shoulders. "You'll be ready for fieldwork by next session. We'll just have to convince your daughter to let you come back."

Maurice joined them on the sofa, then Benjamin arrived and pulled up a chair. Soon they were laughing and sharing stories about their practice sessions at the barn. Frank and Bernice appeared next carrying platters of food they set on the coffee table before pulling up more chairs and joining the conversation.

"Let me guess," Frank said to Aggie. "Julie's reading in bed."

"You guessed right."

"Gotta admire someone who's already got a brain full of information and still finds room to stuff more in."

"I'm lucky she's my mentor."

Aggie was about to say more, but Kat, who had taken a stance next to the piano, was waving a hand to signal for attention. Like Serena, Kat was beautifully turned out. She wore blue pants, a white silk blouse, and a jeweled hairpin. Her makeup was perfect. Aggie was pretty sure she had created what was called 'a smoky eye.'

"Listen up people, Serena's going to sing," Kat announced, making clear they were in for a treat. Serena had seated herself at the piano. Glancing over her shoulder, she acknowledged the room, before turning back to the instrument and beginning the opening notes of a ballad.

Julie was right. Serena had a good voice. Aggie didn't recognize the song, but she wasn't really familiar with modern pop music. After the first number, Serena coyly allowed herself to be coaxed into a second before rising from the piano bench to the sound of hearty applause.

Everyone took a break to refill their plates and glasses, then it was Abe's turn to signal for attention. "Erin and Flora have also prepared some music. I know you'll really enjoy this, so give them your attention, please."

Flora, holding the violin, stepped forward, and Erin rose to stand beside her. Blushing slightly, the younger woman spoke. "Um, the Civil War group is going on their mission tomorrow, and Dad told me about Mr. Buckley's grandfather." She gestured toward Maurice who nodded his head. "I thought it would be nice to do some Irish songs in his honor. I learned two, and Ms. Hopewell practiced with me. The first one is 'The Night Visiting Song.' I thought it sort of fit because you might be visiting at night. It's a love song, but it still fits. The other one is 'The Green Fields of France.' It's not French, though. And it wasn't written by an Irish person, but it's about war and an Irish boy dying. It's a song about World War I, but it really could be any war. So, here they are."

She turned to Flora. The two women exchanged an unspoken signal and began. Serena's voice had been very nice, but, to Aggie's ears, Erin's was more pleasing. The young woman sang with a sweet soulfulness, keeping her eyes toward Flora, as if for reassurance.

When the last note rang out, the room exploded with applause. Erin blushed again, and Flora gave her a hug.

"Marvelous," Maurice exclaimed.

Aggie saw the expression on his face and felt a curious ache in her heart. It was an old wound that sometimes, even now, brought pain. She would never look at a child with a parent's love and pride. It was an emotion life had denied her. Aggie saw Abe watching her and turned quickly to Benjamin. "Wasn't she great?"

"They were both great," he agreed enthusiastically. "Flora is the heart of our little group of rookies. Such a fine person, she and her brother both."

Abe stood and bowed in the direction of the two women. "That was a wonderful send off for our group. Thank you, ladies."

With the program complete, guests rose to their feet, some gathering up cups and plates, others heading to the bedroom to collect their coats. Aggie picked up the platter from the coffee table and carried it to the kitchen where she found Bernice washing dishes. Aggie placed the platter on the sideboard, then grabbed a towel and began drying. From the other room she heard the mild commotion created as people thanked Abe and said their goodbyes.

"Here's the last one," Bernice said, handing her a serving bowl. "Looks like we finished just in time," she added, pouring soapy water from a dishpan into the sink and peering out the window. "Rain's coming."

Indeed, the lights along the pathway that led up the hill illuminated trees thrashing in the wind.

Frank poked his head in the entryway. "Any of those hot dogs left, Bernie?"

"I ate the last one," she answered. "Come on, walk me home. Did you bring an umbrella?"

Almost everyone was gone by the time Aggie returned to the living room, although Serena was lingering near the fireplace as if waiting for someone to offer her a brandy or pay her one more compliment. When neither was forthcoming, she disappeared into the bedroom, emerging a moment later with a wool wrap. She flung an arm around Abe's neck and kissed him on the cheek. Aggie felt a little seed of satisfaction that his only response was a rather distracted pat on her back and a quick move to disengage himself as he walked over to Edgar, who was one of the other stragglers. With a swish of her ponytail, Serena headed out the door.

Edgar had on his overcoat and a wool hat. Abe bent toward him and spoke in a quiet voice. When he spotted Aggie, he gestured for her to join them.

"I mentioned to Dr. Jaworski that you might have twisted your ankle in New York."

Aggie looked from one man to the other. "*Doctor* Jaworski?"

The elderly man looked embarrassed. "I'm an orthopedist. Retired. I do my best to keep up, naturally, but I don't maintain a regular practice. However, if there's anything I can do, I'd be happy to help."

Aggie shot Abe a look then turned to the doctor. "I'm fine," she said warmly. "I just landed wrong coming down some stairs. I don't even feel it now."

"Any pain? Swelling?"

"No."

"Any bruising?" He looked down. "I'm glad to see you're wearing sensible shoes. Some of my female patients insisted on wearing ridiculous footwear that's just asking for problems. But I see you're not in that camp."

"Oh, I'm definitely in the 'sensible shoes' camp," she said, trying not to laugh.

He patted her arm. "Good to hear it. I'll be going then. Our cohort is working with that lovely Miss Elizabeth tomorrow, first thing in the morning. I'll need a good night's sleep to be ready for those challenging little exercises she assigns." He pulled his hat down a bit more snugly on his head and headed out the door.

Aggie was now the last remaining guest. She turned to Abe. "Okay, you and I need to have a conversation. You said, 'All in good time.' I think now is a good time. Before we go into the city and before we return to the 1800s."

To her surprise, he nodded. "Would you like a brandy?"

She gurgled with laughter.

"What's funny?"

"I thought Serena looked like she was waiting for someone to make that offer to her."

He looked momentarily diverted. "Now what makes you say that?"

"Years observing adolescent romantic behavior."

"Is it romantic behavior to offer someone a drink?"

It was her turn to be diverted. "It can be. But I don't think so in this instance," she replied.

"What's different about this instance?"

"You and me. We have an *agenda*. An agenda makes all the difference. So let's have that brandy and get started."

Chapter 26 ~ The Agenda

They sat on the sofa in front of the fireplace. Aggie was reminded of the image on that website she had seen last summer: seniors in front of a fireplace, wine glasses in hand. It had seemed so improbable then. Yet, here she was. True, she and Abe weren't reclining on the carpet, but still, same thing, really. And given that quite a few even more improbable things had happened, she didn't feel the need to spend too much time reflecting on how she ended up in front of a fire, holding a glass of brandy and trying to decipher the expression on the face of the man sitting next to her.

She took a sip and set her glass on the coffee table. "I have questions. Are you going to answer them? Share your thoughts?"

He nodded.

"All of them?"

"Why don't you ask your questions first, then we'll see where we're at," he hedged.

"Okay. What have you been worrying about? What's behind your concern about the drops of water on my blouse? And my fieldwork? And now my ankle?"

He took a swallow of brandy and put his own glass down. "I'm sure you attended to Lillian's lecture the first day you arrived. 'History is not to be changed.'"

"Yes. I listened carefully."

"What she said is true, for the most part."

"What's the part that's not the most part?"

"I think you know. Or at least suspect. I've read your notebook. You're a good observer. You pick up on things." He laughed ruefully. "Also, I've noticed the slightly disreputable crowd you've been hanging out with since you arrived: Julie, of course, but, more importantly for this discussion, Bernice, Sal, and Viola."

"You're talking about intervention."

"Yes."

"Not just a time travel urban legend then?"

Abe picked up his glass, studied the amber-colored liquid, and swallowed the last of it in a single gulp. "Probably not."

"But—"

He held up a hand to silence her. "First, tell me what Viola and the others said to you about intervention. Maybe then we can sort fact from fiction."

"I promised not to talk about it."

He looked heavenward as if praying for patience. "Well, tell me what you think you know, without betraying any state secrets or solemn vows. Did you cross your heart and hope to die?"

Aggie ignored the sarcasm and organized her thoughts. She had another sip of brandy and began. "Lillian's view, I'll call it the traditional view, is that time travelers are observers. We cannot change anything. We can't save a life, or change the course of an event, or move objects back and forth between past and present. In short, we can observe, but not alter, history. Julie, while intrigued with the idea of intervention, shares the traditional view."

"And the non-traditional view?"

"Well, some things are the same. I don't think anyone believes you can change death. At least no one talks about it. Not the time of death. Not the fact of death."

"That's pretty much universal dogma among Remarkables," Abe agreed. "Not even our slightly mystical chapter in California contests that."

"But other types of changes," she paused before plowing on, "the non-traditional view seems to be they might be possible under certain circumstances."

"What circumstances?"

She chose her words carefully. "It's *hypothesized* that a very few Remarkables could possibly affect a select few events. Recent things. Little things."

"You can put your initials in wet concrete," Abe said.

"You've heard this before."

"I've heard it before."

"That leads to another question."

He waited.

"Are they right?"

Abe got up from the sofa, refilled his glass, took a quick gulp, then sat down again. He looked Aggie straight in the eye. "I think so."

Aggie digested this. "How is it you don't know for sure?"

He ran his hand through his hair. "I'm glad you think I'm omniscient, but I'm not."

"I gather from your answer you haven't successfully intervened yourself."

"It's not something I can do."

"You've tried?"

"Of course I've tried. Everyone tries. Over and over. A hundred different times." He shook his head in frustration. "I kept hoping, but it didn't happen. I'm convinced that, for me, it's not going to happen."

"But you're a companion traveler."

"It's a different skill."

They sat a moment in silence staring into the flames. Aggie finished her brandy and set the glass down before asking the next question. "Why do you think I might have the ability to intervene?" There. It was out on the table.

Abe studied her before answering. "In all my years of traveling through time—it started early for me—in all those years, I have known only one Remarkable who, I suspect, has the ability. Before I met you, that is. The rules that applied to the rest of us didn't seem to apply to her. Not in the same way. There were subtle differences, things that didn't add up."

"Like what?"

"I'm sure you've learned the usual axioms about time travel. 'You stand in a mud puddle in the past, and when you return your shoes are clean.'"

"A bullet flies in your direction, but you're evicted before you're hit."

"Exactly. Time is on your side, so to speak. Remarkables are protected. They're never changed. They're never hurt. But with this one traveler, I noticed disparities. The rules didn't quite work. She would return from the past with a torn hem on her dress. A scratch on her arm. And she would be elated. Giddy almost. And when I questioned her, she always had excuses."

"Excuses you didn't believe."

He shook his head and gave a short laugh. "I didn't. It happened too often, and her excuses weren't that convincing."

"And what did you conclude?"

Abe had propped his elbows on his knees. He leaned toward the grate as if to find answers in the fire. "I concluded that the ability to change things—an ability I had hoped for so long to find in someone— did, in fact, exist. Maybe just for small events. Maybe just for very recent events. But still, I was filled with wonder." He turned from the fire to check her reaction before continuing. "But then I realized something I should have considered all along. Intervention has a price. Those who can intervene don't have the normal protections that other travelers enjoy. And there's more. Those that can intervene are vulnerable on *every trip*. Not just trips to the recent past. Not just trips where they try to change things."

"Let me get this straight," Aggie said. "You think if someone has this extra ability, then they also have an extra vulnerability."

Abe nodded. "Someone who can intervene is susceptible to injury."

"You're worried about a torn hem?"

"Well, susceptible to *change*, then. You're right, a torn hem isn't much of an injury. Even a scratch on the arm. But what if something worse happens? And the exposure is there, on every single trip."

"So, with this power, you're working without a net."

"That's about it," he said grimly.

Aggie leaned back against the sofa cushions and crossed her arms, thinking. The fire had been reduced to embers. Abe got up, pulled a few logs from a wood box next to the fireplace and positioned them on the grate. He stayed crouched by the hearth until the flames began to crackle again, then stood up and brushed his hands together.

"I think I'm beginning to understand," Aggie said. "The water stains on my blouse. My ankle."

"Yes," he admitted, starting to pace back and forth. "You see there's reason for concern. When did those water stains occur? Maybe before you went back, and you just didn't notice. And maybe you stumbled on Broadway a few days ago. But maybe you stumbled in 1862, a time when you should have been protected."

"The other person you believe can intervene, it's Viola." It seemed obvious to her now.

He nodded in confirmation.

"Why won't she talk to you about it?" Aggie asked curiously. "Why all the secrecy?"

"She did at first. Then she started getting cagey. Now she just says I should stop worrying and accuses me of being too nosy."

Aggie snorted. "You are too nosy, although I can sympathize with your frustration. But let me ask you this: If the ability to change things is something you hoped for, why are you upset?"

"*Why am I upset?*" He seemed almost angry at the question. "Because as long as it was just a theory, it was wonderful to imagine. Even if travelers couldn't prevent the great tragedies of the past, imagine the good that could be done. Little mistakes could be set right. You'd get a do-over. What does Benjamin, say? The rookie who golfs? You get a mulligan. You could be a Good Samaritan. A Boy Scout. Last winter one of our folks took a nasty spill on a patch of ice. I thought at the time how nice it would be to travel back, just a few hours back, and sprinkle some salt, keep it from happening, save her a trip to the hospital."

"But when theory became reality?"

Abe stopped pacing and sat back down. "I recognized the price. How do you send someone so vulnerable out to change the past? How do you even allow them to do fieldwork? If a disaster could be averted, it might be worth it. If a Remarkable could keep the *Titanic* from sinking or the towers from falling, why not take the risk? But the *Titanic* is always going to sink. The towers will collapse. The concrete has set on those things."

"What about something simple?" she challenged. "Sprinkling salt on the ice, or …," her mind jumped suddenly to Viola in the garden, scolding Carlos to be careful with the knives, "or preventing an accident in the kitchen. Something recent. Something small."

"There's always going to be a risk. Even during fieldwork when events can't be changed. Like a lot of things, the reality is infinitely more complicated than the fantasy ever was." Abe stared into the fire. "Have you noticed there are days when Viola is more tired than usual, or needs her wheelchair? I don't think it's solely the result of being north of eighty years old. I think it's the direct effect of her extracurricular activities. When I try to talk to her, she just pulls out that knitting of hers—"

"Crochet."

"Whatever. She's a damned frustrating woman. She needs to think things through and not just go gallivanting off."

"Does Lillian suspect?"

"No. She doesn't believe it's possible, so she doesn't see the signs."

"She's quite adamant about people not even discussing intervention."

"There were a couple bad incidents early on. Recruits who were desperate to change the past and couldn't. One man fell victim to despair. He was found dead at home, less than a week after leaving us. It was suicide. Lillian blames herself. What Lillian fears is the danger of failure, the anguish of knowing you can't change a tragic event. She has no inkling about what I fear: the danger of success. The danger of a traveler putting herself in harm's way to intervene."

"Listen," Aggie said, placing a hand on his arm and giving him a shake. He turned to look at her. "If it was you who had the ability, what would you do?"

He looked mildly nonplussed. "Well I would at least *consult*—"

"No, you wouldn't," she interrupted him. "You wouldn't at all. You'd keep your own counsel, weigh up the risks and benefits, and make your own decision. You might factor in other opinions, but ultimately, you'd decide for yourself. And I strongly suspect Viola does just that. She's cagey, as you put it, because she doesn't want you to pressure her to stop, and she doesn't want to be barred from fieldwork."

"But she could get hurt."

"Yes, she could. But isn't that her decision to make?"

Her hand was still on his arm. Slowly, he let his finger trace along the narrow band of lace at her wrist then raised his eyes to her face.

"What about the people who care about her? Aggie, you've got to tell me. Can you intervene?"

She shook her head. "I don't know. I've never tried."

Suddenly, the glass at the windows flickered from black to white to black again, and an ear-splitting crack of thunder exploded outside.

Aggie rose to her feet and took a quick look out the casement. "It's not raining yet. But it's going to. I better get going."

"I'll walk you up to your building."

"No. That's silly."

"A gentleman walks a lady home."

"Don't be illogical. If I leave now, I'll make it up the hill. If you come with me, you'll get drenched on the way back."

"But—"

"It's my decision to make," she said firmly before dashing into the bedroom to collect her coat.

He was waiting for her by the door, looking stubborn. "We have more to discuss."

"All in good time," she said with a grin.

He scowled but, scanning her face, saw he couldn't dissuade her. "To be continued, then," he agreed reluctantly.

"Thank you for the lovely evening. The music—" Another clap of thunder rolled from the sky. She shot him an apologetic look and stepped out into the night.

***

Aggie was almost up the hill when the sky opened, and she berated herself for not bringing an umbrella. She was directly across from the barn, and, in desperation, tried one of the side doors. It was open. Gratefully, she stepped inside and ran a hand through her hair. The rain was coming down now in sheets. She'd wait a while to see if the storm passed quickly. If not, she'd just have to face the downpour.

The interior of the barn carried the sweet smell of hay and old wood. A rustling in the rafters overhead indicated the presence of birds nesting near the roof. From a far corner, near the stables, she detected a glow of light.

"Hello?" she called, then realized the pounding rain drowned out the sound of her voice. Walking deeper into the barn, she saw light spilling out from under the door that led to the tack room. She had never actually ventured into the room, and she paused before the door. She was curious, yet hesitant to turn the brass knob. Another flash of lightning created slivers of light in hairline cracks along the walls and a twinkle of brightness from the windows in the barn's cupola overhead.

Suddenly the door opened. Axel stood before her, frowning. Seeing it was her, the frown disappeared, but his face settled into its characteristic, unreadable blankness. Only his eyes moved, shifting to the left and right as if making sure she was alone.

"I'm sorry," Aggie apologized. "I dashed in here to get out of the rain and saw the light."

Axel nodded but remained silent.

"I was on my way back from Abe's when the storm began."

At that, Axel stood back, signaling her to enter. "No umbrella here," he said shortly. There was another roll of thunder, and Aggie saw the lilac bushes beyond the window thrashing in the wind. There were signs that Axel had been at work. A laptop lay open on the table along with pencils, paper, and a cell phone. A half-eaten sandwich rested on a paper napkin. A small pillbox sat near a thermos and mug.

"I'm sorry I interrupted you. Were you working?"

Axel looked at her coldly and, for a moment, didn't answer. "Barn is a good place to practice," he said at last. "Then I make a record."

"You practice at night?"

"Doesn't matter at night or day. Where you go to can be any time."

"Yes, that's true." An uncomfortable silence fell. The rain pounded loudly on the roof. "I better be going," she said and turned to leave, but Axel's hand shot out and grabbed her arm. His grip was not painful. Nonetheless she felt unsettled by his touch.

He looked at her stonily. "I tell you how to go. You don't need umbrella. *Think*. You are a teacher, educated. Not like some of these others. When did the rain start?"

"The rain? Just a few minutes ago. I was almost back to my building, and—" What he was suggesting suddenly hit her.

He nodded when he saw she understood. "Go back maybe ten minutes. No rain. Get to your apartment."

"Ten minutes ago I was still at Abe's cottage. We were talking. If I go back, I'll be in two places." Maybe it was the brandy, or the hammering of the rain, or Axel's hand gripping her arm—maybe it was all those things—but she suddenly felt a little dizzy, ill. "Can I do that?"

Axel shrugged. "Don't think so much about problems. Maybe works, maybe doesn't, but makes no difference." He pulled her toward the door. When she was standing on the threshold before the darkened stables, he released her. "I will close the door. If I watch, you cannot go. You understand this?"

"Yes, I understand." She stepped forward into the darkness.

"Wait," he said abruptly. She turned back to see his square bulk outlined in the doorway. He gestured toward her foot. "Abe says your ankle is hurt."

Aggie blinked. "It's fine," she said shortly. She wondered why Abe confided in this strange man. What else had they discussed? Who was Axel, after all?

Axel grunted. "You go now," he said and closed the door to the tack room.

Aggie waited until her eyes readjusted to the inky blackness. Moving carefully, she worked her way to the side door. She could just make out an old horseshoe nailed to the lintel, a horseshoe like the one over her door at home. It was nailed upside down, like a U. "To keep the luck in," she murmured. She focused on the horseshoe and tried to concentrate on the timeline of this one night. She was still at the cottage. The other guests had left. She was sitting on the sofa with Abe, drinking brandy. They had an agenda. She felt a wave of dizziness and put a hand against the barn wall to steady herself.

Suddenly there was silence. The roar of the rain had ceased. She shivered, drew in a breath, and slipped outside. She didn't look toward Abe's cottage. She didn't want to think about the strangeness inherent in being here, and being there, at the same time. Resolutely, she turned toward her building and walked up the hill. When she reached her apartment, she turned the key with trembling hands and let herself in. Shutting the door behind her, she walked to the glass patio doors. Still no rain. She closed her eyes and willed herself to return to the present. And she was back. It was all back: the sound of the storm, the roll of thunder. Opening her eyes, she saw her patio drenched by sheets of rain. A flash of lightning revealed a thousand rivulets running down the glass.

A great fatigue came over her. It was rare for her to be confronted with too many facts to take in, but that was how she felt. As she put on her nightgown, she reviewed everything Abe had shared with her, then thought about the storm, and Axel, and the stopping of the rain. Simple things, yet impossible to take in. Now you see it, now you don't.

"Stop it," she told herself. Tomorrow would be a big day. Maybe they could help Daniel find the truth about his grandpa. Maybe they could find a precious Mathew Brady portrait of the country's greatest leader. Everything else must be put aside. Power and vulnerability. Mulligans and Boy Scouts. Being here and being there. She would have to figure it all out later.

Chapter 27 ~ The Mathew Brady Greenhouse

There was an air of seriousness on the journey into the city. Even Julie was unusually quiet. Aggie and Abe had exchanged glances as she entered the shuttle bus, but neither said anything. Once in Midtown, Wells worked his way through the crowded streets, then pulled up before the doors to the Yale Club directly across from the west side entrance to Grand Central Terminal. It was a beautiful, late September morning. All evidence of the previous day's rainstorm was gone. Clouds dotted the azure sky, and a gentle breeze ruffled the flags along the street and billowed the dresses and coats of passersby.

"Look," Julie said, as they stepped from the bus. She pointed to a banner flying above one of the station's entrances. "There's some kind of art show at Grand Central."

"I read about it in the *Times*," Aggie said. "It's about portraiture in New York City."

"I'd like to see it," Julie said. She was still staring at the banner but seemed distracted. "When we're done, of course. It's odd, isn't it? Our mission is about portraiture. Maybe we'll discover a photograph of Lincoln that will find a place in a future exhibition."

Arrangements for check in at the Yale Club had been made in advance, so room keys were distributed with quick efficiency. Aggie retained a brief impression of a black and white tiled floor, a man behind a reception desk, a bank of elevators, but her mind was elsewhere. Once in her room, she placed her suitcase on a luggage stand, then zipped open the garment bag. She wanted to change into the blue dress so she would be ready when it was time for her shift.

Lillian had assigned Abe, Serena, Sal, and Kat to the first shift. Aggie, Julie, Bernice, and Frank would go out second. Lillian had left herself and Viola out of the rotation. "Abe advises me there are problems for those of us with mobility issues," she had explained. "We are surveilling at night. The ground is uneven and unpaved. We'll see if there's a role for us, but we're starting with those who can move about more freely."

After changing, Aggie joined her mentor in the room next door. Julie was seated at the window. She had changed as well and was paging through a book of nineteenth-century photographs. Other books were scattered across the counterpane. Aggie selected one and settled in a chair. She opened the book to see a sepia image showing a man loading a wagon.

"The first shift's gone out already," Julie said without looking up from her book. "Abe will companion travel with the first person to show the way. Then they'll go through a rotation or two. If they're lucky, they can cover five or six days."

"How did Lillian set up the shifts?" Aggie asked, her eyes on a photograph of Civil War soldiers outside a tent.

"Serena's very skilled at distance and duration. Abe will probably companion travel with her first to direct her to the homestead. Then she can walk around and scout the area. There's unlikely to be an opportunity for a conversation with Gabe so she'll find places where we can hide and observe the house."

They spent the next hour with the books, studying gray and brown-tinted prints of people long dead and buried. When Julie's phone buzzed, Aggie jumped, the modern sound seeming strangely out of place. Julie checked the screen. "They're on their way back. Abe wants a quick meeting before our shift heads out."

They assembled in a beautifully appointed meeting room that had been reserved for their use. All the first shift members looked tired, and Aggie wondered about the fatigue inherent in surveillance. After all, even the youngest Remarkables were not young.

Sal took charge of the briefing. "We covered five days, just checking in briefly. The next group should set their destination for April 6. The last two days we observed told us something's definitely going on. But Gabe's not digging. He's building." Sal paused and looked troubled. "He's putting up a little greenhouse. It's small, like a shed, but pretty and well-designed. But the glass he's using, it's photographic plates. You can see the faces. That means what Daniel suspected all along is true. Gabe's got those plates. That part's good, but what he's doing with them is not what we expected."

Sal's normally steady voice had taken on a note of distress. "And the whole scene doesn't make sense. He's working carefully, with respect, but he's gotta know what the sunlight will do to those pictures. And he's happy. I've seen a lot of men happy working with their hands, and I'd swear he's one of them. But I don't get it. Why save pictures for ten years, then put them in the sun to fade away?"

No one had an answer.

"Did you see a portrait of Lincoln?" Viola asked.

"No," Serena said. "I was the first one out. Then I went again before we came back. The greenhouse was nearly finished, all the glass was in, anyway, and I got right up next to it and walked around for a while. Lincoln's not there. Just common soldiers."

"So maybe if he's got a Lincoln portrait, he'll bury that one," Kat said, "because that one's valuable. And he's putting the others in the greenhouse because they're not."

Julie started to protest, then just waved a hand as if shooing a fly. "Aggie, when you saw Gabe at the Antietam exhibition, you sensed he was ambivalent about the pictures, right?"

"Yes. I did get that feeling. He said, 'A reminder is not always welcome,' and those that saw the images would not rest easy. But twenty years have passed. We can't know how he feels now."

"Daniel said he maybe took the plates because they were kind of a currency," Frank offered. "They had value. But now maybe they don't have value anymore. Like when Brady tried to sell his own pictures to the government, and they gave him pennies on the dollar."

"Wouldn't a portrait of Lincoln always have value?" Sal asked. He scratched his head. "A day ago, this seemed clear. Now I'm not sure what's going on."

"What's next Lillian?" Viola asked.

"We're still looking for answers," she replied, "so the second shift goes out. Aggie, Julie, Bernice, and Frank. You're up next."

***

Wells parked the shuttle in a discreet little lot close to Morningside Park. Frank was the first to venture out. They had conferred with Serena before leaving the Yale Club and taken down her directions for reaching Gabe's homestead.

"Back in two shakes," Frank said, tipping his cap to the others.

As soon as the shuttle door closed behind him, Aggie pulled out her notebook to review some of her entries. Julie had brought a book to pass the time, and Bernice was paging through the newspaper. Wells had a tablet and was tapping away at the screen. The scene reminded Aggie of study hall.

Frank was back within the hour. "Serena was right on the money with her directions. If you stand at the edge of the park, you're just a hop and skip away. There's plenty of cover for leaving, and when you arrive, there's this bent tree that looks like it's pointing the way. You'll see a livery sign, then down a drive there's a stable and yard and the house. There's some empty land that's part of the orphanage grounds like we saw on the map. It's kind of rural."

Julie leaned forward. "Did you see the greenhouse?"

"Yeah, it's behind the house, near the back porch. I didn't get all the way up to it. Stayed near the stables."

"Anything else we should know?" Bernice asked.

"It's quiet. No one's out. And it's cold. Hard to believe it's April and hard to believe it's Manhattan." He reached across to Julie and pulled her shawl across her shoulders. "You'll need to wrap up when you go out."

"I can go next," Bernice stated. "I need to stretch my legs anyway. What time were you there?" she asked Frank.

"April 6, ten at night."

"I'll target the next night and see if anything's cooking. Wish we had a better idea what we're walking into. We're relying on the gut feeling of a ninety-five-year-old man with a handful of memories and another handful of suppositions."

"Yeah, but that's par for the course every time we're on a mission," Frank retorted. "It's always gonna be a matter of percentages. You take a swing. Maybe you connect and maybe you don't." He paused. "But it's something to see that greenhouse, even if we don't get anything more than that. I didn't get up close, but when the moon came out, you could see the men in their uniforms, young guys, mostly. And there's men with their units. Those boys didn't have it easy. Sometimes you forget your band of brothers aren't just the guys next to you, but the guys that came before."

Julie put her hand against his cheek, then leaned over to give him a hug. Frank looked mildly abashed, but pleased, nonetheless.

"Hey, Wells, did you bring any sandwiches?" He spoke quickly, trying to cover his embarrassment.

Wells reached behind the seat and pulled out a wicker basket. "Help yourself, Frank. There's sandwiches and a thermos of coffee. Hot tea, too."

"I'll eat after my trip," Bernice said, pulling on a canvas jacket and climbing down the steps of the shuttle.

Julie and Frank split a sandwich and had just finished eating by the time Bernice returned. Aggie had no appetite, though she had taken a few bites of an apple.

"There's lilac bushes around the house, like Abe said," Bernice told them. "If you work your way around by the stable, you can cross the yard and be right in among them. I got close in, but then just sat for an hour and didn't see or hear a thing," she added gloomily. "All quiet on the Western Front."

"I'll bet you picked up more than you thought you did," Aggie said. "What did you smell?"

Bernice considered. "Well, you could smell that the greenhouse was new. Wood just sawed. Whitewash put on. 'Too poor to paint, too proud to whitewash,' my granny used to say. At least Gabe put foolish pride away and made that greenhouse look real pretty."

"All I could smell was animals," Frank said, making a face. "Kinda' unsettled my stomach."

"Doesn't seem to have had a lasting effect," Julie said, eying the few crumbs that remained from his sandwich.

"Why don't I head out?" Aggie suggested.

"Yeah, go for it," Frank said. "We'll catch you on the rebound."

Aggie nodded, wrapped her shawl around her shoulders, and stepped from the bus.

"Good luck," Julie called.

Aggie glanced back, smiled wanly, and set off in the direction of the park.

***

Aggie had memorized facts about the year, each one like a strand of silk from a spider's web, a strand that would bind her to the destination. She was uncomfortably aware that she had adopted Axel's focusing technique. She ran through her list like a mantra: FDR is a two-month-old baby. Last summer, President Garfield, the man who had urged Congress to purchase Brady's collection, was assassinated. Darwin will die this year. And Longfellow. And Emerson. When September rolls around, someone will flip a switch in lower Manhattan, and the whole East Side will be illuminated with electric lights, courtesy of Thomas Edison.

She knew immediately she had traveled. The city sounds were gone, replaced by the rattling of tree branches in the wind. Frank was right. It was chilly for April. April of 1882.

It wasn't difficult to find the homestead. The bent tree pointed the way, and the silver moon accentuated the lines and angles that delineated the house and outbuildings. Aggie could see the word 'Livery' painted in an arc beneath the eaves of a small barn. Behind the house, the edge of the greenhouse was visible, its rectangular panes of glass glittering, then fading as clouds scudded across the sky.

Aggie knew she was in the city—the biggest city in the country, even in 1882—yet the homestead seemed curiously isolated with only the suggestion of other buildings far off in the darkness. The moonlight was fierce, accentuating the black-and-white contrasts of the night. The trim around the door and windows glowed white. The lilac bushes beside the house were inky blotches.

A faint thread of sound drifted into the yard. Was it a voice? A cry? Aggie strained her ears, but the sound wasn't repeated. She waited until clouds again obscured the moon then advanced toward the house. She wanted to inspect the greenhouse and check for signs of digging in the yard. Avoiding a patch of yellow light cast from behind one of the curtained windows, she reached the shelter of the lilac bushes.

Her heart raced as she leaned against the rough siding of the house. After catching her breath, she moved carefully toward the rear. When she reached the greenhouse she stopped, staring in wonder at the structure. It was small, perhaps six feet by eight, but had been cleverly constructed, with a steeply pitched roof and a graceful entrance. The bottom portion of each side was wood, but the entire top half was comprised of panes of photographic glass, carefully framed and fitted together to create the elegant design.

The moonlight caused the faces on the glass to gleam as if powered by some inner light. As the wind increased, Aggie pulled her shawl tighter and watched wispy clouds slip across the sky like cobwebs. The flickering light was creating a moving collage on the greenhouse—almost like the film at a Nickelodeon—as first one image, then another, animated the glass. A man with a beard stared into the distance. Two soldiers posed side by side. Aggie's eyes moved from frame to frame. She did not see a portrait of Lincoln.

A sudden banging from the front of the house caused Aggie to jump. Someone was pounding at the door. Wending her way back through the bushes, she peeked out at the front stoop. An African American child of maybe twelve or thirteen, in a pair of rough, hand-sewn overalls fidgeted nervously by the door, moving anxiously from foot to foot. He raised his hand to knock again when the door flew open.

"Did you get the midwife?" The man answering the door was Gabe. Aggie was sure of it. He was older, with gray streaks in his hair and lines across his brow, but Aggie had no doubt it was the same man she had seen at Brady's gallery.

"No sir, no sir." The child was nearly frantic in his anxiety and haste to deliver his message. "I tried to get Bessie, but they say she was called out before supper and wasn't back yet. They don't know where she's at."

"What about the white midwife?"

The white midwife?

"Mr. Gabe," the child's distress was palpable. "She won't come. Her mister told me to get off his porch. He had a gun. He tole' me," the child hesitated, then plowed on, "he tole' me to get the colored midwife for the ... for the 'mongrel baby.' I'm sorry, Mr. Gabe. I'm sorry. I tried to explain about Bessie, and Miz Lula needing help. I tried."

From her hiding place in the bushes, Aggie could see the anguish on the child's face.

Gabe rested his hand on the boy's shoulder, the scarred hand that Daniel had described. "It's all right now, Caleb. It's all right. Run back to Bessie's. Run as fast as you can. Wait till she gets back. Don't matter how long. Wait for her. Then bring her here."

The child took to his heels before the door closed behind him. A scream from inside ripped the silence. Abandoning caution, Aggie moved around the house, peering into each window she came to. The child's anxiety and distress had been contagious. Most of the windows were covered, but at the far corner she saw light spilling from a window whose curtains had been thrust to the side. She looked in.

Gabe was kneeling beside a bed, holding the hand of a woman who lay propped up by pillows, deep in the pains of labor. Like Gabe, the woman was middle-aged. Like Gabe, her black curly hair was streaked with silver. Unlike Gabe, her skin was dark.

Her face contorted in pain. "Gabe, oh Gabe, something's wrong. The baby's not moving anymore. The baby ...." Tears were streaming down her cheeks.

"Someone's going to come, Lula. You're going to be fine." Gabe rose to his feet, moving toward the window. Aggie stepped back behind the screen of lilac bushes. A bloom brushed against her cheek. She saw Gabe peer out into the night, but then another scream came, sending shivers down Aggie's spine. Gabe turned away and disappeared into the room.

For five minutes, ten minutes, there was silence. Dreadful silence. Then a wailing began. Not the wailing of a baby, but a mother's keening of grief and despair. With trepidation, Aggie moved back to the window. Inside, Lula rocked back and forth in the bed holding a tiny form in her arms. A form that didn't move. Gabe stood beside the bed, tears glittering in his eyes. "You're going to be fine," he repeated. "Going to be fine. Going to be ...." He bolted from the room.

The back door flew open, and Aggie crouched into the shadows by the porch. Gabe had walked out into the night, eyes raised to the heavens as if seeking help. Help that wouldn't come. He threw his head back and howled in anger and pain, then turned to the greenhouse. Moonlight and shadows darted across the structure. Gabe reached one hand to touch the glass. In his other hand, he held a gun. The ghostly faces appeared and disappeared as clouds streaked across the sky.

Suddenly he screamed, "Nooo." The hand touching the glass turned to a fist and he smashed the pane, sending a spider's web of cracks across the image. "Nooo!" Raising the gun, he took a step back and fired directly into the side of the greenhouse. A spray of glass flew across the yard, and he fired again. Aggie felt a sting on her cheek. The shards and slivers of glass twinkled in the dirt of the yard like a thousand stars in a midnight sky. She leaned her forehead against the side of the house, tears filling her eyes.

"Who's there?" Gabe screamed. "Did you come to gloat? You think I won't fight for my family?" Gabe peered into the darkness, waving the gun wildly as he turned this way and that. The clouds moved, revealing the greenhouse once again. Many of the panes were shattered, many slivered with crazy lightning cracks.

Gabe lowered the gun and watched the black and silver pantomime. Aggie could hear him crying. It was an awful sound, raw and agonized.

"I'm sorry," he said at last. He reached his hand toward the faces. "You fought with honor. It wasn't your fault." He turned back to the house, mounted the steps to the back porch, and was gone.

***

"Miss? Miss! Are you all right?"

Aggie was back in the present standing at the edge of Morningside Park surrounded by a cluster of saplings and shrubs. Two girls, maybe fifteen or sixteen years old stood a few feet away on the sidewalk looking at her uncertainly. They wore identical school uniforms: gray skirts and sweaters and white button-up blouses. The girl who had spoken to her, the taller of the two, took a step forward, her shyer companion hanging back. "Do you need help, miss?"

Aggie turned toward them and attempted a smile. "Thank you. I'm fine. I was … bird watching. Fall migrations have started."

The two girls exchanged a doubtful look. "She scratched her face in those brambles," the shorter girl whispered to her friend. "Maybe she's got dementia and wandered off, like my grandma does."

The taller girl squared her shoulders, took another step toward Aggie, and spoke slowly, enunciating each word clearly. "Do you know how to get home? Do you want me to call someone for you?"

Aggie cleared her throat. "Thank you, girls. I'm fine. I'm going to call a Lyft when I'm done." She fumbled in her bag and pulled out her cell phone, brandishing it in the girls' direction. The girls looked at each other and nodded, apparently reassured by this evidence of competence.

"Okay, have a nice day," the taller girl said, slinging her book bag onto her shoulder.

"Girls? That was a very nice thing to do. Offering to help."

Radiant smiles appeared on their faces. "Thank you, miss," they said together, and headed back along the sidewalk.

Aggie looked down at her cell phone. She had entered Lillian's number and those of the others before getting on the bus that morning. Quickly, she prepared a group text and hit send before heading back to the shuttle. *We need to talk. Now.* She dropped the phone back in her bag, retrieved a tissue, and dabbed at the scratch on her cheek. It might be a good idea to cover the scratch with a little makeup. Too bad she didn't have any. She could probably borrow some from Julie, explaining to her mentor that she had been evicted into a mass of brambles. Julie wouldn't think anything of it. Not even when she heard about the spray of glass from the shattered greenhouse.

Chapter 28 ~ Provenance

They gathered again in the Yale Club meeting room. The text had triggered a quick response from Lillian who, after reaching Aggie by phone, agreed on the need to deliberate before sending anyone else out. Aggie had been surprised, upon entering the room, to see Axel seated in a corner, a little apart from the others. He hadn't been on the bus and must have found his own way into the city. When Abe arrived, he nodded to Axel before taking a chair next to Aggie at the table. Their eyes met, and he gave her a half smile.

As clearly as she could, Aggie related what she had witnessed at Gabe's homestead.

"Son of a bitch," Sal exclaimed angrily when she finished. "So they were, um, an interracial couple, and the midwife wouldn't show up on that account? Son of a bitch."

Kat shed a few tears in a pretty sort of way and allowed herself to be comforted by Frank who patted her on the back a trifle awkwardly. "The poor baby. It's just so *sad*," she said dabbing at her eyes, "and, like, unfair."

"Are you sure some of the glass survived?" Julie asked.

"Yes, unless he went out again later. I don't think he would have, though. He talked to the pictures of the soldiers. He said he was sorry."

"Well, if some of the plates survived—"

"Then we still have work to do," Bernice interrupted. "Maybe he buries the baby and buries the portraits, and—"

"What's *wrong* with you?" Kat exclaimed. "Don't you have any *feelings*?"

"Yeah. I got a *feeling* he's going to bury the glass plates," Bernice said matter-of-factly. "Isn't that what Gabe's Bible says? He buries Lincoln and Brady's soldiers. Those are the pictures. After what happened he feels threatened. This is the precipitating event Julie was talking about. He buries the ones he didn't smash. He feels bad about shooting them, like Aggie said, and he wants to protect the valuable Lincoln picture. If he's got one."

"What if we've been wrong all along, and he doesn't have a Lincoln portrait?" Julie asked. "It wasn't part of the greenhouse. Maybe the Bible inscription is a metaphor. The Union soldiers were Lincoln's men. Lincoln embodied the Union cause."

"It's all very well to talk about metaphors," Serena stated, "but if there isn't a Lincoln portrait ...." She shrugged. "We have to consider whether those other photographs are worth anything. If what's left is just anonymous nobodies, then we're working on something that isn't historically important, and we should move on."

"We owe Daniel the whole story," Julie said vehemently. The two women glared at each other across the table.

"Don't matter if pictures show famous people." The rough, low-pitched voice had come from the corner of the room, and all eyes turned in Axel's direction. Judging by their startled expressions, Aggie figured some of the others had never heard him speak. Axel's expression was stern, and he seemed to be assessing the group members by a measure no one else understood. "Don't matter. The story makes pictures valuable. Gives them *provenance*."

"What is that supposed to mean?" Serena asked cautiously.

"*Provenance*," Julie said after a curious glance at Axel. "It means derivation or origin." Noting a few blank stares, she took a pen from the table and held it up. "A pen is just a pen unless it was used by FDR or Winston Churchill. If it was, it's valuable." She pointed at Kat, who was wearing a simple, but rather sizeable, diamond pendant. "A gem may have intrinsic value, but if the gem was worn by Elizabeth Taylor or Jackie O, that provenance multiplies its value."

"Look," Serena said abruptly, holding up her cell phone. "All this fancy talk about provenance is ridiculous." She shot a wary glance at Axel, but, seeing no reaction, seemed to gain confidence. "I just googled 'Civil War glass plate negatives.' There's a couple you can buy on eBay, right now. The most expensive one is," she glanced at the screen, "twenty-eight dollars. Don't tell me it doesn't make a difference who's in the picture. Of course, it makes a difference. Provenance or no provenance, if there's no Lincoln, there's no point."

"I have a proposal," Julie said. "Serena didn't see Lincoln, and Aggie didn't, either, but maybe there's a portrait of someone else that's important. Someone they didn't recognize. Sherman or Hancock or Meade. You know I have a good memory but, I'm not good with distance. But if Abe helps me with companion travel, and I go back to the greenhouse before it's destroyed, I could examine each plate, and—"

"That would be pointless," Serena said dismissively. "I spent a lot of time looking at that greenhouse, and there was no one important there."

"But Serena, you don't know all the—"

"Did you hear what I said? *I spent a lot of time.*"

A flash of comprehension appeared on Julie's face followed by fury. "Did you *even once* consider the fact that someone else might need to take a look?"

Aggie was struggling to understand. "What—"

Julie turned to her. "Remember why we needed a sketch artist to draw Gabe? What Kat said about return visits? Carbon copies. How long was that greenhouse standing before it was destroyed? A few hours? Half a day? That's all the time we had to study it. This one," she pointed to Serena, "used up most of that time and made sure there was nothing left to see but carbon copies."

"I didn't know it was going to be smashed, did I?" Serena countered.

"Stop!" The order came from Lillian. "Talk of provenance is premature. Talk of value is premature. I agree with Julie. We owe Daniel the whole story, or as much as we can learn. We can tell him his grandfather and Lula had a child before his own father was born. And we can tell him what happened to that child. I would like to tell him where the child is buried, if that's possible. As for the glass plates, perhaps Gabe held back a portrait of Lincoln, or maybe the Bible inscription is a metaphor, as Julie suggests. Regardless, we continue our surveillance."

"Hear, hear," Viola said, thumping her cane on the floor. "We're Remarkables, aren't we? We're committed to finding answers in history, aren't we? We're not just gold diggers or accountants. When we worked on Ellis Island, did we calculate how much the information was *worth*?" She sent a challenging look around the table. Serena looked unmoved, but most of the others were nodding. Aggie shot a glance at Axel but couldn't tell what he was thinking.

"Lillian and Viola are right," Abe said suddenly. He sounded unusually serious. "There's no reason to stop."

Aggie faced him. *"You roll a one, but a one isn't nothing.* It depends on the game you're playing, doesn't it?"

Abe returned her gaze, and suddenly it was as if there were only the two of them in the room. "Yes. That's my philosophy. That's what I believe. Gabe and Lula and their baby, they are the treasure."

Aggie nodded.

"All right then," Lillian said. "Let's put together shifts for tomorrow. Maybe we can find the end of Gabe's story."

***

But the end, when it came, was not what they had hoped. Taking turns, they watched the homestead hour after hour, observing Gabe's movements through the long day following the death of the baby, and the darkness of another night. Each group of travelers returning to the Yale Club added something to the narrative, but as the surveillance continued, Aggie began to feel claustrophobic in the elegant meeting room where they mulled each new piece of information. Capable staff members removed used coffee cups and napkins, kept the vases filled with fresh flowers, and made sure the table held baskets of fruit and an ample supply of pens and writing paper. It wasn't the Yale Club that caused the gloom Aggie felt each time they convened. It was the cumulative effect of unrelenting sad news shared by each traveler upon return from the nineteenth century.

Neither Aggie nor Julie had seen anything of moment at the homestead, but Bernice had witnessed the arrival of a midwife. The elderly black woman appeared at Gabe and Lula's doorstep in the early hours of the morning. Gabe had murmured to her, and Bernice described how the woman's shoulders slumped, then straightened. She had folded Gabe in an embrace before telling him she would see to Lula.

Sal, with a bleak expression on his face, reported watching Gabe dismantle what was left of the greenhouse. "He used the whitewashed boards from the bottom to make two little boxes. Coffins, I guess. One must be for the baby, and the other one, well, I think Bernice was right. He's going to put the pictures in there, the ones that weren't destroyed. I watched him wrap the glass in muslin and oilcloth. That would protect them long-term."

"Did you see him remove a portrait from the house?" Viola asked.

He shook his head. "Folks, I don't like to say this, but if he's got a Lincoln portrait, I don't think there's any way we can find out. None of us is going to get close or be able to talk to him. Gabe's afraid, real jumpy. He's keeping a rifle next to him while he works. He's a different man than the one I saw before."

Kat, on her return, had little to offer. "It was freezing," she said peevishly, "and nothing's happening."

"We should have been provided with better outerwear," Serena added.

"You get warm as soon as you come back," Julie snapped.

"But it's quite unpleasant while you're there," Serena shot back.

Right before supper, the last shift of the day returned. Aggie knew immediately the news was bad. For the first time since she had met him, Frank looked defeated. "It's all over," he said. "End of the road. Gabe's not burying them by the house. He hitched up the horse. I circled round back to get a better look and saw the coffins and a shovel in the wagon. The kid that works with him got up beside him, and they drove out of the yard and headed south. They're gone, folks. Game over. Abe went out after me and stood by the road to see if he could tell where they were going. But nothing."

Abe affirmed the account. "It was dark. They were swallowed in the night."

"Is there any way to follow them?" Aggie asked.

The others shook their heads. "Some Remarkables can travel in the past in vehicles," Julie explained. "Lillian's very good at it. But the circumstances must be right. There has to be a conveyance you can get aboard and not be particularly noticed like a bus or train. There's no possibility for that here."

"So, Gabe driving off, that's the end of the trail, isn't it?" Sal asked.

Heads nodded.

Lillian looked around the table. "I know some of you are discouraged by the outcome of this mission," she said gently, "but I'm not. We promised Daniel we'd try to find out what happened to the Mathew Brady plates. We did that, and more. Sometimes we focus on an artifact and forget that what we truly seek is understanding. Emerson said, 'What is important is the *journey*, not the destination.' Our journey on this mission will make a difference. To Daniel, of course, but to others as well."

"Will we create oral history the way we did with Ellis Island?" Frank wanted to know.

"We'll talk to Daniel about that," Lillian said. "It's his story to share, or not."

Julie looked distracted. "Emerson died the same month all this happened, you know. April 1882."

"April *what*?" Frank asked softly, looking at her with affection.

"April 27." An abstracted look had come over her face. "Emerson said 'Do not go where the path may lead, go instead where there is no path and leave a trail.'"

"I'm not sure I get your point," Frank said.

"I was thinking Gabe had his own path in mind when he drove off. Someplace specific."

"Of course he had someplace specific in mind," Serena said impatiently. "So what?"

"The Bible inscription says Lincoln and Brady's soldiers were buried at home. So where would home be for them? A military graveyard? An old soldiers' home?"

"What about the Soldiers' and Sailors' Memorial Monument on Riverside Drive?" Lillian asked suddenly. "It was built to honor Civil War veterans, and it's close to Gabe's homestead."

"The time's wrong," Julie said. "The monument wasn't commissioned until 1893, and the first stone wasn't laid until 1900. Teddy Roosevelt was governor and presided at the ceremony."

Frank put a gentle hand on Julie's shoulder. "You're quite a gal, Julie, but this is one time when I don't think any of those things you have stored in your brain are going to help us. We can't research our way to an answer. We needed luck, but she didn't stay with us."

Julie looked into Frank's concerned face and nodded reluctantly.

As if moved by a silent signal, the seniors began to gather their belongings and rise from their chairs.

"I assume tomorrow will be for deceleration?" Viola asked.

Aggie looked to Julie. "I'll explain in a minute," her mentor said.

Lillian nodded. "Yes. You all know what to do. Record everything you observed, everything you learned. After that, you're free to walk around the city or gather supplementary material. Just be back here so we can leave around four. We'll report to Daniel tomorrow evening at the Lodge."

In a few minutes, the conference room had emptied except for Aggie, Julie, and Viola. Abe had left with Lillian, the two of them talking quietly. Axel had not attended any of that day's briefings, and Aggie wondered if Abe would fill him in on the disappointing end of the mission. She also wondered if Axel adhered to Abe's belief that 'rolling a one' didn't mean failure, and she pondered the curious bond that seemed to exist between the two men.

"So, what's deceleration?" Aggie asked.

Julie still looked preoccupied, and it was Viola who answered. "Deceleration is when we know our mission is ending, so we slow down and put the brakes on. It's a transition out of the mission. You write down everything you experienced, details you didn't have time to consider or address while you were on duty. Things you didn't even remember. Of course, that one," she pointed to Julie, "doesn't need to spend much time on that. I've never known her to forget a thing. But for the rest of us, it's essential."

Julie snapped out of her daze and returned to the conversation. "It's essential for me, too. I dictate everything I've picked up. Then Wells prints it out for analysis and sharing."

"Another thing we do is collect what Lillian calls supplementary material," Viola added.

"Frank calls it color commentary," Julie said. "It's when you can't go any further answering the main question of the mission, but you can add information on the time period."

"I'm planning a bit of that tomorrow morning," Viola said. "I've been feeling useless. Lillian was right to sideline me—she had to sideline herself as well—but it was frustrating. I thought I'd ask Wells to drop me at Central Park, so I could look at what it was like when Gabe and Lula were alive. Daniel might like to hear about that. There are a lot of benches, so I won't get overexerted. I want to go early, though, before the City wakes up. If there are too many people around, I'll never get away."

"I'll keep you company," Aggie offered suddenly. "I've already recorded everything from Gabe's homestead."

"That would be nice. I'm heading out at dawn, but I imagine, being a teacher, you won't mind the early start."

Chapter 29 ~ Portraits

Aggie rose before dawn the following morning and pulled on the navy blue dress. She had arranged to meet Viola in the shuttle bus parked in an underground garage on a side street near the Yale Club. When Aggie arrived, she found Viola already seated comfortably on one of the wide seats. She was wearing her period clothing and had stored both her wooden cane and the modern aluminum one behind the driver's seat. "Wells will be down in a few minutes," she said. "He's not a morning person."

Aggie climbed into the shuttle and settled across from Viola who was scanning a glossy magazine entitled *Booties for Baby*. A copy of the *New York Times* lay on an empty seat. Aggie picked up the front section, then realized it was yesterday's paper. At least she could work the puzzle, she thought, reaching for the arts section and fishing in her reticule for a pencil.

Viola glanced up from her magazine. "Oh, I'm so sorry, dear. I did the puzzle yesterday."

"No problem," Aggie said. She found the page with the puzzle and scrutinized the boxes. "Hard one?"

"Not too bad. Will Shortz is always punctilious when it comes to the conventions, lovely man that he is. But sometimes I get tripped up on things that are *trending*, as they say. And I had to ask Frank for that baseball answer. It gave him a nice opportunity to explain at length that the 'Commerce Comet' had nothing to do with either business or astronomy."

Aggie laughed, dropped the paper back on the seat, and pulled out her phone. She tapped on the *Times* news app and checked a few headlines. An afternoon tornado had ripped through a Kansas farm community. The Yankees had won in a late-night, extra-innings showdown against the Red Sox, finishing just before a midnight electrical storm. A new superhero movie was out. Then a headline in the metro section caught her eye: *Brazen Attack on Artist at Grand Central Show*. She tapped the screen and opened the story:

A young caricature artist featured at the Grand Central Portraiture Exhibit was attacked in the early hours of the morning in apparent retaliation for his political cartoons. The artist, Tyrece Vinci, suffered a serious hand injury in the attack which was carried out by intruders who entered the exhibit just prior to the terminal's closing time after distracting security guards posted at the exhibit entrance. Vinci's illustrations, which feature New York celebrities and powerbrokers, have been a popular component of the exhibit. Police report that several of Vinci's drawings were defaced including those in his 'Gangs of New York' series which depict prominent political and financial figures as characters from the 2002 crime drama starring Leonardo DiCaprio and Daniel Day-Lewis ….

Aggie shook her head back and forth, placing a hand against her cheek in distress as she scanned the rest of the story.

"Aggie, what's wrong?" Viola had dropped her magazine and was leaning forward in concern.

"Oh, Viola. There was an attack last night at that Grand Central art exhibit I told you about. One of the artists was hurt. His pictures were vandalized. My sister and I saw him doing sketches last summer at the Javits Center. He's just a kid. Who would do this?"

"You know this young man? You've met him?"

"No, not really. I just watched him doing portraits. He's so talented. The article says his hand was injured! How could this happen? Where was security?"

Viola put a hand on Aggie's arm and gave her a shake. "Aggie. Look at me. Listen. *When did this happen?*"

Aggie looked at her in confusion then glanced down at her phone. "It was last night."

"No. Tell me exactly."

In a flash of understanding, Aggie grasped the import of Viola's question. Her eyes dropped to the phone again. "It was early this morning, just before Grand Central closed. They close at 2 a.m." She looked at her watch. It was nearly six. "It's been four hours."

Viola tightened her grip on Aggie's arm. "There's enough time. But you'll have to decide right now, and you'll have to hurry."

Aggie felt her heart slamming in her chest. When she didn't say anything, Viola shook her again.

"Right now! Decide. You do or you don't."

Aggie met her eyes. "I want to try."

"You know what could happen?"

"I know."

"Okay, then listen. It's always a long shot, and there's no guarantee. But it will help that you don't know him. It may make it easier. And if you're going, you have to go immediately. Before it's too late. Before you can't change it."

Aggie felt a sense of panic. "I don't have a plan."

"You don't have time for a plan," Viola said bluntly. She took a quick look around the shuttle bus, then picked up the flowered aluminum cane and thrust it into Aggie's hands. "Here. Take this. It's the only thing."

Aggie looped the cane's elastic band around her wrist and closed her fingers on the rubber grip.

"Be careful, dear," Viola cautioned. "Now go."

Aggie threw open the door to the shuttle and scrambled out. She looked down at herself and despaired of the long skirt, the woolen shawl. But there was no time to even consider a change of clothes.

Gathering her skirts, she ran toward the ramp that led up to the street. She had almost reached the sidewalk when she plowed into a tall figure. It was Abe. He was dressed in the Yale t-shirt and sweatpants he wore for his early morning walks.

"Aggie." He put his hands on her shoulders to keep her from stumbling. "What are you doing out so early—" He stopped abruptly, and in a split second took in her frantic expression and the cane in her hand. Looking back down the ramp, he saw Viola's anxious face looking out from the shuttle. Comprehension flooded his features along with a look of alarm.

"No," he said. "Whatever it is, you can't go! You're not prepared."

His hands tightened on her shoulders, but Aggie pulled free. With an eerie feeling of detachment, she analyzed the situation, her brain clicking through her options.

She knew he could keep her from traveling just by looking at her. *Another person's concentrated attention holds you in the present.* She could turn on her heels and bolt, but Abe would recover quickly, and she couldn't outrun him—the thought was ridiculous. Words wouldn't help. There was no time to explain, no time to waste in argument. And he couldn't be convinced, anyway. He was a beautiful man, but too stubborn. Just like her husband had been too stubborn.

Well, she could be stubborn, too. She knew what she must do.

She wouldn't need to convince him or outrun him. He was a companion traveler. He could follow her into the past, but not stop her. Go where she was going, but only for moments. Her travel was primary. His was weaker, ancillary. He couldn't seize control of the steering wheel. If he tried, he'd be evicted.

She closed her eyes for a second, as if signaling a willingness to listen to him. A little of the tension left Abe's body, and, almost as if embarrassed to be standing so close, he took a step back. Aggie reached her hand out to him as if she had given up, as if she was willing to have him escort her, without protest, back to the safety of the garage.

As he took her hand, Aggie curled her fingers around his. But she did not move, did not speak, and did not look at him. Instead she focused on Viola's cane which she held in her other hand. In the dim light from the street she studied it. She saw that the flowers on the cane were roses. She

237

didn't know a lot about roses. It was odd, really. She had never grown roses.

"Aggie!" There was a note of fear in Abe's voice. He had realized what she was doing. "Aggie, you can't. You're not protected. You won't be safe, and I can't help you."

"You're costing me time I don't have." She did not raise her eyes from the cane but let him hear the anger in her voice. Resolutely, she closed her mind to him and focused on her destination. It's four hours ago. I am asleep. A tornado wreaked havoc in Kansas. The Yankees won. Someone at the *New York Times* reviewed a superhero movie.

Abe was still holding her hand, but his grip had loosened. She didn't want to think about Abe but tried to convey a silent message: *Give up. Go back.*

She thought about her first trip at the barn and Axel's story about the spider, the strands of knowledge and connection that would bring her to her destination and hold her there. She knew Abe had no idea where she was going or why. If he traveled with her—angry and desperate to stop her—he wouldn't be able to stay. And once he fell away, he wouldn't be able to seek her out again.

Suddenly, she knew he was gone. Whether he had given up or been evicted, she didn't know. She raised her eyes and scanned the street. It lay in darkness, but it wasn't the same darkness. She was still standing at the top of the ramp, but the shuttle bus was gone, and there was something different about the air.

She stepped out onto the sidewalk and headed toward Grand Central. There was an electric feel to the atmosphere. It was palpable, almost a smell. A flash of lightning lit the sky, but the sound of thunder didn't reach her. Instead, she heard the distant rumble of traffic and tires, car horns and sirens. City noises, persistent but indistinct.

She reached the west side entrance of the station in less than a minute. The area was unlit and almost deserted. A construction site across the street was a shrouded skeleton. Tarps draped around the perimeter of the work area flapped in the night like the sails of a derelict ship. A sign on the station door said the side entrance was locked at night, so Aggie moved through the shadows along the sidewalk toward the brighter lights of 42nd Street. She reached the corner, pulled open the heavy door, and headed down the wide ramp to the main concourse.

The giant room was startling in its near emptiness. It's almost two in the morning, she reminded herself. A homeless man shuffled along the corridor by the tracks and disappeared from view. Two young women with backpacks raced off across the open space in the direction of the subway. A group of millennials in business attire galloped down the stairs from the restaurant on the mezzanine on their way out.

For a crazy second Aggie considered accosting them and asking for help, but the idea died in an instant. What good would it do? What would she say? *There's going to be an attack. I need you to come with me. Someone needs help.* Seeing herself through their eyes she knew what they would think and, therefore, what they would do. She was a senior, oddly dressed, babbling nonsense. The men would follow the prescribed set of behaviors used to avoid a mentally disturbed person. Don't make eye contact. Don't respond to the crazy person's pleas. And don't stop moving. Aggie felt a flash of shame knowing she had behaved that way herself. But there was no time for shame. The hands on the brass clock in the main concourse—the clock with four faces of opalescent glass—told her time was running out.

She gathered her skirts again and ran. It crossed her mind that she couldn't recall a day in the recent past—and the not so recent past—in which she had gone anywhere by running. As she approached the entrance to Vanderbilt Hall, she slowed to catch her breath.

With cautious steps, she advanced into the cavernous exhibition space. Aggie saw that the exhibit had been created with a lovely reverence for history. A giant Beaux Arts arch had been erected, spanning the width of the hall. Gilt lettering wove along its framework: *Portraiture in New York: From John Singer Sargent to Cartoon Caricatures.* Beyond the arch, tall panels held framed portraits in all styles and dimensions. The panels had been positioned to create booths and delineate walkways for visitors. A placard at each booth denoted the time period and characterized the portraits inside: *Edwardian Elegance, Faces of the Jazz Age, SoHo Souls.* One booth had the simple title *Mugs* and featured striking black-and-white photos of Depression-era workers.

Where were the security guards? The artwork in the room was priceless. She heard a commotion from the main concourse and looked over her shoulder. A dozen teenage boys were leaping about, tossing a Frisbee back and forth. A security guard was holding his arms up and gesturing them toward the exit. She saw a police officer run up and join the effort.

Then voices from deep in the exhibit drew her attention. Slipping through the barrier with the 'closed' sign, she headed along one of the pathways that led into the maze of booths. Turning a corner, she saw Tyrece Vinci seated on a stool in front of a display of his drawings. Ranged in front of him were three sharply dressed young men. The one in the center, a man with a wide nose, pale skin, and white-blonde hair, appeared to be the leader. He leaned aggressively toward the artist, hissing something inaudible. Aggie recognized the belligerent posture of the bully. Flanked by acolytes, he was confident his victim had no means of escape.

Tyrece started to rise from his stool but was shoved back to his seat. In slow motion, the blonde man pulled a gun from his waistband. Tyrece slowly shook his head and raised his hands in a placating manner.

Aggie moved forward, slid behind one of the partitions, and worked her way closer to the confrontation.

"You think that picture is *funny*?" the blonde man spat contemptuously. He pointed to a large group portrait done in Vinci's signature cartoon style. It showed a gang of ruffians gathered in front of a Manhattan skyline. Aggie recognized Bernie Madoff, Boss Tweed, and John Gotti. Another figure held the banner of the German American Bund. Someone else in the crowd held a cardboard box labeled 'Lehman Brothers.' A small sketched character at the back of the crowd thumbing through a roll of bills resembled the blonde man.

"Stupid nigger," one of the blonde man's sidekicks sneered.

Tyrece didn't react, his eyes never leaving the gun. The ringleader slowly moved the weapon forward, tapping it gently against the artist's forehead.

One of the sidekicks snickered. "Hey, Kasper, check it out. His face's got Frankenstein stitches."

The blonde man scrutinized the scar, waggling the gun in front of the artist. "Tsk, tsk. Not a pretty sight."

With tremendous slowness, Tyrece placed the palm of one hand against the muzzle of the gun and started pushing it, inch by inch, away from his face. The action seemed to infuriate the blonde man, and a look of rage flooded his countenance.

Aggie knew there was no more time. Stepping out from behind the partition, she hooked the curved handle of the flowered cane over the blonde man's arm and yanked as hard as she could. It was almost surprising to hear the explosive report of the gun as it went off before flying from the blonde man's hand and skittering across the floor. For a second, no one moved. The three thugs just stared at her in shocked disbelief.

The flowered cane had been pulled from Aggie's grasp and hung loosely from the blonde man's arm. He stared stupidly at it for a moment, before unhooking it from his sleeve.

One of the other men started to giggle. "Hey, bag lady to the rescue."

The blonde man gave a grunt of anger. Raising the cane, he swung it at Aggie to bat her aside, but Tyrece sprang from his stool throwing himself in front of her. With a sickening thud, the cane hit his head, and he went down.

"No," Aggie cried out, and dropped to her knees. Tyrece lay still, his eyes closed. Aggie put two fingers on the side of his neck and was relieved to feel his pulse. Kasper snorted, threw the cane to the floor, and looked about for his gun.

A voice from the corner stopped him, a voice Aggie recognized. She looked up in shock.

"This you don't need, boy." Axel walked out from behind a partition, Kasper's gun in his hand. Deliberately, he set the weapon on the stool where Tyrece had been sitting and surveyed the scene in front of him with disdain. "What a mess you make. So much mess for no reason. You ask for trouble, Kasper, and you find it."

Aggie was stunned. *How was he here?* Had he companion traveled with Abe? Aggie looked around, but it was clear Axel was alone. *But how could he do that?* How was time making room for both of them?

Axel had addressed the blonde man by name. The two goons had fallen back. In growing astonishment, Aggie realized they knew the old man—knew him and feared him. Kasper shifted nervously, his former bravado gone.

Slowly, Axel took stock of their surroundings then turned to Aggie. "Not good for the knees to be on floor like that." Grasping her by the arm, he pulled her to her feet, then looked her up and down. "Wrap up the hand," he said roughly. "Will stop the bleeding."

Puzzled, Aggie looked down. She was shocked to see a long gash along the back of her hand and blood smeared on her wrist and fingers. "But how—" She stopped abruptly, unable to form a question.

"Bullet grazed you. Lucky nothing worse," Axel said shortly. "Wrap up the hand," he commanded again. With a sense of unreality, Aggie twisted a corner of her shawl around the wound.

Axel's attention had shifted back to the young men. He gestured to the blonde man's companions. "You two, go now. Kasper, you stay." The blonde man flushed angrily. The others, after looking at each other uncertainly, turned and disappeared along the pathway that led out through the exhibit. There was an uncomfortable pause as Axel studied the young man standing before him. "You do better to be out of the business," he said contemptuously. "Leave it to men who don't make trouble so much."

"Leave it?" The young man's voice quavered, but his chin rose in defiance. "*Leave it?* Do you know how much I've expanded the organization? Grown the business?"

Axel glared at him, then with infinite deliberation, pulled something from his pocket. There was a click, and a long shining blade appeared. Axel held the jack knife expertly, with assurance.

"*Wujek*, Uncle … I didn't … listen to me …." Kasper held up his hands in a gesture of conciliation, but, with a swift motion, Axel took hold of the young man's shirt and pulled him close.

"Stop," Aggie cried.

Axel ignored her. His blue eyes glinted like slivers of ice. "You do better to be out," he repeated, holding the knife in front of the younger man's face. "Expand the organization? Make more business? That's no matter. Business is business. This," he gestured toward where Tyrece lay unconscious, "this is foolishness. *Pride.*" He spat out the word.

In a swift movement, Axel's hand moved from the blonde man's shirt to the back of his neck. Gripping a fold of skin, as if holding a puppy, he turned Kasper's face to Tyrece's Gangs of New York portrait. With the hand holding the knife, he pointed toward the picture. "See, *jestes glupcem!* You a fool. You make that true." None too gently, he released the young man and shoved him away.

Still holding the knife, the old man rotated slowly, eyes moving carefully around the exhibit. He sniffed once, as if catching the scent of something unpleasant, and strode toward the wall. Behind a screen, one of Vanderbilt Hall's old wooden benches stood against the marble wall. Leaning over, Axel felt along its surface until his hand reached the place where the bullet had buried itself. He grunted and—wielding the knife as delicately as a surgeon with a scalpel—pried the metal cylinder from the wood. Walking back, he paused, bent over again, and picked up the shell casing.

Reaching Aggie, he took her arm and unceremoniously pulled the shawl from her hand. He was still clutching the knife, and she flinched and tried to pull away. His grip tightening, he scowled, shaking his head.

"We have here a predicament. A mess." He studied her bloody hand. With a sharp movement he snapped the knife closed and stowed it in a pocket of his coat. Then, using both hands, he felt each of her fingers, as if satisfying himself no bones were broken. His inspection complete, he placed the bullet and casing in her palm and curled her fingers around them.

"The woman doctor, Mirlande. She sews up good. What you do now is go back. Carry these back so evidence is gone."

Carry them back? Aggie looked at him in total confusion. He radiated anger, but it didn't seem aimed at her. In fact, there was something else behind his eyes. Almost a look of respect.

"You don't know till you try," he explained impatiently. "Then you try, and, if you still don't know, you try more. You *persist.*" He tapped his chest then pointed at Aggie. "Two of us are here together, in the past at the same time. Everyone says this is not possible. Rules can't be broken. Travel alone is all you get. Travel as companion is all you get." His expression darkened. "I never accept when someone tells me that is all I get. I experiment. I persist. I try many times."

He pointed to her. "You can intervene. This I cannot do. All the changes to this time only possible because you are here. So perhaps you can carry. Objects are small. Only need to take them a few hours away. So you try," he ordered.

"What if it doesn't happen?"

"If no happen, then no happen. Just more of a mess, more predicament."

She nodded slowly. From somewhere outside, a siren wailed. Footsteps and shouting could be heard from the concourse.

Axel turned to the blonde man. He was staring at them with an expression of total confusion on his face, as if they were speaking a foreign language. "Uncle—" he began, but the old man cut him off.

"Go," he ordered, "and do not use this." He picked up the gun and handed it to Kasper. His voice sharpened. "Go. Now." The blonde man shoved the gun in his waistband and sprinted off along the corridor leading to the exit.

Axel faced Aggie. "Now you," he commanded. She ignored him. Stepping over to Tyrece, she dropped to her knees again and assured herself he was breathing normally.

The sounds from outside the exhibition hall grew louder. Axel lifted his shoulders impatiently. "Boy is okay. *Leave now.* No more time left. I go, too. Police will arrive, ambulance."

"You go first," Aggie directed, "I'll follow."

"But—"

It was her moment to be harsh. "*I'll follow.*" She looked up at him, and her voice softened. "Thank you, Axel. I'll be along directly."

He nodded and stepped behind one of the partitions. He was out of sight and, in a fraction of a second, she knew he had left.

At that moment, Tyrece opened his eyes. He stared up at her, but his gaze was unfocused. Gently, she covered his eyes with her hand and formed the intent to return. In the next breath, she knew she was back.

Tyrece was gone. During the hours she had skipped, he would have been discovered, carried off to a hospital, treated. It was still early morning, but the station was open now, and a rush hour crowd was already moving about. Quickly, Aggie moved along the pathway through the exhibition booths, slipped around a barrier, and joined the throngs of people moving in and out of Vanderbilt Hall. Everyone around her was walking, talking, texting, moving out toward the doors on 42nd street or in toward the main concourse.

And here she was, in her odd clothing, observed by no one. Well, maybe not entirely unobserved. At the far end of the gallery, she perceived a broad, square figure, an older man in a dark overcoat. She couldn't really tell, not from this distance, but his eyes looked like blue ice.

From nowhere, she was hit by pain in her hand. She glanced down and saw a slash of dried blood along her wrist. Involuntarily, her fingers closed in a fist, and she felt the metal on her palm. She had carried the bullet and casing back with her.

Chapter 30 ~ Implications

Walking back to the underground garage seemed to take forever. It was like sleepwalking, except for her uncomfortable awareness of a shadowy presence following in her wake. Axel was somewhere behind her in the early morning crush of commuters, but every time she turned to look, he was gone.

When she reached the entrance to the garage, she walked down the ramp, moving from the early morning sunlight of the street into the shade of the underground structure. She paused after a few feet to let her eyes adjust. To her enormous relief, the shuttle was there. Abe was there as well, pacing back and forth on the concrete surface, his entire body displaying an intensity of emotion she had never seen from him. As she watched he balled up his fist and slammed it against the rear of the vehicle, before pulling it back in pain.

For some reason, it struck her as funny, and she started to laugh. "You're going to hurt yourself," she admonished. She had spoken in a low voice, but somehow, he heard. Looking up, he saw her and rushed forward.

"My God, Aggie, how could you be so *reckless*? What the *hell* were you thinking?" He looked her over head to toe, and she winced as his eyes focused on the edge of the shawl wrapped around her hand. "God *damn* it! What happened? Let me see—"

A voice from the shadows interrupted him. "Don't unwrap it," the voice commanded. "Not so pretty, but not so bad. Get some stitches, will be okay." Axel stepped forward, his face, once again, expressionless.

Abe's next words took her by surprise. "You found her then. Thank God. I was afraid you'd be too late."

"You sent him?" Aggie said sharply. "You knew he could … be in the same place?"

It was Axel who answered. "Abe doesn't tell people's business." He stared at her coldly. "You must do the same now. My business is my business."

"But how did you find me? How did you know where I was?" Aggie demanded.

For a moment, she wasn't sure Axel would answer, but then he shrugged. "Not hard. The old woman knows. Viola. She is not one for trusting me, but Abe convinces her."

Aggie's eyes darted from one man's face to the other, trying to make sense of what had happened. A sudden wave of pain and fatigue fell over her. "I think I need to sit down," she said.

Abe flew into action, taking her arm to lead her toward the elevator.

"Wait." Aggie pulled free and went back to Axel. "Thank you for your help," she said quietly, and held out her hand. He placed his own hand under her clenched fist. Aggie allowed her fingers to loosen and felt the bullet and casing drop into his palm. Swiftly, he drew his hand back and put it in his pocket.

Her brow furrowed as her eyes scanned his face, studying the contours of his features. "Conor Pulaski," she said.

He gave a tiny affirmative nod, and, for a moment, Aggie thought she saw a hint of something warmer in his eyes. "My youngest sister, her boy."

Abe looked from one to the other, baffled.

"I don't discuss people's business either," Aggie said with a wry smile.

Axel nodded again. "I am going now. There are many things to arrange." He turned his back on them and walked up the ramp that led to the street. Once again, Abe took Aggie's arm to guide her toward the elevator.

"There's going to be hell to pay," he warned.

"From Lillian?"

"God, no. I'm not going to say a word of this to Lillian," he said as the elevator doors closed in front of them. "But Mirlande will have to know. And she's going to kill us."

***

An hour later, Aggie's hand was stitched and bandaged. Mirlande, indeed, had not been pleased. She had opened the door to Abe's knock and narrowed her eyes as she took in Aggie's wrapped hand and blood-stained wrist. She pulled them both into the room before letting out a stream of Haitian Creole aimed directly at Abe. At the same time, she had taken Aggie into the bathroom, unwrapped her hand, bathed it gently, then seated her on a chair by the bed. She was still muttering as she opened a small doctor's bag and prepared to stitch the gash left by the bullet. Axel had been right. Her hand was not pretty to look at, but no bones had been broken.

Mirlande placed a dressing over her handiwork, before leveling an accusing finger at Abe. "*W ap konn Joj!*" she said sharply.

Abe winced. Aggie gave him a questioning look.

"I'm going to know George," Abe translated. "Like the hurricane. She's saying I'm going to get hit by a storm—get what's coming to me—unless I mend my ways."

"You should have learned from Viola," Mirlande said, reverting to English.

"You can't blame me for Viola," Abe protested. "You know there's no controlling that woman."

Mirlande ignored him and turned to Aggie. "Ms. May, you poor dear, if Abe comes to you with any more *harebrained schemes* to do this, or solve that, or go here, or go there, I want you to tell him to jump in the lake."

Aggie looked at Abe. "Would it help if I said you tried to stop me?"

"Probably not."

Mirlande handed Aggie a small brochure and softened her tone. "Here are instructions on how to care for your hand. I will check on it later. When you get to your room, break a glass in the wastebasket." She noted Aggie's confusion. "It is your explanation for the stitches. Everyone will be nosy. Just say you cut it on the glass. Now go rest," she said firmly. Turning to Abe, she crossed her arms and tapped her foot. "We're only here a few more hours," she said sternly. "Try to stay out of trouble."

Abe walked Aggie to her room and helped her open the door. Once inside, he stepped into the bathroom, and she heard the smashing of glass. He emerged holding a small wastebasket. "I took care of your alibi," he said setting the basket near the door. His eyes roamed around the room. "Can I do anything else?"

She looked around distractedly. "No, not now. But later we need to talk. I have a lot of questions."

"I have questions, too."

"We may need another meeting with an agenda," Aggie said with a small smile. "I think I need to hear your thoughts about people having— how did you put it? —a diversity of skills and abilities."

"And how—as you put it—each one is unique."

He reached out and brushed a wave of hair back from her face, then let his hand linger against her cheek. His voice dropped to a whisper. "I was terrified for you."

She gave a shaky laugh and whispered back. "I was terrified, too."

***

When Abe was gone, Aggie showered, using the disposable shower cap in the bathroom to keep her bandaged hand dry. After toweling her hair, she eyed the bed, but rejected the idea of a nap. Her earlier fatigue was gone. Despite Mirlande's order to rest, she knew she wouldn't sleep.

She got dressed then sat at the writing desk, opened her notebook, and began to record the events in Grand Central. When she finished, she picked up her cell phone, turned it on, and tapped her news app. She scrolled through several stories before finding what she was looking for.

A young caricature artist featured at the Grand Central Portraiture Exhibit was hospitalized overnight after suffering a mild concussion following a fall. The artist, Tyrece Vinci, was apparently rearranging some of his works just prior to closing time when he either tripped or fainted. Security guards posted at the exhibit's entrance only discovered Mr. Vinci after removing a crowd of disruptive late-night revelers who had attempted to move into the exhibit area. Vinci's illustrations, which feature prominent New York celebrities and powerbrokers, have been a popular component of the exhibit....

Aggie turned off the phone and set it aside. She shivered. The other story was gone now. She added a paragraph in her notebook about the changed news item then leafed backward through the pages, reviewing earlier entries.

She stopped at the page she had begun after the Show and Tell session held on her first night at the Lodge. At the top were the two questions she had posed:

What is the role of love? What are its implications?

The rest of the page was blank. She had always intended to answer those questions. But insights had eluded her.

There was a knock on the door. It was Julie.

"I came to see if you were back from Central Park. Maybe we could check out that art exhibit and—oh, my gosh! What happened to your hand?"

Aggie spun out the story Mirlande had provided. She didn't like misleading Julie but didn't see any way of explaining the events of the past few hours. "So, I didn't make it to Central Park, but it's not a big deal. Just a few stitches."

"Not a great way to start the day, for sure," Julie said. "So, do you want to check out the exhibit? Go to lunch?"

"I hope you don't mind, but I think I'm going to take a walk."

"Okay. Do you want company?"

"Thanks, but I was thinking of heading over to the park. To Bethesda Fountain." The plan had formed just as the words came out of her mouth. She gestured toward the picture of Jacob.

Julie picked up the framed photo then looked at Aggie and nodded her head. "I understand. I'll catch you later then."

Aggie stood and was about to close her notebook when her eyes fell once again on the page with the questions about love. "Julie, did you ever look up the definition of love?"

Julie recited without hesitation. "*A deep and intense affection or romantic attachment.*"

"Is that the first definition?"

"Yes. But I rather like the third one: *a feeling of goodwill toward one's fellow man.* It seems a little more inclusive."

"What about empathy?"

"I looked that one up not too long ago. Viola's always talking about empathy. My favorite part of that definition is this: *the ability to sense and share other people's emotions.* Those might not be the most modern definitions, though. They're from my momma's old dictionary that I used as a child."

Aggie smiled. "I don't think I need more modern definitions. The old ones seem fine." She closed the notebook and picked up her key.

When they reached the lobby, Julie put a hand on her arm and regarded her uncertainly. "What you're doing, it's not easy. It can mess you up. That's why Lillian warns against it."

Aggie gave her a quick hug. "I'll be careful," she said and walked out into the sunshine.

Chapter 31 ~ The Better Angels

Aggie felt curiously short of breath as she approached Bethesda Fountain. She wasn't sure why she had decided to do this. She wondered if what Julie said was true. Would seeing Jacob mess her up? Perhaps. But she had not faltered on her way to the park. Somehow, she knew it was time to watch her husband, her lovely angel, as he posed for a picture on that long-ago day.

She paused beneath the arches that faced the terrace. She could see the fountain, but it was early yet. It would be closer to midday when she reached her destination, and there were bound to be crowds. She decided it would be better to view the scene from a higher vantage point, so she turned and climbed halfway up the stairs leading to the upper level of the terrace.

She marveled at the beauty of the stone carvings framing the stairway. She knew that the sculptor, Jacob Wrey Mould, had sought to make each panel different. All four seasons were represented, as were the varying times of day. It was perfect. All of time embodied in this one place. She placed her hand near a carved bird framed by leaves and flowers and focused.

Suddenly, the light grew stronger, as if a cloud had moved revealing the face of the sun. She heard voices and the laughter of children. Looking up, she took in the scene before her. She saw Roscoe first, the center of attention, of course. He was standing at the edge of the fountain, directly in front of the angel, miming her stance, his arms spread like wings. A gaggle of children watched as Roscoe peered over his shoulder, checked the angel, then flapped his arms and swooped toward the little ones. They scattered like a flock of sparrows, whooping and hiccupping with laughter, then returned to watch as Roscoe resumed his pose by the fountain.

Aggie walked back down the steps, all thoughts of keeping her distance gone. A crowd of other visitors were standing about or sitting here and there enjoying sandwiches, sunbathing, snapping photos. Then she heard a voice to her right and stopped.

"Hold still a minute, Mr. Angel. Let me get this shot."

Aggie felt tears sting her eyes. She turned and beheld Jacob, not three feet from where she stood. He was holding his camera and grinning at her brother's antics, a wisp of smoke rising from his cigarette. Raising the camera, he clicked off a few shots in quick succession before taking a drag on the cigarette and blowing out a trail of smoke.

"Your turn," Roscoe called, dropping his arms and bounding over to Jacob. He grabbed the camera and shooed her husband to the edge of the fountain. Jacob stood with his arms at his sides, a resigned expression on his face.

Roscoe gave him a stern look. In a ridiculous French accent, he berated his brother-in-law. "Ah, sir, you must not stand like zee man before zee firing squad." The flock of children listened, fascinated, to this entirely new character. "He is like zee stick in zee mud, no?" Roscoe consulted his small fans for affirmation.

A small boy tugged on his mother's skirt, repeating the funny new words. "Zee stick in zee mud, Mommy."

Clowning for his audience, Roscoe dashed forward and began posing Jacob, pulling his arms out as if they were wings.

Jacob laughed in surrender. "Okay, Monsieur Le Director, take your picture."

And there it was. Roscoe snapped the photo, the same photo she took with her wherever she went. The scene held such natural charm that she found it difficult to resist the impulse to rush into Jacob's arms, kiss him, and laugh at her brother's antics. Her husband was *right there*, laughing and alive. The sun flashed off his glasses, and she could smell the tobacco from his cigarette.

"Come on, Roscoe. This 'stick in the mud' needs a cold drink before we do any more hiking around, and I told Aggie we'd be home for supper."

Roscoe grinned and handed the camera back to Jacob. Some of the children were now experimenting with angel wings of their own, stretching their arms and flapping wildly as if they could soar into the air. "We're angels, we're angels," they chanted, jumping up and down.

"I could make my home right here," Roscoe said. "The munchkins have the Land of Oz. Alice has Wonderland. We angels have Central Park. It's the home of all angels. We belong here."

"The last time anyone set up housekeeping here was during the Depression," Jacob said. "Homeless people came to the park, and a Hooverville sprang up."

"What happened to those people?"

"They were evicted. The judge gave each man two dollars from his own pocket, though. He must have empathized with men who didn't have a lot of choices."

Roscoe turned back for a last look at the fountain. "*Angels in America.* Maybe Tony Kushner felt the same thing. Empathy for men who didn't have a lot of choices. Maybe that's why he put this angel in his play. An angel who heals."

"Maybe we all come to the park to heal," Jacob said. "It's a place of rest. But it's time we got going, kid. Your sister's expecting us home on time."

Aggie trembled. The two men she loved most in the world were walking directly toward her. She longed to fall into step with them, reach for her husband's hand, look into his eyes, and have him *see* her. She knew it couldn't happen. She was not really there, not in any way that mattered. She stood without moving as they passed. Roscoe was chattering away and didn't notice her at all. For a fraction of a second, Jacob's eyes moved across her face, but he walked on without a moment's hesitation.

Aggie watched until they disappeared. Her tears blurred the images around her, and she felt the chill of a late September day. The warmth of that long-ago summer had vanished. She found a tissue and blotted her eyes before turning to leave. A tall figure leaned against one of the columns of the terrace passageway. It was Abe. He shrugged apologetically, unsure of his reception.

"Fancy meeting you here," she said.

He colored slightly. "I thought you might want company for the walk back. The first time you do personal travel, it can throw you for a loop."

"How did you know I was doing personal travel?"

"You didn't look like you were going to rest. And I saw your husband's picture in your room. And ... I sensed it when I touched your face."

"My brother Roscoe took that picture. He was in town for a visit, and Jacob took him to see *Angels in America*. My brother is an actor. He loved the play, and New York, and the angel. He had to see the angel." Aggie laughed softly. "He had to *be* the angel, actually. And he made Jacob pose that way, too."

"So, no regrets?"

"That's the same question Viola asked our first night."

"It's an important question. It's the reason Lillian opposes personal travel and talk of intervention. She's seen—we've both seen—travelers consumed by regret. Regret for things they said or did. Things they ought to have said or done. Loved ones you can't be with anymore. A spouse you can't touch. Sometimes a child. We get older and see how close we are to the end of things, and we want to return to a different point in our lives. Like being away a long time and wanting to go home. It's homesickness. Heartsickness."

"It wasn't that way for me."

"But I saw you crying."

"Yes. There's sorrow, but it was beautiful as well. Beautiful and silly and carefree. Jacob wasn't sick yet, and Roscoe gets everyone around him to smile. It's his great gift. He said —" She stopped abruptly. What had he said? She thought for a moment. It was something important. "He said the park was the home of all angels. That was the church in Seneca Village. All Angels. And you talked about being away a long time and wanting to go home. *Abe, this was their home.* Don't you see? Gabe and Lula. Not here exactly, but Seneca Village. It was their home. Where they met. It's where they would bury the baby and the soldiers."

Abe stared into her eyes trying to follow her reasoning. "But there's no evidence."

"I know. But I think I'm right. Maybe the park has an aura. Maybe it's something else. Listen, I don't believe in angels, but I believe in people. And people I care about—Jacob, and Roscoe, and you—are telling me something. Something about this place and angels and home."

"The people you care about—"

She put a hand on his arm. "We will have that conversation, but right now we need to go look. Are you done walking this morning, or can you go a little farther?"

He drew himself up in mock dignity. "I think I can last a few more miles."

"Come with me then. If we go together, two sets of eyes, I think we can find them."

Abe nodded. "Companion travel it is then, Ms. May. As always, I am at your service."

***

They waited by the 85th Street entrance to the park. A quick call to Julie verified the entrance existed in 1882.

"You could have googled it," Abe pointed out.

"Julie's faster than googling if it's something she's read about."

Aggie had worried about her appearance. After her shower she had pulled on jeans and a stretchy knit top that hugged her body. "I'm not wearing period clothing," she fretted.

"It won't matter," Abe said. "I saw Gabe set out that night. It was cold and late. No one will be about. And if they are, well, your hair isn't too long," his eyes moved over her body, then he unzipped his sweatshirt and handed it to her, "and this will hide your, um, figure. From a distance you'll look like a man. A short man, I mean." He stopped, embarrassed.

She smiled at his discomfiture.

"Maybe you should take off your earrings, though."

Aggie tried to unfasten the gold hoops, but her bandaged hand made it impossible.

"Here, let me do it," Abe said. He fumbled a bit but was able to remove the earrings. "How did you put these on in the first place?"

"I put them on when I woke up. Before I got shot," she added dryly.

Aggie pulled on the sweatshirt and zipped it up. Abe dropped the earrings in his pocket. "We're ready."

They chose a tree near the pathway. Abe held out his hand, and Aggie grasped it. Without saying a word, they focused on the details of the bark.

Aggie concentrated on the destination. She knew the year, the month, the day. The time was not hard to reckon. A flood of confidence filled her. A lifetime of observing and recording, calculating and analyzing, told her they were on the right path.

The sun's disappearance and the sudden buffeting of wind signaled their arrival. Abe's fingers curled more tightly around her own, and their eyes met. The tree that had sheltered them was gone, but they remained screened by a cluster of saplings. A rattle of harnesses and the sound of horse's hooves drew their eyes to the narrow road.

"It's Gabe," Aggie whispered.

The wagon rolled slowly along pulled by a ghostlike dappled gray as shadowy and dark as the leaden sky overhead. Gabe sat on the narrow wooden seat with the young boy Aggie had seen at the homestead.

"Where will they go?" Abe asked.

For the first time, Aggie hesitated. "I thought it would be here. It's where All Angels was. But maybe they're going to where his home used to be or ...." Something was trying to enter her mind: an elusive memory of someone's words. *A sense of hope. The hope of having a normal, happy life.* "He's going to Summit Rock," she said with sudden conviction. "Maurice told us where they would be. Those youngsters he saw. Gabe and Lula. It must have been. It all fits. Everything we've been looking for. It all comes back to this. They want their baby to rest in the place they still thought of as home. The place that represented hope to them."

"Let's go look."

"Hurry," Aggie said urgently. "I want you with me, so we can both be witnesses. I don't want you evicted before it happens."

They darted forward, following the winding path into the park. A spit of rain blew against them, and the wind tore at their clothing. Abe put his arm around Aggie's shoulders and pulled her along. In a few hundred yards they saw the wagon standing empty at the side of the lane.

"This way," Aggie directed. A set of stone steps led upward, and they climbed together, reaching the top as thunder rolled across the crest of the hill. Aggie looked about, turning in a circle. No one was there. She turned an agonized face to Abe, but he was calm.

"Down there," he pointed, leaning close to be heard above the wind. "They can't dig in the rock. They went to the base."

Carefully, they inched their way back down. Abe pulled Aggie to a stop in a thicket of shrubs. Peering out, they saw Gabe, leaning on a shovel, his head bowed. The hole at the foot of the giant slab of rock was ready. Two small, white boxes rested at Gabe's feet. Aggie caught her breath. Each coffin was adorned with a slender branch of heart-shaped leaves and purple buds. Lilacs. She reached for Abe's hand and held it tightly in her own.

She was startled to hear Gabe speak. "I'm sorry you won't have the view. But it's a good place to rest. No one will bother you here. No one will move you out or say you don't belong."

"The angels will be watching over them, won't they Mr. Gabe?" the boy asked.

He rested his hand on the boy's shoulder. "Yes, child."

"Mr. Lincoln's better angels, isn't that so?"

"Yes. Mr. Lincoln's better angels."

"Want me to say a prayer for them now?"

"Yes, say a prayer for all of them."

The boy nodded. "What's the baby's name, Mr. Gabe?"

"His name is Lincoln. We named him after the president."

The boy considered this then squatted down and patted one of the little boxes. "You rest well now, baby Lincoln."

Gabe crouched next to him, and together they moved the coffins into the hole, placing one on top of the other. As they worked, the boy recited a prayer. A soft patter of rain had begun, and Aggie couldn't hear the words. As the prayer ended, Gabe began to shovel.

When the hole was filled, he knelt and smoothed the ground. As he got to his feet, a burst of wind bent the branches of the shrubbery where Aggie stood with Abe. Gabe's eyes widened. His grip on the shovel tightened.

"He sees us," Aggie whispered.

Slowly, Abe removed his cap and bowed his head in respect. Aggie lowered her eyes. Hearing no sound, she glanced up to see Gabe regarding the two of them as if considering what to do. He inspected Abe's tall figure and bent head, then Aggie's shorter form. His eyes lingered on her injured hand—the bandage visible.

"Let's go, child," Gabe said to the boy. "These folks don't mean any harm." With that, he shouldered the shovel, turned, and headed back toward the wagon.

At the same moment, Aggie felt the pressure of Abe's hand disappear. He had been pulled back. Now alone at the base of the rock, she walked to the burial site and knelt on the wet ground. The rain had already begun to erase any sign of digging, blurring the lines the shovel had created in the soft dirt. She used her uninjured hand to smooth the earth as Gabe had done. It was a familiar movement, like being at home in the spring and pressing the soil around a new shoot in the garden. She rose and turned her back to the granite wall, then closed her eyes and formed the intent to return. When she felt the sun on her face, she opened her eyes. Abe was there, waiting for her.

Chapter 32 ~ Debts

Aggie and Abe arrived at the Yale Club to find preparations underway for the trip back to Connecticut. As they crossed the lobby, the elevator door opened, and Lillian and Serena emerged, followed by Wells pushing Viola in her wheelchair. Seeing Aggie and Abe together, Serena threw her hair back and rolled her suitcase out the front door. Lillian didn't move. Her eyes had fastened on Aggie's bandaged hand, and she frowned.

"What happened?" she demanded.

Wells jumped in before Aggie could respond. "Mirlande said Ms. May cut her hand on a glass, and it needed a couple stitches."

"So silly of me," Aggie said shaking her head. "I went to get a glass of water to take my medications, but it slipped out of my hand and shattered." Lillian regarded her suspiciously.

"But you got everything accomplished this morning?" Viola asked, searching Aggie's face.

"Yes. I got everything accomplished."

"No harm done then," Viola said calmly.

"Daniel's coming to the Lodge tonight?" Abe asked, drawing Lillian's attention.

"Yes. He'll be with us this evening." She stopped and gave Abe a sharp look. "You found something."

"Aggie found something," Abe said. "I followed. We can explain tonight."

Lillian looked from Abe to Aggie, and a smile lit her face. "I was afraid for my old friend. Afraid we wouldn't have enough answers to give him peace."

The elevator doors opened again, and Sal emerged. "Hey folks, are we set to go?"

"Almost," Lillian said. She turned back to Aggie and Abe. "Get your luggage. I'll speak to the concierge and get us checked out."

Back in her room, Aggie packed her notebook and Jacob's picture then rolled her suitcase into the hall. She saw Julie waiting by the bank of elevators. Uncharacteristically, her friend didn't immediately burst into speech. Instead, she raised her eyebrows and gave Aggie a questioning look.

"I saw Jacob," Aggie said simply. "And my brother, when he was a young man."

Julie placed a tentative hand on Aggie's shoulder. "Are you okay?"

"I'm okay. But Julie, there's something else. When I returned, Abe was there. And suddenly, I knew where to look for Gabe, and the baby, and the portraits."

Julie's eyes widened. "You found them?"

"We found them together. We're going to tell everyone about it tonight at the Lodge, when Daniel is there."

Julie grinned, and Aggie found herself enfolded in one of her mentor's enthusiastic bear hugs. Releasing Aggie, she shook her head in wonder. "Yes, wait till tonight, so Daniel can hear it first. But, gosh, Aggie. *Gosh almighty.*"

***

They gathered in the library. Daniel wore a coat and tie. Lillian looked regal in a loose-fitting, black dress, her snow-white hair cascading around her shoulders. Maurice, Elizabeth, and a handful of the rookies were present as well. Erin, Carlos, and Angel sat on the carpet. Mirlande and Wells stood together in the doorway. Axel was not in attendance, although somehow Aggie was sure Abe had told him everything.

Lillian gave no introduction, simply gesturing toward Aggie. With very little preamble, Aggie related what had occurred at Summit Rock. Abe added a few observations but left most of the telling to her. She kept her eyes on Daniel's face as she spoke, making sure he was following the narration. "The baby's name was Lincoln. He would have been your uncle," she explained.

A look of peace tinged with sadness settled on the old man's face. *"Lincoln buried at home. Brady's soldiers to stand guard. With the angels as our witnesses.* What was written wasn't allegory. It was plain truth."

"So, they didn't have a portrait of Lincoln?" Kat asked.

"No, dear," Viola said gently. "The inscription is about the baby."

"But the other pictures are there, right?" Kat went on. "And they have that 'provenance' thing. What about them?"

"What happens now is up to Daniel," Lillian said. She glanced at her friend with affection and compassion. "The story is his."

There was silence for a moment, then Erin spoke up. She sat near Maurice's chair, with her arms wrapped around her knees. "Mr. Buckley, do you want the baby reinterred? Like, buried somewhere closer to you?"

Daniel shook his head. "My grandparents brought him to the place they wanted him to rest. The place they considered home. It was a home they had lost, but they saw it as a sanctuary for the baby and a fitting place for the soldiers." He looked at Maurice then back at Erin. "Your pa told me you sang some Irish ballads."

Erin colored and nodded.

"And these are your brothers? Lillian says you help look after them."
She nodded again.

Daniel looked around the circle of faces, then turned back to Erin.
"Well, tell me. What would you do if the decision was yours?"

Erin looked to Maurice. "Tell the man what you think," he said. "He
wants your opinion."

"Your grandpa and Lula were trying to make a home, weren't they?"
Erin asked. "And he was a good man and a good father?"

"I knew that when I was young," Daniel said, "and I know it even
more now."

"And the baby died because of the Civil War, didn't he? Because of
what it was about?"

"I would say that was so," Daniel agreed. "It was after the war. The
fighting was over. No one attacked them, but no one came to help. So
maybe it wasn't really after the war. Maybe the war was still going on.
Some might say it's still going on today. You understand what I'm
saying?"

Erin nodded. "If the decision was mine," she said slowly, "I'd tell
their story. As long as no one would try to move the baby or the
pictures."

"No one will move them," Lillian assured her.

"Then I would make sure people knew about Lula and Gabe," Erin
said with growing conviction. "And knew about the baby, and why the
baby died. Telling their story would be a way to give them honor."

Daniel gazed at the unlined face of the young woman, then at the
many older faces around the room. He reached out a hand to Lillian, and
she grasped it in her own. "A way to give them honor. That sounds right.
That's what we'll do."

***

Julie sat in the rocker in Aggie's room watching her pack. "I'm going
to miss you."

"I'm going to miss you, too. What made you decide to stay?" Aggie
asked curiously. "Don't you usually go home between sessions?"

"I'm not staying all the way to January. Dorothy and I will spend
Christmas together. I'm just staying a few extra weeks." She hesitated.
"Frank is staying, too. He asked me if I wanted to check out the new
sports bar in town and maybe catch a post-season game."

"And do you want to? Check out the new sports bar, I mean?" Aggie
tried to keep a straight face.

Julie started laughing. "We've always been like brother and sister, but
maybe it's time to explore the parameters of that."

"Well good for you!"

"What about you and Abe?"

"What do young people say? 'It's complicated,'" Aggie replied matter-of-factly.

"But you like him, don't you? And he likes you. Anyone with eyes can see that."

"I like him, but I didn't come here for romance. And I don't know him. *Really* know him. We've worked together for a month. We get along. Most of the time, anyway. I think I'm content with things the way they are. Just finding out about the Remarkables, adjusting to time travel, that's enough for me. Maybe some time down the road—"

"*There was never any more inception than there is now. Nor any more youth or age than there is now; and will never be any more perfection than there is now.*"

"What's that from?" Aggie asked suspiciously.

"Walt Whitman. *Song of Myself.* Notice the repetition of the word *now*?"

Aggie picked up a throw pillow and flung it at her friend, hitting her squarely on the side of the head. Julie dissolved in giggles.

"Good shot!"

"I grew up with younger siblings," Aggie said. "I have good aim."

***

Aggie left her suitcase at the Lodge along with the luggage of the other Remarkables heading home that afternoon. A lunch buffet had been set out in the dining room, but she wasn't hungry. She had already visited Maurice and his children, Elizabeth, and Lillian to express her thanks, but she wanted time for a few more personal goodbyes.

She made a quick visit to the restroom and, before leaving, pondered the new survey posted on the bulletin board. The question of the day was simple:

Which adjective is sadly underused with respect to seniors?

1. *Intrepid*
2. *Audacious*
3. *Dynamic*
4. *Perceptive*

Someone had penciled in a comment stating she'd "belt the next person who used the expression *sharp as a tack*." Aggie put a check mark by the first choice before heading outside.

She found Viola relaxing in an Adirondack chair near the gazebo. Bernice stood nearby, fiddling with what looked like a complicated pair of binoculars.

"Birdwatching?" Aggie asked.

"Drone watching," Bernice said excitedly. "Wells brought us this gizmo for field testing. It just got delivered. It's a prototype."

"He said one of your former students helped develop it," Viola added.

"Conor Pulaski. He got a scholarship from Hytech where my sister works, and I put Wells in touch with him a few weeks ago."

"Check these babies out," Bernice said admiringly, holding up the binoculars. Aggie saw immediately that they were not traditional binoculars. A long muzzle was attached on one side, along with what looked like an antenna.

"How do they work?" Aggie asked.

"Beats me," Bernice shrugged. "Wells is going to explain it to us. He said something about syncing it up to a laptop so you can hijack a drone and send it off course—like into a hornet's nest or down a well."

"Now, now," Viola said in a soothing voice. "Let's not get carried away. We just need a little privacy around here. Becoming a new Bermuda Triangle would invite attention and defeat the whole purpose."

"You're no fun," Bernice groused, then scanned the horizon. "Not much to see today, anyway. I'm going to walk up the hill, Vi. I'll be right back." She strode off, binoculars in hand.

"We never had much time to discuss what happened in New York," Aggie said when Bernice was out of sight.

"You don't need to tell me, you know. The ability to intervene is a blessing, but it's a burden as well. Not just because you risk injury. Soldiers accept that risk. So do first responders. But Abe gets quite agitated about that, and after I had a few little mishaps, I realized I shouldn't share everything with him and cause needless anxiety. And I couldn't explain that the real risk is emotional. You don't succeed every time. And when you don't, it stays with you. You agonize over the 'what ifs.'"

"Is that why you said it would be easier because I didn't really know Tyrece?"

"Yes. It's simpler that way. Your judgment is unclouded."

"I'm going to have to think about that."

"Of course you will. I'll be here in January. We can talk when you're ready."

They sat together until Bernice came wandering back, then Aggie rose and bade the women farewell. She had two more visits to make.

She found Axel in the barn. He was seated in front of the wooden table in the tack room, cleaning a rifle.

"You won't need that," Aggie said from the doorway. "Conor sent Wells a device to deal with the drones. It sends them off course."

The old man's eyes moved to her face, then back to the weapon. "Sometimes is good to have options."

"Are the drones because of you? Because of your ... business?"

He shrugged. "Abe finds out there is a club for children. Drones are mostly from that. But maybe not all. Is not a good idea to count on things that are *mostly*."

"I wanted to thank you again for helping me at Grand Central."

He nodded.

"Is Kasper Conor's brother?"

Axel grunted. "No. Different family. Kasper is one who will need watching."

"Did you know he would be there when Abe asked you to find me?"

"Doesn't matter whether yes or no. Abe says you need help, so I go. I owe him. I owe you. I pay debts. Works out I help my business, too, and keep Kasper out of trouble."

Aggie was taken aback. "Why do you owe *me*? Because of Conor? He earned that scholarship on his own."

Axel swiveled in his chair. "On his own? You keep him from being expelled. Probably with lies," he added shrewdly. "You teach him science."

His voice, usually cold and harsh, softened. "Conor is my youngest sister's boy, her only child. She never want him in my business. Never take any money from me. Why did you help him? I don't understand this. Conor was always wild. Smart, good brain, but always in trouble. Then he changes. Why?"

"He showed me who he really was. That gave me an opening. But you don't owe me a debt for that. I was Conor's teacher. What I did, that's just what teachers do."

Something occurred to her. "You said you owe Abe a debt, too." It felt like prying to ask, but she did anyway. "Is it something related to law enforcement? Is that how you crossed paths?"

Axel set the rifle down. His hands lay still. "Not that. That is something else. The debt I owe him is older business. He won't tell you. We meet, first time, in Poland. Many years ago."

"Poland? That's where—" Aggie stopped.

Axel's eyes met hers. "Yes, the debt is from there. We meet while searching the past, same time, same place. *Oswiecim*. Auschwitz. We hunt for our families. His grandparents. My father. We find them on different sides of the fence."

The ice had returned to his eyes. "When I was a boy, my father says he is part of the resistance. Always I have pride about this. Then I learn the truth. You say about Conor that he shows you who he really is. I see my father in the past—collaborator, liar—he shows me who he really is, too. He looks me in the face, not knowing the old man he sees is the boy he lied to. I see who he is, what he does, how he laughs at the misery of others." Axel spat on the floor. "I am not a good man, but I am not like my father. The day I meet Abe is the day I learn all of this. It means a debt. Later when we crossed paths, I help him, and he helps me. We talk about history. Men who are evil. Men who try to stop evil."

Axel turned from her and resumed work on the rifle. He had nothing more to say.

"Thank you for telling me," Aggie said quietly. He didn't look up as she left the room.

From the barn she headed down the path to Abe's cottage, stopping at the gate. Abe was in the yard. He wore jeans, a denim shirt, and a rather battered fedora. He had a trowel in his hand and a worried expression on his face. A large bucket stood at his feet filled with soil and a nice lilac split with half a dozen tall branches covered with heart-shaped leaves. The click of the gate latch made him look up.

"Thank goodness you're here," he said, looking relieved. "They made it sound so easy, but I'm not convinced it's going to work. This is from behind the barn because the garden club members said ones from a nursery can get *stressed*, and they're hard to find in the fall. But splitting it off the mother plant was a nightmare. Erin thought it would be good for me to do it myself," he said, looking rather affronted, "but the whole process seemed unnecessarily brutal. Apparently, fall is the best time to divide and transplant lilacs, but that can't be right. It's going to get *cold* and how this is going to *take*, I don't know."

Aggie struggled to keep from laughing. "First time doing this?"

"How did you know?" he asked sarcastically.

"Where are you going to put it?" she asked looking around the yard.

"It's not for *here*," he said appalled. His face softened. "It's for you. To take back to your garden. You said you don't have any."

She walked across the yard and crouched down to inspect the split. "It looks fine. It's a good divide. I know just where to put it, too." She rose to her feet and patted his arm in a reassuring way. "And fall is fine for dividing lilacs. You can do it in the spring as well, but fall is better. Thank you, Abe."

His eyes rested on the ugly scar on the back of her hand. "It's not enough."

"It's perfect."

263

"Wells said he'd put it in a wagon to bring up to the Lodge then load it on the bus." He gave the bucket a last look and turned to her. "Can you come inside a minute? I have something for you. Your earrings. I put them in my pocket that day in the park and forgot to return them."

She followed him into the cottage. The room was as before. The violin was out, and a pile of books sat on the table. Abe went to the bedroom and emerged a moment later with the earrings. She reached for them, but he held up his hand. "Let me do this. I think I've figured out how they attach."

"My hand functions perfectly, you know," Aggie said dryly. "Mirlande says it's all surface damage."

"Shh, I'm concentrating." She felt his hands moving gently against her cheek and ear—first one side, then the other. "Okay, done," he said with satisfaction. He studied her face. "What time are you leaving?"

"Three."

"You didn't come for your earrings, did you?"

"No. I didn't remember you had them."

"So, a different agenda?"

"Well, I wanted to say goodbye, of course. But on the way here, I saw Axel. He gave me some history. He said he owed me a debt because I helped his nephew. The boy was my student, brilliant, but troubled. He's okay now, though. Axel said he owes you a debt as well."

Abe frowned. "Many years ago, we saw things no one should have to see. He believed it created a debt, a debt for life. I've told him he owes me nothing. The guilt was never his. But he persists in that conviction. Several times over the years, I've taken advantage of that conviction. I did it again in New York. I don't know if it was wrong, but I couldn't have you hurt. I prevailed upon Viola to tell us where you went and what you were trying to do. As it turned out, Axel knew something about that mess at Grand Central because his associates were there. He had reason to go on his own, but he went for me as well, and for you. His way of thinking is that life is about debts. Debts owed and debts paid."

"Aren't we all in debt? To each other. To those that came before and those that will follow. We're all part of the whole. You can't draw lines around who matters and who doesn't."

Abe reached for her hand—the scarred one—and held it carefully in his own. For a moment they just stood that way.

"Hey there folks." Wells was in the doorway. "I came for the plant. It's that one in the bucket?" Suddenly he noticed their silence and Aggie's hand in Abe's. "Um, sorry to interrupt," he said, looking embarrassed. "I'll put the plant in the wagon, okay? Aggie, is your suitcase at the Lodge? We're, um, going soon."

"Yes, I'm all set," she responded with amusement. "I'll walk back up with you."

"Uh, right," Wells said and disappeared from the doorway. They could see him through the window, hoisting the bucket into a wagon.

Aggie turned back to Abe. "We have more to talk about, but there will be time. I'll be back in January."

"Then I look forward to our continued discussions." He looked suddenly restless, like he had more to say.

"What is it?"

Abe released her hand, pulled the fedora from his head, and slapped it against his thigh in sudden frustration. "Viola says you have to be in charge on this, Aggie. 'All the way down the line.' Traveling. Intervention. How much to share and how much to keep to yourself. I mean, I understand I blew it with her, trying to direct—she actually said *control,* and Bernice used the word *dictate*—and that's why she stopped saying anything to me about intervening. But then she said that was all water under the bridge, and the important thing was to get off on the right foot with you going forward, and—"

Aggie started laughing. Abe stopped talking and eyed her warily. Aggie tried to control herself, but his baffled expression set her off again. "I'm sorry," she finally managed to say. "I just would love to have been a fly on the wall when you had this discussion."

A reluctant grin appeared on his face. "You can laugh all you want but being called on the carpet by those two was more than a little unnerving."

"I think you'll recover," Aggie said. Then, on an impulse that struck like lightning, she took his face between her hands and kissed him.

Stunned by her own action, she took a step back. Abe stood completely still, his eyes seeking hers, one eyebrow raised in a query. Amusement appeared on his face as he waited for her to speak.

"Abe, I ...." She stopped, at a total loss for words.

"I hope you don't regard that as a mistake," he ventured.

She tilted her head to the side and considered. "It was a trifle unexpected, but it wasn't a mistake."

"Good," he said, "because this isn't either." With that, he kissed her back.

Aggie's kiss had been over in a flash. Abe took his time. Only a deliberately loud rapping on the doorframe caused them to step apart.

Wells stuck his head in the door again, displaying an exaggerated caution that made Aggie smile. "Uh, we've really got to get going here."

"I'll be right out," Aggie said and turned back to Abe. She could feel her heart pounding and knew her face was flushed. Abe looked a little flushed himself, she thought.

"Abe ... I want to talk about how this will work going forward. I just need time."

"Until January?"

"Until January." They regarded each other solemnly, then Aggie extended her hand. Now it was his turn to laugh, but he took her hand in his own, and they shook.

Aggie looked down at their clasped hands, then up at Abe. "Are you ... sensing anything?"

He held her hand for another beat, then released her. "From you? All the time." The familiar grin, the confident Indiana Jones grin, had returned.

"Then I expect you to keep me posted," she said.

"Of course. And you'll keep me posted, too? On the lilac. On how it's doing?"

"The lilacs will be fine," she laughed. "A rookie dug them up, but a veteran will plant them."

***

It was mid-November, a week before Thanksgiving, when Larry, a former student now working as a mail carrier, rang her bell. "Hi, Ms. M. You're a popular lady today. There's too much stuff to fit in the mailbox. I didn't want to just leave things outside 'cause there's rumors of snow." He held out a fat stack of envelopes and magazines.

"Thank you, Larry. Have a nice Thanksgiving if I don't see you."

"You too, Ms. M." He hitched his mail bag higher on his shoulder and set off again, whistling.

She watched as he hiked back along her driveway. A few hardy chrysanthemums still bloomed in the garden, and her own patch of Brussels sprouts was flourishing in the cold weather. The lilac bush was also doing well. She had planted it directly outside her kitchen window where it would get full sun.

Eva's student teacher had done a magnificent job caring for the garden and house and had left a note expressing her gratitude:

I planted some bulbs as a thank-you. Daffodils, tulips, and hyacinths. Hope you like them. Call me anytime you need a house-sitter. Or pet-sitter. Hubble is so sweet ....

Aggie had snorted at this and shot her cat a cynical look. "Ran a scam on that nice young student teacher, didn't you?" He yawned in response, stretched, and repositioned himself on the window seat to take better advantage of a patch of sun.

Walking back to the kitchen, she did a quick sort of the mail, setting aside the magazines, dropping the advertising flyers in the recycling bin, and carrying the rest to the kitchen table. The first item she opened was a thank you from the Potatuck Historical Society. She had sent a donation to help pay for fall plantings around the statue of the Civil War soldier on the green.

Next she read a note from Dr. Sterling reporting that the bloodwork from her recent wellness visit was normal. He had tutted at the scar on her hand but accepted the story about the broken glass.

"We need to take care as we age, Aggie. Our attentional reference frames change. Any other problems? Tripping? Clumsiness?"

"Nothing like that."

He studied the screen of his laptop. "You've lost weight. That's good news. Did you join a gym? Take up a new hobby?"

"No to the gym, but yes to the hobby. Nothing big," she assured him. "I'm just doing more walking. And I joined a community theater group."

"Excellent. So you're—"

"*Fine*," Aggie said and knew it was the truth.

The doctor gave her an inquiring look. "Did you follow my advice? Find inspiration from Einstein? Or Thoreau?"

"Actually, I found a measure of inspiration in Whitman."

"*Keep your face always toward the sunshine and shadows will fall behind you,*" the doctor recited.

"Exactly," Aggie said.

The next item in the stack was a card from Roscoe with a picture of the Bethesda Fountain Angel on the front:

Thanks for your call, sister dear. It was fun wandering through memories of that day in New York. Yes, I found some other prints from that same visit. I was so young and gorgeous. But weren't we all, really? I will send along copies as soon as I figure out what today's equivalent of a Fotomat is. Ah, Aggie. I cried looking at the pictures of Jacob, though he would not have wanted that, I know. What a sweet man he was.

Min says you had a good experience at that senior retreat, and you're planning to go back. I can't believe you had classes with Elizabeth Stevens! THE Elizabeth Stevens. Odd she decided to work with community theater. Especially (forgive me) community theater for oldsters. But lucky for you. CALL ME. See you at Christmas. Love, Roscoe.

Next, Aggie opened an oversized envelope with the Lodge's address printed in the corner. Inside was a new wall calendar, like her old one, with beautiful photographs of flowers on every page. The photo for

January depicted a spray of red roses in front of a window looking out on snow-covered trees. There was also a note in Abe's scrawl:

Saw this and thought of you. I read the January message and believe it is apt. How are the lilacs doing? Oddly, I'm actually interested in the answer. See you in a few weeks.

Aggie ran her hand over the words, then refolded the note to read again later.

The last item in the pile was a fat manila envelope from her sister. Minnie had a gift for stuffing an envelope with photos, newspaper clippings, raffle tickets, recipes, and anything else she wanted to share. Aggie emptied the contents onto the table. She admired a photo of her nephews ranged in front of the newly restored pickup truck then pulled her sister's note from the pile of other items:

Dear Aggie,
Can't wait for Christmas. I've already started an Excel spreadsheet. We have to catch Roscoe's show, of course, and the boys want deep dish pizza and a trip to the Museum of Science and Industry (me too). Speaking of travel, Hytech is sending me to New York for a training conference in the spring. I think I can wrangle an extra day or two to spend with you. New York in the springtime! What could be better? Lilacs, cherry blossoms, and bagels! I've enclosed a list of Central Park walking tours. Wouldn't that be fun? They all look wonderful especially the one on Seneca Village. I got interested because I read this long article (enclosed) about a child that was buried there in the 1800s along with glass plate negatives from Mathew Brady, the Civil War photographer! Amazing, huh? One more thing ... be sure to look at the article about the artist we saw at Comic Convocation. And check out the photo of his sketches. I think the one on the end LOOKS JUST LIKE YOU! Always knew my big sister was a superhero. LOL. The boys were so tickled. Let's talk soon.
Love, Minnie.

Aggie unfolded one of the newspaper clippings that had tumbled from her sister's envelope. She spread it flat, and Daniel's ancient eyes met hers. He had been photographed at Summit Rock, leaning on a cane and holding his Bible. Lillian was with him, and they were surrounded by a group of men and women, young and old, black and white. The caption stated they were from local community, religious, and park conservancy groups. By the time Aggie finished the article, she had to get up and bring a box of tissues to the table to wipe her eyes.

The second clipping offered an in-depth look at several of the contemporary artists whose work had been displayed at the Grand

Central exhibition. There was a nice full-color photograph of Tyrece smiling shyly next to a panel displaying some of his superhero portraits. One depicted an elderly, dignified Batman, another Captain America with a lined face. The third portrait showed an older woman in a navy blue wizard's robe. The woman had red hair, round wire-rimmed glasses, and a rather stubborn look on her face. Her hand, disfigured by an ugly scar, grasped a cane covered in carved pink roses.

Epilogue ~ New York City, April 1889

Gabe and Lula strolled along the pathways of the park, her arm tucked into his. She had a bonnet on, and a parasol open for welcome shade. It was warm this April, so different from the stormy night years before, the night the baby was laid to rest. It had been a long time before Lula could rise from her bed. And longer still until she was strong enough to emerge once more into the world. But the years that followed had been kind. There was the miracle of another child. Now, as they walked together, their boy scampered along beside them, chasing butterflies and stopping now and then to gape at the statues.

A few remarked on the couple and their son. The man's pale face contrasting with the woman's dark complexion, the child seemingly unaware of anything other than the beauty of the day and the enchantments of the park.

The family made this trip when they could, taking the train into the city then walking from Grand Central Station. Their old homestead was gone now. The el train and Morningside Park had hastened the disappearance of the blocks of shanties and saloons on the Upper West Side. But this was their real home, their childhood home.

They had shown their son where his brother lay. Lula always brought flowers to set on the place where he slept. Your brother is safe here, they had told the child. He is protected here.

"Who protects him?" The boy wanted to know.

"The angels, baby," Lula said.

"Like the angel at the fountain?"

"Yes, my son," Gabe answered, "and the president's better angels."

"Who else?"

"The soldiers who fought for a more perfect union. They are with him, too."

"Who leads the soldiers?" the child asked. He had heard the words before and knew what came next.

"The president leads the soldiers," Gabe answered. "He was your brother's namesake. He is with him now and watches over all of them."

"The angels, the soldiers, the president," the child recited as he skipped along the path. He was silent a minute, considering the familiar story. "Did you see any angels? What did they look like?" the boy asked his father.

These were new questions. Lula looked to her husband to see how he would add to the tale.

"Yes, I saw them, but only for a moment," Gabe said. "There were two of them, companions. They came to be witnesses. One of them was tall. He removed his hat to show respect."

"The angel had a hat?" The child laughed, intrigued by this new detail. "What about the other one?"

Gabe thought a moment. "The other had a hand that was hurt, maybe from a battle."

"Your hand was hurt from a battle, but then the hurt was gone." The boy stated this with confidence. His parents had assured him it was so. "Is it that way for the angel?"

Gabe took one of the boy's hands. Lula grasped the other.

"I am sure it is that way for the angel, my child. I am sure the angel is fine."

About the Author

Bette Bono has worked as a political analyst, Harvard-trained lawyer, public school teacher, and teachers' union steward. When she isn't writing, she may be found working in her garden, wandering through a park or nature preserve, visiting a historic site, listening to people tell their life stories, or exploring local libraries. Bette lives in Connecticut with her family.

ALL THINGS THAT MATTER PRESS

FOR MORE INFORMATION ON TITLES AVAILABLE FROM
ALL THINGS THAT MATTER PRESS, GO TO
http://allthingsthatmatterpress.com
or contact us at
allthingsthatmatterpress@gmail.com

If you enjoyed this book, please post a review on Amazon.com and
your favorite social media sites.
Thank you!